THE GYPSY MOON

BOOKS BY GILBERT MORRIS

THE HOUSE OF WINSLOW SERIES

The Honorable Imposter
The Captive Bride
The Indentured Heart
The Gentle Rebel
The Saintly Buccaneer
The Holy Warrior
The Reluctant Bridegroom
The Last Confederate
The Dixie Widow
The Wounded Yankee
The Union Belle
The Final Adversary
The Crossed Sabres
The Valiant Gunman
The Gallant Outlaw
The Jeweled Spur
The Yukon Queen
The Rough Rider
The Iron Lady
The Silver Star
The Shadow Portrait
The White Hunter
The Flying Cavalier
The Glorious Prodigal
The Amazon Quest
The Golden Angel
The Heavenly Fugitive
The Fiery Ring
The Pilgrim Song
The Beloved Enemy
The Shining Badge
The Royal Handmaid
The Silent Harp
The Virtuous Woman
The Gypsy Moon

CHENEY DUVALL, M.D.[1]

1. *The Stars for a Light*
2. *Shadow of the Mountains*
3. *A City Not Forsaken*
4. *Toward the Sunrising*
5. *Secret Place of Thunder*
6. *In the Twilight, in the Evening*
7. *Island of the Innocent*
8. *Driven With the Wind*

CHENEY AND SHILOH: THE INHERITANCE[1]

1. *Where Two Seas Met*
2. *The Moon by Night*

THE SPIRIT OF APPALACHIA[2]

1. *Over the Misty Mountains*
2. *Beyond the Quiet Hills*
3. *Among the King's Soldiers*
4. *Beneath the Mockingbird's Wings*
5. *Around the River's Bend*

LIONS OF JUDAH

1. *Heart of a Lion*
2. *No Woman So Fair*
3. *The Gate of Heaven*
4. *Till Shiloh Comes*

[1]with Lynn Morris [2]with Aaron McCarver

05A

GILBERT MORRIS

the GYPSY MOON

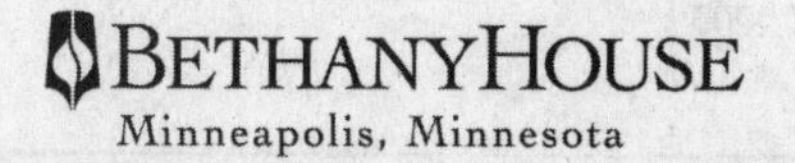

The Gypsy Moon

Cover illustration by William Graff
Cover design by Melinda Schumacher

Scripture quotations are from the King James Version of the Bible.

Published by Bethany House Publishers
11400 Hampshire Avenue South
Bloomington, Minnesota 55438

Bethany House Publishers is a division of
Baker Publishing Group, Grand Rapids, Michigan.

Printed in the United States of America

Library of Congress Cataloging-in-Publication Data

Morris, Gilbert.
The gypsy moon / by Gilbert Morris.
p. cm. — (The house of Winslow)
Summary: "Dr. Gabrielle Winslow joins the Underground in Holland to help smuggle Jews out of the country. She teams up with an OSS agent to rescue her uncle in Berlin. Will they succeed in bringing him out of Germany only to be trapped in Holland?"—Provided by publisher.
ISBN 0-7642-2687-8 (pbk.)
1. Winslow family (Fictitious characters)—Fiction. 2. World War, 1939-1945—Netherlands—Fiction. 3. Holocaust, Jewish (1939-1945)—Fiction. 4. Americans—Netherlands—Fiction. 5. Refugees, Jewish—Fiction. 6. Netherlands—Fiction. I. Title II. Series: Morris, Gilbert. House of Winslow.

PS3563.08742G97 2005
813'.54—dc22

2005004891

I would love to dedicate a book to every single one of you who have bought a Winslow novel. Since I can't do that, let me mention a few of you who have been so supportive of the series:

—To *Betty Southworth* of Warner Springs, California

—And to *Jack and Shirley Werst* of Wapakoneta, Ohio

—To a special friend, *Gerald Squires* of Yreka, California

—To *Maryan Wolfe,* my good friend from Covina, California

—*Mike Hollingshead* of Malvern, Arkansas—can't think of a better man!

—And here's to you, *Ivy Iorio* of Niagara Falls, New York

—To *Anne Lahti,* who keeps me supplied with the best jam in the world!

—And to *Horace and Betty McKenzie* of Monroe, North Carolina, my very good friends.

GILBERT MORRIS spent ten years as a pastor before becoming Professor of English at Ouachita Baptist University in Arkansas and earning a Ph.D. at the University of Arkansas. A prolific writer, he has had over 25 scholarly articles and 200 poems published in various periodicals and over the past years has had more than 200 novels published. His family includes three grown children. He and his wife live in Gulf Shores, Alabama.

Contents

PART FOUR
August–October 1940

THE HOUSE OF WINSLOW

★ ★ ★ ★

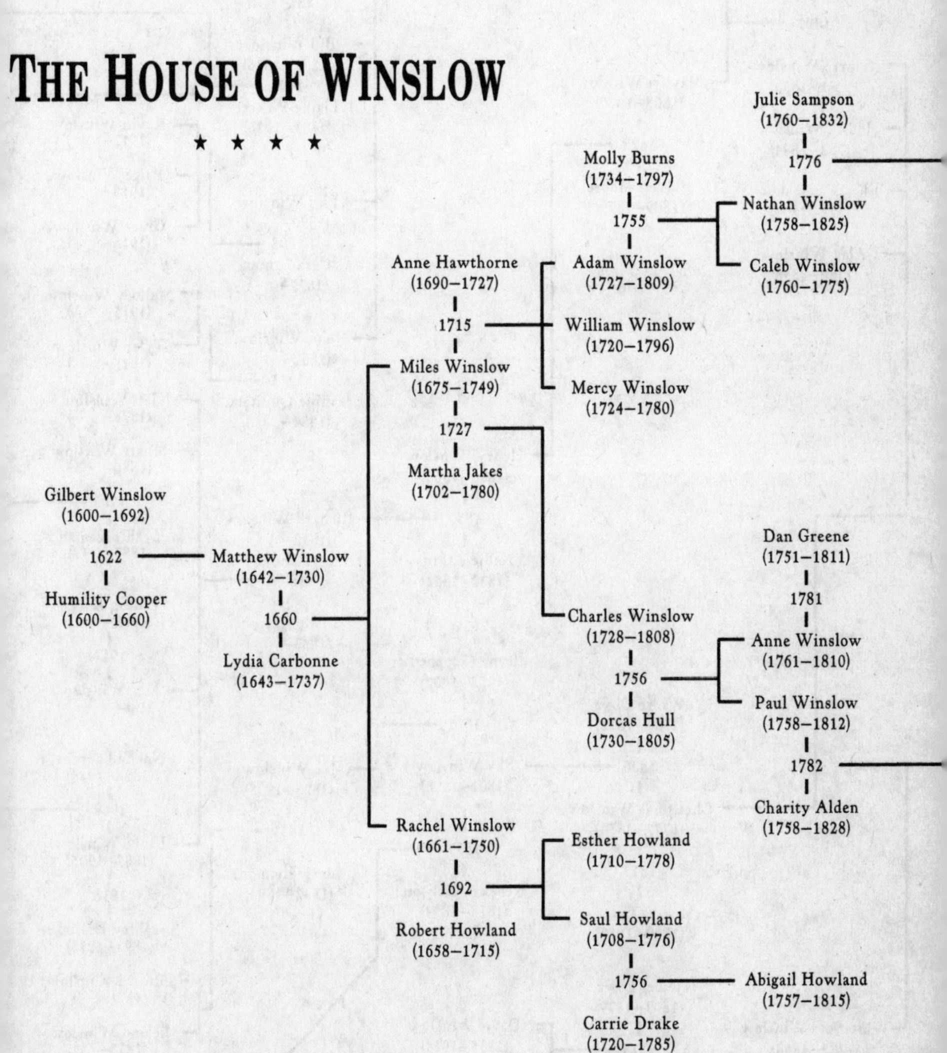

Julie Sampson
(1760–1832)
1776
Molly Burns
(1734–1797)
Nathan Winslow
(1758–1825)
1755
Anne Hawthorne
(1690–1727)
Adam Winslow
(1727–1809)
Caleb Winslow
(1760–1775)
1715
William Winslow
(1720–1796)
Miles Winslow
(1675–1749)
Mercy Winslow
(1724–1780)
1727
Martha Jakes
(1702–1780)
Gilbert Winslow
(1600–1692)
Dan Greene
(1751–1811)
1622
Matthew Winslow
(1642–1730)
1781
Humility Cooper
(1600–1660)
1660
Charles Winslow
(1728–1808)
Anne Winslow
(1761–1810)
Lydia Carbonne
(1643–1737)
1756
Paul Winslow
(1758–1812)
Dorcas Hull
(1730–1805)
1782
Charity Alden
(1758–1828)
Rachel Winslow
(1661–1750)
Esther Howland
(1710–1778)
1692
Saul Howland
(1708–1776)
Robert Howland
(1658–1715)
1756
Abigail Howland
(1757–1815)
Carrie Drake
(1720–1785)

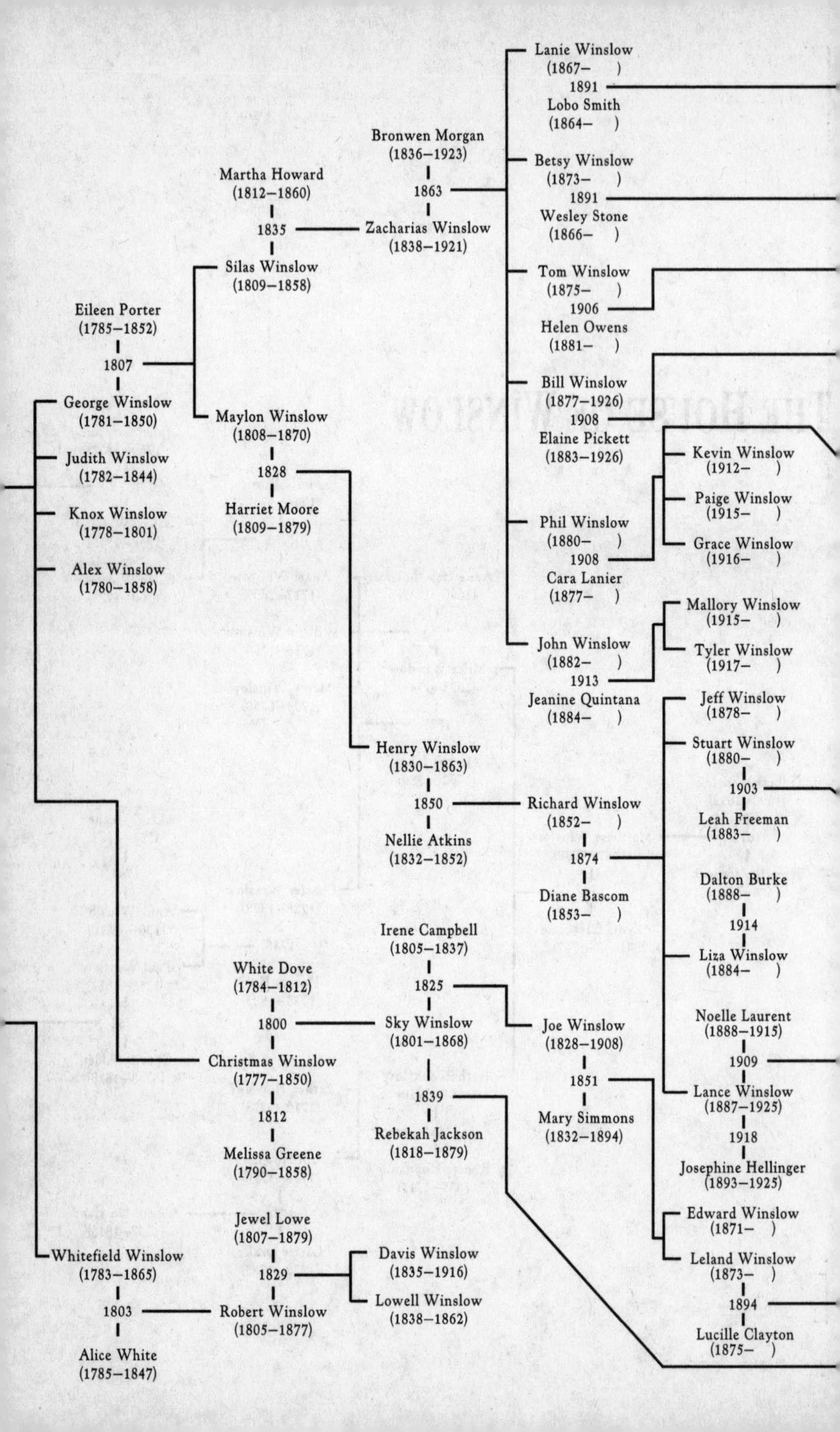
Lanie Winslow
(1867–)
1891
Lobo Smith
(1864–)
Bronwen Morgan
(1836–1923)
Betsy Winslow
(1873–)
1891
Wesley Stone
(1866–)
Martha Howard
(1812–1860)
1863
1835
Zacharias Winslow
(1838–1921)
Tom Winslow
(1875–)
1906
Helen Owens
(1881–)
Silas Winslow
(1809–1858)
Eileen Porter
(1785–1852)
1807
Bill Winslow
(1877–1926)
1908
Elaine Pickett
(1883–1926)
George Winslow
(1781–1850)
Maylon Winslow
(1808–1870)
Kevin Winslow
(1912–)
Judith Winslow
(1782–1844)
1828
Paige Winslow
(1915–)
Knox Winslow
(1778–1801)
Harriet Moore
(1809–1879)
Phil Winslow
(1880–)
1908
Grace Winslow
(1916–)
Alex Winslow
(1780–1858)
Cara Lanier
(1877–)
Mallory Winslow
(1915–)
John Winslow
(1882–)
1913
Tyler Winslow
(1917–)
Jeanine Quintana
(1884–)
Jeff Winslow
(1878–)
Stuart Winslow
(1880–)
Henry Winslow
(1830–1863)
1903
1850
Richard Winslow
(1852–)
Leah Freeman
(1883–)
1874
Nellie Atkins
(1832–1852)
Dalton Burke
(1888–)
Diane Bascom
(1853–)
1914
Irene Campbell
(1805–1837)
Liza Winslow
(1884–)
White Dove
(1784–1812)
1825
Noelle Laurent
(1888–1915)
1800
Sky Winslow
(1801–1868)
Joe Winslow
(1828–1908)
1909
Christmas Winslow
(1777–1850)
1851
Lance Winslow
(1887–1925)
1839
1812
Mary Simmons
(1832–1894)
1918
Rebekah Jackson
(1818–1879)
Melissa Greene
(1790–1858)
Josephine Hellinger
(1893–1925)
Jewel Lowe
(1807–1879)
Edward Winslow
(1871–)
Whitefield Winslow
(1783–1865)
Davis Winslow
(1835–1916)
Leland Winslow
(1873–)
1829
1803
Lowell Winslow
(1838–1862)
1894
Robert Winslow
(1805–1877)
Lucille Clayton
(1875–)
Alice White
(1785–1847)

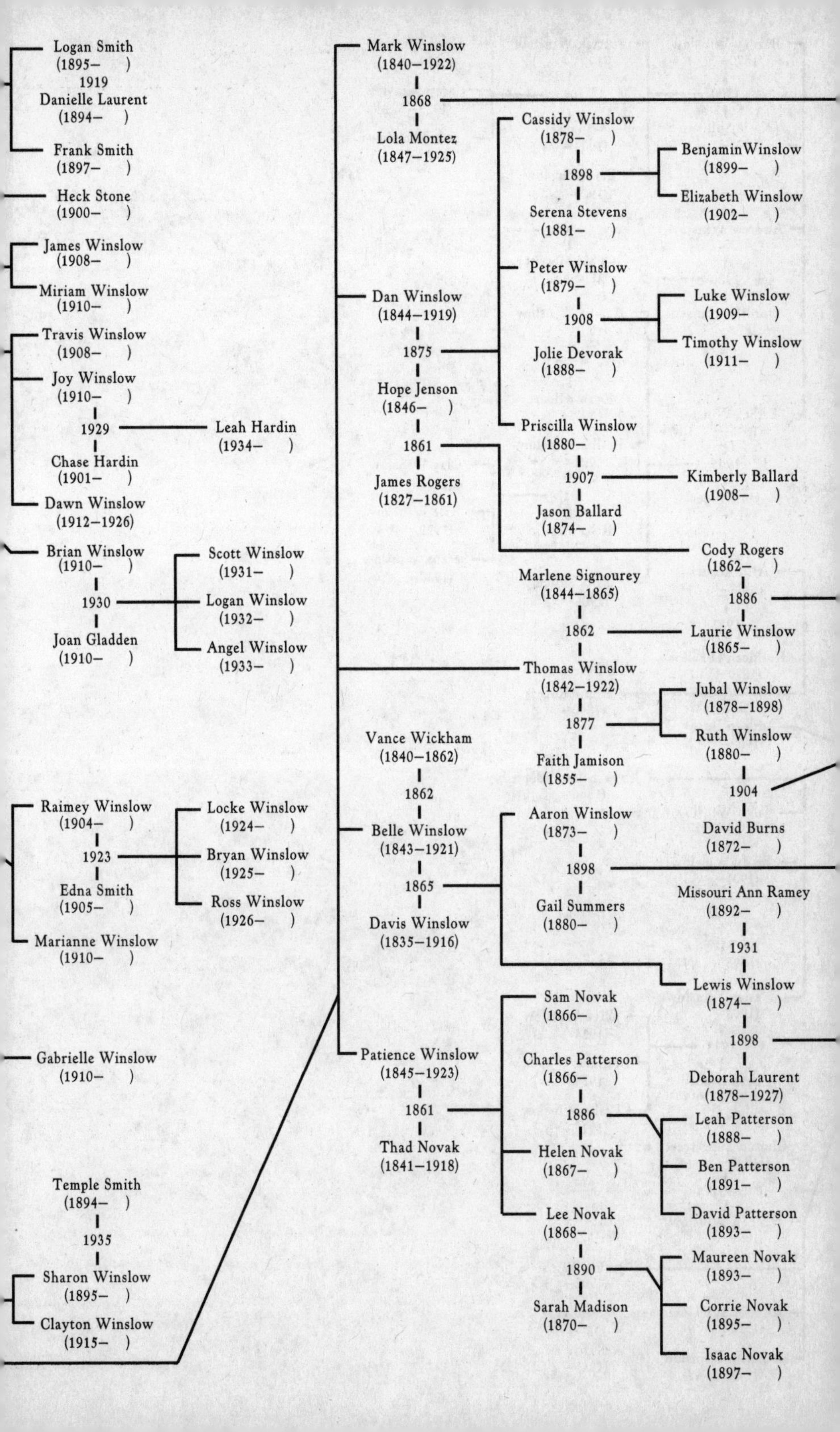

Logan Smith
(1895–)
1919
Danielle Laurent
(1894–)
Frank Smith
(1897–)
Heck Stone
(1900–)
James Winslow
(1908–)
Miriam Winslow
(1910–)
Travis Winslow
(1908–)
Joy Winslow
(1910–)
1929
Chase Hardin
(1901–)
Leah Hardin
(1934–)
Dawn Winslow
(1912–1926)
Brian Winslow
(1910–)
1930
Joan Gladden
(1910–)
Scott Winslow
(1931–)
Logan Winslow
(1932–)
Angel Winslow
(1933–)
Raimey Winslow
(1904–)
1923
Edna Smith
(1905–)
Locke Winslow
(1924–)
Bryan Winslow
(1925–)
Ross Winslow
(1926–)
Marianne Winslow
(1910–)
Gabrielle Winslow
(1910–)
Temple Smith
(1894–)
1935
Sharon Winslow
(1895–)
Clayton Winslow
(1915–)
Mark Winslow
(1840–1922)
1868
Lola Montez
(1847–1925)
Dan Winslow
(1844–1919)
1875
Hope Jenson
(1846–)
1861
James Rogers
(1827–1861)
Cassidy Winslow
(1878–)
1898
Serena Stevens
(1881–)
Benjamin Winslow
(1899–)
Elizabeth Winslow
(1902–)
Peter Winslow
(1879–)
1908
Jolie Devorak
(1888–)
Luke Winslow
(1909–)
Timothy Winslow
(1911–)
Priscilla Winslow
(1880–)
1907
Jason Ballard
(1874–)
Kimberly Ballard
(1908–)
Cody Rogers
(1862–)
1886
Laurie Winslow
(1865–)
Marlene Signourey
(1844–1865)
1862
Thomas Winslow
(1842–1922)
1877
Faith Jamison
(1855–)
Jubal Winslow
(1878–1898)
Ruth Winslow
(1880–)
1904
David Burns
(1872–)
Vance Wickham
(1840–1862)
1862
Belle Winslow
(1843–1921)
1865
Davis Winslow
(1835–1916)
Aaron Winslow
(1873–)
1898
Gail Summers
(1880–)
Missouri Ann Ramey
(1892–)
1931
Lewis Winslow
(1874–)
1898
Deborah Laurent
(1878–1927)
Patience Winslow
(1845–1923)
1861
Thad Novak
(1841–1918)
Sam Novak
(1866–)
Charles Patterson
(1866–)
1886
Helen Novak
(1867–)
Leah Patterson
(1888–)
Ben Patterson
(1891–)
David Patterson
(1893–)
Lee Novak
(1868–)
1890
Sarah Madison
(1870–)
Maureen Novak
(1893–)
Corrie Novak
(1895–)
Isaac Novak
(1897–)

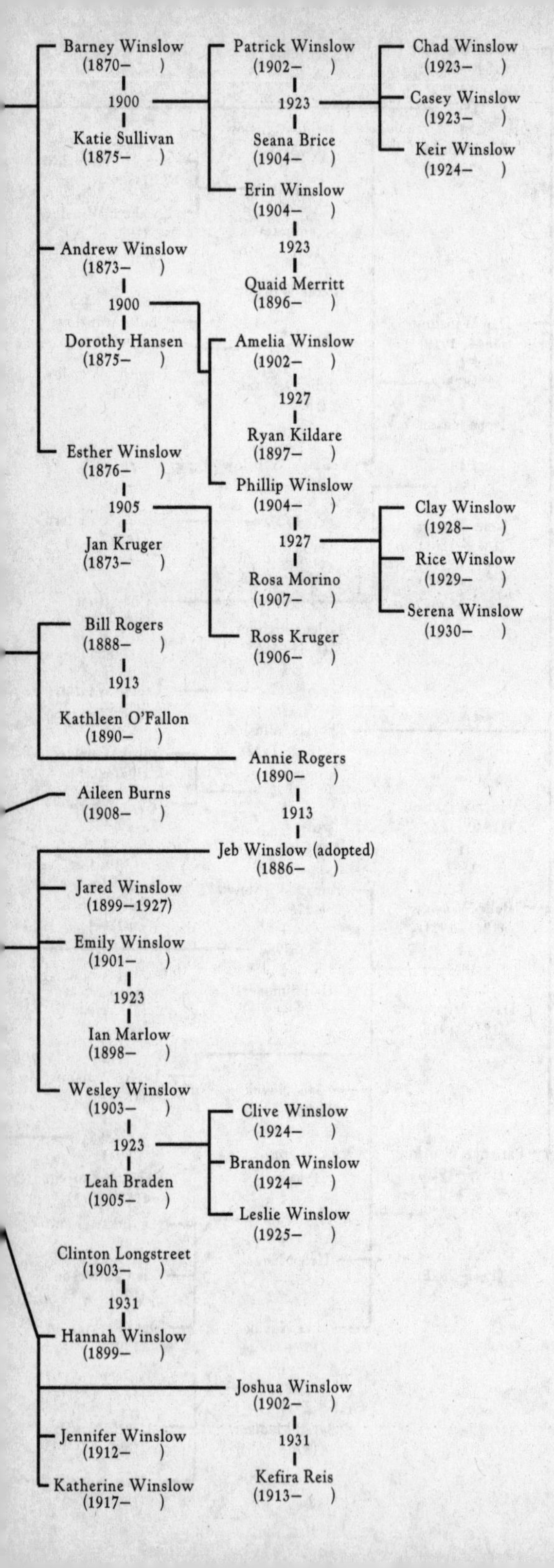

Barney Winslow
(1870–)
1900
Katie Sullivan
(1875–)
Patrick Winslow
(1902–)
1923
Seana Brice
(1904–)
Chad Winslow
(1923–)
Casey Winslow
(1923–)
Keir Winslow
(1924–)
Erin Winslow
(1904–)
1923
Quaid Merritt
(1896–)
Andrew Winslow
(1873–)
1900
Dorothy Hansen
(1875–)
Amelia Winslow
(1902–)
1927
Ryan Kildare
(1897–)
Esther Winslow
(1876–)
1905
Jan Kruger
(1873–)
Phillip Winslow
(1904–)
1927
Rosa Morino
(1907–)
Clay Winslow
(1928–)
Rice Winslow
(1929–)
Serena Winslow
(1930–)
Ross Kruger
(1906–)
Bill Rogers
(1888–)
1913
Kathleen O'Fallon
(1890–)
Annie Rogers
(1890–)
1913
Aileen Burns
(1908–)
Jeb Winslow (adopted)
(1886–)
Jared Winslow
(1899–1927)
Emily Winslow
(1901–)
1923
Ian Marlow
(1898–)
Wesley Winslow
(1903–)
1923
Leah Braden
(1905–)
Clive Winslow
(1924–)
Brandon Winslow
(1924–)
Leslie Winslow
(1925–)
Clinton Longstreet
(1903–)
1931
Hannah Winslow
(1899–)
Joshua Winslow
(1902–)
1931
Kefira Reis
(1913–)
Jennifer Winslow
(1912–)
Katherine Winslow
(1917–)

PART ONE

May 1925–November 1938

★ ★ ★

CHAPTER ONE

A Dark Prediction

★ ★ ★

Gabrielle slipped down into the tub until she was completely submerged in the warm, soapy water. She lifted her legs toward the ceiling and pointed her toes while singing, "Tea for two and two for tea, just me for you and you for me . . ."

Gabby didn't have the best voice in the world, but it was strong, and she knew all the lyrics to every popular song coming over the radio. This particular one had been the smash hit of 1924 both in America and in England, and now a year later it was still a favorite. Gabby loved to sing, and one of the keen regrets of her life was that she did not have a good enough voice to sing on the stage or in films. As she relaxed in the soapy water, soaking up the heat and looking up at her polished toes pointed at the ceiling, she thought of the time when her mother had gently broken the news that she would never be a professional singer. She had been twelve years old, and it had broken her heart for at least a week.

Sitting up abruptly and splashing the water to rinse off the soap, Gabby pulled the plug and stepped out onto the bath mat. Grabbing a fluffy white towel, she rubbed herself vigorously, then tossed the towel over a rack. Quickly, she slipped into a chenille robe that had once been a deep royal blue but now was faded to an anemic lavender. Leaving the bathroom, she scurried down the short hall and went into her bedroom and peered out the window.

"Good! It's not going to rain anymore." The first week of June had been particularly wet for southern England, and she had been afraid that a downpour such as they'd had the previous evening would spoil her date with Greg. But the skies were clear, and there was no sign of anything but fine weather. From where she stood, she could catch a glimpse of the English Channel. She was intensely sensitive to natural beauty, and for some time she drank in the sight of the rough waves, the occasional boat going by, and the branches blowing in the breeze.

Turning, she moved to the rosewood table that had belonged to her grandmother. She selected a record from a tall stack and wound up the gramophone. Each year her mother made a trip to America, her home, and she always returned with all the latest records. Gabby sang along as she decided what to wear. "It had to be you, it had to be you. I wandered around and finally found the somebody who could make me be true. . . ."

She looked through her underwear drawer, tossing a flattening brassiere to the side with a snort of disgust. "Silliest thing I ever heard of! Women ought to look like women," she muttered. The last few years had produced some strange garments in women's dress. Women were now supposedly freed from their "bondage," but for some reason this meant they had to look like men. They had cut their hair short and disguised their feminine shapes as much as possible. Gabby pulled out the camiknickers she had bought only the week before, the latest fashion in underwear. The one-piece garment combined a camisole top with attached knickers. Gabby stared at herself in the full-length mirror. "It looks stupid, but it's what everybody is wearing," she murmured.

She put on a white pleated skirt and a soft green loose-fitting jumper with a low neckline. She draped an emerald green scarf around her neck, pulled on her beige stockings, and slipped into a pair of dark green low-heeled shoes. Moving closer to the mirror, she studied her face critically. As usual, she was not overly impressed, but she did have nice eyes—large, almond-shaped, and a warm brown that appeared almost golden at times. Her mother used to tell her, *"The eyes are the windows of the soul; people can see right through to your soul, Gabby."* She surveyed her straight nose and broad forehead and shook her head with disgust. But she brightened up at how her hair looked. She liked her abundant curls and the rich chocolate color with a trace of auburn that glowed in the sun. Her friends were always complaining about their thin or straight hair, but she had no complaints with hers.

She stepped back from the mirror and admired her trim figure with satisfaction but sighed, wishing she were shorter than five-seven. She had always admired diminutive women like her best friend, Helen Stempson, who was only five feet tall. More than once her mother had told her to straighten up and be what God made her to be.

Gabby picked up her cloche hat and pulled it down over her hair. She personally thought cloche hats looked stupid, but everyone wore them, and this one had seemed to her the best of a bad lot. After examining her complete outfit from every angle in the mirror, she put her hat back on the bed and sat down at her desk.

She removed a small red leather book from the back of the bottom drawer and opened it to the marker. Grabbing a pen, she wrote:

> *So, this is my first grown-up date. I have a new outfit, and Daddy and Mum say I can stay out until eleven. They wanted me to come back by ten, but I argued them out of it.*

Gabby hesitated for a moment, chewing on her lower lip, before beginning again. Unconsciously her tongue appeared at the corner of her mouth, a childhood habit she had never shaken.

Greg Farnsworth isn't the most handsome boy I know, but he's not hideous either. At least he's tall and got rid of his pimples this year. I wonder if he'll try to kiss me when he brings me home—and I wonder if I'll let him.

"Gabby, are you ready?"

Gabby quickly slammed her journal shut and shoved it into the drawer. "Come in, Mum."

Her mother poked her head into the room.

Gabby stood up and struck a pose. "Do you like my outfit?" she asked eagerly. "Do you think Greg will like it?"

"I think he'll love it." Josephine Winslow, at the age of thirty-two, looked like she was in her twenties. She was a tall woman with green eyes and reddish hair and a strong, attractive square face. She had married Lance Winslow after the death of Gabby's mother and for a time had wondered if she could fill the role of mother as well as wife. Despite her doubts, everything had turned out successfully. Although there were times when Gabby mentioned her birth mother, Noelle Winslow, she and Josephine had grown very close. Josephine had met Gabby's father during the Great War, when she was a journalist from New York and he was a pilot with the Royal Flying Corps.

Now Josephine kept up her career and did a great deal of traveling, though England had become her first love. She had only distant relatives in the States and found her greatest pleasure was in being at their home in Hastings on the southeastern coast of England.

"If he doesn't like it, he would have to be blind and a moron," Jo said with a smile. "Turn around and let me see." Gabby turned, arms extended. "I can't believe this is the gawky, long-legged creature that kept bringing frogs into the house just a year ago, it seems."

"Oh, Mum, it's been longer than that!" Gabby protested.

"Well, as long as you don't start collecting snakes, I suppose I can bear it." Jo shook her head as she looked at the walls, which were completely covered with specimens, including butterflies in glass-covered frames, birds' eggs in frames with small sections—each bearing a tiny egg with a label underneath it—and flowers that had been dried and mounted. "We won't ever have to worry about decorating a house. You've got enough specimens to fill Windsor Castle."

Gabby giggled. "I guess I have, haven't I? Look at what I did this morning. Come over here."

Jo went over to the table, which was cluttered with books and a microscope. At Gabby's insistence she looked down into the scope. "I can never see anything in here," she protested.

"Yes, you can. Just look and concentrate."

Jo Winslow obediently peered into the lens. "I see it, but I don't know what it is."

"It's a butterfly wing. Isn't it beautiful?"

Jo straightened up. "Yes, it is. But I think I'd rather see the whole butterfly than just a microscopic section of it." She walked to the window and looked out at the sea for a moment. Then she turned and said, "I want us to have a mother and daughter talk."

"Oh, Mum, please not now!"

"No kissing," Jo said firmly.

Gabby tightened her lips. She was an obedient girl and had given her stepmother and father little trouble. As a matter of fact, she was so caught up with her science studies and collections that she had given little thought to boys until this year. She had been a rather gawky adolescent just a short time ago, but a single year had wrought as much difference in her as one saw in a caterpillar and a butterfly. The angular, bony edges had been replaced with graceful curves. Her skin had cleared up and now possessed a pleasing silkiness about it. She had inherited her French mother's figure along with her father's strength and bone structure, which combined to make her an attractive young woman.

"No kissing," Jo repeated.

"Just one, Mum? Please!"

Suddenly Jo laughed. "I was only teasing, Gabby. You're

fifteen years old, and you have a smart head on your shoulders. You have more sense than I do, actually. I'd hate for you to know what a flibbertigibbet I was when I was your age."

"What's a flibbertigibbet? Is that an American word?"

"Yes, it's American for *fool*—which I was when I was fifteen. I was quite boy crazy."

Gabby came over and put her arm around her stepmother's waist. "I can't believe that. You're the smartest woman I know."

"Well, I'm not fifteen any longer. Let's go downstairs and let your father see how beautiful you are."

Gabby grabbed her cloche hat and asked, "What was your first date like, Mum?"

"It wasn't nearly as exciting as my first date with your father. Now, come along."

They walked down the stairs and turned left into the living area, a beautiful room with a low ceiling supported with exposed beams. The ceiling was so low that Lance Winslow often sported a red spot in the middle of his forehead when he forgot to duck. The house had been built in the 1600s, and it had been the delight of both Lance and Jo to work lovingly on it until it was filled with antiques and reflected a warm aura of hospitality.

"Well, so this is the man-killer!" Lance Winslow came out of his chair and moved over to get a better look at his daughter. He was a tall man with an athletic figure, and at the age of thirty-eight, he still had most of the fast reactions he had had as a fighter pilot in the war. He was wearing a pair of baggy gray trousers and a dark blue shirt that brought out the color of his eyes. "Why, you look good enough to go to a horse race."

"Daddy," she protested, "I look better than *that*!"

"Yes, you do. In fact, you look so good I'm going to have to have a serious talk with Greg. I'm going to tell him to have you back by ten o'clock. If he objects, I'll tell him I've got a forty-five and a shovel and that no one will miss him very much."

"Daddy, you can't say that!"

Lance laughed at her horrified expression, then came and put his arms around her. He gave her a hug and said, "No, I don't suppose I will. But you look beautiful." When he released her, a frown crossed his face. "It's going to be hard to go away and leave you."

"Well, I've tried hard enough to go with you before, but you wouldn't let me."

Jo spoke up. "It's going to be a long, hard trip. I want us all to go to the States next year when we have plenty of time. This trip we have to make now is going to be nothing but tiresome travel and work."

Lance worked for an aircraft firm and was often sent on assignments to other countries for months at a time. Jo worked as a journalist wherever she hung her hat, but she was also writing a book about the new jazz music in America and wanted to do some research.

"I wouldn't care. You'd see," Gabby said. She dreaded these times when her parents had to leave her alone. They usually tried to space their trips out so that one or the other of them would be home, but this time there was no possibility of that.

"But, dear, you love to go to Holland and visit with your aunt Liza. You know you do," Jo coaxed.

"But it's not the same as being with you."

"It will only be for two months. You had a wonderful time with your friend Betje when you were there last year. Why, you told us you had the best time of your life. And before you know it, we'll be back."

Gabby quickly covered her disappointment. "I know, Mum," she said. "I'll miss you, but don't worry about me. Betje and I will have a good time, and I always like staying with Uncle Dalton and Aunt Liza."

Liza was the only sister of Gabby's father. She had married Dalton Burke, who had become a scientist of some reputation and taught at the university in Amsterdam. They had a beautiful house, which was very old, and Gabby did love spending time with them. She had been there three times, beginning when she was very young, and now knew quite a few people. Though it had been hard at first, she had learned to speak Dutch passably well, thanks to her friend Betje.

"Oh, I'll be fine, Mum. Don't you worry about me. And, Dad, you go over and tell 'em how it's done. Don't let those Yanks give you any trouble!"

Lance's face registered his relief. He had been worried about leaving Gabby for two months, but Jo had convinced him there would be little fun for her on this grinding trip. "I'll tell you what," he said. "Your mum and I will work as hard as we can and try to get back early. We'll pick you up and go to Paris for a holiday. How would that be?"

"Really, Dad?"

"Really."

Gabby squealed and threw her arms around her father's neck. She squeezed him hard before releasing him. "That'll be super! We'll have the most fun ever. Why, Mum and I could go to all the stores and see the latest fashions. Maybe we can find ourselves some new outfits."

"We'll see about that," her father said, winking at her. "We'll stop off and see your grandfather on the way. He gets lonely now. We don't get to see him very often, but he thinks the world of you." Noelle Winslow's father was getting on in years and did delight in his half-English granddaughter.

"That will be wonderful," Jo said. "You know, if you ever become a doctor, he'll take all the credit for it."

"Ever since I was a little girl, he's been telling me I ought to be a doctor," Gabby said. "But a better one than he is, he always says."

"I doubt if anybody is much better than your grandfather. But I know he misses your grandmother and gets lonely, so it would be nice to make that stop and spend some time with him."

At that moment a muffled roar filled the room, and Lance said, "If that's your young man, it sounds like he's driving a lorry, and a big one, instead of a car."

"He's got his license and everything, Daddy," Gabby

said. "And he's a very careful driver."

They waited for the knock on the door; then Jo opened it. "Hello, Greg. Come in."

Greg Farnsworth was a tall, lanky young man of seventeen. He was not filled out yet and was not handsome, but there was a homely charm about him. He was almost as tall as Lance and had to stoop carefully under the dark exposed beams.

"Hello, Mrs. Winslow. Good evening, sir."

"Hello, Greg." Lance came over and shook his hand. "How are your parents?"

"They're just fine. Gabby tells me you're leaving soon."

"That's right. We'll be going to the States tomorrow."

"I wish I could go. If you go to California, do you think you'll see any movie stars?"

"I don't think we'll do much stargazing." Jo smiled. "It'll be mostly work, and plenty of it."

Greg turned his attention to Gabby and smiled in admiration. "You look great, Gabby."

"Why, thank you, Greg."

"A new outfit?"

"Yes. You really like it?"

"It's the cat's pajamas, as they say in the States. Are you ready?"

"I'm all ready."

Gabby got her hat, and as the two went out the door, Lance called out, "We'll be waiting up for you. Be home before eleven."

Jo waved at the young people and closed the door, then turned to her husband. "I believe you're more nervous than she is about her first date."

Lance came over and put his arms around her. "You women don't understand what it's like to be a father trying to keep a fifteen-year-old girl in line."

Jo leaned against him. "Tell me about it. Is it really all that hard?"

"Almost as hard as keeping a beautiful woman like you in line. Come on. Let's go finish packing."

★ ★ ★

"Greg, slow down. You're driving too fast."

"Fast! Why, this isn't fast at all." He was proud of his bright red roadster. The car was so small he had no trouble reaching around and putting his arm around her. "You're out with the best driver in England. Relax and enjoy yourself."

Gabby did not resist and leaned against him. The roar of the small engine made it necessary for them to shout against the wind, and as he sped along the narrow, winding road, they encountered little traffic. She liked the touch of his arm around her, and she was feeling very excited. He had taken her to dinner at a very nice restaurant in downtown Hastings, and then they had gone to see *The Gold Rush,* starring Charlie Chaplin. They had both laughed themselves weak over the comedian's antics, and afterward they had gotten ice cream before heading home.

They shouted at each other over the noise of the engine and the racing wind. When they were less than a quarter of a mile from the street where the Winslows lived, Greg made such a sharp turn that Gabby had to grasp wildly at the frame of the car. "Where are you going?"

"Why, I couldn't take you home from your first date without a trip to Lovers' Grove."

Gabby instantly grew alert. Lovers' Grove was a large, heavily wooded park. During the daylight hours nannies pushed babies in their perambulators along the shady walkways, and at times Gabby had gone there herself looking for specimens for her collections. At night, however, the park was known as a place where young men took unsuspecting young women for their own selfish purposes. "I'm not going to Lovers' Grove with you," she protested. "Take me home."

Greg merely laughed and slowed the car as he followed the serpentine road that led deep into the grove of large trees. "Why, you're not a little girl," he said. "It's not going to kill you."

But then the headlights picked up some movement, and he muttered, "Blast, somebody's here!" They got closer. "Looks like a bunch of gypsies."

Gabby was intrigued by the sight. They were all sitting around a blazing fire, singing a song with a haunting melody. Three wagons were grouped behind the small gathering, and horses grazed on the tall grass nearby. "Come on, Greg. Let's go visit them."

"Not on your life!" He shook his head firmly. "They're thieves and even worse. I'm getting out of here."

But Gabby opened the door and stepped out, ignoring his protests. "Oh, come on, you're a grown man, aren't you?" she mocked him. "Don't tell me you're afraid!"

He glared at her and shut off the engine. "This is your idea, not mine," he complained as he opened his door and got out.

As Gabby approached the small band of gypsies, the music fell silent and a tall man came toward her.

"Good evening. Welcome to our home," he said in a strongly accented voice, bowing deeply.

Gabby could see by the light of the fire that he was wearing a brilliant yellow shirt with a red kerchief around his neck. Gold earrings hung from his earlobes, and his white teeth flashed against his dark skin.

"We didn't mean to interrupt, but we saw your fire and heard your singing. It was very beautiful."

"We are pleased to have you. I am Duke Zanko. You like music? You will hear plenty of music. And if you want your fortune told, my wife can do that. And we have some beautiful jewelry for a beautiful young lady."

As Gabby and Greg moved closer to the fire, Gabby felt a surge of excitement. She had seen bands of gypsies before in her travels with her parents and had always been curious about their mysterious ways. She looked around the gathering and noted at least a dozen adults and considerably more children. Several of the women held small babies, and their eyes seemed to flash as the two visitors came closer.

"This is my wife, Marissa," Duke Zanko said, gesturing

at a young woman with dark eyes and large gold earrings dangling from her ears. He shrugged his shoulders sadly and said, "I have not had much luck with wives. I've worn out two. I got this one young so I could bring her up myself—and teach her to do nothing but please me."

Marissa laughed, displaying her very white teeth.

"Perhaps you came to visit our camp because of the full moon," Duke said, looking up through the branches. "Gypsy men and women always fall in love when there's a full moon, a gypsy moon." He winked at Greg. "Maybe it'll work the same for you!"

Greg laughed and Gabby was glad the darkness would cover the red she felt creeping up her face.

Marissa stood up and came closer to Gabby as the rest of the group started talking among themselves and lining up to get a bowlful of something cooking in a large iron pot over the fire. "I married him because he is old and rich," Marissa told Gabby. "When he dies I will take all his money and find me a strong young man."

Duke laughed. "You will not find another man like me. Someday you'll appreciate what you have in me."

Marissa grinned and took hold of Gabby's arm. "Come. You will eat with us," she invited.

"Oh, we couldn't do that," Gabby protested, although her mouth was watering as she inhaled the delicious aroma coming from the cooking pot.

"Yes, you will be our guests. Please . . ." Before Gabby could say more, a young woman came over and handed both of them bowls filled with stew.

"Why, thank you," Gabby said as she and Greg sat down and joined them. They found the stew delicious, and as the rest of the group ate, Duke pulled out his fiddle and began to play. Two other men joined him as they finished eating, one of them on a zither and another on a stringed instrument that neither Greg nor Gabby had seen before.

Several young women began to dance, and they were soon joined by young men. Their shadows cast by the flickering fire flitted across the ground, and the air was filled with laughter and music.

A rather short but well built young man came over to Gabby with his hand extended. His hair was as black as a raven, and his eyes seemed almost as dark. "Come, you dance with me. My name is Pavko."

"Oh, I can't dance!"

"Go on," Greg urged. "You want to be a gypsy? Here's your chance. Maybe that gypsy moon will bring you happiness."

Gabby allowed Pavko to pull her up to her feet. She felt self-conscious at first, but soon she found herself relaxing as she learned the simple steps of the dance. All the people watching were clapping their hands, and the music filled the night air. Finally, she pulled away and said, "Thank you. I'm afraid I'm not as good a dancer as you are."

Pavko laughed. "You are a wonderful dancer for a *gaji*."

"What is a gaji?"

"That is what we call girls who are not gypsies."

Gabby sat back down beside Greg, and the two visitors listened as the lilting music danced on the warm summer air deep in the grove of tall, ancient trees. During a break in the music, Marissa took Gabby's hand in her own and said, "I will tell your fortune."

"I don't believe in fortune-telling," Gabby said with an apologetic smile. "I believe people make their own fortunes." Nevertheless, she did not resist when Marissa started examining the palm of her hand.

"You are going on a long journey. You will meet a man with blond hair."

Gabby was amused with the familiar prediction.

"Be very careful of him," Marissa continued. "He will not be good for you. Later you will meet a dark-haired man, and he is the man you want."

Gabby saw Greg smiling, and she returned it. Gabby pulled some coins out of her purse and thanked the woman.

"We'd better get going," Greg said. "Your dad will skin me alive if I don't get you home on time."

"I'm afraid so." Gabby started to get to her feet when she noticed a very old woman moving slowly toward her. The small woman wore a scarf over her head and large gold earrings.

"This is Madame Jana," Duke told her. Intersecting lines formed a network about the woman's face, and her lips were drawn tightly together. Though her eyes were practically closed, there was a dark glitter that showed she was alert.

"Good evening, Madame Jana," Gabby said. "How are you?"

The elderly woman did not answer, nor did she move. Gabrielle tried not to squirm under her unsettling gaze. Finally, Zanko said, "She is a Christian. Some say she is a prophet. Very wise."

Gabby was surprised at his words. She had assumed the whole group believed in fortune-telling and mysterious ways. A silence settled on the group as Madame Jana rested her hand lightly on Gabby's forehead. Gabby froze, not knowing what the woman would do. The old woman closed her eyes and began to pray for Gabby in a language Gabby could not understand. When she was done, she opened her eyes and seemed to look into the depths of Gabby.

"You are a believer, child. I feel the spirit of Christ in you."

Gabby's uneasiness turned to surprise. "Yes, I do believe in Jesus."

The woman dropped her hand to Gabby's shoulder. "You will need great courage, daughter," she said quietly. "A dark time lies before you, but Jesus will never forsake you. When you think all is lost, He will bring you the strength you will need. He will make a way for you through the danger that awaits you."

With trembling hands she took a gold chain from around her neck and handed it to Gabby. "This is very old," she said, "and the Lord tells me to give it to you. It is not magic. It is to remind you that you are not alone—that somewhere an old woman is praying for you when you feel that all is lost. Go with Jesus and do not fear." As she turned and moved away, the group resumed their quiet chatter.

"She is a strange one," Duke said as the woman disappeared into the darkness. "But I tell you, she is a praying woman. She never gives up! Do not let her words fall to the ground."

Gabby had laughed at Marissa's fortune-telling, but she was truly frightened by this woman's prediction and told Greg she was ready to go. They said good-night to Duke and his wife and went back to the car.

"Well, that was definitely strange," he said as they left the area. "What did you make of the old woman?"

"I don't know, Greg," she said as she touched the gold chain the woman had given her.

"We're lucky they didn't rob us blind. They're all thieves, you know."

She did not answer as Greg drove out of the park and headed for the Winslows' house. When he stopped in front of her house, she opened the door and said, "You don't have to come in, Greg. Good night."

"Hey, wait a minute—"

"Good night, Greg."

Somehow the old woman's words and her prayer had shaken Gabby. She had thought she might like a good-night kiss on her first real date, but now she was preoccupied with other disturbing thoughts. She entered the house and found her parents drinking coffee in the kitchen.

"Well, that wasn't very late after all," her father said with a smile.

"Did you have a good time, dear?" her mother asked.

"Oh yes, it was very nice." Gabby had an impulse to tell them about the group of people at Lovers' Grove, but for some reason she did not. She had not had a chance to look carefully at the gift that Madame Jana had given her, but somehow she knew she would not forget this night or the necklace for a long time.

"You'd better go to bed, dear," Jo said. "We have to leave early to get you to the wharf to board the ship for Amsterdam."

"Yes, I know. Good night, Mum. Good night, Dad."

She kissed her parents, went upstairs, and took the necklace out of her purse. At the end of the gold chain hung an old coin, nearly an inch in diameter. It was worn thin, but she could still make out the figure of a woman wearing a long robe and some words in a foreign language under the figure. She held it in her hand and thought about the old woman's strange prayer. Gabby quickly pulled her diary out of her desk and began to write down the woman's words of warning and of encouragement as closely as she could remember. She could not understand why she was so moved by the woman, but after she had gotten ready for bed, she got down on her knees and prayed for courage. For some reason she could not fathom, she found herself praying for Madame Jana.

Glancing out the window, she saw the huge silver disk and thought of Greg's words. *"That's a gypsy moon."* For a long time she stared at the argent globe before finally dropping off into a deep sleep.

★ ★ ★

"It won't be long, dear," Jo said. "We'll be back before you know it." They were standing on the wharf, and the blast of the boat's loud whistle had already given the first warning for its imminent departure. She kissed Gabby, then stood back and watched as Lance put his arms around her. He held her tightly before finally releasing her.

"Don't forget about that trip to Paris when we get back," he said.

"I won't, Daddy." Gabby felt a strange reluctance to walk up the gangplank and board the ship. It was not unusual, for she always hated saying good-bye to her parents. Still, this time something seemed to hold her back. She had a sudden desire to cry out, *"Take me with you. Let me go with you!"* but she knew that was impossible. She turned and walked up the gangplank and found a place along the rail and waited as the last passengers boarded. As the ship slowly pulled out, she looked down at her parents and waved. They waved back, and she could hear her father calling out, "Don't forget Paris when we get back!"

She called back but knew they could not hear her, for right then the ship's whistle gave another loud blast. Then it slowly turned as the tugboat pulled it out away from the dock. "I hate good-byes," she muttered. "Why do people ever have to say good-bye?"

CHAPTER TWO

A SUMMER INTERLUDE

★ ★ ★

As Gabby pulled the brush through her hair, she remembered the first time she had visited in the Netherlands. She had been only nine years old, and she had come expecting to see a land filled with windmills and tulips and wooden shoes. She had thought she'd see people in fancy costumes looking like the colorful pictures she had seen in her storybooks, and treelined canals and tall, thin houses with fancy gables.

A smile touched her broad lips as she thought about how disappointed she had been to find that no one wore wooden shoes. On that visit and subsequent ones, she had discovered that no other country in Europe offered so much variety or so many picturesque sights in such a small area. She had been pleased to find there actually were windmills, as well as acres and acres of tulip fields with colors so bright they almost blinded the eye. She saw castles and cathedrals, canals and museums, and had fallen in love with the place instantly.

Putting the hairbrush down, she let her glance run around the small upstairs room with the single window that looked out on the main street of Oudekerk aan de Amstel. The small village was only fifteen or twenty minutes by car or thirty minutes by bus from the center of Amsterdam. Her uncle had often told her they had all the advantages of country living while being almost in the center of a great city.

The room itself was decorated with bright yellows and blues and filled with beautifully constructed furniture hand-crafted by Dutch artisans. Paintings of the Flemish school—but not originals—ornamented the walls. An original painting by Franz Hal would have cost as much as a dozen houses.

Her room was warm and cozy. *This room fits Holland,* she thought. *It's a small country, and this is a small room. Everything here is pretty and petite—except the cathedrals.* She checked her appearance in the mirror and then went down the narrow stairs to the kitchen, where she found her aunt and uncle waiting for her.

"Are you ready for the festival, Gabby?"

Dalton Burke was a short man who tended to be overweight. He had very fair hair and blue eyes, in the manner of most Dutch adults, and his smile warmed his whole face. Gabby had often thought he looked like a middle-aged baby or even a smiling cherub. His appearance was deceptive, for he was one of the foremost scientists of Europe, with an international reputation for his expertise. Although he taught at the university, he spent much more time on research than he did in the classroom. He came over now and gave her a squeeze and a kiss on the cheek. "You're getting to be such a big girl. We'll have to make sure you get plenty of food while you're here with us."

Gabby kissed her uncle on the cheek. "You'll have me as fat as a pig if I stay much longer, Uncle Dalton. I've only been here two days, and I've already had enough food to last me a week!"

Liza Burke, at the age of forty-one, was four years older than her husband. She was also taller by an inch and had auburn hair and blue eyes. She resembled Lance Winslow, her baby brother. She had married Dalton Burke after a long courtship, for she wanted to be certain they were compatible. Dalton needed someone to look after his personal life, and she was more than glad to fill the role. His mind was too busy with the scientific world of formula and theory to worry about everyday trivia. He would have occasionally gone off to work wearing one blue sock and one green one if she did not check his attire each morning.

"I've fixed your favorite breakfast, dear. Sit down and eat."

Aunt Liza's breakfast was indeed a bracing way to begin the day. Along with bread and rolls, there were thin slices of cheese and ham, preserves, a boiled egg for each of them, and plenty of freshly brewed tea. They even had orange juice, which many people did not drink due to the high cost.

Dalton Burke was a rather messy eater, and by the time the meal was half finished, his waistcoat was covered with crumbs. Once, Gabby reached over and laughed as she brushed them away with her napkin. His blue eyes twinkled, and he grunted, "I certainly do need a keeper. It's a good thing I married your aunt Liza. No telling what I would be like if I hadn't." Although he spoke English well, he had an interesting accent that he had picked up while studying at a German university.

Dalton spread a generous amount of jam on a roll and bit off an enormous hunk. "Have you thought about what we discussed yesterday, Gabby?"

"Yes, I have."

"So you still want to be a doctor?"

"I think so." Gabby smiled. "It sounds silly, but I couldn't decide for a long time whether to go into show business or become a doctor."

Liza laughed. "That's like trying to decide whether you want to be a brain surgeon or a housewife." She was a sweet-faced woman, who was very fond of her brother, Lance. She and Dalton had never had children, and Liza's maternal instinct had drawn her toward Gabby. The vacations the young girl had spent with them had brought the two of them close. "You could live with us and go to medical school here," she suggested.

"I expect Mum and Dad will want me to get my training in England, but I'll visit here often and see that your tie matches your socks, Uncle Dalton."

Liza shook her head. "Your uncle has received offers to teach at Oxford, but he has turned them down. I wish we'd go. Then we'd be closer to family." She looked over at her husband and shook her head slightly. "There's trouble coming in this part of the world, Dalton."

Many people in Europe were saying those exact words. Germany was struggling to recover from the terrible depression and financial crash following the Great War, when the German mark became practically worthless.

"It will be fine, dearest," Dalton said, reaching over and taking Liza's hand. He squeezed it and smiled cheerfully. "Germany has been flat on its back ever since the end of the war, but things are looking up now. You'll see. All will be well."

Liza did not agree. "Your mother doesn't think so." Dalton's mother, Dorcas, lived on the outskirts of Oudekerk in the house where he had been born. She was a strong woman, a devout Christian with solid opinions.

"Mother and I don't agree a hundred percent on everything," he said.

"She is a wise woman," Liza said firmly. "You should listen to her more."

Dalton was an incurable optimist, always expecting the best outcomes. He seemed to push the matter out of his mind and leaned toward Gabby. "You must be careful at the festival." He underscored his statement with a wink.

"Careful, Uncle Dalton? Careful of what?"

"Why, the young men." He laughed heartily. "Young men have no respect today. Why, when I was a young man—"

Liza laughed and interrupted him. "When you were a young man, you behaved like all other young men—very badly."

"I'm afraid I did," he admitted. "Would you believe that I held your aunt's hand without asking permission of her parents?"

"How shocking!" Gabby laughed. "Before I let anybody hold my hand at the festival, I'll make him come and ask your permission."

★ ★ ★

Betje van Dych caught Gabby's arm and laughed at her. "Hurry up," she said. "We'll be late. All the good-looking boys will be taken."

Betje was two years older than Gabby, but they had become fast friends on Gabby's first visit to the country years ago. On the two subsequent trips, their friendship had deepened, and now the two young women were very close. Betje was a solidly built girl with a full figure that drew the eyes of young men. Her blond hair was cut rather short in the American fashion, and her blue-green eyes sparkled with life. She was very emotional and thought far too much about boys—or so Gabby thought. "Come on," she said. "You're walking as slow as a snail!"

Gabby snickered. "Snails don't walk. They crawl."

The two were moving quickly along the streets of Oudekerk, caught in the stream of people. The sun beat down, and tulips and other flowers were everywhere, providing brilliant color in window boxes and in small yards. The air was full of chattering and singing and laughing as the crowds made their way to the festival.

"I always forget what this festival celebrates," Gabby confessed.

Betje laughed and nudged Gabby with her elbow. "It's another excuse to get drunk, for young men to find young women, and young women to fight them off—for a while."

Gabby was very different from her friend and was often shocked by her seeming lack of morals. "That's not true!" she protested. "It has to celebrate something."

"Why can't it just celebrate love?" Betje asked with a grin. "Look. See that tall fellow over there?" She indicated a young man who was walking in the same direction on the opposite sidewalk. "He keeps looking at us. Do you want to meet him?"

"Betje, don't be silly! For all you know he's already got a girlfriend."

"That's half the fun of it. One of us could take him away from her. She shouldn't let him run loose if she wants to hang on to him."

The young man had seen the two girls giggling and crossed the street. He had dark blue eyes and clean-cut features, but when he came close, Gabby smelled alcohol on his breath.

"Good morning, ladies. You've come to the festival, I see. May I escort you?"

"Why, we're married women," Betje said with a straight face. "You wouldn't want to get involved with a married woman."

He smiled and winked. "I wouldn't mind as long as your husband doesn't have a pistol."

Betje laughed and continued to tease him as they continued along their way.

They were soon joined by another young fellow, a short, muscular young man of some eighteen years, Gabby judged. He was wearing a colorful shirt and had already been sampling the wares of the drinking houses. His name was Hans, he said, and he talked Betje into stopping for refreshments. He led them into a small place called Bistro Klein Paardenburg. It was crowded and filled with noisy talk and laughter, and Gabby noticed that many of the patrons were eating *rolpens*—a combination of minced meat, fried apples, and red cabbage. Gabby was not hungry, but her three companions gobbled down *saucijzenbrood*—a flaky roll of pastry surrounding a piece of sausage. They also had beer, which Gabby refused. Instead, she had a drink similar to apple cider, which was very good.

After they had eaten their fill, the quartet left the restaurant and joined a larger group of young people, some of whom Betje knew. For the rest of the morning, the two girls enjoyed themselves tremendously at the outdoor festival. At noon they went to a sandwich shop and squeezed around the only empty table. Hans had drunk more than was good for him and insisted on putting his arm around Gabby. He leaned over her, and before she could move, he picked up the old coin that hung by the golden chain from her neck. She had worn it since Madame Jana had given it to her. She had laughed at her own superstitions, but still the words of the ancient woman had remained with her. *"It is to remind you that you are not alone—that somewhere an old woman is praying for you."*

"What is this? A good luck charm?" he asked.

"Not exactly. Just a gift from an old gypsy woman."

"A gypsy? Did she tell you your fortune?"

Before she could answer his question, Hans suddenly kissed her noisily on the lips.

Betje laughed. "Now you're getting into the spirit of things."

Gabby pushed Hans away angrily. "Don't you do that again!"

"I forgot to tell you," Betje said to Hans. Her eyes were somewhat glazed, for she had been sampling wine and beer and even stronger drinks throughout the morning. "She's a good girl." She winked at her own escort, whose name was Frans. "Not like me."

Such talk made Gabby ill at ease, and for the rest of the afternoon she tried in every way she could to get Betje to stop drinking so much. Betje simply laughed at her efforts, saying, "I'm going to have a good time."

"You won't have a good time if you get in trouble, and that's what could happen if you get drunk."

"I can take care of myself," Betje snapped. She usually was a cheerful girl, but sometimes alcohol made her quarrelsome. "If you don't like what's going on, go home to your aunt and uncle."

Gabby felt a great concern for Betje, for she knew her

friend was not careful with men. "I think I will," she said. "I'll see you tomorrow."

As Gabby turned her back on the group, she could hear Betje's scornful tone. "Come on, Frans. There's a lot to see yet."

Gabby felt sad as she walked back to Dalton and Liza's house. She worried about Betje and had tried more than once to talk to her about her soul. Betje had simply laughed, saying, "Let old people worry about religion. It's not for me."

★ ★ ★

"You didn't stay very long at the fete, Gabby," Liza said. "Didn't you have a good time?"

"Oh, I did for a while, but then—" She broke off. "I just thought I'd rather come home."

Liza Burke had a keen insight into people. She had been glad when Betje and Gabby had become friends when they were little girls, but during the last few years she had watched Betje, who was the daughter of one of her good friends, turn wild. Now she said gently, "Betje has changed, hasn't she?"

"Oh, I don't know, Aunt Liza. She's always been a little wild." Gabby plopped down on the couch.

"I'm afraid it's more than that now," Liza said as she sat next to Gabby.

Gabby looked up. "What do you mean?"

"I shouldn't tell you this, and I don't do it as a matter of gossip. It's just something you need to know. Has she told you about her abortion?"

Shocked, Gabby just stared at her aunt, unable to speak. Finally, she said, "No, she hasn't."

"She probably will. It didn't mean a great deal to her. She was seeing this young man and became pregnant. She came to your uncle and wanted him to help her—that is, help her get rid of the baby. He refused, of course, and she became very upset."

"But she found somebody to do it?"

"Yes, she did. It broke her parents' hearts. She has a brother and sister who are as good as can be, but there's a wild streak in Betje that grieves me." She put her hand on Gabby's arm. "I hope you don't think I'm gossiping to tell you this."

"Of course not, Aunt Liza. I'm glad you told me, but I feel so sorry for her."

"I suppose part of it is the times. Everything is so unsettled these days. There's talk of wars and revolutions everywhere you go. Betje told me once that she was going to enjoy life as much as she could before it crashed down around her ears."

"I've heard that before, but it doesn't make any sense. If things are crashing down around your ears, that's the time to look to God."

"Exactly right!" Liza gave her niece a warm, approving look. Then she shook her head. "I hate to think about your going home. We'll miss you so much."

"Dad said in his letter that they'd be coming back sooner than they thought. I'm looking forward to skiing in France. But of course I'll miss you and Uncle Dalton."

"I hope you'll come back soon for another visit. You liven this house up."

"I'll try, Aunt Liza, but I'll be studying to be a doctor pretty soon."

"You'll be a good one too. You're intelligent, and you're sensitive. Those are the two traits a doctor must have, so Dalton says."

"I've got so much to learn."

"Don't you worry. With your bright head, you'll learn all of it and more." Liza leaned over and kissed her niece on the cheek. "Tomorrow we're going into Amsterdam to see all the museums we can. You'll like that, won't you?"

"Oh yes! Will Uncle Dalton go with us?"

"Yes, he promised to take the day off so we could all go together and have a good family time."

★ ★ ★

Gabby's time in Holland had gone by so quickly she could hardly believe it was practically time to return to England. She picked up the telegram that had come a few days before and reread it. *Finished quicker than expected. Will board ship soon. Be ready for France. Dad.* A good feeling came over Gabby as she read it. She had been happy with her uncle and aunt, and she and Betje had made up after their disagreement and spent the days pleasantly enough. But she missed her parents and was anxious to go to Paris and see her grandfather.

As she straightened the room and made the bed, she sang "It Had to Be You" under her breath. She reflected on some of the articles she had recently read in the newspaper about life in America. *It sounds like they've all gone crazy,* she thought. *Throwing off all restraint. I wouldn't like that.*

Gabrielle Winslow liked stability more than adventure. She had found it at home with her parents, as well as in the home of Dalton and Liza Burke. The world outside seemed to be spinning wildly around. The Great War had ended, but still the nations were jockeying for a position of power, while the people in America seemed to be on an unending search for new ways to indulge themselves. She could hardly believe the stories she read of what the wild, crazy youth in the States were doing. She had absolutely no desire for such things.

As she finished making the bed, she glanced out the window and saw her uncle hurrying down the brick walk that led to the front door. *Why would he be coming home? I thought he had classes all day.* It was unusual for him to come home during the day, and she hurried downstairs to see what was up.

As she reached the foot of the stairs, she saw her uncle

and aunt huddled together, speaking in hushed tones. When Dalton noticed her, he broke off suddenly, his face twisted into a strange expression.

A cold hand seemed to grab her as she looked from her uncle to her aunt. Both of their faces were stretched taut, and both were pale. Suddenly, her aunt's face seemed to break, and tears ran down her cheeks. As Liza put her hands over her face, Gabby suddenly knew what the news was and began to shake with fear.

"Is it . . . is it Mum and Dad?"

Dalton came forward and gently put his hands on her shoulders. He had tears in his eyes, and he struggled to get the words out. "You . . . you must be brave, my dear one."

"What is it?" Gabby felt stiff, as if she had been paralyzed. Her lips were numb, and she could hardly speak.

"There was a terrible storm, and their ship—" Dalton broke off and pulled a handkerchief from his pocket and wiped it across his face. He was a sentimental and emotional man, and his lips quivered as he continued. "The ship, my dear, went down."

"Maybe they're in a lifeboat."

Dalton glanced at Liza before turning his gaze down to his shoes. "Maybe so, dear," he whispered.

Liza joined the two of them and put her arms around both. For a moment Gabby could not even weep, and then the enormity of the situation overwhelmed her, and she began gasping out great sobs. Her aunt's arms tightened around her, and she knew that all hope was gone—that her life would never be the same again.

★ ★ ★

Dalton Burke held the Delft china cup with both hands. The fragrance of the strong tea wafted up, but he paid no heed to it. His ordinarily cheerful face was drawn tight. As he looked over toward his wife, he was worried about the weight she had lost since the devastating news. *It's been two weeks,* he thought, *and I still can't believe they're dead.* He had been very fond indeed of Liza's brother and his wife. They had been most kind to him, and because he had few relatives, the loss had hit him almost as hard as it had Liza. "We must do *something,* dear," he finally said.

"I know, Dalton. I haven't been able to think. It's almost as if the sun has gone out. I . . . I feel so bad for poor Gabby." Liza clasped her hands together and stared down at them. She had slept little over the past two weeks, and her cheeks were sunken from the weight loss. She looked across the table with grief in her eyes. "I can't believe that Lance and Jo are gone! So quick . . . with no warning at all!"

"It's hard to make any sense of it. Of course death can take any of us, at any time, but when we're the ones left here, we realize how fragile life is."

"Did you show Gabby the letter from the Maritime Board?" They had received a formal notice stating there were no survivors from the wreck. There had been no hope in any case, but this had closed a final door on the lives of the two people they loved so dearly.

"No, I hate to do it. It takes away her last hope."

"I don't think she really has any hope. She's like a ghost, Dalton."

"I know. She's going to be ill if she doesn't start eating soon."

"They were her life. I don't know how she's going to bear it or what she will do."

"Do you think she will go back to England?"

Liza shook her head. "She hasn't said a word about it, but I don't think so. She has no other family there."

"There's her grandfather in France. She might go to him."

"He's quite old and feeble, unable to take care of himself. He couldn't take on the responsibility of raising a young woman."

Dalton was quiet, and for a time the two just sat there. Their marriage was happy, but they had been disappointed that they had not been able to have children. Liza had been pregnant three times, but each pregnancy had ended prematurely in miscarriage. Now he suddenly knew what must be done. "She must stay with us, Liza."

She raised her eyes. "That's what I've been thinking, but we'd be taking on a lot of responsibility."

"Perhaps, but she needs us—and we need her."

Liza reached across the table, and the two clasped hands. Tears came to her eyes, and she whispered, "She has no one but us, Dalton. We must take her in! I'm sure that's what Lance and Jo would have wanted."

★ ★ ★

Gabby was walking through one of the tulip fields close to the village. Ordinarily, the vibrant colors would have thrilled her, but now they might as well have been gray or black. Ever since the terrible news of her parents' deaths, she had been dazed with grief at her loss. Part of her moved and ate and drank and slept, but another part of her was completely cut off from all that was alive in the world. She had not known that grief could be so terrible. At first, she felt as though a sword plunged into her heart every time she thought of her parents. Now she felt trapped in a huge, dark void, with no color or sound of any kind. The feeling of crushing despair would overtake her at times, usually at night as she tossed on her bed. Even now, as she walked past the beautifully flowered field with the blue sky overhead and the warm breeze on her face, she might as well have been locked in a prison cell for all the beauty of the world that surrounded her.

A flock of crows passed over, their sharp cries falling to the earth. Gabby glanced up, but the sight of them did not stir anything within her. Over to her left a windmill slowly turned its majestic blades. Where there had once been ten thousand windmills in the Netherlands, there were now only about three thousand remaining. This particular one was pumping water away from the land into the sea.

Ordinarily, Gabby would have stopped and watched the blades turn. She might even have gone over to look inside and see how the pump operated, but this held no charm for her now. She walked along the well-beaten path until she came to a grove of trees and then stood still. Fond memories, which she tried to block, seemed to climb over the walls that she attempted to build and flooded her mind. She thought of the time her father had taken her up in an open airplane. She had been delighted with the exhilarating experience, and he had laughed at her joy as she gazed down at the earth far below. She could see his face as clearly as if he were standing before her. She thought of her stepmother, Jo, always laughing, always eager to spend time with her, and she remembered the many times Jo had read aloud to her.

The creaking of the windmill suddenly brought her to her senses, and she cried out, "Oh, God, I don't know what to do! Help me! I can't live with this grief!"

But the only response was the groan of the windmill and the raucous shrieks of the crows overhead. Gabby's mind went back to her date with Greg the night before she left England, back in May. She could clearly see the horses and wagons in Lovers' Grove, the dark faces of the people who greeted her and Greg, their flashing smiles as they sat around the fire. She heard the wild music of Duke Zanko's violin—and then she remembered the ancient face of Madame Jana and her prayer. And she heard her voice again, saying, *"A dark time lies before you, but Jesus will never forsake you. When you think all is lost, He will bring you strength."*

With trembling fingers, Gabby grasped the gold coin that hung from the necklace she had worn since that day. She held it tightly and tried to call out to God, but it seemed that the heavens were brass. Finally she blinked her tears back and said, "I have no one else to turn to, Jesus, so I'm trusting you."

She turned and stumbled home, where she found her aunt and uncle waiting for her.

"We must talk to you, dear," Liza said. "Come in."

"What is it, Aunt Liza?"

Liza led her into the low-ceilinged living area and pulled her down to sit beside her on the sofa. Dalton stood a few feet away beside the window, his eyes full of concern. "We've been talking about you, dear, and your uncle and I want to know if you want to go back to England."

Gabby thought of her home in England, the only one she had ever known, but the idea of going back to it without her father or mother was unbearable. "I don't want to," she whispered. "I don't think I could bear it. But I have no other choice."

Dalton came over and sat down on the other side of her, taking her hand. "We very much want you to make your home with us, Gabrielle. We're your family, and you're like the daughter we never had."

Tears suddenly flooded Gabrielle's eyes, and she threw her arms around her uncle's neck. He held her tightly, and she felt her aunt Liza's hand stroking her hair. She wept then as she had not wept since she had heard the tragic news. The three sat there embracing one another until Gabby was exhausted and could cry no more.

As she continued to cling to her uncle, he said, "You will live here with us. You will finish secondary school here and then go on to college. There's a fine medical college in Amsterdam. You'll become a doctor, and we will be a family for one another."

Gabby gave her uncle a tight squeeze and then turned to her aunt. As the two clung to each other, Gabby felt the security her heart had longed for. It was like coming into a safe harbor after a terrible storm. *I can stay here, and they'll take care of me*. The thought was comforting, and she knew that somehow she would survive even this terrible loss. Again she thought of Madame Jana's words and knew that they had come true by way of her aunt and uncle.

CHAPTER THREE

DR. WINSLOW

★ ★ ★

During the nine years since the death of her parents, Gabrielle Winslow had found not one home but two in the Netherlands. She lived, for the most part, with her uncle Dalton and aunt Liza, but Dorcas Burke, Dalton's mother, had also proved herself to be a safe harbor for a young woman making her way in life. Dorcas lived only a few miles from Dalton and Liza, and this distance was easily manageable for a girl on a bicycle or later as an aspiring medical student with an automobile of her own.

As Gabby looked across the dining room table at Dorcas, she felt a warm sensation of comfort as she realized she couldn't have made it through those difficult years had it not been for the great-aunt she now called "Grandmother." Dorcas had invited her to use the name, saying, "You seem more like a granddaughter to me than a niece. And since I have no other grandchildren, that makes you extra special."

A smile spread across Gabby's lips as she waited for Matilda, the housekeeper, to serve breakfast. She felt deep love and admiration for the woman sitting across from her. Dorcas Burke was not tall and had gained weight over the years. Her silver hair was done up in a simple arrangement, and her blue eyes were as clear as those of a young girl. Her face was far younger-looking than her sixty-five years. She wore her age as gracefully and as lightly as most women wear a spring bonnet. And she had a depth of strength that Gabby had leaned on time and time again through the years. Dorcas always seemed to have the right word for whatever Gabby was facing.

"We may starve to death before we get any of those *pannekoeken,*" Dorcas teased.

Gabby had learned years ago that her great-aunt loved her housekeeper like a daughter, but they constantly gave each other a hard time.

Matilda, a tall, gaunt woman with stern brown eyes and salt-and-pepper hair, responded in Dutch. "I'm comin', aren't I?" She came to the table and put two sugar-dusted, apple-filled pancakes on each plate. Dutch pancakes had become Gabby's favorite.

"These look delicious, Matilda!" Gabby said. Her Dutch had become very good over the years, and she spoke with hardly a trace of an accent. Her German was quite proficient as well. French was another language she spoke well, but not as fluently as Dutch.

"Some people don't appreciate!" Matilda sniffed and went into the kitchen, her head held high.

"Matilda's having proud thoughts," Dorcas said loud enough for the housekeeper to hear. "I shall have to remember to pray for her to become more humble." She winked at Gabby and then bowed her head and asked a quick blessing on the food. Dorcas ate heartily, and as she did, she fired a series of direct questions at her great-niece.

Gabby was accustomed to this routine and answered each question as clearly as possible as she savored the delicious filling in the pancakes. When she had first gotten to know Dorcas, she had been somewhat put off by the woman's rather intimidating manner. But Gabby had quickly discovered that deep down, the woman had the most enormous heart she had ever encountered. She loved her son and his wife, and she loved Gabby—she just loved people in general—although she shied away from physical affection. She loved God most of all, which was apparent to anyone who knew her. At the church she attended with Dalton, Liza, and Gabby, her voice seemed to fill the building with praises. It was there that Gabby had learned that this woman had a deep love for God and for others, for she was always giving an encouraging word to someone or helping in a practical way.

Suddenly, Dorcas fired a question as if it were a bullet from a gun. "What about your men friends?"

Startled, Gabby paused, holding a fragment of the pannekoeken on her fork. "My men friends?"

"Yes. Are you keeping appropriate boundaries in your relationships?"

Gabby knew exactly what she meant and realized she'd better answer directly before the woman rephrased the question and embarrassed them both. She was sure her face was already flaming red.

"Of course, Grandmother."

"Well, that's good to hear. I thought so, but since you've become my only granddaughter, I have to be sure you don't fall into the evil ways of this terrible generation. I'm certain you know there's no real love involved in these adulterous habits many young people have fallen into."

"Yes, I know."

Dorcas changed subjects quickly, as was her custom. "Are you proud that you're now a full-fledged doctor and finished with your studies?"

"It's wonderful to be a doctor, but I don't know if I'll ever be finished with my studies."

"But you received your degree."

"Yes, of course, but I want to do more advanced studies."

"Hmm, I don't see what for. You're working in a hospital and treating sick people. Isn't that what you wanted to do?"

"Yes, but I need to know so much more. The medical field is always encountering new challenges."

"I suppose you're very proud now that people call you *Doctor*."

Gabby laughed. "I was for about two days, but that didn't last. I quickly realized how little I knew."

"I'm glad to hear it. Don't be proud, Gabrielle. God hates pride. More people stumble in life over pride than anything else."

Gabby smiled at the woman's wise words and finished her breakfast, drinking the last of her tea. "Don't forget, I'll be using the wagon and Samson again this year."

"You're going to the fete again rigged out like a gypsy? I think it's foolish," Dorcas scolded.

For several years Gabby had taken part in the local church's annual event to raise money for overseas missions. Two years after her parents' death, the pastor had asked her if she could come up with a plan to raise money. Gabrielle had always been interested in dramatics, and as she had thought about what to do, a small wagon at her great-aunt's barn had caught her attention. She came up with the idea of converting it into something resembling a gypsy wagon. Dorcas even had a horse named Samson that the hired man used to plow the garden.

Gabby's first effort had been very successful. She had dressed herself in colorful flowing garments, complete with big gold earrings, and pretended to tell fortunes. The people who came to the event enjoyed her act because it was new and different, and their contributions had been generous. She had continued this every May, and as the event grew closer every year, Dorcas made the same comment. "It doesn't sound Christian to me. I don't believe in fortune-telling."

"Oh, I don't either, Grandmother," Gabby answered now. "It's just for fun. I know many of the people who come, and I tell them silly things that make them laugh."

Gabby got up from her chair and went around the table to kiss her great-aunt. "I'll make sure Oskar knows I'll need the wagon this afternoon."

Dorcas reached up and laid her hand on Gabby's cheek.

She was thinking back to the frightened young fifteen-year-old who had just lost her parents. She had seen her grow up into a twenty-four-year-old woman with such maturity and poise. She had found her place in the world of medicine, and Dorcas Burke was tremendously proud of this young woman—of her character as well as her beauty.

As Gabby left the house, she waved at Oskar Grotman and paused long enough to say, "Oskar, will you get Samson and the wagon ready for this afternoon?"

"Ja, you be a gypsy again, will you, miss? I mean Doctor." He grinned. "I forget. You still seem like a little girl to me."

Gabby smiled. "Miss is fine. Yes, I'm going to play the role of a gypsy again, but first I need to check on my patients at the orphanage."

★ ★ ★

Deman van der Klei, the director of the Vermeer Orphanage, greeted Gabby warmly. "Ah, Dr. Winslow, I'm so happy to see you."

"It's good to see you, Herr Director," Gabby responded.

"I would like to introduce you to Reverend Karel Citroen, our new pastor."

Gabby turned to the tall, strong-looking man with blond hair and nodded. "I welcome you to the congregation, Reverend."

The man bowed slightly and smiled. "I'm sorry I don't recognize you. It will take me a little time to become acquainted with everyone."

"I'm sure. I've enjoyed your sermons very much," Gabby said with a smile. "But now you must excuse me. I must hurry to the infirmary."

"Of course, Doctor," Van der Klei said. The two men watched as the shapely young woman moved down the hall and turned up the stairs.

"She's young to be a doctor," Reverend Citroen remarked.

"Yes, she got her degree only a few months ago."

"Her Dutch is impeccable, but I heard the slightest of accents. Is she Dutch?"

"No, she is English. The niece of possibly the most famous man in this country—Dalton Burke."

"Yes, I've heard of him. A prominent scientist indeed." Citroen cocked his head to one side. "She's a very pretty woman," he observed. "Not married?"

"No, but don't waste your time. Many young men have tried to court her. She's a very dedicated physician and hardly has time for a social life. She works full-time at the hospital, yet still finds time to take care of our children here and never charges a guilder."

"She sounds like an admirable Christian."

"Yes, that she is."

Citroen, who was unmarried and accustomed to the admiration of ladies in his congregation, smiled. "I hate to see a lovely woman be alone. She needs a husband and a family."

The director shook his head. "I suppose you're right, Reverend, but she has withstood some rather high-powered courting, I understand."

Citroen smiled. "It only takes the right one."

* * *

Gabby met Mrs. van der Klei at the infirmary. The director's wife was an attractive woman of thirty-five, who smiled nervously as she came forward. "I'm so glad you're here, Dr. Winslow."

"Is there more sickness? Anything critical?"

"It's Nicola. She has a very high fever."

"I'll see her at once," Gabby said.

Gabby walked rapidly to the girl's bedside, followed by Mrs. van der Klei. They found the girl lying flat, her cheeks flushed. She smiled, however, when she saw Gabby.

"Good morning, Dr. Winslow."

"Good morning, Nicola," Gabby said. "You're not feeling well today?"

"Not very well."

Gabby took the girl's temperature and examined her. She had already become a very proficient doctor and was a favorite at the orphanage. It had been a joy for her to work with the children, a relief from the difficulties of the city hospital in Amsterdam, where she had worked as an intern.

"Nicola, do you know anyone who has had the measles recently?"

The girl nodded her head and then said, "Ohhh," as she realized why Gabby had asked the question.

"*Oh* is right. I'm afraid that's what you have."

"Good heavens," Mrs. van der Klei exclaimed. "That means all the children will get it!"

"Not necessarily, but it might not be a bad thing if they did."

"Why, how can you say that, Doctor?"

"Most children are going to contract the measles at some point, and they might as well get it as early as possible."

Nicola's eyes had grown large. "The measles? Will I have spots?"

"I'm afraid you will, but they won't last long, and we'll take very good care of you."

"Will you come back and see me every day?"

"Every single day. Now, you lie there while I go check on your friends."

As they moved on to the next bed, Mrs. van der Klei shook her head. "I don't know what we'd do if it weren't for you, Dr. Winslow. The children so depend on you. You always seem to brighten their day."

"Why, you would have another doctor," Gabby said pleasantly.

The woman shook her head. "The one we had before you came was very gruff. The children didn't like him at all, but they all love you."

Mrs. van der Klei accompanied Gabby as she examined the rest of the children. When they had seen the last one, she asked, "Are you going to the fete this afternoon?"

"Oh yes," Gabby said. "I always look forward to it."

"Are you going to dress up and tell fortunes again?"

"Absolutely." A small dimple appeared to the left of her mouth, and humor danced in her eyes. "It's my one chance every year to behave foolishly. Everyone expects a doctor to be so sober all the time, so it's really fun for me."

Mrs. van der Klei laughed. "You do it very well. I remember you told my husband's fortune last year. It almost convinced him that you really could predict the future."

"Nothing like that. It's all nonsense, really." Gabby's lips stirred with a pleasant expression. "Will you be there, Mrs. van der Klei?"

"Yes, of course."

"Then perhaps I'll tell you your fortune."

Gabby turned to leave, but Mrs. van der Klei said, "Say, have you met the new pastor, Reverend Citroen?"

"Yes, your husband just introduced me to him downstairs."

"So fine looking and such a good preacher." She arched an eyebrow. "There's a catch for you."

"A pastor doesn't need a doctor for a wife. He needs someone who can go to teas and be sociable with the members of his congregation. But I'll tell his fortune. Maybe I can match him up with a suitable girl. Maybe Doreen Hoffmeyer."

"But she's so—plain."

"A minister's wife *should* be plain. Movie stars are the only ones who need to be beautiful." Gabby laughed and shook her head. "Now I'm being foolish. I'll see you later."

* * *

"Are you leaving soon, Gabby?" Dalton asked. He had run into Gabby as she came down the stairs. His glasses were pushed up on his head, and his clothes were disheveled, as usual.

"Yes, in about twenty or thirty minutes."

"Are you going by my mother's?"

"Oh yes. I have to stop there for my gypsy costume I keep there."

"Come and have a cup of tea with me before you leave. I need to talk with you."

"All right, but I can't take long. I must be at the church as early as possible. I have to make money for the missions, you know."

Dalton smiled. "I know, but this won't take long."

The two went into the dining room, where Liza joined them around the heavy walnut table for a cup of tea. Dalton had gathered some papers together that he needed his mother to sign. "Be sure you bring them back with you," he said. "Mother's getting a little forgetful lately."

"I'll take them, but I think you're wrong, Uncle. Her mind is as sharp as ever," Gabby said.

"Is that fellow Lang Zeeman going to the festival with you?"

"Yes, he is. And I've got to go, or we'll be late." She kissed her uncle and her aunt and then left the house.

As soon as she was outside the door, Liza said, "I don't think Zeeman is good company for Gabby."

"No, but how do you tell her that?" Dalton shrugged. "He's handsome, and his family's rich. And Gabby does seem to have a mind of her own."

"That may very well be, but you know as well as I do that he's a wild young fellow. He's very careless in how he treats others, and he's not a Christian. I'm worried about Gabby."

Dalton was troubled also about his niece's relationship with Lang. After sharing their concerns for several minutes, they prayed for Gabby. They were both intensely proud of their niece's achievements and wanted to help her in any way they could. "Does she ever talk about her parents with you?" Dalton asked.

"Never. Has she spoken to you?"

"Not once in all these years. It's like she's buried all her memories of the past."

"I think they're too painful for her, Dalton."

"I'm not sure that's good. I wish we could have recovered her parents' bodies and had a proper burial. I think it gives us a focal point for our grief, helps us to begin the healing process."

"But there was no chance of that. They went down with the ship."

"I know, so she never really had a chance to say good-bye to them."

The two sat silently for a time, and finally Liza said, "She's a very strong woman and a fine Christian. She'll be all right, but I wish she were interested in someone besides Lang."

* * *

Gabby stood in front of the mirror in her great-aunt's extra bedroom, checking out her gypsy costume. She had used dark foundation on her face and hands and had covered her dark hair with a bright-colored scarf. Gold earrings glittered as she moved. She pulled on a vest over her brilliant green blouse and fastened the gold coins she had sewn on for buttons. Her aunt Liza had helped her make her outfit years ago. She topped the outfit with the necklace she always wore—the one Madame Jana had given her in another lifetime, it seemed. She twirled around and watched the long skirt brush the top of her black kid boots. She plucked a silk shawl from the shelf and draped it over her shoulders.

"Would you like your fortune told?" she asked her reflection with a thick accent, trying to mimic Duke and Marissa's accent as well as she could. "You will have good fortune." She laughed and shook her head. "You would never have made it on the stage. It's a good thing you became a doctor."

While Gabby knew she wasn't talented enough to act professionally, she did love to dabble in it when the opportunity presented itself. She had often recruited friends and staff at the orphanage to help her put on skits and short plays for the children, complete with costumes and makeup. Her great-aunt was kind enough to let her keep everything she needed for these plays in the closet in the spare bedroom.

She left her bedroom now and found Dorcas out digging in the garden.

"You look like no young woman should look," Dorcas said.

"But, Grandmother, I look like a gypsy, don't I?"

She sniffed. "Foolishness, I say!" She got to her feet carefully, saying, "Oskar said Samson is harnessed. You be careful, now."

"What can happen to me at a church festival, Grandmother?" Gabby leaned over and kissed the woman on the cheek. "I'll come home and tell you all about it tonight."

"Plain foolishness! God doesn't need our help collecting money."

Gabby laughed. She was accustomed to her great-aunt's tart remarks about parties.

She went to the old carriage house that had once kept a buggy and the horses for transportation. Now the place had a musty smell, but she found Samson already hitched up to the wagon. She remembered how she and Oskar had labored over it, putting false sides on it, making it into an authentic-looking gypsy caravan. It had windows now and was painted red and green and yellow. She walked over to the horse and stroked its nose. "Samson, are you ready to go?" She dodged and laughed as he tried to nibble at her fingers. Lifting her long skirt, she climbed up into the seat. "Oskar, have you seen Lang?"

"He's waiting out in front. I told him you'd be right there."

Gabby took the lines from him and slapped them on the back of the horse. Samson moved out slowly. He was getting older now but was still capable of pulling the wagon, at least as far as the church. When she reached the front of the house, she turned slowly into the drive and saw Lang leaning against his car. He came over to the wagon.

"Well, I'm here, but I don't like it."

"I wish you'd let me dress you up too. You'd look handsome in a bright red shirt and earrings."

"I'm not dressing up and that's final." Lang Zeeman was a fine-looking man of twenty-six. He had once been in medical school, but he had dropped out, abandoning his studies out of sheer laziness. He was witty, and his family had plenty of money, so there was no reason for him to feel insecure. He had the reputation of being rather wild, and the sleek, powerful car he drove gave evidence of his exorbitant taste. He was very fond of Gabby.

He clambered up in the wagon seat beside her, grumbling, "I don't see why you want to do this. It'd be much easier just to make a contribution."

"I *am* going to make a contribution," she said. She clucked at the horse, which started up at once. It was May, and the weather was cool but pleasant. The sun sent its yellow beams down, and as the wagon rumbled over the cobblestones, the two rocked gently from side to side.

"You should have become an actress. You like to dress up and play roles so much."

"What roles do I play?"

"Oh, you play being a fortune-teller, and you play being a doctor," he teased her. "I think you see yourself in a drama always—the great doctor Gabrielle Winslow rushing to save those threatened with death by plague!" He laughed and put his arm around her, pulling her close and kissing her on the lips.

She quickly pulled away.

"You're not too good at playing love scenes, though. Too shy."

"Lang, somebody will see us!"

"What if they do? We're courting, aren't we? As a matter of fact," he said almost gruffly, "we've been courting so long

I feel like I've got a long white beard."

Gabby laughed at him and pushed him away. "You stay on your own side of the seat. At least in daylight."

Lang brightened up. "Oh, all I have to do is wait until dark, and then you'll come to my manly arms!"

Gabby rolled her eyes and turned her attention back to the road. She had mixed emotions about Lang. He seemed serious enough at times, but the way he lived troubled her. She found herself drawn to him, for he was charming and highly intelligent. He worked in his father's factory, and one day he would own it, but still there was something that kept her from making a commitment. She knew he cared for her, but she didn't know if his interest was anything more than temporary. She also was aware that he had dated a number of women, which bothered her greatly.

⋆ ⋆ ⋆

The fete was a rousing success, and at the end of it, Reverend Citroen came across the park to applaud her efforts. "Congratulations! You must have taken in a bundle. You were busy all day."

"Yes, Reverend, I was busy, but I had lots of fun. I know the missionaries will make good use of the money we made."

"I know you're right about that." He put his hands in his pockets. "A few of us are going to get together tonight to celebrate a successful fund-raiser. I'd like you to come if you could."

"Oh, I'm sorry. I have another engagement."

"Well, some other time, then. Thank you so much for all your efforts. They're greatly appreciated."

As the pastor turned away, Lang approached Gabby. "Guess who I found down the way. An old friend of yours."

He turned and grinned as a woman appeared from behind him.

"Betje!" Gabby exclaimed. "What are you doing here?"

Betje was wearing an artistic sort of dress, loose fitting but gaily colored. She laughed and said, "Why are you so shocked that I would come to a church event? Where have you been? I haven't seen you for so long."

The two women embraced and spent a few moments catching up while Lang stood by idly. Betje had become an artist. She had spent several years learning to paint in France. It was also apparent she had picked up some bad habits, and Gabby noticed a hardness in her friend she hated to see.

"Listen, we're going out on Frederick's boat. You must come with us—you and Lang."

Gabby shook her head. "You know I can't do that." Frederick Godfried was a wealthy friend of Lang's who owned a yacht, albeit a small one. The boat had earned a bad reputation, for it was the scene of frequent parties that ended in drunkenness and immorality, so it was believed.

"Come along," Lang said. "You need to relax. We'll have a good time."

Betje nodded. "Gabby, you work all the time. You need to have some fun once in a while."

The argument went on for a considerable time, and finally Betje grew angry. "You're going to be a stale, dried-up old woman!" She turned and walked away, leaving Lang alone with Gabby.

"She put it badly, but she's right. You need to learn to relax and have some fun. Besides, nothing bad will happen on the yacht. I promise you that."

"I don't think you can promise that, Lang. You know what Frederick is like. You've been on that boat before, haven't you?"

He flushed. "Once or twice."

"And people were always drinking and partying and doing all kinds of things, weren't they?"

"We don't have to take part in any of that."

"I wouldn't find it much fun to be around a bunch of people who are drinking."

Suddenly, Lang stepped forward and put his hands on

her arm. "Look, you know I want to marry you, don't you?"

Gabby was startled at his words. Lang had tempted her before, testing her virtue, but she had always drawn a strict line. Now she stared at him. "You've never mentioned marriage before."

"Well, it's time I settled down. I think we'd have a good marriage. You know I care deeply for you." When she was silent, he added, "And I believe you care for me."

Gabby was confused by his sudden mention of marriage. She did like Lang Zeeman very much, but it was a big leap from liking someone to marrying him. She felt as if she were on a huge cliff about to step off into nothingness. For lack of a better answer, she said, "It's something we'll have to talk about, Lang."

He took her in his arms and kissed her. His lips were demanding, and she gave herself to him for a moment. She was not unaware of the desire she felt for his affection. She had never denied that part of her nature and thought women who did deny it were foolish. She was stirred by his kiss, and when he drew his head back he laughed.

"You see. There's a tiger in you somewhere. Come along. I'll take you home. You can get out of that garb, and then we'll go out for coffee and talk about it."

Gabby nodded with relief. "That will be fine." She pulled all her things together, and they went to the edge of the park, where the horse and wagon waited. On their way to her great-aunt's house, they spoke lightly of how the evening fund-raiser had gone, but Gabby's thoughts were elsewhere. Her relationship with Lang was the most serious thing she had faced since the loss of her parents. She had thought of marriage often and prayed that God would send her the right man. She knew that Lang Zeeman was not a Christian, although he was a member of the church. She kept up the light banter with him but knew she would have to make a decision soon.

CHAPTER FOUR

A Change of Direction

★ ★ ★

Gabby strolled along the dike, looking out over the choppy water held back by the structure in the never-ending battle with the ocean. The August sun beat down strongly, warming the back of her neck and nearly blinding her as it struck the water. Blinking, she turned away and continued walking slowly, occupied with fond thoughts of this country she had come to love so dearly. Ever since she had made her life in Holland, she had been intensely aware of the constant struggle between water and dry land. She often found herself quoting Coleridge's "Rime of the Ancient Mariner" under her breath: "Water, water, everywhere . . ." She had heard one Dutchman summarize the goal of the country in one sentence: "It is to possess the land where water wants to be."

She had studied her history well and knew that little by little the country was sinking into the sea. In fact, half of the country now sat below sea level. The Dutch had fought for centuries to stave off the attacks of the sea and to control the rivers, which were prone to flooding. They had constructed an amazing system of dikes, along with canals and pumps to drain the land. Without this elaborate system, much of the country would be under water, including the main cities and ports.

Overhead, a flock of sheldrakes scored the summer sky, which was as blue as she had ever seen it and seemed solid enough to strike a match on. She had recently been reading about the social changes that the challenging sea had made in the Dutch way of life. As flooded lands were reclaimed for farming, some fishermen adapted their skills to growing crops, and later many of these farmers became industrial workers. Gabby had always been aware of the Dutch character and admired their courage, their tidiness and humor, and the smugness and the conservative streak that ran through them. She believed, as did others, that the Dutch had been formed by the waters surrounding them.

Gabby stopped by an orange cat lying on the dike that had been watching her approach with heavy-lidded eyes. It rose and stretched and then pressed against her leg. When she bent over and stroked it, it purred loudly.

"Nice kitty," Gabby said. She stroked it again, and suddenly the cat jerked away and slashed at her with its claws. The claws caught in her sleeve and ripped it, and she jerked up. "Aren't you a fine one!" she muttered. "See if I ever pet you again." The cat looked at her and then lay down like a sphinx, paws out straight and head held high, looking out at the canal.

Gabby shook her head and laughed. She continued her walk along the dike and then turned and crossed one of the many bridges that spanned a still stream. She stopped at the top of the arch and looked down. The water was so clear she could see her facial features, and she studied them for a moment almost clinically. *I'm twenty-four years old now,* she thought, *and where am I going? I'll never win a beauty contest, but that's all right. I don't want to anyway.* The thought amused her, and for a time she sat there taking in the sight of the three windmills that stood like silent sentinels watching the sea. Usually, the blades turned slowly, sucking the water up from the land and pumping it drop by drop back into the sea in an endless cycle. She had always loved the windmills—they seemed to have a graceful beauty for all their size. No sight stirred her more than a series of windmills spinning rapidly in a stiff breeze.

She crossed to the other side of the bridge and leaned over to pick up several small stones. She tossed one of them into the stream and watched the circles spread from the spot where it had hit the water. She threw another stone a little farther down the stream. She listened for the *plop* and watched the concentric circles form. They struck against the first ones, creating small areas of confusion that disturbed the pattern. The circles reminded her of life. *When you throw one stone,* she thought, *it's very simple. It sends out circles with nothing to interfere, and everything is orderly and neat and systematic. But when you throw another stone, that pattern is broken.* She impulsively threw the rest of the stones. They scattered, and there was no pattern of geometric circles at all. Simply confusion. *That's the way it is. But life isn't one stone falling into the water making a pattern. It's a dozen or twenty, and soon everything is confused.*

"Oh, God," she prayed quietly, "it's so hard for me sometimes to see a pattern in my life. If life were only like that one stone making one set of circles, I could understand. But it's not like that. There are so many things about my life and about being a Christian that I don't understand, and I'm troubled about them, Lord. But I know that you are never confused and that you're not the author of confusion. So even when my life becomes confused and shattered, I know you understand each tiny thing that touches my life. And you have said that all things work together for good to those who love you. So, Lord, let me love you so that the patterns of my life will always be under your gracious and merciful hands." She smiled and looked up. "Thank you, Jesus, for listening to this foolish person!" Gabby had never been able to establish a regular prayer time. She preferred to pray spontaneously, dialoguing with her Lord whenever she felt the desire to commune with Him.

She watched until the patterns in the water were completely dissipated, and then she continued on her way, looking up at the opaque sky, where a pale sun cast down its beams with a benevolent warmth.

★ ★ ★

"You haven't said anything lately about your plans, Gabby."

Looking up from the sink where she was washing dishes, Gabby regarded her aunt with a questioning look. "Well, there's nothing much to tell, Aunt Liza."

Liza Burke picked up a Delft saucer and polished it carefully before putting it in the cabinet. "I haven't said anything before, but it seems to me that you're not very excited about your engagement to Lang."

Gabby started to answer but then pressed her lips together and moved the small dishrag around the surface of the bowl. The heat had raised a fine sheen of perspiration on her brow, and a tendril of her luxurious brown hair fell over her forehead. She brushed it away with a quick gesture. "Well, he's been in the army for two years. We haven't seen all that much of each other. It's been difficult, but then, I suppose it's difficult for all couples while the men are serving their time in the service."

Gabby's answer did not satisfy her aunt. She turned and studied the profile of this young woman who had come to fill such a large part of her life and that of her husband. Being childless, Liza had once turned her interests to other things, but since Gabby's parents had died, she had poured herself out for the young woman. Never a day passed that she didn't thank God for her. "I don't mean to be critical, dear. It just seems that you're not very excited about your upcoming marriage."

Gabby swirled the dishrag around, dipped the dish into the rinse water, and set it on the drying rack. "It's just hard to be engaged to a man while he's serving somewhere far away." She whirled around and asked her aunt, "Are you unhappy that I'm engaged to Lang?"

"Your uncle and I just want you to be happy."

"Well, I *am* happy. Of course, it's simply not my way to set off sparks. I wish I could be as romantic and overflowing as the movie stars in those silly movies."

"Well, I certainly wouldn't want you to imitate them," Liza said with a smile. She was troubled, however, about Lang. Although she did not let it show in her features, she was thinking of the many conversations she and Dalton had had concerning Gabby's relationship with Lang Zeeman. They seemed to be the only ones who were concerned, for Zeeman was handsome, wealthy, and likely to do well in the world of business. His father was not in good health, and one day Lang would run the large factory and have control of the family fortune. They had often spoken of something in the young man they found disturbing. "He's not steady, Liza," Dalton had said many times. "And he's too easy in his ways. You know how many affairs he's been accused of having with other women."

Liza had never mentioned Lang's freewheeling history to Gabby. He did go to church fairly often, but there was little to indicate any true devotion to the Lord.

Her aunt's silence troubled Gabby. She truly loved Liza and Dalton Burke. They had taken her in when she had nobody, and she not only owed them her devotion but was glad to give it. Now she suddenly laid the dishrag down and put her arm around Liza's waist. "It's all right," she said quietly. "Don't worry about me."

Liza returned Gabby's smile and said no more, but she felt a heaviness in her heart she could not deny.

★ ★ ★

Three days had passed since Gabby's conversation with her aunt concerning Lang Zeeman, but Gabby couldn't get the brief encounter off her mind. When such things happened, she usually assumed there was a reason for it. Every night she prayed, "God, show me if there's something I need to know about our engagement. I want to please you in this as in all other things." She spent hours walking along the canals and delighting in the tulip fields. She thought about her relationship with Lang and tried to put it into perspective. She remembered throwing the single stone into the canal and watching as the clear symmetrical circles made their way outward from the first tiny splash. She longed for the same simplicity in her own life. But then she also remembered how the other stones had disturbed this pattern. She felt there was a parallel to this in her life, although she could not put her finger on it.

Lang was by far the most fascinating man she had ever met. His dramatic good looks and charm drew people to him—especially women. Gabby was aware that he had known many women, but she had resolutely decided not to let that bother her. It was her conviction that when a man and a woman came together in marriage, they needed to shut the door on the past. Of course, she had nothing in her past to shut out, but she felt a disquietude in thinking of the many young women Lang had dated. They had not been innocent flirtations—she knew that, for Betje had kept her informed. Betje, in fact, had warned her, "You can't expect a man like Lang to stop looking at other women. They look at him, and he's a man. He's going to look back. So don't let him break your heart."

Betje's warning had disturbed Gabby more than she had indicated. To her, marriage was a lifelong promise that united a man and a woman in a sacred circle, and all others were shut out. It was not that they were isolated from the world, but she had exalted ideas about marriage. She was convinced that God chose a particular man for a certain woman and that God had a specific man for each woman. She was too easily embarrassed to ever express her views to Lang, for she felt he would laugh at her and call her a romantic. But still she treasured the idea in her heart, and she was terrified lest she make the terrible mistake of choosing the wrong man. She had seen enough loveless marriages in which the man and the woman simply went through the routine of living together without any trace of real devotion and with no excitement.

Maybe I'm expecting too much, Gabby thought. She was walking through the center of the village, stopping from time to time to look in a store window. *Maybe I'm too romantic*. The idea startled her, for she considered herself a logical person with a scientific mind. The study of medicine was not romantic in the least, but it required the faculties to be completely given to logic and reason. Still, she had another side that embarrassed her a little. She loved romances, and she sometimes wept in the cinema over heroines dying graceful deaths in the arms of a handsome lover. She knew that beneath her smooth professionalism lay a romantic side, but she had never learned how to show it to anyone else.

"Buy a pretty ring, miss?"

The sound of a voice at her elbow startled Gabby, and she turned quickly to see a young woman standing beside her. One quick look revealed that the woman was a gypsy, for she wore the colorful dress, long skirt, and gold earrings that they commonly wore. She was a strikingly attractive woman with olive skin, large lustrous eyes, and hair as black as a raven. "This ring, it would look so beautiful on your finger. Try it on, lady."

As always, Gabby was fascinated by these people, so she didn't turn away. She took the gold ring, set with a flashing green stone.

"You like it?" the woman asked, watching with eager eyes.

"Very beautiful indeed, but I don't think I could afford it."

"Oh, you must have the ring!"

Gabby did like the ring very much, and when she asked the price, she laughed and said, "Oh, I couldn't afford anything like that!" As she had expected, the gypsy began to bargain with her, and finally she bought it for much less than the original price. When she handed over the money, she said, "Did you ever happen to meet a gypsy named Duke Zanko?"

The eyes of the young woman flew open. "Duke Zanko! You know him?"

"I met him years ago in England. You have met him, then?"

"Met him! He is the leader of my band."

Instantly, Gabby grew excited. She had fond memories of her brief encounter with Zanko. "Is Madame Jana still with your band?"

"Oh yes. She is very old, very wise."

An impulse took Gabby, and she asked, "Please, would you show me where your band is camped?"

"Yes, I will take you. My name is Maria."

Maria led Gabby down the street and cut through a side street. When they were clear of the village, she pointed at a grove of trees. "There is our camp," she said. "Duke Zanko, he will be glad to see you, lady."

"I doubt if he will remember me. It's been many years."

"Perhaps he will not, but Madame Jana will remember you. She never forgets anything."

As Gabby approached the camp, she felt a strange excitement. Of all the memories of her life in England, perhaps her meeting with Zanko and Madame Jana was the clearest. She didn't know why, but she could remember every word that had been said, and she still wore the necklace that Madame Jana had given her. She had sometimes thought herself foolish for believing that an old woman, after all these years, would still be praying for her, but somehow she felt sure the old woman had kept her promise.

Now as they approached, Maria called out, "Zanko, a visitor for you!"

Gabby glanced around and noted that there were four gaily covered caravans, perhaps the same ones she had seen in England. The camp was busy with women cooking over fires and children playing. Over to one side a young man with coal black hair was playing a fiddle with great energy.

In front of him two teenage girls were dancing, their colorful skirts making a splash of color as they whirled and dipped.

"Welcome to our camp," Duke Zanko greeted.

He looked a little older, with a few new lines on his face, but his hair was still dark. He had grown a heavy mustache, but Gabby would have known him anywhere. When he bowed from the waist, she extended her hand, and surprise flashed in his dark eyes. He bent over and kissed her hand with a courtly gesture.

"You don't remember me, I think," Gabby said.

Zanko released her hand and studied her face carefully. "We have met before?"

"Many years ago in England. I came to your camp with a young man."

His eyes narrowed. "That was a long time ago. I would not have known you."

"I would have known you anywhere, Duke, and I still remember Madame Jana."

"She is old now, but she has spoken of you many times. I have heard her pray for you. She never forgets."

"Could I see her?"

"Yes, certainly. Come this way. She is not well, you understand." His face grew sad. "She will take her long journey soon, I think."

"She's dying?"

"As she says, we are all dying, but her turn may come quicker than others. Come."

Zanko stopped before the back of a wagon, where a pair of steps led up to the door. He mounted the stairs and opened the door a few inches. "Madame Jana, are you awake?"

"Yes, I'm awake."

"You have a visitor."

Zanko turned and put his hand out to help Gabby up the stairs. She climbed the steps and then ducked and stepped inside. For a moment she could see little in the dimness, but then her eyes adjusted. A lamp attached to the ceiling was burning, throwing its amber light over the woman who lay on a cot on one side of the caravan.

"I'm sorry to disturb you, Madame Jana, but I—"

"Sit down and give me your hand."

Gabby pulled a three-legged stool forward and extended her hand. As the old woman took it, Gabby studied the familiar ancient face. Jana was wearing a kerchief even in bed, and she seemed very tiny and frail. Her face had a few more wrinkles than it had had years ago, but her eyes were as bright as they had been that first night in the lovers' grove.

"I am Gabrielle Winslow. I met you many years—"

"My daughter, I have prayed for you often." The voice was as strong as the grip that held Gabby's hand.

The old woman reached with her other hand to enclose both of Gabby's hands between the two of hers while her eyes searched Gabby's face. She did not speak for a long time, and then she said, "I always knew I would see you again. God had told me so."

The enormity of this statement took Gabby's breath away. She did not know what to say, but she felt the power of this weak old woman who was endued with such spiritual strength. "I have thought of you so many times over the years, and your prayers have been a comfort."

Madame Jana smiled. "You have grown into a fine woman. Have you married?"

"N-no." Gabby could not understand why the word was so hard to say, and she hastened to say, "But I am promised to one who will be my husband."

The woman's eyes grew darker, and the intensity of her gaze troubled Gabby. This frail woman had a power she could not understand, and the silence that filled the wagon made her feel intensely uncomfortable. She felt the need to defend herself, but she did not know from what.

"God knows your past, and He knows your future, my daughter. But you are concerned with the present."

The old hands tightened on Gabby's, and she felt lightheaded. She listened as the old woman continued.

"For some reason, God put you on my heart that night many years ago. This old woman is not good for much, but she knows when God has a task for her. And the Lord Jesus has given me to prayer and called me to seek the goodness in your life."

Gabby sat absolutely still, conscious of the old woman's frail hands holding hers, unable to move away from her eyes. She had no confidence in fortune-telling, and she was well aware that there were those among the gypsies who were thieves and worse. All of this, however, was shoved aside, for here in the dim light of this gypsy caravan, Gabby Winslow knew she was in the presence of one of God's servants. The power of God rested on Madame Jana, and Gabby listened as she spoke for some time about the love of God and the way He directed the lives of His children.

Finally, Madame Jana pulled on her hands and whispered, "Lean forward, daughter."

Obediently, Gabby did so, and the old woman placed her hands lightly on each side of Gabby's head. The old woman did not speak for what seemed like a long time, but Gabby's head seemed to tingle where the ancient hands rested on the sides of her face. She began to tremble, and tears filled her eyes, although she could not explain why.

"You still wear the necklace I gave you."

"Yes." Gabby pulled the necklace from beneath her blouse and held it out. The light caught the gold, and it glowed dully in the semidarkness. "I've always worn the necklace you gave me, Madame Jana, and I have believed in your prayers."

"You are faithful, child, and God will be with you. But you must not make a mistake. You are thinking of going through a door, but you must not pass through it, for God has other plans for you. You will close one door, but another door will open. Go through that door. God will be with you."

Suddenly, without doubt, Gabrielle knew that the exhortation had to do with her intended marriage to Lang Zeeman. She heard no voice, but she knew that God had spoken to her through this woman.

Finally, Madame Jana pulled Gabby forward and kissed her forehead. She seemed weak then, exhausted, and her eyes closed for a moment. It took all her strength, it seemed to Gabby, to open them, and she said, "Now, tell me about yourself."

Gabby spent over an hour in that gypsy caravan, speaking her heart to the old woman as she had never spoken it to anyone, not even her dear aunt Liza. The old woman prayed for her again, and she knew that the direction of her life had changed.

"I do not think we will meet again on this earth, my daughter," Madame Jana whispered. "I go to meet my heavenly husband soon, but until that moment comes you will always be in my heart."

"Oh, Madame Jana!" Gabby cried, tears forming in her eyes. She kissed the withered cheek, and they said their good-byes.

She turned blindly and left the caravan, wiping her eyes with her handkerchief. She found Duke Zanko standing a distance away, waiting silently. "She is a wonderful woman," Gabby said.

"The wisest and the best I have ever known."

"She . . . she said we will not meet again."

"She is rarely mistaken." Zanko's face was sad, and he shook his head. "I do not know what I will do without her."

★ ★ ★

It was nearly two weeks later before Gabby told her aunt and uncle about her conversation with Madame Jana. Gabby was subdued at supper that evening, lost in her thoughts. When the meal was over, before her aunt could rise to clear away the table, she said, "I have to talk to you."

Instantly, both Dalton and Liza grew alert. Gabby had been pleasant enough recently but was obviously preoccupied with something that was bothering her. Liza had noticed it first, and when she had called Dalton's attention to it, he had watched her closely as well. They had not spoken to her but had prayed much about whatever trouble she was going through.

"You've probably noticed that I've been . . . rather quiet lately."

"Yes, we have noticed," Liza said. "Is something wrong, dear?"

"Not *wrong* exactly, but I've made a decision." Gabby lifted her head and met the eyes of her aunt and then her uncle. "I've decided not to marry Lang." As she watched, she saw relief wash through both of them and knew that this pleased them both. She considered explaining why she had made this decision, but that seemed unnecessary. She was not sure they would understand her respect and affection for Madame Jana, and she felt a moment's pang at the woman's death. Earlier in the week Duke had sent Maria to the orphanage to give her the message that Madame Jana had died and he hoped she would attend the funeral.

Gabby thought back to the funeral at the camp outside the city. It had been unlike any she had ever attended. No minister was there to lead the small group in a service. An old man had spoken a eulogy, and then several people had explained what Madame Jana had meant to them. Gabby had felt like an outsider at first, but as the people told of their relationships with Madame Jana, she felt a kinship with them. She was surprised when Duke Zanko asked her to speak, but she willingly and fervently told the gathering of her great respect and love for the old woman.

Now her thoughts returned to the present, and she said simply, "Lang and I are not suited for each other. I believe you've known that for a long time."

"Are you certain, Gabby?" Dalton said gently.

"Yes, I'm very certain."

Dalton Burke glanced at his wife, and Gabby saw something pass between them. She was curious and asked, "What is it, Uncle Dalton?"

"We've known that you've been troubled, dear, so we

didn't want to add to your difficulties. But I must say that we are relieved. We did not feel Lang was the man for you. But something else has come up that we must talk to you about."

"Oh?"

"I've been offered a post, a very important position, and Liza and I have decided we cannot pass it up."

"A position with another university?"

"Yes, at the University of Berlin."

Gabby stared at her uncle, and then her eyes went to her aunt. "You're moving to Germany?"

"It's been a hard decision, but they have offered me such wonderful conditions. I'll be free to continue my research, and all of the financial burdens will be gone."

Gabby listened as her uncle spoke eagerly of this opportunity, his eyes shining. She knew he was an impulsive man, and though he was a scientific genius of international repute, he sometimes made decisions rashly. She studied her aunt and saw that Liza Burke was not as happy about this decision as Dalton was. When her uncle finished explaining his new position, she said, "Are you sure this is what you want to do?"

"Yes. Oh, I know there are some things about the new Germany that will have to be rectified, but it will happen in time. Germany was nearly destroyed after the war, but now new things are happening. It's going to be a new world."

"So much has changed in the last couple of years," Liza said. "It wasn't all that long ago that Germany had a chancellor, a president, and a parliament. Now one man fills all those functions."

"I'm still not convinced that's a good idea," Gabby said. Adolf Hitler now had more power than Stalin or Mussolini, and a story in the newspaper a few weeks ago said that he was more powerful than Genghis Khan had been when his career was at its peak.

"I know you're worried about Hitler," Dalton said, "but ninety percent of the voters approved his presidency back in 1934."

"Still, ten percent of the voters dared to vote no," Liza said quickly, "and a million of them expressed their dissatisfaction by tampering with the ballots."

"I don't think it's good for Germany, Uncle Dalton," Gabby said. "Hitler can make war or peace. He can create new laws and abolish old ones. Why, he can even execute suspects and pardon convicts. He's legislature and executive all in one, and I don't think that's good for the people."

Dalton was a great scientist but somewhat stubborn about his political views. He had attended the university in Germany and had become good friends with many of those who were now leaders under Adolf Hitler's new regime. He remembered them as men of intelligence and daring. "Germany needs a strong hand at the helm," he said. "There are enough wise Germans who won't allow him to get too far off the track."

Liza leaned forward and said, "To get back to the subject at hand, we would like very much for you to go with us, Gabrielle. I know you've made a life here, and your friends are here, but we'll be very lonely if we have to leave you behind."

Gabby at once saw that her aunt was troubled, but she suddenly remembered something Madame Jana had said the first time they'd met. She had not understood it at the time, but now her advice came back with startling clarity. *"You will close one door, but another door will open. Go through that door. God will be with you."*

Instantly, Gabby knew that this was the door Madame Jana had spoken of. She had no desire to go to Germany. She was frightened of some of the changes that were happening in that country. But as she looked at her aunt and saw the pleading in her eyes, she knew what she must do.

"But, Uncle Dalton, what about your mother?"

Dalton's eyes grew sad. "She will stay here. We tried to get her to go with us, but she refuses. She says this country is her home, and she will spend her remaining days here. We will do all we can to help her with money, of course."

"But will you go with us, dear?" Liza asked, her eyes filled with hope.

"Why, of course I'll go with you. You're my family." She saw tears come to her aunt's eyes, and she felt assured that this move was God's plan. The image came back quickly of the stones thrown into the water and how many things confuse life's patterns, and she prayed, *Oh, God, I don't know what this move will bring, but help me never to step outside your will.*

CHAPTER FIVE

A FANCY AFFAIR

★ ★ ★

Even after serving eleven months at the Berlin City Hospital, Gabby still felt out of place and ill at ease. Part of the problem was that the procedures were so different from what she was accustomed to. She had been unprepared for the strict and military precision the director and others demanded of her work. She also found the staff distant and hard to get to know. Her previous experience had not prepared her for this, for no matter how intense the training, there was still a homelike warmth in the medical family in the Netherlands.

As Gabby walked down the hall of the third floor of the hospital, making her rounds, she spoke to the interns, the doctors, and the occasional patient that she met. Her German was excellent, and though she still spoke with an accent, and always would, she was comfortable with the language. She often felt that the language somehow exemplified the difference between Germany and Holland. The German language seemed sharp to her, guttural at times, while Dutch was a more gentle language, at least in Gabby's opinion. She missed Holland terribly. She missed the windmills, the enormous fields of colorful tulips, the laughter of the people at the festivals, the Burke house, and especially the woman she knew as "Grandmother."

"I congratulate you, Dr. Winslow."

Startled out of her reflections, Gabby turned quickly to see Dr. Gunther Schultz, the director of the hospital. He was a tall man, muscular, with iron gray hair and a pair of very sharp blue eyes. He would have been handsome except for an ugly scar that disfigured the right side of his face. A dueling scar, Gabby had been informed. Gabby had been terrified of Schultz at first, for he had been strict and unsmiling for the first two months she was on duty. Gradually, Gabby had come to understand that he was testing her, and since she was the only female doctor on the staff, she understood. After two months on the job, he had finally smiled at her and said, "You are a fine doctor. I am proud to have you in our hospital and in our country."

Now Schultz had a smile on his usually tight lips. "I've been looking over your reports. They look very good indeed. Yes, very good indeed."

"Thank you, Dr. Schultz."

"And tonight you are going to the reception and ball, I understand?" He spoke of the reception for scientists, an august occasion that the German leadership used so well to bring their top leadership together. The Germans loved ceremony, and the reception would be impressive, with the best food and music available. "You will be going?" he repeated.

"Yes, my uncle has asked me to attend with him and my aunt. I understand my uncle is receiving an honor of some sort in acknowledgment of the work he's doing for Germany."

"You must be very proud of your uncle. Ah, there is a real scientist!"

Gabby smiled. She made a very attractive picture as she stood before the director, unaware that part of his resistance to her at first had been her good looks. Schultz felt that attractive women would be a nuisance and an impediment to his hospital. Neither did she know that his observation over a period of time had led him to the conclusion that she was unaware of her attractiveness.

Gabby had a beautifully fashioned face, all of its features generous and capable of robust emotion, all of them graceful. Her expression now held a hint of her strong will and pride that was reflected mostly in her eyes and at the corners of her lips.

"I'm very proud of my uncle, of course," she said, "but I'm not fond of receptions and balls. They're too big and impressive for me, Doctor. I get overwhelmed."

"Yes, that is my feeling also, but this one will be different."

"Different? In what way?"

"The führer will be there."

By an act of will Gabby managed to keep the sharp feeling that surged through her from showing. She had learned to control this fear she had of the political situation in Germany through long practice. Everywhere she went a latent excitement would often break out into a livelier scene at the mention of Germany's new gains. The year 1937 had brought a new air of enthusiasm to Germans. In 1935 Adolf Hitler had reestablished obligatory military service in Germany. A year later, he had marched his troops into a territory that was supposed to be a demilitarized zone. This action violated the Treaty of Versailles, but Hitler, in a speech to the Reichstag, the German parliament, had called it the end of the struggle for German equality. He had finally declared outwardly that Germany was no longer bound by old treaties.

Hitler was becoming a rising star. He had used the 1936 Berlin Olympics to highlight the progress of Germany since the Great War. The games had been staged with German efficiency and superiority. Yet at least for Hitler and his cabinet, they had been darkened because of the Jews who were among the visiting athletes. Also Hitler, who called the Negroes an inferior race, had been embarrassed and enraged by a Negro athlete from Ohio State, Jesse Owens.

Owens had dominated the track events as no man ever had, and the German leadership had simply chosen to ignore Owens's amazing victories.

Several months ago, Germany had attacked the undefended town of Guernica in northern Spain. Hundreds of people, mostly civilians, were ruthlessly killed by German bombs. The fascists denied that German pilots were involved, but everyone knew who was responsible for the atrocity.

"Dr. Winslow, I should be interested to know more about your political views," Dr. Schultz said. "After all, as the führer says, we German and you British come from the same bloodline. We should be close allies."

Gabby smiled diplomatically. "I know so little about politics. I'm probably the most ignorant student of it in the world."

"It is impossible that you should be ignorant of anything." He checked his watch. "I will hope to see you at the dinner."

★ ★ ★

That evening Gabby dressed carefully for the ball. Her aunt had taken her shopping and had insisted on buying her a beautiful blue gown. It had delicate patterns that clung closely to her upper body and then dropped loosely to the top of her gold kid sandals. She wore a simple pearl necklace as her only jewelry.

As they entered the reception room, she was greeted by Dr. Schultz. "You look very nice. You never look like this on floor duty." His bright blue eyes sparkled, and he turned to tip his head to the Burkes. "I am so happy to see you again, Professor, and you, Mrs. Burke." The Burkes had met the doctor when Gabby had given them a tour of the hospital.

The Burkes greeted Schultz warmly, for he had been kind to Gabby during her time in Germany, and this was enough to win their approval.

The three moved around the enormous hall, admiring the decorations and greeting acquaintances of Gabby's uncle from the university. A huge stage occupied the end of the room, and a row of red flags with swastikas hung over it. When people started to take their places in the chairs that were lined up in rows, Gabby and her aunt and uncle found seats near the front. The seats were soon filled and the ceremony began.

Gabby was interested in the proceedings, and she applauded enthusiastically when her uncle was introduced. He said a few words in appreciation of the honor, and as he returned to his seat, Gabby whispered to her aunt, "He feels completely out of place at a thing like this, doesn't he?"

"Yes, but he's pleased at the honor they are giving him."

Privately, Gabby thought Dalton Burke was more at home in a laboratory, but she said no more.

The speeches went quickly, most of them being brief, and finally the main speaker, Adolf Hitler, rose. The audience leaped to its feet as he came to the podium, and the air was alive with excitement. Many were extending their hands and crying, "Heil Hitler! Hail to our führer!" Gabby did not take part in this, nor, she noticed, did her aunt, although she could see her uncle was excited.

After a long time of applause, the crowd seated itself, and Hitler began to speak. Gabby studied him carefully. She had seen so many pictures of him, for the world's eyes were on this man who now stood before her. She was close enough that she could see his features clearly, and she was curious about what he had to say. She was surprised that as he began his speech he spoke in an even, conversational tone. This changed quickly, however, and soon his voice began to crackle with passion—a passion that connected with the huge audience like a surge of electric current.

Hitler spoke of Germany with obvious pride, and he concluded his address by saying, "We are Germans, and our destiny is to rule! Our young men have mastered the art of war, but you, my friends, must master the art of science. Whether by arms or by the test tube, we must all lay our talents on the altar of the Fatherland."

The audience rose to its feet and applauded loudly as Hitler waved to his admirers. Dalton turned to Gabby, his eyes glowing, and shouted over the noise, "It's wonderful to have a leader who understands and cares about the importance of science. So many don't."

Gabby nodded but did not reply. She had found the speech rather depressing, and she wished that the evening were over.

The people made their way into the adjoining ballroom, where the orchestra was already starting a waltz. The crowd was abuzz with conversations about Hitler's speech as everybody headed either toward the hors d'oeuvre table or the dance floor. Gabby knew almost no one outside of her professional colleagues, and except for Dr. Schultz, she had seen none of them at the reception. She had met a few people at the church she'd been attending, but none of them had been invited to this stellar event.

She was standing with her back to the wall watching the dancers waltz while her uncle and aunt were engaged in conversation with another couple several yards away. A movement caught her eye, and she turned her head to see a man approaching her with his eyes fixed on her. She had never seen him before, for she would have remembered such an incredibly handsome man. He came to stand before her and did a half bow.

"I beg your pardon," he said with a smile, "but I would consider it an honor if I might have the next dance."

"Why, certainly."

"My name is Erik Raeder—and you are Fraulein Winslow."

She smiled. "How did you know my name?"

"I made it my business to find it out."

Raeder was a tall man, just a little over six feet, well built and with a military posture. He might have served as the model for the perfect German male. His blond hair had a slight curl, he had blue eyes with long lashes, and he was very clean cut. Gabby's first impression was that he had an ease about him that came to those accustomed to being obeyed. He wore a navy blue suit that fit him as if he were poured into it, and the snowy white shirt made a startling contrast to his tanned features. As he led Gabby to the dance floor, she said, "I'm afraid I'm not a very good dancer."

"That doesn't matter. I'm an excellent dancer. I shall teach you as we go."

"Well, you don't lack confidence, Herr Raeder."

"Actually, I do. It took me all this time to steel myself to ask you for a dance."

Gabby laughed. "I don't believe that for one moment, Herr Raeder."

"I suppose if I came to these events often enough, I would gain the confidence to ask a beautiful woman for a dance without hesitation."

"Or you could make a career of offering your services to women in need of a dance partner."

"I shall keep that in mind," he said with a smile. "When my business fails, I will have something to fall back on."

The idea was preposterous, and Gabby was amused as Erik continued to outline his future career as a professional dance partner.

Gabby was acutely conscious of his hand on her back and of the strength of his other hand as he held hers. He was a fine dancer, and Gabby, for all of her protests, was actually a good dancer herself. As they moved around the floor, Gabby found herself enjoying Erik's light remarks. She wanted to know more about him, and when the dance ended, she agreed to get some refreshments with him.

He led her to a relatively quiet corner and then went to get drinks. He came back with two glasses, and Gabby said, "Oh, I forgot to tell you, I don't drink alcohol."

He looked at her in disbelief and then laughed. "That will make it very difficult for you. No alcohol at all? Not even a stein of good German beer?"

"I'm afraid not."

"You must be one of those Salvation Army women I see pictures of. I believe you're out to win converts."

Gabby admired the easy wit of the man. It actually was socially awkward to be a nondrinker, for everyone in Germany, it seemed, drank beer. He left and then returned shortly with a glass in hand. "Here, lemonade. I guarantee no alcohol at all. When you're finished, I must beg another dance of you."

As the two sipped their drinks, Erik asked what she did. When she told him, his eyes opened wide with surprise. "A doctor!"

"Yes, I am a physician at the Berlin City Hospital."

"Well, Doctor," he said, "I've been having this pain in my side, and I don't feel too well in the morning. What do you prescribe?"

"Take an aspirin and go to bed."

"Ach, you doctors are all alike!"

"And what do you do, Herr Raeder?"

"Please, it would be nice if you would call me Erik."

"Very well, Erik, and my friends call me Gabby."

"Gabby . . . that's an unusual name."

"It's short for Gabrielle."

"Ah, very pretty. Well, as for what I do, I am a wastrel. A prodigal son, you might say."

Her eyes narrowed, and she shook her head. "No, you're too well dressed. You haven't been feeding with the swine, and you have no spirit of repentance about you."

He laughed. "You doctors! You have become too good at reading people. Well, my father owns a business, and one day when I am old and fat, I will have to go to work in it."

"It sounds very dull."

"Yes, it is, but let us hope that will be a long time off and I can continue to be a wastrel for many years."

As the evening went on, a number of men, mostly older than Gabby, asked her to dance. Erik kept returning to her side every time she left the dance floor, however.

"Well, are you enjoying the reception?" her uncle asked her after she did a fox-trot with one of the other gentlemen.

"Very much."

Liza smiled and put her hand on Gabby's arm. "I've

noticed you spending a lot of time with Erik Raeder."

"Who is he, Aunt Liza?"

"You don't know?" Dalton asked.

"He said his father owns a business. He didn't get very specific."

He laughed. "His father is Baron Rudolph Raeder. You see that couple over there beside the pillar? That's the baron and his wife. He was called Rudy Raeder in the war. He was a fighter pilot, and he's a close friend of the führer. Very high up in the Party. His family is quite prominent."

Looking over, Gabby saw a tall, strongly built man with an equally tall, rather thin woman. They stood out even in this august company. "He didn't tell me he was from such a family."

"They're a very powerful force in German politics," Dalton said.

Suddenly, a stir to their left caught their attention, and Gabby turned to see Hitler and another man approaching, along with four men in matching uniforms who appeared to be bodyguards. The short man with a sharp face whispered something to Hitler, and Hitler turned toward Gabby and her aunt and uncle, then came forward. The small man said, "My führer, may I present one of the premier physicists of Germany, Professor Dalton Burke."

Hitler stretched his hand out and smiled, and Dalton took his hand, struck speechless. "I have heard of your fine work, Professor," Hitler said. The aide went on to introduce Liza, and then the aide, who seemed to know everything, said, "And may I present Fraulein Gabrielle Winslow—or *Dr.* Winslow, I should say."

Hitler stood directly in front of Gabby. She did not know what to do, but she put out her hand. Hitler took it and bowed over it with military precision. "Ah, Dr. Winslow, you are British, I understand."

"Yes, sir, I am."

"And what do you think of our new Germany?"

Gabby knew she must not offend this man. His eyes were strangely hypnotic, and the pressure of his hand seemed electric. Truly, Adolf Hitler was the most unsettling man she had ever met. "I am little qualified to judge politics," she ventured, "but I have seen the excitement in the air everywhere, sir."

He smiled, his eyes aglow. "I admire the British. The Nordic strain is in them." Hitler continued to speak of his admiration for the British and then concluded by saying, "I welcome you to the new Germany, Fraulein, and both of you, Professor and Frau Burke. We appreciate your work for the Fatherland."

As Hitler and his entourage moved away, Gabby stood speechless. Her aunt took her by the arm and asked, "What did you think of him, dear?"

"For some reason I find him frightening."

"I thought he seemed very nice."

Gabby did not answer. He had certainly seemed pleasant on the outside, but she had the strangest feeling about him. She wanted to ask if they could leave, but she knew it was much too early for an acceptable exit.

★ ★ ★

Across the room, Baron Rudolph Raeder and his wife, Hilda, were speaking with Erik. "Who was the woman you were dancing with—the one in the blue dress?" his mother asked.

"She's a doctor at the city hospital. Originally from Britain. She's the niece of Professor Dalton Burke." He laughed and said, "She's quite entertaining. I'm taking her to see the sights of Berlin later this week."

Baron Raeder gave his son a direct look. "One day her people will stand in the way of the Fatherland. Make no alliance, my son."

Erik laughed. "She's a good-looking woman and plenty smart. That's enough for me, Father."

CHAPTER SIX

The Danger of Power

★ ★ ★

The snow under her skis looked like powdered white glass, and the brightness made Gabby squint. Erik had introduced her to the sport, and now she loved it. Exhilarated, she sped down the mountainside, crouching low over the skis, poles under her arms, and shifting her weight to change direction. She had never gone down such a steep slope before, and she was filled with a delicious mixture of fear and awe as the wind whipped across her face and bit at her lips.

"You can't win. Give up!"

Erik had pulled up beside her. He was an expert skier—she had found he was good at every sport, it seemed—and now the wind blew his blond hair wildly, and his teeth blazed white against his sunburned complexion.

"Be careful!" he yelled. "I'm going to take a shortcut, but you go straight on down."

Gabby watched as he sailed ahead of her and then veered off to her left. A perverse notion took her, and she followed. He did not know she was behind him, and she was delighted to think that she might even beat him to the foot of the slope.

As she sped recklessly downward she thought of how close they had become. Ever since the night of the reception, he had taken her to concerts, operas, plays, and short excursions into the countryside.

Gabby often asked herself how she really felt about him. She could not deny the strong physical attraction between them. He had kissed her at the end of their first date, when they had gone to hear the Berlin Symphony. Gabby had been shocked at the emotions that had raced through her at his tender embrace. She had put her hand on his chest, feeling herself slipping beyond control, and he had laughed at her. *"You've got to learn to relax, my dear Gabby,"* he had said. *"There's more to life than taking a patient's temperature."*

A large rock formation loomed ahead, and she followed Erik as he expertly turned to the right. She came precariously close to the outcropping, but with a wild twist of her body she managed to avoid it. Her heart was racing as she sped down the straightaway, but even so, she was thinking more of her relationship with Erik Raeder than she was of skiing down a dangerous slope.

The two weaved through the powder, and then Erik abruptly threw himself to the left. Gabby had no time to follow suit but shot by him. She had not gone more than fifty meters when she heard a stifled cry and a noise she did not recognize.

He must have fallen! At once she threw herself sideways and skidded to a stop. She looked back up the mountain and saw no sign of Erik. She slipped out of her skis and ran clumsily back up the slope, her skis under one arm. She finally spotted him as he struggled to get up. One ski was still attached to his boot, but the other one was missing.

"Erik, are you all right?" she cried. She made her way to his side just as he collapsed back onto the snow. His eyes were closed, his lips drawn tightly together. "Have you broken something? Can you move your legs?"

Gabby had no time to ask further questions, for suddenly

Erik's arms shot up and he pulled her down on his chest and kissed her firmly with his icy lips.

She felt relieved that he was not hurt. She was pressed tightly against him and could not move, for his arms were strong. Finally, she turned her head to the side and gasped, "Let me go!"

He laughed and released his grip. He sat up, his eyes sparkling. "That's a good treatment you have for a fallen skier. Kiss me again. I feel a weakness coming on."

She hit him on the chest as he grabbed at her, but she was helpless against his strength. He flipped her around so that she lay in the snow, her arms pinioned to her sides. "As they say in the American movies, you're beautiful when you're angry, even in those silly goggles."

Gabby giggled. She couldn't help it. They must have both looked ridiculous in their goggles with his sole ski waving in the air as he lay on his stomach. "You are insane! You could have been dead. I was scared to death!"

"Were you?" He leaned forward and kissed her lightly on the lips again. "That's good news." He gently pulled her goggles off and then did the same with his own. He put his cheek next to hers and simply held her.

This was an unusual moment for Gabrielle Winslow. Here on the side of a mountain, lying in the snow, being held by the tall, strong man she had become so attached to, she felt a sense of longing. She felt as if she had been seeking love all of her life. She had not found it before—not even with Lang, she could finally admit—but now as Erik held her firmly, yet with a tenderness she had learned was part of his character, she felt safe and secure, and she longed for even more.

This longing frightened her. Erik was two men, it seemed. One was the typical German man of strength and discipline and iron, but he also had a tender side to him, and he showed it to her from time to time. If she had not seen it, she would have refused to date him at all. But it was there, and she tried to understand the balance of these two influences—his tenderness and yet the steel of his Nordic character.

"You know, Gabby, I think I feel more for you than I should," he said quietly. He pulled his head back so he could look into her eyes.

She could see the clean handsomeness of his features, and she let her eyes linger on his eyebrows, his eyelashes, his perfect cheekbones. She wondered how a man with such masculine strength could be so beautiful. "Then . . . you had better stop," she said.

"How can I stop? Is love a thing you can turn on and off like a light switch?" He pulled her up to sit on the snow next to him and then removed her ski cap, watching her luxurious wealth of hair fall about her shoulders. He had always loved her hair and had told her so many times. He ran his hand through it and said huskily, "I can't stop loving just because someone tells me to."

Gabby could not answer. She felt helpless, caught between two conflicting emotions that were keeping her from thinking clearly. She well understood that Erik's parents were opposed to their relationship. They were polite enough, but there was a wariness in both of them, and she wondered now if she should mention her concerns to Erik. But he gave her no chance.

"Come on," he said. "We were lucky not to break our necks. Why did you follow me?"

"Because I wanted to."

"Did you?" Erik pulled her to her feet and put his arms around her. "That pleases me very much. I hope you will always want to follow me. Because if you don't, I'll follow you."

"Let me go," she said with a giggle. "We need to find your other ski."

They looked up the mountain and found it buried in the snow not too far away.

"Let's be more careful this time," Gabby said as they both got back into their skis and put on their goggles.

"You're right about that," he said ruefully. "I was a fool

to take such chances, and you were no better following me. Are you ready?"

She adjusted her hat, and the two started down the slopes at a more sedate pace. After they reached the lodge, he said, "My parents are expecting us for a visit. Go change clothes, and I'll have the car ready."

"All right, Erik." She spoke lightly enough but inwardly was frightened, as she always was when she fell under the eyes of the Raeders. Still, she had promised to go with him, and now she had no choice.

Gabby spent two days at the Raeder mansion just outside of Berlin, and she was glad when the visit was over. Erik's parents had not said anything specifically that made her feel uncomfortable, but the very correctness with which they treated her spoke of their disapproval louder than words. She said her good-byes, and Baron Raeder said stiffly, "You must come again." His words were polite, but they were spoken with such formality that she felt as if he were shutting a door. His wife simply said good-bye and didn't even pretend to extend another invitation.

As Erik drove her home, they avoided the subject of his parents. They talked instead of the fun they'd had skiing and of other mountains where he had skied. When he pulled up in front of her aunt and uncle's house, he shut the engine off and turned to face her. "So now you go back to work."

"Yes, I have to make a living."

Erik reached over and took her hand. He held it for a time quietly, then looked up and said, "What is that necklace you wear all the time?"

"I got it many years ago from an old gypsy woman."

"She sold it to you?" He was surprised. The German Party considered gypsies "undesirables." He frowned as he asked, "Who was she?"

"Just an old woman. She didn't sell it to me—she gave it to me." Gabby hesitated. "She was very strange, Erik. She told me I was going to have a difficult time, and she was right, because my parents died almost immediately after that."

"She told your fortune?" he asked, disbelief in his voice.

"No, I don't believe in that. She was actually very close to God, and I believe she was telling me the truth. She gave me this necklace and told me she would be praying for me."

"So she was a Christian?"

"Yes, she was." She hesitated and then added, "I met her again after I came to Holland. Just a chance encounter. I went out to visit her, and she said she had been praying for me for years. She died shortly after that."

He released her hand and picked up the coin that hung from the golden chain around her neck. "It's a beautiful old piece. Do you know what it means?"

"I have no idea." She suddenly looked up and saw the moon high in the sky. "That's a gypsy moon."

He turned to look. "It's very beautiful. Why do you call it a gypsy moon?"

"The leader of the gypsies told me that a full moon is a gypsy moon. He said gypsy men and women always fall in love when there's a full moon."

"Well, that's foolish! What if they're in love and the moon isn't full?" He laughed and reached over to pull her close, then kissed her cheek. "There's something about you I don't understand. There's a resistance. I feel it when I kiss you. You give yourself to me for a moment, and then you hold back. Why is that?"

"I don't know, Erik."

"I think you do. Have you had an unfortunate love affair? Are you afraid of men?"

Suddenly, Gabby realized there was some truth in his question. "I . . . never had a love affair. Not a real one, but I came very close to being in love with a man once. We were engaged, actually. I thought I loved him, but I was wrong. He wasn't the man for me. I suppose I'm afraid of making a mistake, and no one can afford that."

Erik shook his head. "We make mistakes all the time, Gabby. The only people who make no mistakes are those who live in a cave and won't come out—people who are afraid to take a risk for something they truly want." He used his finger to tilt her chin toward him and kissed her with passion.

As she responded to his affection, she knew that the heart of this man had a wildness in it, which almost seemed to consume her at times.

He pulled back and said, "One day I'll ask you to marry me."

She had wondered, of course, what it would be like to marry him, but she thought it was much too soon to get serious. They had only known each other for a few months. Now that the word *marry* had been spoken aloud, she felt a shock run along her nerves. "But we're too different."

"Of course we're different. I'm a man and you're a woman."

"Oh, it's more than that, and you know it! Your family would never accept me."

Erik did not argue, but he said firmly, "They can change."

"But, Erik, there are . . . things in Germany—political things—I don't understand, and I'm afraid of them."

Erik stroked her hand, and for a moment he did not answer. Finally, he lifted his eyes and said, "There are some things in this new order that I do not accept myself. My father blindly accepts whatever the führer proposes, but Hitler is only a man and subject to error."

"That's what bothers me. The men and women on the street, the working people, everyone seems to think he's . . . almost like a god. That whatever he does is right."

"Strong men always elicit that sort of feeling from people. You don't know what it was like in Germany after the war. It was terrible. Money became worthless. People were starving in the streets. We didn't know which way to turn, and then Hitler came along. And he made things work. He's a man of destiny, Gabby. He will make Germany the strong nation she once was."

"But he's breaking treaties, invading other countries.

There's something wrong with that, isn't there, Erik?"

"Yes, I think there is, but he's a relatively young man and new to all this power. He'll gather some wise men to advise him. It'll be all right."

"I should go in."

He turned so he could look straight into her eyes. "Don't be afraid of me, and don't be afraid of Germany. If you and I love each other, we'll find a way. I love you—I'm sure of it—but I sense your fear, Gabby. It won't stay. My love for you will send it away. You'll see."

Gabrielle got out of the car, and they were silent as he walked her to the door. She turned to him and smiled. "Thank you for the wonderful time."

He leaned over and kissed her lightly. "We will have many times like this. Things will work out for us. You will see, my dear."

Gabrielle watched as he turned and went back to the car. Their conversation had excited her and frightened her at the same time, but she knew that somehow the future was rushing toward her at a furious speed, and there was nothing she could do to control it.

★ ★ ★

"You look tired, dear. Didn't you sleep well?" Liza asked.

Gabby's aunt was right. It had taken her a long time to drop off to sleep, and even then she had not slept soundly. Erik's mention of marriage had filled her mind with many thoughts. Fitfully, she had tossed on her bed, waking several times, and had risen the next morning with swollen eyes and feeling groggy.

"Not very well, I'm afraid."

"Perhaps after breakfast you can lie down and take a nap."

Gabby laughed. "I need to get to the hospital."

The two women looked up as Dalton entered the room and greeted them cheerfully. He sat down at the table and told them excitedly about the research he was doing at the university. He was working on developing a new kind of power that involved splitting the atom. It would be so much more powerful than any of the known energy sources that Gabby could hardly comprehend the scope of the project.

Gabby said little but listened as her uncle spoke of the progress that was being made and how Germany would become the envy of the world when this discovery was made public. She was puzzled about her uncle, for he was a genius in his field, but he appeared to have little sensitivity to some things. She knew he read the newspaper and was familiar with the excesses of the Nazi machine that was growing stronger every day. A man of his intellect should have been able to see some of the troubling developments, but he seemed blind to them. She could not understand why he would not be more concerned about the use of such power in the hands of the Nazis.

After her aunt left to go to the store, Gabby said, "Uncle Dalton, doesn't it worry you that Hitler doesn't seem to have any morals?"

"Morals, my dear? Why, whatever do you mean?"

"I mean he's not a man of honor. You must know that. He's ignored every treaty that Germany has made. Why, the whole world knows that his ambition is leading Germany straight into difficulty."

"Oh, my dear, that's the way it is with politics and new movements." He picked up the newspaper. He had little confidence in women as far as political affairs were concerned. He admired and was tremendously proud of Gabrielle's skill in medicine, but he was quite sure she didn't understand the way Germany operated.

"I wish we'd never left Holland," she blurted out.

"What's that? Why, Gabby, I can't believe you would say that! You're doing so well here. You've made such progress, and so have I."

"Progress isn't everything. I'm afraid of what's going to happen in this country. Why, Germany has given Hitler absolute power, and that kind of power can be very dangerous. I can't believe they would let a single man act as both president and chancellor. Germany is being run by a dictator!"

"You're right about that, but power isn't always dangerous. Not if it's used wisely."

She saw that it was impossible to reason with her uncle, so she fell silent while he turned his attention back to the newspaper.

"Are you going to the rally at Nuremberg?" he asked as she took her dishes to the sink.

"No, I don't think so."

"You should. It sounds like it's going to be a wonderful spectacle."

"I'd really rather not, Uncle."

★ ★ ★

Gabby had no intention of going to the rally at Nuremberg, but Erik had been trying to persuade her to go with him.

The day approached, and finally she gave in, partly out of curiosity but more so out of a desire to be with Erik.

The two of them drove to Nuremberg in his big automobile. The streets of the city were lined with storm troopers, and all the church bells were pealing loudly for the huge rally. They stood in the crowded streets watching as Adolf Hitler and his entourage arrived, and the opening of the National Socialist Congress began.

Gabrielle was stunned by what she saw. A foreboding sea of Nazis turned out in Nuremberg. The size of the congress was staggering. Hitler reviewed a parade of six hundred thousand men who pledged absolute loyalty to the führer. Hundreds of trains transported army and paramilitary units to Nuremberg, and the men were housed in thirteen tent cities. Many European celebrities attended the political festivities, including Benito Mussolini.

Hitler dominated the event, of course, and Gabby noted

that Erik's face nearly glowed as he stood tall and straight beside her. As she looked out over a sea of steel helmets toward where Hitler stood on a white platform, she felt weak. The night before she had dreamed of Madame Jana. The old lady's face had appeared before her, her eyes filled with compassion and yet with warning. Now as she looked out over the massive display of armed men, she knew all this was wrong.

There before her hung three towering black banners, each with a large swastika in the middle. Hitler stood behind the microphone, a faint figure from her vantage point far back, and yet the personality of the man filled the air.

Erik turned and smiled at her, but when he saw her pale face, he asked, "Don't you feel well, Gabby?"

"I'm fine," she assured him, but she knew in her heart that all was not fine. An overwhelming sense of foreboding at what was happening in Germany closed in upon her, but she did not know what to do or where to flee.

* * *

Three weeks after the Nuremberg rally, Gabby returned home after a hard day at the hospital. She entered the house and at once was met by her aunt, whose face was tense with strain. "Gabby, something terrible has happened."

"What is it, Aunt Liza?" Gabby put a supporting arm around her. "You look ill. Is something wrong with Uncle Dalton?"

"No, it's Otto and Hulda."

Otto and Hulda Marx were close friends of the Burkes. They were a Jewish couple with three children. Otto was a well-to-do manufacturer, and they had visited often in the Burke home. Gabby liked the couple very much and was especially fond of their children. "What's the matter? Are they ill?"

"No, they've been arrested."

"Arrested! That's impossible!"

"I'm afraid it isn't, Gabby, and even worse, their children have been taken from them."

"What's the charge? I can't believe it!"

"I just got word from Hulda's sister. The court has arrested them because they refuse to teach their children Nazi ideology, so they took their children away."

"I can't believe it," Gabby said. "What does Uncle Dalton say?"

"He's gone to see what he can do, but it's very serious, I'm afraid."

"Where are the children?"

"They've been taken under the charge of the State. Here, this is part of the ruling that will explain it all."

Gabby took the sheet of paper that her aunt handed her. It was a lengthy statement delivered by the judge, and she read one section aloud, her voice tense with pain and disbelief: "'The law is a racial and national instrument entrusting German parents with the education of their children only under certain conditions, namely, that they educate them in the fashion that the nation and the State expect.'"

Gabby looked in disbelief at her aunt, who was visibly shaken by this turn of events. "This is terrible! This means that the State will break families apart if parents don't agree with Nazi doctrine."

"Dalton is hoping he can do something."

Gabby straightened up. "I'll go see what Erik can do. His family has great influence."

★ ★ ★

"But, Gabby, I can't interfere with the policies of the government!" Erik protested. He had gotten a frantic call from Gabby, and now the two were seated in a small café on the outskirts of Berlin not far from the hospital. He had listened as she explained the problem, and then he had read the judge's ruling. "This is very serious. These Jews, they're friends of yours?"

"Of course!"

"What do you expect me to do, darling?"

"I expect you to go to your father and see if he can do something. He's a powerful man. These are good people, Erik."

"I'm sure they are, but you know my father is very rigid when it comes to politics."

"Rigid!" Gabby exclaimed, eyes flashing. She usually kept her emotions under careful restraint, but now anger scored her face. "It's not right, Erik, and you know it's not! The Marxes are not enemies of the State. They're not political at all, as far as I know."

He held his hand up, but she would not be quiet. There was a fire in her he hadn't seen before. She usually presented an appearance of cool reserve, but her anger was evident today. He tried to quiet her, but she wouldn't stand for it.

"I'm going to do something," she promised. "I just don't know what."

Alarm swept across his face. "Gabby, these are dangerous things you are saying."

"Dangerous! It's dangerous to try to keep a family together? If it's dangerous, then what kind of a leader is this Adolf Hitler?"

Erik looked around the room and saw that her voice had reached others in the café. Several people had turned to stare with frowns toward Gabby.

"You must quiet yourself, Gabby—"

She got up and walked out without another word. She was furious and frightened and at the same time determined that nothing could stop her from doing what she could to right this terrible wrong.

★ ★ ★

Gabrielle tried, but she was powerless. She was a foreigner, not even a citizen. She attended the trial, and her heart was broken as the Marxes' children were taken from the courtroom weeping, their parents having been sentenced to a short time in prison along with a stiff fine.

As she watched them being led away, a sense of fear came over her. She left the courtroom and returned home. When she told her uncle about the trial, he was shocked but said, "These matters are beyond us."

"I hope decency isn't beyond us, Uncle Dalton." This was the first time Gabby had spoken anything close to sharply to her uncle, and his eyes opened with surprise.

"I'm going to do what I can. I've already written letters, but I will write more," he said, trying to comfort his niece.

Gabby did not answer, but from what she had observed of the rising Third Reich, she knew well what little effect the letters of one man who wasn't even a German would have on Hitler's loyal henchmen.

When Erik called her the next day, she put him off. He begged her to meet him for coffee, but she simply said, "I have to work today."

"You mustn't turn away from me," he pleaded.

Gabby's only thought was, *It's probably the first time in his life that he has ever begged anyone for anything.*

"I'm sorry, Erik. I need a little time. I'm very disturbed about this whole situation."

But as the days passed, things did not get better. She did not see Erik again, and she had the suspicion that his parents had heard of her activities and had pressured him to stop seeing her. It hurt her deeply, for she had been falling in love with Erik. She knew it was happening, yet at the same time, she knew it would only bring misery to both of them. Their love was strong, but it was becoming apparent it might not survive their political differences. As to what she would do, she had no idea. Then her mind was made up when she received a call from an American newspaperman who had been acquainted with her stepmother. His name was Frank Templeton, and he called on a Thursday morning in November asking urgently to see her. She agreed, and at noon she met with him in a small café near her home. He was waiting for her at the door.

"Hello, Dr. Winslow."

"Mr. Templeton."

"Just call me Frank." He was a short man, not young. He had thinning gray hair, and his face was red from drinking too much the night before. "Here, I've got a table," he said. "Sit down, please."

He ordered something to eat, and to be agreeable, Gabrielle ordered some soup. While they were waiting for the food, Templeton spoke of her stepmother. "She was the best newspaperwoman I ever knew. Better than any man. I still miss her."

"It's kind of you to say that, Frank." She leaned forward and asked, "Why did you want to see me? It wasn't just to talk about my stepmother."

"No, not exactly, but in a way it is." He hesitated and then grinned. "You'll never believe this, but I wasn't always a fat old slob. I was lean and mean back in the early days and very much in love with your stepmother."

She stared at him. "She spoke of you often, but I didn't know you two—"

"Oh, she never knew it. I wasn't the marrying kind, and even if I had been, she did much better with your father. I met him several times. He was a great man."

"Thank you," she said. She listened as Templeton continued to speak of how much he admired her parents, and then he said, "Look, you'll say it's none of my business, and it probably isn't, but I came for the sake of your stepmother. I think you'd best get out of Germany."

Gabrielle grew absolutely still. "What have you heard?"

"Rumors about your taking up for the Marx family. It's made waves, especially since you're tight with Erik Raeder. What about that? Are you two engaged?"

"No!" Her retort was terse. "What is it that you want to say? Please just say it, Frank."

He put his elbows on the table and clasped his stubby

hands together. "Things are going to get bad, I'm afraid. I got a tip from an inside source that something's going to happen tonight."

"What's going to happen? What are you talking about?"

"It's no secret how Hitler feels about the Jews. Your friends the Marxes are just the beginning. The crackdown's going to begin tonight."

"I can't believe it, and yet from what I've seen, I suppose I ought to."

"If you want to come with me tonight, what you see may convince you more than anything I could say."

Gabby lifted her head. "All right, Frank, I'll go."

"It might be dangerous, Miss Winslow."

"I'll go. What time shall we meet?"

"Meet me here at six o'clock."

★ ★ ★

It was already dark by six o'clock when Gabby met Frank Templeton in front of the café. It was cold, and she was wearing a warm wool overcoat and gloves. Templeton got out of his car, muffled up to his ears also. "Can't stand this cold weather," he said. "I'd like to be back in Georgia, where I grew up. Believe me. They know how to have hot weather there."

"Where are we going?"

"To the Jewish quarter. Come on."

Templeton apparently knew Berlin well. They drove in silence until he indicated they had arrived at their destination. When they got out of the car, he led her through the silent streets until he finally pulled her to a halt. "Wait a minute! You hear that?"

Gabby had heard shouting and screams in the distance. "What is it?" she whispered.

"I think it's the beginning of Adolf Hitler's war against the Jews. Come on."

They had not gone more than a hundred yards when

suddenly Frank grabbed her arm. "Hold on." He pulled her over into a shadow, and as Gabby looked down the street, she saw brown-shirted storm troopers breaking the windows of shops.

"What are they doing?" she whispered in horror.

"Those are Jewish shops," he said tersely. They continued down the street, staying in the dark shadows as much as they could.

That night Gabby and Templeton saw hundreds of homes and places of worship set on fire and ransacked. The men who looted and killed were mostly dressed in civilian clothes, but as Frank Templeton pointed out, many of them wore the boots normally worn with Nazi uniforms, and they drove Party cars.

When they had seen more than Gabby could have ever imagined in her worst nightmares, Templeton said, "Let's get you out of here. I've gotta try to get this story out of Germany. It won't be easy."

Gabby sat in the car silently as Templeton drove her home. She was stunned by the brutality she had witnessed. She could not blot out the terrible scenes of the Jews, young and old, being beaten with truncheons, some of them killed.

When Templeton stopped in front of her house, he said, "You need to get out of here. I'm afraid the violence is only going to get worse."

"What about you?"

"It's my job to tell America what I see. They'll throw me out of Germany sooner or later, but it's no place for a woman. Let me know if I can do anything for you."

"Thank you, Frank."

"I think about your stepmother a lot."

"I appreciate that," she said. Gabby went into the house and found her uncle in the library. "I've got to talk to you, Uncle Dalton."

"Why, of course, dear."

"Where is Aunt Liza?"

"Here I am, dear." Liza came in and noticed Gabby's pale face. "What is it?"

Without sparing any of the gruesome details, Gabby told them of the horrors she had just seen. She gave them a moment to take it all in and then said, "I'm leaving Germany."

"Leaving Germany!" Dalton gasped. "Wherever will you go?"

"Back to the Netherlands. There's nothing for me in England. I don't know anyone there, but I think I'll be able to get my position back in Holland. I'm sorry to leave you two. I wish you would go with me."

"Perhaps we should, Dalton," Liza said tentatively, looking toward her husband with fear in her eyes.

"No, we must stay here. I can't leave my work. And you don't have to go either, Gabrielle. Germany needs good doctors."

"I'm leaving Germany," she insisted, her voice steady, though her face was pale. "I can't stay and watch what's happening here."

★ ★ ★

The announcement for final boarding was made, and Gabrielle said a last good-bye to her uncle and aunt. As she started toward the door that led out to the airfield, Erik suddenly appeared.

"Gabby, you can't go away!" he pleaded, his face tense with strain.

"It's useless to argue, Erik. Our worlds are too far apart. I can't agree with what's happening in your country. I've seen terrible things, and it's only going to get worse."

"I can't argue politics." He took her by the shoulders. "All I know is that I love you, and we can work it out."

Gabby had somehow known this moment would come. She looked up into the face of the tall man and saw the strange melding together of compassion and love and pity, but it was tempered with something hard, which she knew would only grow harder. "Good-bye, Erik," she said, pulling away from him and turning around. He called her name, but she walked steadfastly out of the building and toward the plane that was warming up on the field. An attendant took her hand and helped her up the stairs, and when she reached the top, she turned and looked back at Erik. He was standing as still as a statue, and she could see the despair in his face. She saw his lips frame her name, and then desperately she turned and entered the plane. As the door shut behind her, she knew that this part of her life was over forever.

PART TWO

May–August 1940

★ ★ ★

CHAPTER SEVEN

"The Lights Are Going Out"

★ ★ ★

An ominous specter hung over Europe like a dark cloud—the creation, it seemed, of a single determined man. Adolf Hitler had mobilized the German people, and like a juggernaut, his troops swarmed over Germany's neighbors. In the fall of 1938, the German army took over western Czechoslovakia almost unopposed. In March of 1939, all of Czechoslovakia was overrun by German troops. In August 1939, Germany and the Soviet Union signed a nonaggression pact, which stunned the rest of the world, and all of Europe began mobilizing for the inevitable.

On September first, a mighty German force of over a million men swept across the Polish border. Britain and France immediately declared war on Germany, and the world knew that the war to end all wars had not worked. Another more threatening dark shadow was falling over the earth. Later that month, the Soviet Union invaded Poland from the east. The poor country didn't stand a chance against its invaders, and by the end of the month, the eastern third of the country was occupied by the Soviet Union, and Germany controlled the rest.

In November, tiny Finland was swallowed up by the Soviets, and in April of 1940, the Nazis entered Denmark and Norway.

As she walked briskly down the street, Betje thought about how dramatically her world had changed over the last couple of years. With Hitler and his massive military machine aggressively sweeping destruction throughout Europe, the entire world watched nervously, wondering which nation the dictator would conquer next.

She glanced up and saw a bullfinch fly swiftly past and then drop down into a feeding box. Always captured by beauty of any kind, Betje paused and admired the bird's amazing colors. For a time the bird pecked at the seed with sharp, quick motions, then turned a bright eye on Betje and froze.

"I'm not going to hurt you," Betje whispered. Her artist's eye took in the blue-gray back and the rosy breast of the small bird and she mused out loud, "I wonder why we appreciate the colors on birds more than in other parts of nature. Right overhead the entire sky is blue and beautiful. It must be that we admire beauty more in small things than in large ones."

The small bird cocked its head, uttered a short muted cry, then rose in the air with a flutter of wings. Betje stood still, turning to watch until the bird disappeared into a grove of trees across the road. "All you have to worry about is a few seeds to eat and a place to stay when night falls." She shrugged her shoulders impatiently. "I wish it were as easy for me—and for everyone."

Slowly she walked toward the house of Dorcas Burke, but she was troubled by the contrast of the beautiful bullfinch and the blue sky above with the political chaos of the spring of 1940 that filled her thoughts. Betje turned through the gate of the glistening white fence that surrounded the redbrick house that was half covered with ivy. Oskar Grotman was busily digging in one of the flower beds.

"Hello, Oskar," she said as she approached him. "What are you planting now?"

At age sixty, Oskar was still a strong, active man. His hands were huge, and the shovel looked like a toy in them. His small blue eyes contrasted with his large wide mouth, and his chin was as blunt as a piece of granite. When he spoke, his voice was coarse but friendly enough. "Planting geraniums," he muttered. He pointed with his shovel, holding it as if it weighed no more than a straw.

Betje looked at the gaily painted wagon that had been pulled out of the carriage house. It remained inactive all year except for the festival that came in May, and now it gleamed with fresh red and yellow paint. "Is Gabby home yet?"

"Not yet. I've been cleaning up the wagon for her—greasing the wheels so they won't squeak." His eyes glowed, and his big lips stretched into a broad smile. "Every year she do this thing—dress up like a gypsy. You go with her this year, Miss Betje?"

"Yes. I told her I would." She gazed at the geraniums for a moment and then suddenly asked, "What do you think of Germany, Oskar? Will the Germans invade the Netherlands?"

Anger flared in his eyes, and his lips drew into a tight line. "Ja, the filthy Boche are coming!" He shook the shovel in the air, his grip so tight his knuckles turned pale. "And I vill kill them like I did in the Great War."

Betje had always liked the older man. He had often taken her and Gabby fishing when they were growing up. She remembered walking along the dikes holding one of Oskar's huge hands while Gabby held the other one. He had told them stories of his service in the war and the changes he went through when he returned home. He had medals he was very proud of and still wore on special occasions.

"You're a Christian, Oskar. Isn't killing Germans a sin?"

"It's not a sin to kill lice!" He took the shovel in both hands and drove it into the dirt. He said no more, but he was clearly enraged.

He must have been a fierce warrior back in his fighting days, she thought.

Betje turned and walked up the path made of crushed oyster shells to the house. She knocked on the door and it opened almost at once. "Hello, Matilda."

"Hello, Miss Betje. Come on in."

"How is Grandmother today?"

Betje couldn't help noticing how much Dorcas Burke's housekeeper had aged lately. Matilda had never been a beauty, but now with old age creeping up, her cheekbones stood out atop hollowed cheeks, and deep wrinkle lines marked her face.

"She's having a good day," Matilda said. "Go on in. She's in the sitting room."

Betje walked down the short hall and then turned into the sitting room. Yellow sunlight flooded through the windows, enlightening the features of Dorcas Burke, and Betje thought, as she often did, *I hope I can look as good as she does when I'm seventy-one. I'm already almost halfway there!* "Good morning, Grandmother." Betje had always loved Gabby's great-aunt and thought of Dorcas like her own grandmother.

"Good morning, Betje. Come and sit."

The sunlight touched the old woman's hair, giving it a silver glow. She was wearing a pale blue dress fastened at the neck and at the wrist. Her gaze was direct, and as she lifted her voice and called for tea, Betje admired the strength still evident in her. Betje sat down and questioned Dorcas about her health.

"At my age, I'm good," she said. "The Lord has given me a good life. I have Jesus, and that's the best anyone can have."

Betje smiled as Dorcas told her about the Scripture she had been studying lately. She knew that soon enough the older woman would ask her directly about her own spiritual life, and sure enough, after Matilda had served the tea, Dorcas gave her an encompassing glance.

"I'm praying that you will find Jesus," she said directly. "I will never give up, Betje. You will have to say yes to God one day."

"Don't preach at me, Grandmother!" Betje pretended to be angry, but actually she respected Dorcas Burke as much as she did any human being. She had known hypocritical Christians before, but this woman had lived her religion faithfully under Betje's careful scrutiny.

"I only preach because it's important," Dorcas insisted. "God has a wonderful plan for your life, but He can't share it with you until you say yes to Him."

"Yes, yes, I know." She changed the subject, saying, "Gabby talked me into going to the festival with her this afternoon. She's going to do her gypsy act again."

"Yes, of course. She always does."

"I may even try my hand at doing a little fortune-telling myself this time. I've watched her do it often enough, and I've got nothing better to do today."

"I've never liked her doing that fortune-telling," Dorcas said. "I used to get angry about it, but not anymore. I know Gabby just does it to raise funds for the church. She has a good heart."

"This may be the last year she'll do it."

"You mean because of Germany and that madman Hitler?"

"Yes. He's going to take over the world, it seems."

"He could never do that."

Betje sipped her tea and shook her head. "Nobody's been able to stop him yet."

"God will stop him," Dorcas said with a confidence in her voice.

Betje did not argue, for she actually agreed that the only one who could stop Hitler was the Almighty himself. She got up and looked out the window. "Does Gabby ever talk about what happened to her when she was with your son and his wife in Germany?"

"She never speaks of it."

"Something must have happened there," Betje remarked, and her eyes narrowed as she thought hard. "She's changed. Something has made her different. For one thing, she won't have anything to do with men anymore. Someone must have wounded her heart."

"You could take a lesson from her."

"You think I like men too much? Well, maybe I do. What's not to like?"

"Moderation in all things, young lady!"

Betje laughed. "All right. Go on and preach to me, Grandmother. I know you're going to, and we might as well get it out of the way."

Dorcas looked fondly at the younger woman and spoke of Jesus and His love for sinners. Tears rose in her eyes as she spoke of the cross. She dashed them away and said firmly, "One day you will find the Lord Jesus."

As always, Betje felt uncomfortable when Dorcas Burke spoke to her of Jesus. The same thing happened when Gabby tried to get her to turn from her ways. Deep in her heart, she knew that both women were right and that her life was wrong. Although she had known many who called themselves Christians who did not seem to live up to that claim, she was never able to deny the reality of the faith of Dorcas and Gabby. Uncomfortably, she shifted and poured herself some more tea. "Have you given any thought to going to stay with your son in Germany?"

"No, I won't do that."

"Hitler's going to invade Belgium and Holland, Grandmother." She waited for the old woman to reply, but when she said nothing, she said what everyone in Holland already knew. "He wants France, and he has to come through the Low Countries with his armies to get at it."

"I will never leave my home." The words were firm, and Dorcas Burke's lips formed a tight line. The Germans might occupy Holland, but they would find this old woman who sat across from her as adamant as a human could get.

They heard the front door open and close, and then they heard Gabby greet Matilda. The two women waited in silence until Gabby entered the sitting room. She greeted Betje and gave her great-aunt a kiss.

"I see you've come to go to the festival with me," Gabby said to Betje.

"Of course. I told you I would."

"I've heard that the queen might be there."

"So they say."

"Are you still going to let me dress you up in a costume like mine this year?"

"I'll wear a costume, but you're not going to dye my hair! I like it blond."

"I can cover it up with a colorful kerchief." Gabby perched on the edge of a chair. "Grandmother, Betje has been doing such good work at the orphanage."

"So you told me." Dorcas turned her eyes on Betje. "You've been teaching the children to paint. That's good. They need all the love and attention they can get."

Betje suddenly felt uncomfortable. She had worked hard with the children but preferred not to be complimented about it. "I get bored," she said. "There's nothing else to do."

"I know just the thing for your boredom," Gabby said. "We're starting to work on another skit for the kids at the orphanage, and I think you'll like the part I've got for you."

"That's fine, as long as I don't have to wear one of those ridiculous wigs you keep in the spare bedroom."

"It's a deal. Come on. I'll show you the costume I wore for the last skit. The children laughed until they were practically rolling on the floor."

"All right, and then you can make a gypsy of me!"

* * *

Gabby stood back and admired her handiwork. "You look just right, Betje. You make a fine gypsy."

Betje laughed and turned to look at herself in the mirror. She tucked a stray piece of blond hair back under her kerchief and fingered the gold earrings that hung heavily on her earlobes.

The two were both dressed in colorful blouses and full

skirts. They had spent a fair amount of time lining their eyes with eyeliner and darkening their eyelids with brown shadow.

"Come along," Gabby said after they'd checked their reflections from all angles. "We don't want to be late."

The two women left the house and found that Oskar had already hitched up the horse to the wagon for them. As they climbed up onto the seat, Oskar handed the lines to Gabby, saying, "He's getting old, so don't hurry him." He patted the horse fondly. "I remember when he was only a colt."

"I'll bring you back something nice from the fete, Oskar. Thanks for painting the wagon. It looks beautiful."

"Go on," Oskar said gruffly. "Do your fortune-telling."

Gabby slapped the horse with the lines, and he obediently moved into a brisk walk. As the wagon rolled along the road near the canal, the two young women spoke of the festival. It was a beautiful day, and people called out to the two women as they passed, smiling at their appearance. A young boy ran over and said, "Tell my fortune, Miss Gabby."

"You're going to be rich and famous and marry a beautiful girl and have twelve children."

"I don't want to hear that! That's for old people."

Gabby laughed as they left the boy behind. She told Betje about one of the children at the orphanage, a girl named Leida, who was having great emotional troubles. "She lost her father and mother in a train accident," she said sadly. "She cries herself to sleep every night. I know what that's like. It took me a long time to get over the loss of my parents."

"I don't think you ever really did get over it."

"No, I guess not."

They rode in silence for a moment, listening to the horse's rhythmic cadence. Suddenly, Betje asked, "What happened to you in Germany? You weren't the same after you came back."

"It wasn't a happy time, Betje. I don't like to think about it."

"It was a man, wasn't it?"

Gabby was startled that Betje had come to that conclusion. "Yes, it was," she said.

"Who was it?"

For some reason Gabby felt she was finally ready to tell her friend about those days. She had tried to forget about them, but from time to time, a song on the radio or a laugh she heard in a crowd reminded her of Erik Raeder. The months apart had not removed the memory of his passionate kisses. They came back with a startling reality, even though she knew she had done the right thing in leaving.

"His name was Erik."

"What did he look like?"

"Very handsome."

"Well, tell me about him. Did you love him?"

"I . . . I thought I did, but it never would have worked."

"Did he love you?"

"He said he did, Betje."

Something about Gabby's voice caught at Betje, and she realized that talking about it was hurting her friend. Quickly, she put her hand on Gabby's arm. "I'm sorry," she said. "I know you were terribly hurt by it, but you have to put things like that behind you."

"I wish I could, but how do you do that?" Gabby said, her eyes sad. "Our memories are not at our command, Betje. I mean, we can't forget something just because we will it."

"You have to try."

"I have tried, but he loved me. How can I forget that?" She waved at a couple passing by on the sidewalk. "Oh, I know he's with some other woman by now—maybe even married. But I think he really did love me, and when a man loves a woman, that's the best compliment he can pay to her."

Betje did not speak for a moment. The hooves of the horse clattered on the cobblestones, and people heading for the festival were laughing as though no threat from Adolf Hitler loomed on the horizon. "You need to have more fun,

Gabby. I still remember part of a poem I read when I was just a girl:

"Gather ye rosebuds while ye may,
Old Time is still a-flying:
And this same flower that smiles today
Tomorrow will be dying.

"That's what I believe," Betje said. "You have to grab whatever happiness comes to you. There's not much of it."

Gabby shook her head. "That same poet once said, 'Forgive me, God, and blot each line out of my book that is not Thine.' Gathering flowers isn't the same thing as loving a man. I want something that will last for a lifetime."

"Nothing lasts. I wish it did," Betje said poignantly.

The women fell silent until they pulled into the park, where people were already gathering for the fete. Betje looked at her friend and tried to speak, but she felt too sad. She knew she had stirred unhappy memories, and she did not want to hurt Gabby. *I wish she were happy,* Betje thought. *But then, who is?*

★ ★ ★

Reverend Karel Citroen moved through the crowd, smiling and greeting those he passed. He was somewhat surprised at the size of the crowd, for given the shadow of a German invasion that hung over the Low Countries, he had thought the festival might be poorly attended. But as he walked across the grass, he thought, *Maybe people need things like this more during hard times than when everything is going well. God help us. We're going to need all the good humor and happiness we can grab.*

He was startled when a hand seized his arm, and he turned to find himself looking into the eyes of Gabby's friend Betje.

"Tell your fortune, sir?"

He smiled at the engaging young woman. Her hair was

done up under a red and blue scarf, and her loose costume did not hide her attractive figure. "Yes," he said, "as long as it's a happy one."

"I tell only what I see in the hand," she said, one eyebrow raised.

Betje pulled him over to sit next to her and took his hand in hers. She began to rattle off a patter of events to come in his life, but he paid little attention to the charade. He was thinking instead about Betje's real existence. *Such a waste of a life,* he thought. *She has so much to give, so much talent, but she wastes it all looking for pleasure. She'll never find what her heart really needs that way*. He spotted Gabby over Betje's shoulder and saw that she had found a customer. He felt a touch of envy as Gabby held the man's hand and studied his palm.

Betje looked up at the pastor and saw that he was no longer smiling. "Beware of blond women. They'll lead you astray." She let his hand go and said, "You're too good-looking to be a preacher." Her remark obviously embarrassed him, which pleased her. "Come along," she whispered, pressing herself against him. "Let's go to the tavern. I'll let you buy me a drink."

"I don't think so, Betje."

"Ah, you're missing all the good times. What you need is a woman."

Citroen was accustomed to her teasing, and for a few moments the two observed the hubbub around them. Gabby's customer finally left and she approached them.

"Hello, Gabby," he said. "It looks like business is good today."

"Yes. Everyone wants their fortune told." She grinned. "Has Betje been telling you yours?"

"I've been trying to get him to go out with me. I'd like to show him what life is all about. Poor fellow! He's missing out on everything." Betje laughed as she whirled and moved quickly to grab the hand of a tall young man who was passing by. "Tell your fortune, sir?"

Karel turned to Gabby after Betje's customer got settled

into a seat and said quietly, "I worry about Betje."

"So do I, Pastor."

"It's nice of you to be such a loyal friend to her." He watched her as she cheerfully greeted some friends. When she turned back to him, he said, "Playacting agrees with you. You really come alive when you do this."

"It is fun. I really look forward to it every year." She suddenly sobered. "You don't think it's wrong to pretend to be fortune-telling, do you?"

"I suppose there's no harm in it as long as it's only that—just pretend."

"Grandmother's never liked it much, but I guess she's decided it's just silly."

"It probably is, Gabby, but we need some silly things in our lives—especially now."

Gabby looked at the crowd, at the bright colors of the costumes, the blue sky overhead, and the beautiful flowers. "It seems impossible that war could ever touch this place, doesn't it?"

"I'm afraid it's very possible," Karel said soberly. He noticed the crowd parting to let an entourage through and pointed. "Look, there's the queen. It looks like she's getting ready to make a speech. Let's get closer so we can hear."

Queen Wilhelmina was a sweet-faced middle-aged woman who always appeared cheerful. She loved her people, and they adored her. Gabby had once seen her riding along the street on a bicycle. She had waved as if she were an ordinary person, and Gabby had waved back. She had never forgotten that, but now as she pressed closer with the pastor by her side, she saw that the queen looked weary. "She looks worried, doesn't she?"

"Don't we all."

Queen Wilhelmina began to speak, and for several minutes she spoke of her pleasure at being at the fete and how important it was to keep such events alive. Suddenly, however, a cloud passed over her face, and she dropped her head. Startled, the crowd fell silent, and when Wilhelmina finally looked up, there was pain in her fine eyes. "A dark day, my friends, has come to our country. Just a few moments ago I received word that the German air force has attacked our Dutch cities. After our country, with scrupulous conscientiousness, had observed strict neutrality, Germany made a sudden attack on our territory without any warning."

The crowd quickly burst into worried conversations, but as the queen continued, they quieted. "Our gallant air force has fought off waves of gliders carrying German troops, but they are being overwhelmed by superior numbers. . . ." She spoke for some time of the invasion, in a firm voice that carried easily on the still air. "Our nation has been overrun by other nations in the past, and even though we are being invaded, we will never, never, never give up our liberty!"

★ ★ ★

Betje had come to stand beside Gabby and Karel to listen to the queen speak. When the royal entourage left, she said bitterly, "I'd like to kill every German in the world!"

"Not all Germans are evil," Karel responded.

But Betje was furious. Her face was pale, and she shook with anger. "They're not *human*!"

"A statesman once said as the Great War began, 'The lights are going out all over Europe. We shall not see them turned on again in our lifetime.'"

Karel took Betje's arm and looked straight into her eyes. "God will not forget us. He will not allow the world to fall into darkness."

"That's right, Betje," Gabby said. "God is still on the throne!"

day [illegible]
mountains [illegible]
[illegible]
[illegible]
[illegible]
man.
[illegible]
[illegible]
[illegible]
[illegible]
[illegible]
[illegible]
[illegible]
[illegible]
[illegible]
[illegible]
[illegible]

CHAPTER EIGHT

OPERATION JONAH

★ ★ ★

Major Ian Castleton sat at his desk, his eyes closed, half dozing in the heat. He slapped at the large fly that circled his head. "Blast!" He straightened up. For a time he stared hopelessly at the mass of papers on his desk and wished he were out fishing for trout instead of serving England in a stuffy office. He laughed at his disloyal sentiment. "Can't go fishing with the Germans taking Europe by storm!"

The door popped open, and a skinny sergeant stepped inside. "Colonel Flynn to see you, Major."

"Well, show him in, Sergeant."

Castleton got to his feet. He was a sturdy man of thirty-four, but his prematurely gray hair made him look much older. He stepped around his desk and saluted when the officer entered. "Good morning, Colonel."

Colonel Colin Flynn returned the salute. "Hello, Ian," he said with a smile. He came over and shook the hand of the shorter man. Flynn was tall, well over six feet, lean and fit. His face showed lines of fatigue, however, and there was a tense nervousness in all of his actions.

"Will you have a whiskey, sir?"

"I shouldn't, but I will."

"My sentiments exactly." Castleton opened the liquor cabinet and pulled out a bottle of whiskey and two glasses. He filled each of them and handed a glass to Flynn. He held his own up and said, "To victory."

"To victory."

The two men drank and then sat down. "I've been working on the movement you spoke of, Colonel," Castleton said.

"About Operation Jonah?"

Castleton shook his head, and a weary disgust seemed to touch his features. "I don't think it has a prayer."

"Neither do I, but it's got to get done."

Castleton rose and got the whiskey bottle. He offered it to Flynn, who shook his head as he went to look out the window. Castleton poured his own glass half full again and drank it down, shuddering as the raw alcohol bit at his throat. He slammed the glass down, anger washing across his pale features. "Another impossible task assigned by the powers that be. Who dreamed up this little gem?"

Flynn mentioned a name as he watched a squad that was drilling on the parade ground. He turned and grinned. "That startled you."

"Well, he's capable of thinking up such a harebrained idea. I suppose we'll have to try it."

Colonel Flynn leaned back against the wall and folded his hands across his chest. "Numbers won't work with this one, Ian," he said in his high-pitched voice. "It'll have to be a small group."

"You're right. As a matter of fact, it'll all pretty much depend on one man."

"Yes, with some good backup."

"I've gone over the dossier of every man we've got, but I hate to make this choice."

"Well, you do have to make it, so who will it be?"

Castleton walked over to a battered filing cabinet and yanked the drawer open. He shuffled through several files, pulled one out impatiently, and handed the manila folder to the tall man. "He's my pick."

Flynn sat down at Castleton's desk and opened the folder. He read slowly, his head bent over the stack of papers. Ian Castleton watched him carefully. He was not at all happy about this Operation Jonah. For one thing, he did not like the name. It sounded like a failure by definition. The silence grew thick in the room, interrupted only with the buzzing of the fly that circled his head. He waved it away impatiently but did not speak until finally Flynn looked up.

"Are you sure he's on *our* side, Ian?" the colonel asked sarcastically.

"He's a maverick, but he's done some very difficult things."

Colonel Flynn studied the paper again and shook his head doubtfully. "Well, I don't think a spit-and-polish officer would serve in this case. I'd better meet him. Is he on the station?"

"Yes, he's between assignments. But when I heard you were coming, I kept him available."

"Have him come up, will you?"

Picking up the phone, Castleton's voice crackled, "Sergeant, find Captain Bando and get him here at once." He put the phone down and slumped into a chair, looking miserable.

"Dailon Bando. What kind of name is that?"

"He's a Welshman."

"A Welshman?"

"Yes, to the bone. His friends call him Dai."

"Most Welshmen are pretty emotional, Ian. We can't have that for an operation like this."

Ian Castleton laughed shortly. "He's emotional, all right. Got a bit of a temper, loves poetry, has a sentimental streak that he covers up." He paused for a moment and ran his hands across his face in a weary gesture. "But he's hard as nails, sir. He's into the martial arts—a black belt, I understand. He's the best shot in the service, and he speaks French, German, Dutch, and two or three more languages, I think."

"What makes you think he can pull this thing off?"

"I'm not so sure he can."

The answer ruffled Colonel Flynn's nerves. "Then why are you recommending him?"

"Because he's the best I've got." He rose and poured himself another whiskey. "I'm drinking too much," he said, looking at the glass. He carefully poured the liquor back into the bottle and shoved his hands into his pockets. "I gave him a test."

"A test? What kind of test?"

"I told him to try to get the file marked *Operation Jonah* out of my safe. That was two days ago, and it's still there. I checked it this morning. But I didn't expect he would succeed. Security here is as tight as a jug."

The two men sat talking about other special projects they had taken on. The two were often reassigned from their usual duties and directed to the most difficult and dangerous work, which required top secrecy. Both Castleton and Flynn had come up the hard way, and now with the war pressing in upon them, they were working day and night as Hitler pushed his way through Europe. It was not a service with any outward rewards. There were no pictures in the newspaper of the men and women who succeeded. The very essence of these private armies was to keep their agents as far from the newspapers as possible.

The door opened, and the sergeant announced, "Captain Bando is here, sir."

"Send him in."

Both men stood up as the captain came through the door. "Reporting as ordered, Major."

"Bando. Captain, this is Colonel Flynn."

"Hello, Captain," the colonel said. He sized up the officer who stood at attention before him. The man's age was hard to fix. He could have been anywhere from twenty to forty. He had coarse black hair and a squarish face with rough features. He was not at all handsome, but he guessed that women would call the man masculine or even virile looking. His eyes were strange, a light green that glowed against his rather dark complexion. He had high cheekbones

down to the barracks we've assigned them to. I don't know if they're there or not."

"Thank you very much, sir."

Bando followed the sergeant to a low rectangular building with no identifying characteristics. The sergeant opened the door, and after Bando stepped in, he said, "There's one of them right over there."

"Thank you, Sergeant."

The barracks was hot, almost stifling, and Bando wiped sweat from his face as he approached the man. "Good afternoon."

The man he spoke to was short and stocky with light blond hair and a pair of steady blue eyes. "Hello. You have come to take us to our new assignment?"

"I'm afraid not. I'm Captain Bando. I need to question you a little."

"Question? About what?"

"Let's start with your name."

"Mogens Roosevelt."

"Any relation to the American president Roosevelt?"

"Maybe a cousin. Very distant. What is it you want to know, sir?"

"Have you ever visited a little town called Oudekerk aan de Amstel, near Amsterdam?"

"No, but one of our group comes from there. That's him over there playing draughts. The lanky fellow."

"Thanks." Bando approached the man and said, "My name is Bando. I understand you know the town of Oudekerk aan de Amstel."

"I know it very well indeed. That's my home. Why are you asking?"

"Your name is?"

"Lieutenant Lang Zeeman." There was suspicion in Zeeman's eyes, but he reluctantly agreed when Bando asked him to step outside.

When they were outside, Bando said, "I'm doing a job for a special unit, and I need to know a bit about your country."

"Are you going there?"

"I expect I will, but I can't say why. What about you, Lieutenant?"

Bando listened as Zeeman described the air battles he'd been in. "We had no chance at all," Zeeman concluded. "I shot down three Germans, and then I went down myself. I was in Rotterdam when it was leveled. Hundreds have died, maybe thousands. Eighty thousand people are homeless." Bitterness tinged Zeeman's voice, and his anger was scarcely contained. "But they will not win," he declared.

"You've come to England to join the RAF?"

"Yes."

"That's very commendable, Lieutenant. Now, our conversation must be kept absolutely secret. It could be fatal to me and my group if it got out."

"Of course, sir. Why is it you want to know about Oudekerk?" he asked curiously.

"I need to find out all I can about a man named Dalton Burke."

His eyes opened wide with surprise. "Dalton Burke!"

"Yes. I don't suppose you knew him?"

"Knew him? I certainly did. I was very close to the family. As a matter of fact—"

When Zeeman broke off suddenly, Bando's eyes narrowed. "What is it, Lieutenant?"

"Well, it's rather personal."

"I'd like to hear it if you don't mind."

"Well, I was going to marry his niece. The fellow is a traitor for going over to the Germans, but I'll say this for him. He loved that girl and would do anything for her."

"Is she in Berlin with him?" Bando demanded, sensing a break for exactly the kind of information he needed.

"No, she lived with him and his wife there for about two years, but she didn't like it. She's back home in the Netherlands. She's a doctor. Works in the hospital in Oudekerk."

Carefully, Bando said, "This is going to take a while, Lieutenant. I need to learn everything you know about this family. Come along. I'll buy you a meal."

Lang Zeeman was mystified. He ate his meal and found that Bando was a most thorough investigator. Zeeman answered question after question, and finally, after an hour of this, he burst out, "Why do you want to know all this, Captain Bando?"

"I'm afraid I can't tell you that, but I mean no harm to Dalton Burke. You can be sure of that."

Zeeman hesitated. "He's basically a good man but rather foolish in his politics. His wife has much better judgment, I think."

Dai continued to question Zeeman, and after another half hour, he smiled and put his hand out. "You've been a great help, Lieutenant. I wish you good fortune. I think the RAF is lucky to have you."

"Will you let me know, if you can, how it turns out?"

"I'll do that."

"And if you happen to meet Gabrielle Winslow, tell her I still think of her."

"I'll do that too."

★ ★ ★

Bando returned to his quarters and for a long time simply sat in a chair replaying the entire conversation in his mind. Finally, he got up and pulled some old letters from a chest. He sat down and read several of them before returning them to the drawer.

He went directly to Major Castleton's office, and when he was admitted, he said, "I'll be leaving at once—for Holland."

"For Holland? But why?" He listened intently as Bando explained his plan and then said, "All right. It sounds like you're on to something. Make sure you've got all your radio contacts arranged. You'll be all alone when you leave England." He suddenly dropped his official manner and said, "If you can pull this off, Dai, it'll be a big thing."

Dai Bando sobered for a moment. "We'd both better believe in miracles, because that's what it's going to take to do this job."

CHAPTER NINE

An Emergency Case

★ ★ ★

As the world watched, the dark shadow of Nazi tyranny spread out from Germany and swallowed up nation after nation, and there seemed to be little that the free world could do to stop it. As the Bible put it, men's hearts were failing them for fear, and all over the world, men and women were crying out to God for deliverance from Hitler and his ruthless hordes. Resistance was hopeless against the mighty German army, and on May fifteenth, the Dutch commander-in-chief, Henri Gerard Winkelman, directed his troops to give up in order to prevent further bloodshed and annihilation. That day the Netherlands succumbed to the relentless barrage of superior German force. Later in the month, King Leopold of Belgium ordered the Belgian army to capitulate to Germany.

Throughout most of May, it became difficult to listen to the radio, as there was little to report but bad news as Germany swept forward victoriously and the Allies fell back. Gabby had a glimmer of hope, however, as she listened to the radio while she ate her lunch late in May. As she put her dishes in the sink, she heard that French and British troops that had been trapped on the beach at Dunkirk in northern France were evacuated by what seemed to be miraculous forces. The British sent boats of all kinds, both military and civilian, by the hundreds across the Channel and rescued the trapped soldiers at Dunkirk. "It was clearly a work of divine deliverance," the announcer said with enthusiasm. Still, while avoiding news of complete disaster, he had revealed that the Allies had suffered nearly one hundred thirty thousand dead, wounded, or captured. Thousands of guns and costly supplies were abandoned at Dunkirk.

As Gabby headed out to her car, a convoy of trucks crammed with German soldiers crawled by. She paused and examined the faces of the German soldiers. She was always surprised that they did not look like monsters, for she knew of the cruelty of the Germans as they overran their neighboring countries. One of the soldiers noticed her and pulled off his helmet, revealing his blond hair, which was cut very short around the ears, with the longer hair on top slicked back. He smiled at her and called out, *"Guten Morgen, Fraulein."* He had a nice smile and looked very young. Without thinking, Gabby raised her hand and waved, whereupon the other soldiers began whistling and shouting at her. The roar of the engines drowned out most of their remarks, and the column soon passed, leaving a cloud of dust to settle on the street.

The movements of German troops had become fairly commonplace around Amsterdam, but still the sight of the flags bearing the hated swastika never ceased to cause a chill to run down her spine. The sight of the youthful German soldier's face gave her pause, and as she settled into her car and started the engine, she thought, *He looks like a nice boy that I might have dated when I was younger, and yet I've seen with my own eyes that he and his comrades are responsible for brutality beyond comprehension.*

She pulled out of the driveway and headed toward the hospital. Traffic was light, and it had proved to be a banner year for tulips. As she passed between the fields, she enjoyed the acres of brilliant yellow and crimson flowers that stretched for miles. It was one of the things she loved most about Holland, especially in the spring, along with the greenness of the grass and the slowly turning peaceful windmills. But the German occupation stood in stark contrast to the surrounding beauty. She had already heard stories of Jews being snapped up during midnight raids and disappearing, and rumors circulated that they were being sent to concentration camps. Horrible stories leaked out of the torture and death of Jews and others the Nazis called "inferior races." She shuddered at the thought that the very nightmare she had left Germany to escape was now here in Holland.

Ten minutes later, Gabby pulled up in front of the hospital. As she entered the building, she was greeted at once by one of the nurses, Hilda Schmidt, who, despite her German ancestry, hated Hitler and the occupation as vehemently as the Dutch did.

"Hi, Hilda," Gabby said with a smile. Hilda was an attractive middle-aged woman with strawberry blond hair, and Gabby liked her a great deal. Her husband had been killed while fighting the Germans. Her face was now set, and a sadness prevailed over her features.

"You'd better go see Hans Dent."

"Is he worse?"

"Not physically, but he's ready to give up. It's hard for a young man to lose his leg."

Hans Dent had been one of the defenders of Holland until his leg was destroyed by a close-up blast from an automatic weapon. He had almost bled to death, and Hilda and Gabby had fought hard to save him.

"I'll go see him right now," she said and then added, "You need to take some rest, Hilda."

"And you also. You're tired. Did you sleep at all last night?"

"Enough. We've got to keep going. The patients depend on us."

"Ja, listen to your own voice." Hilda managed a smile before she turned back to her mound of paper work that never seemed to grow smaller.

Gabby moved through the hospital until she reached one of the wards where the more severely wounded lay. She moved down the line of beds speaking cheerfully to each man, as she always did, and finally came to stand beside the bed of Hans Dent. He was twenty-two years old with the typical Dutch appearance—blond hair and blue eyes. He had little life in his features, however, and sounded exhausted as he said good morning to her.

"Good morning to you, Hans. Let me see how you're doing." She folded the sheet from his legs and carefully pulled part of the dressing back from his stump. "We'll change the dressing later this afternoon," she said as she pressed the gauze back into place. "I must say I'm proud of myself. I did a fine job."

"Thank you, Dr. Winslow."

The reply was weak, and Gabby put a hand on his forehead under the pretense of checking for a fever. Although she was not nearly old enough to be his mother, she was surprised, as always, at the maternal love she had for these young men. She pushed his hair back off his forehead. "What are you worried about, Hans? You're going to be well."

"I'll have only one leg."

"That's true, but it could have been worse. They do wonders with artificial limbs these days, and I left a good pad of flesh there. You'll adjust well. You'll be able to go hunting and fishing and maybe even skiing. You'll be fine."

Dent remained silent, but obviously something was on his mind. Finally, he blurted out, "What will my fiancée say? She agreed to marry a man with two legs."

Suddenly, Gabby understood the emotional turmoil that had drawn Dent's face into a mask. She put her hand on his shoulder and squeezed it. "Let me ask you this, Hans. If your fiancée had lost a leg, would you cease to love her?"

"No!"

"And she won't cease to love you. You must get well, and you'll marry and have children, and you'll have a good family. Your loss of a leg will be a badge of honor. You can tell your children you lost it fighting for Holland."

"I guess you're right," he said, although he didn't sound very convinced.

Hilda came into the room, and soon the two started working their way through the wards together, checking wounds and watching for signs of complications such as infection, which if not caught immediately could take a soldier's life quickly. Gabby noticed that Hilda was even more quiet than usual. She commented on her friend's mood when they finally took a break for tea.

"I must tell you something about your friend Betje," Hilda told her.

"Betje! What is it, Hilda?"

"She's hiding a young couple in her apartment. They're Jews." Hilda's eyes glinted, and her lips drew tight with fear. "If the Germans find them there, Betje will be sent to a concentration camp or even shot."

Gabby's thoughts were a whirlwind at the news. "I'll go see her as soon as I get off work."

"She must be more careful," Hilda said. "These Nazis are beasts. They would kill her like a fly!"

★ ★ ★

As soon as she entered the apartment, Gabby knew that Hilda had told her the truth. A young couple was standing in the middle of the room, their faces tense, watching her anxiously.

"This is Abraham Stein and his wife, Sarah," Betje said, "and this is my good friend Dr. Gabrielle Winslow."

"I'm glad to know you," Gabby said. She made herself smile, for she didn't want to make the couple any more nervous than they already were. "Don't worry," she said, "I'm safe enough." She saw relief wash over the face of the woman, who was no more than twenty-five.

"We're a little bit cautious here, Doctor," Abraham said.

"That's good." She turned to Betje. "You don't need me to tell you to be careful. You know what would happen if you were found out."

Betje's brother had been killed in the German invasion. A hard bitterness reflected in her eyes, and she was far more sober than her usual smiling self. "I've read the notices. Anyone concealing Jews will be shot. The swine!"

"Do you have any plans for getting them out of Holland?"

"Yes. They'll be leaving tonight well after dark. I have a friend with a boat who will be taking them out."

Gabby resisted the impulse to tell her again to use caution. "Is there anything I can do?"

"You'd better stay out of this, Gabby," Betje said. "It's too dangerous. If they think you're involved, you could lose—"

Gabby cut her off. "It's as dangerous for you as it is for me."

Betje simply shook her head, and after bidding the three good-bye, Gabby left the small apartment. She got into her car and drove to her great-aunt's house.

Matilda greeted her, then said, "Dorcas has had a bad day. Maybe there's something in your black bag that can help her."

"I'll see what I can do," Gabby said, but she knew there was no medicine for the ailment her great-aunt had. She was simply getting old. Still, there might be something she could do to help her feel more comfortable. Entering Dorcas's bedroom, she found the old woman sitting in a rocker reading her Bible.

Dorcas looked up. "So you remembered your grandmother."

"I'm sorry I didn't get by yesterday. I worked until very late." She leaned over to kiss her cheek and then sat in the other chair. She told her about some of her patients at the hospital, for Dorcas found it interesting, as well as an inspiration, to pray for those who were suffering worse than she was.

Gabby told her about Hans Dent and how the man was

afraid his fiancée wouldn't want to marry him now that he had lost a leg.

"If the woman loves him, one leg more or less won't make any difference."

Gabby laughed and leaned forward, patting Dorcas on the knee. "That's what I love about you, Grandmother. Everything's either black or white. No gray areas."

"There are too many gray areas, if you ask me. Now, tell me about that young man with a shoulder injury you mentioned the other day. How is he doing?"

Gabby stayed until Dorcas started looking weary and then said, "No argument, now. I'm going to get you ready for bed, and I've got some tonic I want you to take. It will help you feel better."

"I don't need a tonic."

"You mind the doctor."

As soon as she had her great-aunt safely tucked in bed, she asked, "Have you heard from Dalton and Liza?"

"No, I think the Germans are holding up all the mail. They were always so regular in writing."

Privately Gabby agreed, but she said only, "Have you thought about what we talked about the day before yesterday?"

"I'm not coming to live in your house." Dorcas looked up at Gabby defiantly. "I will die in this house, as is proper."

"You're a long way from that." She leaned over and kissed the withered cheek. "I'll be by to see you tomorrow. I'll bring you something good to eat."

"Good night, love," Dorcas said. She closed her eyes, and her breathing quickly grew deep and slow.

Gabby left the room and stopped in the kitchen to speak to the housekeeper. "She's asleep, Matilda. I'll stop by tomorrow, but meanwhile"—she rummaged in her bag and pulled out a bottle—"put a teaspoon of this in a glass of water and have her drink it in the morning and then do it again in the afternoon."

"Yes, that I will do."

As she left her great-aunt's house, a weight seemed to

fall on Gabby's shoulders. She drove home in the darkness, praying that God would give Dorcas many more years of life, but in all truth, she was worried about the old woman.

★ ★ ★

Time passed quickly for Gabby. Besides working hard at the hospital and making her daily visits with Dorcas, she also provided medical care for the children at the orphanage twice a week. Sometimes she grew so tired she could hardly stay awake. The casualties of war had been heavy, and the hospital was filled with wounded men in addition to the usual load of patients.

When she arrived at the orphanage on Monday, Gabby stopped by Deman van der Klei's office to greet him before going to the infirmary. The director of the orphanage was on his phone, clearly unhappy over something. When he hung up, he ran his hands through his thick blond hair and shook his head. "I don't know where all this is heading, Dr. Winslow." The Germans had cut back on the supplies necessary to keep the orphanage running.

"God will prevail. Don't worry."

She sat down for a few minutes and let him blow off some steam before seeing to her duties.

At three o'clock that same afternoon, Gabby was sitting in her small office at the hospital. It was hot, and she was soaked with perspiration and longed for a long hot bath. She responded to a knock on the door and smiled as her pastor entered. "Good afternoon, Karel," she said and then motioned him to sit down. He drew a chair up close to her desk, and she asked, "Would you have some tea? Coffee, perhaps?"

"Nothing for me, thank you. How are you? You look tired."

"So do you. Everybody looks tired these days."

The two sat there talking for a time. Karel Citroen came to the hospital almost every day to visit the wounded. The church had grown under his leadership, and there were a great many older people he visited faithfully as well. Gabrielle had come to admire this man a great deal. He was, in her judgment, one of the finest ministers she had ever known. He was a scholarly man, yet his sermons were not dull. He had a sparkling wit that kept his congregation alert, and besides this, he was a fine musician, playing both piano and violin expertly.

Gabby had taken part in a number of church activities, and the two had worked long hours on various projects, often late at night. She had wondered why he had never married, for she knew that many of the women in the village had their eye on him.

During a lull in the conversation, Gabby noted that Karel seemed a little on edge. "Is anything wrong, Karel?"

"I'm not sure."

"That's odd. Are you sick? Something troubling you physically?"

"No, it's a matter of the heart."

Gabby blinked with surprise. "Of the heart? What do you mean?"

He faced her squarely and took a deep breath. Then he said calmly, "You must have noticed that I've come to care for you, Gabrielle." He always called her Gabrielle, disliking the shortened form of her name.

He had spoken in such an ordinary tone that Gabby thought she might have misunderstood him. "Care for me?" she echoed. "What do you mean?"

"What does a man mean when he says he cares for a woman? I love you. I'm not romantic, but I guess I don't need to tell you that."

She could not restrain a smile. "Well, you certainly aren't romantic. Haven't you ever seen a movie? You're supposed to do more than simply barge in and say you care for me."

Karel smiled. "You'd see through me in a moment if I tried singing love songs and writing poetry. I admire and respect you more than any woman I've ever known." He reached over the desk and took her hand and kissed it, something he had never done before. "No, I'm not romantic, but if you could come to care for me, and we could be married, I think you might teach me a little more."

"But I don't love you, Karel."

His eyes sparkled. "You'll love me after we've been married awhile. I'm very lovable."

Despite his light manner and his unorthodox approach, she knew Karel was very serious. He often acted lighthearted to help people get through difficult situations. It was as if he were afraid to let himself go emotionally. She desperately wanted to find some way to respond in a way that would not hurt him. She was trying to form an answer when suddenly the door flew open and Hilda burst in. "Doctor! You must come quickly!"

Jumping to her feet, Gabby asked, "What is it, Hilda?"

The nurse started to speak, but suddenly a large figure filled the doorway. A stern-faced man in a German staff officer's uniform stepped inside, brushing Hilda roughly to the side. "I am Oberleutnant Mueller. Our commandant has been shot. You must come at once."

"Of course."

Gabby followed the burly officer down the hall with Hilda at her side filling in details. "He's already in the operating room ready for you."

"You must save him. You understand, Doctor?"

"I will do the best I can for your commandant, exactly as I would do for any other patient."

Mueller turned and glared at her, anger flaring in his eyes. But when he saw that she was calm and returning his look with determination, he nodded. "Do the best you can, Doctor. You must save him."

Gabby directed the German to the waiting room, and she and Hilda scrubbed up. Hilda was an excellent operating nurse, and Gabby was glad she was on duty. The two pushed through the doors into the operating room and greeted the anesthesiologist.

"He's ready, Dr. Winslow," the man said. The patient was lying facedown on the operating table, sheets draped over all of his body except his shoulder.

"Thank you, Gregor."

Gabby listened to Hilda rattle off the patient's vital signs as she studied the entry point of the bullet. It had taken him high on his back on the left, and she knew there was some danger that it had punctured a lung. Quickly, she went to work probing for the bullet and soon said, "It looks good. It missed the lung."

Removing the bullet proved to be relatively simple, and she dropped it into a pan and started to close the wound. "You can bandage the wound now, Hilda. I'll speak to Lieutenant Mueller."

She left the operating room and found Mueller waiting nervously, his face tense. Pulling the mask from her face, Gabby said, "He's going to be all right. The bullet missed the lung." She watched as relief washed across his stern face. "He will need to stay here for a couple days."

"Certainly. I will assign guards to watch over his room."

"As you wish. How did this happen?"

"A civilian appeared out of nowhere and shot before we could stop him."

"And the civilian? Where is he?"

Mueller's face hardened, and his eyelids pulled down over his eyes slowly, giving him a cruel visage. "He is dead, of course! He's fortunate. I would have hanged him!"

★ ★ ★

Gabby was getting ready to leave when Hilda came into her office and said, "The German officer, he is awake. Do you wish to see him?"

"Yes. Is he doing well?"

"Perfectly well. He's very strong." Hilda shook her head. "It's a shame the assailant missed the heart."

"Come, Hilda, we mustn't speak like that."

Gabby went down the hall and past the two German guards stationed outside the private room that had been assigned to the commandant. They watched her as she went into the room but didn't stop her, as she had already been introduced by Oberleutnant Mueller. She started to greet the man, but a shock ran over her when she realized she was looking down at Erik Raeder!

She had thought of this man so often, but now as she stood speechless staring down at him, she saw recognition come into his eyes, and he smiled.

"Hello, Gabby," he whispered.

"Erik! I didn't know—" She could not finish, for her ability to think failed her at the shock of seeing him. She could not believe that this man whom she had loved—or thought she had loved—was lying in the bed.

"You're surprised to see me," he said. "But I knew you were here. That's why I had them bring me here—I knew I'd be in good hands." He reached for her hand. He squeezed it, but then his eyes began to close as the medication took over. "I always knew," he whispered faintly, "that you would do me good, Gabby. Thank you for saving my life."

She was so stunned it was difficult for her to answer. "You must sleep," she said, not wanting to speak further.

He struggled to open his eyes and squeezed her hand again. "You are more beautiful than ever. I never forgot you," he said before his eyes closed and his grip relaxed.

Gabrielle laid his hand on his chest and then found that her legs and knees were weak and that she was breathing rapidly, almost hyperventilating. She quickly walked from the room, and the thoughts that ran through her mind were as wild as any she had ever had.

★ ★ ★

For two days Gabby walked about almost in a state of shock. She stayed busy enough with her work and her visits with her great-aunt, but beneath these activities her mind went back to the room where Commandant Erik Raeder lay. She tried to act professional each time she stopped in to check on his progress, but she couldn't help but think back on their time together in Germany.

Each night she lay awake, asking herself, *Why am I so upset? It's all over*. And yet she could not put Erik out of her mind, which bothered her so much she almost forgot about the proposal, such as it was, from Karel Citroen.

Finally, on Thursday, she wrote the order for Erik to be discharged. As she went from one ward to the next, she was surprised to encounter Erik in the hallway, fully dressed and in his uniform. She had not seen him in a Nazi uniform, and the sight of it sent a cold chill through her.

His face, however, seemed to blot out that sight. He smiled and came to stand in front of her. "You don't take very good care of your patients, Doctor."

"Why do you say that, Herr Commandant?"

"Herr Commandant! Not Erik?"

"We're very formal in this hospital."

"I see that."

She stood for a moment, aware that he was studying her face. "I won't be here long, Gabby. I'll be going to the front soon. General Bruno Rahn will be in charge of the occupation forces. He's been ill but should be here soon."

"I see. You must be very careful. You were very fortunate that the bullet missed your lung."

"I know I was lucky, and I had good care. You're an excellent doctor, Gabby." He waited for her reply, but when she was silent, he went on, "I would like to see you sometime. Perhaps we could have dinner."

"That wouldn't be wise, Erik." Feeling the need to bring closure to her relationship with this tall, handsome man she had once had such strong feelings for, she said, "What we had is over."

"Love is never over. You know, since I've been here, I've been thinking of a poem that I memorized when I was just a boy in school."

"What poem is that?"

"I'm sure you know it. By the Scottish poet Burns." He spoke slowly, his eyes fixed on her.

"O my luve's like a red, red rose,
That's newly sprung in June;
O my luve's like the melodie,
That's sweetly play'd in tune.

"I always think of you when I remember those lines, Gabby."

She dropped her eyes. "You mustn't say those things to me, Erik. I must go." She turned and went into the next ward, and as she did, she was protesting with all the vehemence of her spirit, *I can't feel anything for him. It's all over! It has to be!*

CHAPTER TEN

AN UNUSUAL PICNIC

★ ★ ★

Gabby had just finished her rounds at the hospital when Betje tracked her down.

"Do you have a free moment, Gabby?"

"Of course. Let's get some cold tea and go outside."

The two women got some tea from the kitchen and found seats on an iron bench under a spreading chestnut tree. The branches threw a welcome shade over the bench. As soon as they sat down, Betje said, "I suppose you're surprised to see me here."

"A little bit, but I'm glad. How have you been, Betje?"

"All right." The answer was weak, and her usually merry eyes were sober. She took a sip of her tea. "You know what I've been doing."

"About the underground? Yes, I've been worried sick about you."

"Don't worry about me. It's the Jews who are in trouble. They're killing them like flies in concentration camps. It's a sure death for them to go there."

"We don't actually know that. That is, we don't have proof."

"A few have miraculously gotten away. They say the Nazis are working them to death in slave labor camps. Those who can't work are being beaten and shot by firing squads. As for families, they tear children from their parents, husbands from wives. They're monsters!"

A floppy-eared hound of mottled mustard colors came loping across the yard, catching their attention. They watched as he chased a squirrel into a small grove of trees to the north of the hospital. When the yard was quiet again, Betje asked, "Have you heard about Saul Nimitz and his family?"

Instantly, Gabby grew alert. Nimitz had been her favorite professor at the university in Amsterdam. He was a brilliant man, warmhearted, always willing to help, and she had always been grateful to him for his assistance. She had been in his home and knew his wife, Irma, and their children, Sarah and Aaron.

"What's happened to them? Are they ill?"

"No, but I learned they're going to be picked up by the Nazis."

For a moment Gabby could not speak. Her throat seemed to close as she thought of the happy times she had enjoyed in their home. "I can't believe it. He's not political at all."

"He's a Jew. That's all that matters."

"How'd you find out about this?"

"We have a cleaning woman who's a member of our covert cell group. Gretchen keeps her ears open as she does the cleaning. You'd be surprised how a person like that becomes almost invisible. The Germans don't think about a cleaning woman being a member of the underground. If they caught her, they'd kill her instantly."

Gabby sat utterly still as she tried to digest the information. "We've got to do something!" she said vehemently. "We've got to get them out of here."

Betje laughed. "I came here wondering how to convince you of that, and here you are ready for anything." She leaned forward onto her elbows. "You're like two women—one very careful and cautious, backing off from anything involving the emotions, but underneath that there's a fiery rebel. I'm glad to see it."

"Never mind me. What about Saul and Irma and the children?"

"They've got to get out before this weekend, but I can't figure out how. It's not as easy as it once was, Gabby. The Germans have placed a line of guards around the city. Nobody can get in or out without a pass."

"Where would they go if we *could* get them out?"

"A fisherman would take them to England. The Germans are smart enough but stupid in some ways. The fishing boats go out every morning. The guards don't count them. So if we could get the Nimitz family to one of the canals, their boat could mingle with the other boats. Twenty-two fishing boats would go out and twenty-one would come back. They'd never know the difference."

"All right, I'll help." She tapped her fingernails on the bench while a plan began to form in her mind. "As a matter of fact, I believe I might even know a way that would work."

"It's got to be nearly foolproof. They'll shoot you if they catch you, Gabby."

"I know."

"Aren't you afraid?"

"Fear has nothing to do with it. I need to do the right thing. You know, I think if Jesus were here, He would have been a member of the underground."

Betje laughed. "That almost makes me want to become a Christian." She got up and said, "I'll keep in touch. Think through your plan from every angle. I'm counting on you."

From that moment on, Gabby knew her life would never be the same. Up till now she had avoided any thoughts of joining the underground, determined as she was to continue her work as a physician and keep herself available to the orphanage and the sick. But as of July 14, 1940—as she later recorded in her journal—she knew she was going to have to do much more.

★ ★ ★

Gabby was hungry when she left the hospital that evening, and she did not fancy going home and cooking, so she stopped at one of the cafés. She had become fond of a small place called La Belle Époque. It had only eight tables and a six-stool counter, and the room was decorated in turn-of-the-century decor. The food was not expensive and very good. She gave the waitress her order—sauerkraut with bacon and sausages—and sat back to let the fatigue seep out of her.

She closed her eyes for just a moment and opened them to see Erik Raeder walk through the door. He came straight to her table and smiled. "May I join you?"

Actually, Gabby didn't think that was a good idea, for it was not smart for a Dutch woman to be seen with a German officer. But she had little choice, so she nodded and said, "Of course."

"You wouldn't go out with me, so I followed you," he said. "I know it puts you in a bad position, but I had to see you, Gabby."

"Why don't you order something, Erik?"

"All right. What do you recommend? What are you having?" She told him what she was having, and he told the waitress he would have the same.

He ordered wine, and when the bottle was brought, he offered her some. When she refused, he smiled. "Still no alcohol, eh?"

"That's right."

"You don't change, do you, Gabby?"

"Of course I change. Everybody does." As she studied him, she saw that he was even better looking than she'd remembered. He was aging well, and she had to admit that the Nazis knew how to design uniforms. The perfect fit revealed his muscular build nicely. He was tanned, and his eyes were clear. "Your wound doesn't bother you?" she asked.

"Not a bit. I had an excellent doctor." He sipped his wine as the waitress set Gabby's plate of food down in front of her. "Go ahead and eat. I'll catch up when mine comes."

"I am hungry," she said. "It's been a long day." She ate, enjoying the spicy food, and when he asked about the hospital, she told him about several cases. He also inquired about the orphanage, and she wasn't surprised that he knew about her movements.

"Erik, I wish you would help. If you could do anything for the orphanage, I'd appreciate it."

"Why, of course. Help in what way?"

"The supplies are being cut way back, and the children are suffering. They don't need to be punished like this. They are innocent."

"Of course. I will see to it at once that things are better."

"Thank you very much."

Erik's meal came, and he ate heartily. After they had finished, he continued to drink his wine while she drank strong black coffee.

"Gabby, do you hate me?" he asked quietly.

She looked up and saw that he was totally serious.

"Of course not. Why do you say such a thing?"

"We are hated, we Germans. I regret it."

She could not think of a reply. "I don't like what's happening. I think Germany could do so much, but the people running the country are being misled."

"I know that's what you think, and I've told you before, there are things I don't like about some of the leadership. Some of us are protesting. Right now events are moving to change things."

Gabby had learned enough about Adolf Hitler to know that Erik was dreaming. Hitler, in her mind, was a maniac, and she had told her great-aunt, "If ever a man was filled with demons, it's Adolf Hitler." She said none of this, however, for it would be useless and could put her in serious danger. The Nazis did not tolerate people who spoke out against Hitler. She still could not believe how clearly she remembered the good times she and Erik had had together.

Suddenly, he asked, "Do you remember when we were skiing and I fell down?"

"Yes, of course I remember."

"You came over and thought I was hurt. I pulled you down in the snow with me and kissed you."

Her cheeks grew flushed. "I remember that too."

"Do you, Gabby?" He reached over and took her hand before she could move and held hers firmly. "I've forgotten nothing."

"But I suspect you've had other girlfriends since then."

"They meant nothing. I've never been able to forget you, Gabby."

She hesitated. She did not know how to speak to this man any longer. It bothered her that she still thought of him, of his caresses, and she tried to change the subject. She finally said quietly, "Those days were in another world, Erik."

"It's the same world. Thc political climate has changed, but some things never change. Love never changes. I've collected poems that say what's in my heart about you—that love never changes."

"I don't understand you, Erik. You're a soldier engaged in a terrible war, but there's something better in you than that. Something finer."

"I'm glad you think so. I don't want you to hate me, Gabby."

She pulled her hand back, and he released it.

"Have you heard from the Burkes?" he asked.

"No, I think the occupation forces have stopped the mail."

"If you want to write to them, I will see that the letter reaches them."

"That would be kind. Thank you."

Gabby rose, and Erik rose with her. He looked tall and strong in his uniform, and a pang went through Gabby as she thought, *He could be so good. How can men like him give themselves to be the tools of Hitler's evil designs?* "Good night," she said as they walked toward the door.

"I'm going to ask you out again."

"Please don't, Erik."

"I'm a determined man. I don't give up easily. Good night, Gabby."

She got in her car and drove home. She was shaken by the incident and knew that Erik had spoken the truth. He was a determined man, and it was painfully obvious that he still had deep feelings for her. "I can't let this go on," she murmured. "I've got to do something to let him know that we can never be together."

★ ★ ★

Betje looked around the room, which was no more than a cellar at the hospital where old equipment was kept. The cell group met there sporadically, never on a regular schedule, but Betje had felt it was necessary this time. She glanced around, her eyes touching on Jan ten Boom, a small, average-looking man with brown hair. He was in his midtwenties and loved practical jokes. He was fond of girls and wrote the most horrible poetry that Betje had ever read, but he was a key member of the team. He looked absolutely innocent, but underneath his jovial manner lay a sharp mind. Next to Jan was Gretchen Holtzman, a sixty-two-year-old woman who cleaned for the Germans and kept the group posted on bits of information she picked up. Across the room sat Groot Dekker, a huge older farmer, and Gottfried Vogel, almost as large. Vogel was a pharmacist and a man with a fiery temper who needed watching. The final member was Karel Citroen, the pastor. He did not seem to fit in with the group, but Betje had learned, despite her antagonism toward Christianity, that he was a man of iron convictions and had been very helpful in their clandestine work.

"What's up, Betje?" Jan said. "I've got a date. I can't stay here long."

"Your date can wait, Jan," Betje said with a smile. "I've

got a date too, but we needed to meet. We've got to do something about the Nimitz family."

"You're right about that," Karel agreed. "If Gretchen's information is correct, they plan to pick them up this weekend."

Gretchen sniffed. "It's correct. They think they're the only ones who speak German. Stupid pigs!"

"Exactly what did they say, Gretchen?" Dekker put his hamlike hands together and looked capable of ramming his head through a brick wall.

"The one called Mueller, he said it's time to pick up the family. He said this weekend would be the best time."

"We'll have to get them out before then," Vogel said. In his dignified manner, he smoothed back his iron gray hair. He was a clever and fearless man who had come up with several good schemes for sneaking Jews out of Amsterdam.

"I've been talking to Dr. Winslow," Betje said. "She has a plan. She's working on the details, and she's going to get back to me as soon as she's got everything worked out."

"I don't trust her," Gretchen said. "She's good friends with the commandant."

"No she's not!" Betje snapped.

"She is too," Gretchen said. "I have a friend who saw them eating together at La Belle Époque."

Betje defended her friend quickly. "He came in and sat down with her, and there was nothing she could do about it. Besides, that may be a good thing."

"How can it be a good thing to be a friend of a German?" Groot Dekker demanded.

"It wouldn't be except for someone like Gabrielle Winslow. She could do the same thing you're doing, Gretchen—pick up information from Raeder."

"They knew each other in Germany, didn't they?" Karel asked. "Do you know anything about that?"

"I've always thought they were in love, but I'm not sure," Betje said. She understood that Karel's concern was personal. "She doesn't care for him now, though, Pastor."

Citroen looked down at his hands for a moment and then

addressed the group. "We'd better be quick. We've got to get those people out before it's too late."

"I'll talk to Gabby tonight, and then I'll be in touch."

The meeting was over, and one by one, at intervals of several minutes, the members left the room, each one using a different hospital exit so they wouldn't raise suspicion.

★ ★ ★

"We've got nine Jews who have to get out of Amsterdam right away," Betje said as soon as they were alone in Gabby's office at the hospital. Betje was wearing a pale green dress and looked pretty, Gabby thought. "There's the Nimitz family, and then there are five others. We can't put this off any longer. We've got to do this quickly."

"All right. I've been thinking about a way to do it, and here's what I've come up with," Gabby said. "I'll get permission from the Germans to take a group of children from the orphanage out to the fields over past the big dike for a picnic. There are lots of trees there—a forest really. We'll mix the Jewish children in with the children from the orphanage, and the parents can play the part of staff members, and we'll stay until late—almost dark. Then you and Karel or whoever else you want to join us can slip away with the Jews and take them to a fishing boat. Did you get a boat lined up?"

"Yes. I made contact with a fisherman who's sympathetic to the Jews. He's agreed to be available whenever we need him. He's just waiting for final details."

"And you're positive he's truly sympathetic?" Gabby asked. "There's no chance he could turn on us?"

"Absolutely. I'm certain."

"Okay, then. I think we've got a plan that will work."

Betje nodded. "It should work. It's better than any plan the rest of us came up with. Will you go along on the picnic?"

"Oh yes, I will."

"It's pretty dangerous smuggling that many people at one time," Betje suggested.

"God will be with us."

Betje stared at her friend. "You really believe that, don't you, Gabby?"

"I know it's true. You'll find out one day that God is faithful."

Betje hesitated and seemed on the verge of saying something, but then she closed her lips and said, "All right. You set it up. I'll have the boat ready on Thursday. Will that be all right?"

"I think so. Get it all ready. It'll have to go like clockwork."

★ ★ ★

Gabby looked up from her desk as Hilda led a tramp into her office. His clothes were worn, and he nervously twisted a soft cap in his hands. He had not shaven recently, and even from where she sat, Gabby could smell his rank body odor. "Who is this?" she demanded skeptically.

"The director said we could hire someone to do some of the rough work," Hilda told her. "This fellow came along asking for work, and Dr. Carstens hired him and gave him a room in the basement."

It irritated Gabby that Berg Carstens had hired such a man. They certainly needed extra help for some of the dirty work in the hospital as well as some outside work, but surely there must be someone better than this.

"What's your name?" she asked.

The man seemed not to hear her. He was looking around with a blank stare. His lank dark hair obviously hadn't been washed in months, and his beard looked like brittle wire. "What's the matter?" Gabby said more sharply. "Can't you talk?"

"Uh . . . ja . . . talk."

Gabby exchanged a sharp glance with Hilda. "Do you

have a name?" she demanded.

"They call me Petric."

"Petric what?"

"Just Petric. That's all."

"Wait outside," Gabby directed.

"I work here?"

"Go outside."

As soon as the man left, Hilda said, "I know. He's a bum, and I think he's slow mentally, but Dr. Carstens said he's cheap."

"I don't like it, Hilda."

"Neither do I, but he looks strong enough. If he could do some of the heavier lifting and empty bedpans, we could use his help."

Gabby shook her head. "All right. I guess I don't have a choice if Dr. Carstens already hired him. See if you can get him to wash himself, and keep a close eye on him for the next few days."

★ ★ ★

For the next two days, the man called Petric seemed to appear every time Gabby turned around. He had cleaned himself up somewhat, although he always wore the same tattered clothes. Hilda told her that she had insisted he wash them and found out that he only had the ones he wore. "I gave him some of my brother's old clothes, but he won't shave."

"Does he do a good job here?"

"Oh yes. He's very strong. You just put him to a task, and he goes right at it."

"He's either slow of wit or suffering from a mental illness. I don't know which," Gabby said. "We'll have to watch him all the time."

"I'll keep an eye on him, and I'll warn the others to do the same. But I'll say this: he's not afraid of work."

★ ★ ★

Gabby talked to the director of the orphanage and asked for permission to take the children on a picnic near the dike. She explained that some friends of hers were going to accompany them, so they wouldn't need any staff members to go with them. She also told him she wanted to keep the children out past their usual bedtime so they could enjoy the beautiful sunset. Once she got the director's approval, she sent a message to Erik asking for permission to take the children past the perimeter that the Germans had set up around the city. Erik at once sent back passes for all parties involved, along with a note asking her to meet him for dinner. She responded that she would love to do so sometime in the future.

Having the pass made the first part of the plan simple, but the scheme required considerable arrangement so the timing of the whole plan would work without a hitch. She made contact with Betje and gave her all the details of the plan. Betje would arrange for some of the members of the cell to accompany them and help with the escape.

Gabby arranged to get two flat-bottomed trucks to transport the children, but she was relying on Betje to firm up her plans with the fisherman.

On Thursday, Gabby was tense and had difficulty concentrating on her patients. Once, early in the afternoon, she almost ran into Petric, who was mopping the floor. He looked up at her with blank eyes but said nothing.

"Watch what you're doing, Petric."

"Ja, I watch." He seemed to have only a rudimentary understanding of the language, and she reminded herself again to keep an eye on him. Something about him gave her concern, but her thoughts were on the plans to save the Nimitz family from the Nazis.

Late that afternoon when she got home, Gabby opened her drawer and took out the pistol that had belonged to her father and carefully loaded it. Troubled that she would have to take such a precaution, she wondered if she would really have the courage to shoot a man if necessary.

She stopped for a quick visit with her great-aunt but said nothing about the plan that was soon to be set in motion. Gabby did not want to burden her with more problems. It was best for Dorcas's protection that she know nothing of what Gabby was about to do. The old woman seemed to be growing weaker and didn't even get out of bed for the visit.

"Is something wrong, Gabby?" Dorcas asked her.

The old woman's got sharp eyes! "No, of course not. I'm just tired."

"Come here. I want to pray for you."

Gabby went over and knelt by the bedside. She felt the warmth of the old woman's hand on her head. Dorcas prayed quietly, and then when she was done, she said, "Go with God, my darling."

"Of course, Grandmother."

★ ★ ★

Everything was going according to schedule. The children were being loaded into the trucks in front of the orphanage. The Jews were dressed in clothing similar to what the staff at the orphanage wore. There were four adults, including Saul and Irma Nimitz, and five children, who fit in easily with the orphans. The orphans had been strictly warned to say nothing to anyone about the strangers.

Gabby's senses stood on alert when she looked up to see a military staff car pulling up in front. Her heart sank when she realized Erik was sitting beside the driver. She quickly instructed everybody to act naturally. "Don't be frightened," she said. "Just chitchat and laugh as if it were a picnic, which it is."

Erik got out of the car and nodded his head to Gabby. "I thought I might join your picnic," he said, smiling. "I haven't been on a picnic in a long time."

Her heart seemed to freeze, but her training in dramatics stood her in good stead. She smiled brilliantly and said, "What a good idea! I'm so glad you came, Erik. It's a good thing we have plenty of food. I remember how much you always ate."

He laughed. "It'll be good to get away from my job for a short spell."

"Will you come in your staff car?"

"Oh yes. They insist on having guards with me after that fool shot me."

"Very well. I think we're about ready to go."

"Fine. I'll follow the trucks, and when we get to the perimeter, just show the guards the pass that I sent."

"Okay."

"If the guards give you any trouble, I'll handle it."

"Thank you, Erik."

They had no trouble at all passing through the lines. The guard's eyes widened at the sight of Commandant Erik Raeder, and he snapped to attention and said, "Heil Hitler!" giving the traditional salute. Erik returned it, and the small caravan passed on through.

As soon as they arrived at their destination, Gabby organized the children and got them started on a game, with the Nimitzes and the two other adults acting as supervisors. Betje and Pastor Citroen soon arrived in a separate vehicle. Gabby introduced Erik to Pastor Citroen.

"It's good to meet you, Pastor," the commandant said. "Gabby has told me about the good work you're doing with these orphans."

"Thank you, Herr Commandant."

Betje said nothing at all but immediately went to join in the games, for which Gabby was thankful. She knew the rage that seethed in her friend and wished she were not there. However, Betje was needed to help get the group to safety.

Erik was delighted when Gabby enlisted his help in setting up the food tables. The two guards kept well back, but their eyes were cautious as they watched the goings-on.

Gabby called to the children when it was time to eat, and they quickly came running from all directions. After supper, the adults gathered the children around for a quieter game, and then they moved to an area where there were no trees so they could watch the sunset.

Betje pulled Gabby aside and said, "We've got to get our group away. Can't you do something with that German and his guards?"

"I'll take Erik down to the canal."

"Good. If you can keep their attention away from this area, Karel can get the Jews on their way. Keep Erik occupied until I let you know we're ready to go. We'll get everybody loaded into the trucks while you're at the canal, and hopefully Erik won't notice that some of the adults are gone. Can you do that?"

"I'll try."

Getting Erik to go to the canal was not difficult. "There's a very pleasant spot down by the water," she told him. "Would you like to watch the sunset with me?"

"Excellent!" The two walked down to the canal, closely followed by the two guards.

"I'd like to get rid of them," Erik whispered as they walked.

But Gabby was glad they were accompanying them. It would make it impossible for Erik to try to hold her hand or kiss her, but it would give Karel the necessary time to get the Jews to their meeting point with the other members of the cell, who were hiding in the woods waiting for them.

The canal was not large, no more than thirty meters across, but it made a pleasant sound as the water gurgled past. The guards stayed far back and began smoking, and Gabby could hear them shooting the breeze. She looked up at Erik and said, "This is nice."

"It is. It's very peaceful here."

"How are your parents?"

"Very well."

Gabby was grateful to him for not sharing any details of their lives with her. No doubt they were happy that she and

Erik had broken up. They were quiet as they watched the sunset and listened to the faraway sounds of the children laughing.

"That's a nice sound," Erik said quietly. "You love children, don't you?"

"Of course I do."

"Not everyone does."

Somehow the subject turned to poetry, and Gabby shared snippets of some of her favorite poems with him. As she quoted "I Held a Jewel" by Emily Dickinson, he reached over and took her hands.

"It's the first time we've been really alone in a long time," he said, "and I've wanted to see you so much."

Gabby knew he was going to kiss her and knew that she must permit it. When he put his arms around her, she lifted her head and took his kiss. His lips were firm but demanding, and for a moment she surrendered. *It's just an act,* she told herself. *That's all it is. Like an actress in a movie kissing another actor.*

She was the first to pull her head away, and she forced herself to smile. "I shouldn't have let you do that."

"I don't think you could have stopped me, Gabby. Tell me, do you ever think about me?"

Gabby could not lie. "Yes, I do, Erik. I have many times."

"I'm glad to hear it." He dropped his hand down from her shoulder and held her hand in his warm, strong grip. "I would never have known what love was but for you."

"Surely you've been in love with other women."

"No, I haven't. You're wrong about that."

"Come, Erik, I know better."

"Oh, I've known other women, but they've really meant nothing. You're the only woman I ever wanted to spend the rest of my life with. I hope you believe that, Gabby."

She did believe him, but she was spared having to answer, for suddenly Betje approached, saying, "We've got to get back, Gabby. The children are getting tired."

"Yes, we need to get them home."

Erik muttered, "What terrible timing!" But he followed

them back to the trucks, which were already loaded.

Gabby was afraid something could go wrong at this point, but Erik simply said, "I'll leave you here, and I'll call you tomorrow."

"All right, Erik. Thanks for furnishing the pass."

Erik and the guards got into the staff car, and it roared off. As it disappeared, Betje said, "That was well done."

"Did the others get away?"

"They're halfway to the boat by now, I expect. They'll be all right." She grinned and said, "It doesn't hurt to have the enemy in love with you. We'll have to use that again, Gabby."

"I'd rather keep Erik out of it as much as possible after this."

"Gabby, this is war. People have to do things they don't want to. But anyway, it worked fine this time."

They got into the trucks and rode back to the orphanage. After they ushered the kids back into the building, Gabby started for her car. As she opened the door, she saw a shadow—just a flicker—beside the building. Suspicion and fear assailed her, and she hastily reached under the driver's seat and pulled out the pistol. It was dark, with only a sliver of a moon overhead, a mere thin crescent, but she advanced silently toward the figure, which now was frozen in place. She held the pistol in both hands straight in front of her and commanded, "Stay right where you are." She came closer and shock ran through her as she saw who it was. "Petric, what are you doing here?"

When he didn't answer, Gabby insisted, "Who are you? What's your real name?" She saw intelligence flicker in his eyes, and she knew that this man who called himself Petric was not who he pretended to be.

CHAPTER ELEVEN

THE PRISONER

★ ★ ★

Even in the darkness, Gabby could see something was different about the man she had known as Petric. He was standing straighter than he had at the hospital, and there was no hint in his features of a man of slow wit. His dark eyes were sharp and penetrating, and she knew she was in danger, even though she was the one holding the gun.

Still holding the pistol straight out, she commanded, "Put your hands up or I'll shoot you."

"You don't have to do that," he said as he raised his arms. "I'm no danger to you."

Even the voice was different! There was no slurred or faltering speech, no reaching for words. As she wondered whether she should call for help, she felt her finger tighten on the trigger. She had no desire to shoot anyone, so she loosened her finger and took a step back. "Who are you? You're not who you say you are. You're a spy."

"I'm a spy all right, but not a very good one." A hint of a smile lifted the corners of the man's lips. He kept his hands in the air and made no attempt to move toward her. "If I were a good spy, I wouldn't have let you catch me."

"You're working for the Germans. I know that."

"That's not true. I'm with foreign intelligence for England."

She shook her head. "I don't believe you." He started to take his hands down, and she yelled, "Don't you do that, or I'll shoot you!" in a voice that was higher pitched than she had hoped.

"I wish you wouldn't do that. I've come all the way to this country to meet with you, Dr. Winslow. I'm actually sympathetic to your cause."

"That's not very likely."

"But it's true."

"All right. Prove it. Let's see some identification."

The smile broadened on the man's face, and he shook his head. "I may be a very bad spy, but not bad enough to carry information around with me. But if you'll give me a chance, I can prove my identity."

"All right. Turn around and lock your hands behind your neck." She waited until he did so and then said, "All right. Turn left and walk that way."

Obediently, the man turned and walked slowly through the darkness. She directed him until they came to a sturdy shed built of stone with a heavy oak door.

"Get in there!" Gabby directed.

"What is this place?"

"It used to be a storage room. There's nothing in there now." A malicious thought touched her. "Except a rat or two. They won't bother you if you let them alone."

He turned, keeping his hands behind his head. "What are you going to do?"

"I'm going to get some of my friends. Now get inside."

Gabby waited until the man had stepped inside and then quickly shut the door. She closed the hasp and stuck the large spike through the opening. Quickly, she ran back to the front door of the orphanage through the darkness. She was breathing faster than usual, and she was relieved when Karel opened the door just as she got there.

"Come quickly!"

"What is it? What's wrong?" he asked, clearly detecting the alarm in her voice.

"I've caught a man who I think is a spy."

"A spy!" The pastor stared at her. "Who is he? How did you come upon him?"

"He came to work at the hospital. He called himself Petric. I didn't like him from the beginning," she said between breaths. She saw him glance toward the gun. "This was my father's. I brought it in case we ran into trouble tonight."

"Where is he? What have you done with him?"

"He's locked in the old storage shed around the east side of the building," she said as she pointed. "He can't get out, but we've got to do something."

"I think we'd better have a meeting of everyone in our cell." The term he used, *cell,* referred to the small group of underground agents. There were many such cells all over the Netherlands, particularly around Amsterdam and Rotterdam. "Come along. We'll call the others."

As they went into the building to use the phone, Gabby had a grisly thought. "If he is a spy, we'll have to shoot him, won't we?"

Without breaking his stride, Karel said softly, "I expect we will."

* * *

Groot Dekker was the last member of the cell to arrive. The rest had gathered outside the orphanage, and finally he drove up in a rickety pickup he used to haul his produce to town. They all watched as he got out, the truck sagging with his weight.

"What is it?" he asked as he approached. "Did the Jews get caught?"

"No, it's nothing like that," Betje said. "We've caught a spy."

"We're not sure of that," Karel corrected.

"A spy! Is he a German?" Dekker demanded. He made a huge shape in the darkness, outlined by the single light outside of the orphanage. He doubled his hands up into huge fists. "I know how to handle him."

Jan ten Boom was almost jumping up and down with excitement. "Dr. Winslow, she caught him," he said. "The man came to work at the hospital, but the doctor was suspicious even when he was first hired." Jan quickly told the rest of the story.

"We'll have to get rid of him," Dekker declared.

"I'm not sure that he is a spy," Gabby said. "He claims he works in foreign intelligence for the British."

"We're wasting time," Betje said. "Whoever he is, he'll have a chance to prove it." She had taken an automatic pistol she had hidden in her car and now held it loosely. "Come along." She turned on her flashlight and led the way around the side of the orphanage. Almost all the lights were out inside the large building, and the beam of the flashlight made a white cone as the group moved through the night.

Betje stopped in front of the shed and pulled the spike out. She flipped the hasp and stepped back, pulling the door open. "Come out of there!" she commanded harshly, her pistol poised.

Gabby also had her pistol aimed at the man but had taken her finger off the trigger. She watched nervously as the prisoner stepped outside. He blinked when the strong light hit his face and turned his head to the side.

"That's pretty bright," he said. "Would you mind not blinding me?"

"Never mind giving orders," Betje said stridently. "You're in trouble."

"If you'll give me a chance, I believe I can convince you that I'm not a German spy."

"You'll have to prove it," Gottfried Vogel said. He stood tall and ominous in the darkness, his iron gray hair giving him a patriarchal look. "What's your name?" he demanded.

"Captain Dailon Bando."

"Bando! What kind of a name is that?" Vogel snorted. "It's German, I suppose."

"Not at all. It's Welsh."

"Your life is on the line unless you can prove you're not a German spy," Betje said authoritatively.

She kept the gun on him, but the man called Bando simply smiled. "I'll tell you one thing that ought to convince you. If I were working for the Germans, you'd all be dead."

"What do you mean by that?" Betje demanded.

"I've watched you smuggle two groups of Jews out, and that's only in the short time I've been here. If I were a German, you would all be in an interrogation room right now, probably being beaten with something harder than a rubber hose."

"Why are you spying on us?" Gabby asked. "Why didn't you tell me you were working for the British?"

"Because when I came, I didn't know who was safe to talk to. You can't just walk up to someone and say, 'Hello there. I'm a British spy.' You wouldn't have believed me." He smiled at Betje. "You probably would have shot me with that pistol."

A silence fell over the group, and Gabby looked at the others, sensing their doubt. At first she had been afraid they would shoot the man without any kind of trial whatsoever, and that would have been painful to her, as she hated violence. "You'll have to give us more than your word, I'm afraid, Captain."

"Yes, you will," Betje added. "And if you can't prove it, I'll shoot you myself."

"I can prove who I am easily enough. Can any of you work a shortwave radio?"

"I've been operating one for two years now," Jan said. "I have my license."

"All right. I've got a radio hidden in the barn outside the hospital. I keep in touch with my team. If you can hold off shooting me long enough, I think you'll have enough evidence to convince yourselves I'm not working for the Nazis."

"All right. You'll have your chance," Betje said. "Does anyone have anything we can use to tie him up?"

Groot, the farmer, pulled a length of heavy twine from his pocket.

"Gottfried, tie his hands behind his back," Betje instructed. "All right," she said as two of the men tied his wrists behind him. "We'll all go with Bando. You'd better be telling the truth."

"I am," he said. "It would be a bad night to die."

"Any night's a bad night to die," Betje said.

"Some are worse than others. Come on. These cords are cutting off my circulation."

* * *

"It's there up on those boards over the rafters," Dailon Bando said, pointing with his nose.

The group stood in the barn, which used to be used for horses. The floor was covered with hay, and a musty smell permeated the air.

"I'll get it." Jan climbed the stairs built into the side of the barn and scooted over the boards laid over the rafters. "I got it!" he yelled.

"Bring it down here," Betje told him. She waited until Jan came down and set the square radio on an ancient table sitting by the wall. "Do you know how to work it?"

"Of course I know how to work it. I'm an expert." He looked at the prisoner, who had said nothing all the way from the orphanage. "What are the call letters?"

"A-J-N-C-O."

"What's your code name?"

"Jonah."

Jan grinned. "That's not a good sign. Jonah came to a bad end."

"He was all right at the end of the story," Bando said.

Gabby watched the face of the prisoner as Jan set up the radio and began calling, speaking into it and waiting for a reply. Bando, if that was his real name, looked at her, his eyes locking with her gaze. As she held it defiantly she realized she was more disturbed than the prisoner was. He was not a handsome man, she decided, but there was a virile strength in him. She felt somehow embarrassed or even frightened at the intensity of his gaze and was relieved when she heard the radio crackle in return.

"Jonah, identify yourself" came a voice over the radio. "Jonah, what is your mother's first name?"

Everyone looked at Bando, and he said, "It's Bronwen."

Jan spoke into the microphone. "Bronwen."

"Tell them to give the name of the agent in place," Betje spoke. She held the pistol trained on Bando, even though he still had his wrists bound.

They all waited until Jan made the demand, and there was a moment's pause. Then the voice spoke clearly, "Daily attacks intent—bandits at new direct organization."

The transmission stopped abruptly, and Jan cried, "They've broken the transmission."

"That's all you'll get, but it's all you need."

"What does it mean? It made no sense at all."

"It does if you take the first letter of each word."

Betje, who had a phenomenal memory, repeated the message. "Daily attacks intent—bandits at new direct organization."

"That's me. Dai Bando. Everyone calls me Dai."

A silence fell over the group and then Betje lowered the pistol. "Cut him loose. I think he is who he says he is."

Groot Dekker pulled out a knife and cut the cords.

"Welcome to Holland," Betje said with a smile.

"Thank you, Miss van Dych."

"You know my name?"

"Oh yes, I know all of you."

"Why have you come here?" Betje asked. She put the weapon away but still watched Bando closely.

"I'd like very much to tell all of you, but it goes against my orders. I can tell only one person, and then it will be up to that one person to do as they please with the information."

"Which person is that?" Betje asked.

"Dr. Gabrielle Winslow."

Gabby felt the pressure of the group, and she blurted out, "Why me?"

"I can only explain when we're alone, Doctor."

"Is everybody satisfied that this man is who he says he is?" Betje demanded.

The group murmured their agreement, and Karel said, "I'm glad we didn't have to shoot you."

"That would probably go against your ministerial ethics, Pastor."

He grinned. "I'd like to know more about your mission, but I doubt if I can get it out of Gabby. She's a very private person."

"A very good thing to be in these dangerous times, Pastor."

"All right. Let's break up," Betje said. She turned her eyes on Gabby. "Are you ready to hear what our newest member has to say?"

"I think I'd better be."

"Don't shoot yourself with that pistol," Betje said with a grin. "You need to take lessons. All right, everyone, let's get out of here. Thanks for your help tonight. We won't meet again until I get word to you."

Gabby waited until they had all disappeared, and the silence fell between her and the tall man who watched her carefully. "You want to talk here?"

"That's fine with me. Do you want to sit on the hay?" he asked, pointing to some hay bales near the door.

"Sure." They got settled in the semidarkness. "Go ahead, Captain. I'm listening."

"I'd rather you called me Dai. Of course, it will have to be Petric when we're at the hospital or around other people."

"Is that a common name in Wales? Dailon?"

"Fairly common."

Gabby nodded, and he said nothing further.

"Well, I'm waiting to hear about this mission of yours and why you can tell only me about it."

"Did you ever hear of a man named Owen Bando—the same last name as mine?"

Gabby was startled. "Why . . . my father spoke of a man called Owen Bando! He flew with him in the war."

"Yes, he did. That was my father. I don't think he ever saw your father after the war, but he never forgot him. I'd be interested to know what your father said about him."

"Well, Dad didn't like to talk much about the war. When he did, it was usually to mention some friend that he had made, one of the fliers or the mechanics he had gotten close to. But I do remember he spoke very well of your father—more than once. He liked him a great deal." She thought hard for a moment. "He said Owen had a keen sense of humor and made him laugh even when things were terribly dark. And he liked to play practical jokes."

"Yes, my dad was like that."

"Does this have something to do with your mission, Dai?"

"In a way it does. I would have come anyway, but when I found out you were involved with my mission, it made me want to come even more. You see, your father saved my dad's life on a mission once. A German was on his tail, and he was sure he was a dead man, when suddenly the German plane blew up. He looked around and saw that your father had broken away from his own fight and came to help him. He always felt like your father gave him life, so I heard a lot about him. As a matter of fact, I still have all of the letters they exchanged."

"Letters from my father to yours?"

"Yes."

"I-I'd like to see them sometime."

"Of course, Doctor. I don't have them with me, but as soon as I get back to Wales, I'll get them to you."

"I'd like that very much."

He shifted to find a more comfortable position on the

hay. "I'm going to break the first rule of successful espionage."

"What's that?"

"Don't tell anyone anything that you don't have to."

"That sounds like a good rule. But I don't know much about spying."

"I'm going to break the rule because, well—in the first place, I'll have to tell you sooner or later anyway. In the second place, I need your help, and you can't work in the dark. I've come to you because my assignment is to get your aunt and uncle out of Germany."

"Aunt Liza and Uncle Dalton?"

"Yes."

"I . . . I can't believe it!"

"I know a little bit about your family and all I could find out about your uncle. He's needed on our side. He's like a secret weapon. My superiors tell me he could do terrible damage to the Allies if he gives his keen scientific mind to the Germans, which is what he seems to have done."

"He's a very simple man, Dai. He means no harm, but he's easily swayed. He's a good man. You have to believe that."

"I believe it if you say so. You know him, and I don't. Will you help me, Doctor?"

Gabby hesitated and then said firmly, "Of course—and by the way, my friends call me Gabby."

CHAPTER TWELVE

"GROW OLD ALONG WITH ME"

★ ★ ★

Betje dismounted from her bicycle and balanced it against the fence. As she headed toward the hospital, she noticed Dai Bando—or Petric, as they were strictly enjoined to call him—loading supplies onto a truck. She paused for a moment, thinking over the past three weeks, during which time she had become very well acquainted with the Welshman. She smiled and changed directions to greet him.

"Hello, Petric," she said when she neared the truck.

Bando turned and glanced at her, then put the box he was holding on the bed of the truck. "Hello, Betje." His cap was pulled down over his forehead, and his whiskers had grown shaggy. He looked exactly as he wanted to look, much like a bum. He stooped over, even though no one else was there to observe him, but he knew he had to be cautious. "What are you up to today?"

"I'm here to see Gabby."

"She's probably making her rounds now."

"Good. Why don't you come over in the shade with me? We can get to know each other."

"That wouldn't be too wise," he said.

"Why not?"

"Someone might be watching from one of the windows."

Betje shifted her weight to one foot. She reached up and tousled her blond hair while she studied Dai skeptically. "It's good that you're being careful. How about if I help you load your truck?"

"Better not. That wouldn't look right either."

"Why don't you show me the ducks down in the canal?" she said with a laugh.

"All right. A break would be nice. You go ahead, and I'll meet you there."

Betje nodded and followed the sidewalk that went around the hospital. Behind the hospital was a small grove of trees lining one of the numerous canals that drained the land. She could see one man fishing a ways off in the distance, but other than that, it was an isolated spot. She waited until Dai stepped out of the trees and came over to her. He took his hat off and pulled a handkerchief out of the hip pocket of his baggy pants and wiped his forehead.

"Hot today."

"Sit down and let's dabble our feet in the water."

"You go ahead. I don't think I ought to be dabbling much. If anybody should happen to come by, I'd have to have my shoes on and get back into my act."

"Well, sit down with me anyway. I want to know more about you."

He sat down cross-legged while Betje took off her shoes. She sat down very close to him and kicked some water at him. "You're going to drown me," he protested.

"Wouldn't be a bad idea on a hot day like this." She took hold of his arm and pressed herself against him. "I like you, Dai."

He laughed. "Don't be so shy and retiring, Betje. Just come right out and say what you mean."

"When I like a man, I like him a lot. Why don't you and I go out some night and have some fun?"

"And when people see you out with a half-wit, what will they think?"

"How about if we have a picnic in some secluded place?"

Dai grinned at her broadly. He had liked Betje from the first time he had met her. She was a loyal member of the underground, and aside from that, she seemed to have only one aim in life, and that was having a good time. As she clung to him, he knew exactly what her invitation meant.

"This job is too big, Betje, and dangerous. If we can pull it off, it'll be a miracle. And it's going to take all of my attention." He tried to pull his arm away, but she held it fast. She laughed up at him, and he saw that she was enjoying her game. He let his arm remain where it was, acutely aware of her figure and the invitation in her eyes.

"Did you ever read the story of Joseph in the Bible?" she asked suddenly.

"Why, sure."

"You remember when he got sold as a slave into Egypt?"

"Yes, into the house of Potiphar."

"That's right, and Potiphar had a wife, didn't he?"

"Sure did. She gave Joseph a hard time."

"I've always thought she wasn't much of a woman."

"Well, her morals certainly weren't what they should have been."

"If I had been married to Potiphar, Joseph would have been in trouble." Without warning, she put her hand behind his neck and pulled his head down until they were nearly nose to nose. "What kind of woman do you want, Dai?"

"I guess every man has an idea of the woman that would make him happy," he said thoughtfully as he gently pulled away. "It's usually not one woman but the combination of the qualities of many of them."

"What does that mean?"

"I mean he sees one woman with a beautiful figure, another who is generous, another who will be faithful to death. So he makes up a composite of all of these."

"That's not very fair, is it? He'd never find a woman perfect in all those ways."

He shook his head. "I guess when he finds the woman he wants, he has to give up some of those things—but he probably finds some other qualities he likes. I guess every man wants sweetness and honesty in a woman."

"Have you ever had both of those things in a woman?"

"I . . . thought I did once."

Betje tightened her grip on him and pulled him so close he could smell the sweetness of her breath. "I think you did find it and you walked away—or she walked away. Most of us do that. Then we're desperate to fill that void, so we rush into another relationship and wind up with just a wreck of a love." She sighed. "Do you think you'll ever find a woman who'll make you happy?"

"I hope so. Every man hopes that. Our life is made up of little things, Betje. Little pleasures that don't shake the world. Maybe a beautiful sunset that makes you want to cry. A good friend you can count on to the very death. Things to remember when you're old."

Betje suddenly felt sad for him. As she pulled his head down and lifted her face, she felt his arms go around her. She leaned toward him while he kissed her, and she sensed his strong desire. The pressure of his arms told her he was lonely and maybe even discouraged, and she decided he might have a wild side if he would allow it to break out. At the same time, though, from what she had learned about him in the last couple of weeks, she felt sure that this man was decent and would never mistreat a woman.

Ordinarily, she would have prolonged the kiss. She could tell he was struggling to control his desires. She knew all the tricks to stir a man, but she suddenly had no desire to try to take advantage of Dailon. She pulled back and studied his face.

"You know how to make a man want you, Betje."

"I guess so." As she looked into his eyes, she recalled all the men she had known and wished it were not so. She straightened up and murmured, "A woman can ruin a man, Dai. You can never do anything about that. Don't try to."

A touch of sunlight came out and bathed her face, and her eyes seemed innocent. She dropped her head and put her cheek against his chest. He knew she was saddened and grieved, and with an unusual gesture, he stroked her hair. He said nothing, nor did she, but finally she pulled back and said almost roughly, "I've got to get going." She yanked her feet out of the water and kicked them until they dried before putting on her shoes. As she stood up, she said, "Don't look for things in women that they can never give you, Dai."

He watched her as she left and pondered her last statement. He decided there was much more to Betje than what appeared on the surface.

Betje walked back to the hospital and found Gabby just coming off her rounds.

"You got a minute, Gabby?"

"Yes, let's step outside."

They went outside, and the two talked of matters that affected the covert cell. They had to take these moments when they could. As they talked Gabby saw Dai walk across the green grass. Her eyes followed him, and her thoughts were interrupted when Betje said, "He's good at what he does, isn't he?"

"Yes. He goes around muttering in Welsh, making everybody think he's a half-wit. He's actually very intelligent."

"He's very good-looking, isn't he," Betje said.

"Oh, I suppose so. Not handsome like a movie star but very masculine."

"Did he ever make a pass at you?" Betje asked, her eyes wide.

"No!"

"Did you ever make one at him?"

"Betje! You know I would never do that!"

Betje laughed. "You ought to try it sometime, Gabby. It might be good for you."

"Don't be foolish!"

"Someday you'll find a man worth giving everything for. You've always held back—for as long as I've known you. A man deserves all you have, Gabby."

"There's something wrong with that, Betje. You know I don't believe that's right."

"I've got to go. I'll see you later."

Gabby watched her friend leave and then turned to see where Dai had gone. She found him not far away, turning over the dirt in a flower bed. She walked across the lawn, noting the greenness of the grass and thinking of how the beauty of the world about her was so different from the world that man had made. She came up to Dai and said hello to him.

"Hello, Gabby." He kept his head down and didn't stop working.

"Betje just left."

"I know. She . . . talked to me."

"Is that safe?"

"Don't worry. It's all right. We went over by the trees on the canal."

"I don't think that's very wise, Dai. You're supposed to be an idiot—not courting women."

"We were very careful that no one saw us."

"I think it would be smart to be even more careful in the future."

Dai dug a shovelful of earth and dumped it to one side. "We've got to make a move to contact your uncle," Dai said as he continued digging. "Have you written to him?"

"Yes, I have. But his letters to me are censored. I don't even know if he gets those I write. I couldn't put anything in a letter, could I?"

"No, I don't think so. It's going to take more than that."

"You don't understand, Dai. I tried everything I could, and so did his wife. Neither of us wanted to go to Germany. Both of us were afraid of Hitler and what he stood for, but Uncle Dalton is naïve when it comes to politics. He's almost like a child. Oh, I know he's a genius in his field, but when it comes to some matters, he's really quite simple."

"We've got to change his mind about leaving the country."

"I just can't think how. It seems to me—"

The sound of an automobile approaching at a high speed caught Gabby's attention. She broke off and saw it was the German staff car that Erik always traveled in. It was too late to hide, so she waited there until the car stopped.

Erik got out of the passenger door and came over to her. "Good afternoon, Doctor," he said as he gave her a slight bow.

"Good afternoon, Commandant." She turned and addressed Dailon. "I'm not going to stand for this type of behavior. You'll either straighten up, or you'll have to leave. You understand me?"

Dai nodded and mumbled his words. "Ja. No more, Miss Doctor."

Gabby turned her attention back to Erik and said, "Come inside. I just had to have a word with this fellow."

"Why do you keep a man like that around?" he asked as they started toward the door.

"The director hired him. It's very hard to find people to do the hard physical labor, and he works cheap."

"He could be dangerous, Gabby. He could harm you."

"Oh, I don't think so. He's not dangerous."

Erik took her arm and turned her around. "I can't stay. I just stopped to ask if you would have time to see me. I know you won't go out, but perhaps I could come to your house."

"You think *that* would be private?"

"I don't like sneaking around." Erik shook his head. "It's not right. I won't be here long, and I need to have a little time with you, Gabby."

"Well, you can't come to my house. I have a reputation to guard. If the commandant of the occupation force came to my house, why, not a person would speak to me. I'm sorry, Erik, but that's the way it is."

"I see. But I'm not giving up. I'll figure out a way even if I have to put on a false beard."

She smiled. "I'd like to see that."

"Gabby, tell me. Don't you have any feelings in your heart for me?"

Had she been wise, she would have said no instantly. But she wanted to be honest with him. "I . . . think at one time we had a chance, but the world's moved on. We're two different people now."

"I think you're wrong." Erik stepped toward her but caught himself. "I'll call you tonight. If I have to sneak around in the dark for you, I will, but I insist on seeing you, Gabby."

She didn't answer. She just watched as he got in the car and his guard drove away. She was sick at heart, for she knew that no good could come of trying to regain what they once had.

★ ★ ★

For two days Gabby did not hear from Erik, which was a relief. Neither did she speak to Dai. She had to be careful not to be seen talking to him too much, or his cover might be blown. She stayed busy spending more time at the orphanage than usual and staying overnight with Dorcas one night. When she came out of the hospital on Thursday it was late, and dark had already fallen. As she walked toward her car, she was startled when Dai suddenly appeared beside her.

"You get around as quiet as a cat," she exclaimed.

"Yes, I'm a sneaky fellow. It has served me well a time or two."

"Do you need to talk?"

"Yes. Get in your car, and I'll scrunch down so nobody will see me."

"Scrunch? Is that a Welsh word?"

"No, it's American, I think. Those Yankees have a language all their own."

Gabby smiled as they both got in the car, with Dai down on the floor until they were well clear of the hospital. As she drove, he said, "Tell me more about your uncle. Everything you can think of."

"Dai, I've told you everything."

"There must be some things you haven't thought about in years. I need to know everything I can about Dalton Burke."

"If it were just Aunt Liza, you would have no trouble. She would leave in a minute."

"Suppose I kidnapped her. Would he leave then?"

"Are you serious?"

"I suppose not." He sighed. "Would you pull over here? I need to walk back to the hospital." He waited until she had stopped the car, and then he moved from the floor to the seat. "I don't think kidnapping would be a particularly good plan. He needs to come of his own free will, Gabby."

She was very much aware of the strength of the man beside her as he went on to discuss various possibilities. She knew they would not have sent a weakling for this job, but his mission was far from her mind at the moment. When he fell silent, Gabby asked abruptly, "Are you married?"

"No."

"Engaged or anything?"

"Not engaged and not anything—whatever that means."

"Why haven't you married?"

Dai smiled. "I never met anyone I'd want to grow old with."

"What an odd thing to say."

"Do you think so?"

He put his arm over the seat behind her. She felt it brush her hair and did not know whether it was an accident or not.

"Isn't that what love is?" he said. "Wanting to be with somebody always?"

"I suppose so, but usually we think of Hollywood love stories. You know, a beautiful girl falls in love with a handsome man, and the violins start playing."

"Nonsense made by idiots who dream too much! I think Robert Browning had the right idea."

"What do you mean?"

"I'm sure you've heard his poem about mature love. 'Grow old along with me! The best is yet to be. The last of life, for which the first was made.'"

"Yes, I've always loved that poem."

"If he had written nothing else, he did well to put into

words what some of us feel." He peered out the window to make sure no one was nearby. "What about you? Have you ever met anyone like that?"

Gabby looked down at her hands, and he knew he had touched on a sensitive issue.

"I didn't mean to pry—well, I suppose I did."

When she met his gaze, her wide eyes looked sad. "I thought I found someone like that twice."

Dai felt a great compassion for this woman. He knew enough of her story to know about the tragedy she had had to face in her life, and now he pulled her into an embrace. She was not crying, but she seemed close to it. He was afraid she would start sobbing if he said the wrong thing.

"I don't know what's wrong with me," she whispered. For some reason, she remembered a time when she was a little girl and she ran to her father after skinning her knee. He had picked her up and held her in much the same way Dai was holding her now. She wished for a moment she was still a girl, full of sweet happiness, but she knew that was forever gone. She tried to pull away, but he moved his head forward to kiss her. She put her hand against his chest and said, "Don't do that!"

"Gabby, you've had a hard life. I don't know exactly what you've gone through, but it's obvious that it hasn't been easy. But you can't hide behind that stethoscope forever."

"I nearly made a terrible mistake twice, Dai. I'm just not one of those people who know how to love, I suppose. I'm not going to make another mistake. Now, please get out of the car!"

He had not known this woman long, but he was convinced she had a good heart, and he didn't want to push her. "Good night, Gabby," he said quietly. "I'll see you later."

She gripped the steering wheel as he shut the door and disappeared into the darkness. *Can I ever care for a man?* she thought. *I don't even know what it means to love.* She had always thought it meant the world turning over, the difference between living and not living. She had always hoped for a full heart and even for wild, emotional feelings. She longed for a deep and abiding love between herself and a man, but as she sat in the darkness, she was afraid it would never come.

Putting her head down against the wheel, she began to sob. She felt empty and all alone in the world. "Oh, God," she cried out, "I don't know who I am or what I am. Please help me!"

Some loud frogs in a nearby pond broke into a melancholy chorus. She straightened abruptly and dashed the tears from her eyes. She put the car into gear and roared away, as if to flee from something she could not face.

PART THREE

August 1940

★ ★ ★

CHAPTER THIRTEEN

THE EXECUTION

★ ★ ★

Oberleutnant Mueller entered the room, his eyes bright with anticipation. He snapped to attention and said with excitement tingeing his voice, "Commandant, General Rahn has arrived!"

Erik had been laboring over the papers that lay on the desk before him, and he looked up with less excitement than Mueller had anticipated. "You must not call me commandant anymore, Mueller. General Rahn is now the commandant."

"Yes, sir, of course."

"Where is the general?"

"He is on his way here. I had Conrad show him to his quarters first," Mueller burst out. "Now we will see some efficiency around here."

Erik smiled slightly and leaned back in his chair. "I am sure of that."

"Oh, sir, I did not mean that *you* were inefficient."

"That would be true enough." Colonel Erik Raeder got to his feet and strolled to the window. He looked out for a moment in silence, then said quietly, "I was not cut out for this work. I will be leaving soon to go to a field command, which is my desire."

"You have done an excellent job, sir," Mueller said quickly, "but I know you yearn for action."

Erik was watching a group of sparrows that were competing for the crumbs he threw out each morning for them. Even as he watched, a tremendous fight broke out between two of the minute creatures. They were rolling in the dust, pecking and squawking and scratching at each other. The humor that lay not far beneath the surface caused him to smile. "Seems to me a poet once said that even birds in their nest agree, so why shouldn't we? But those little fellows are fighting with as much ardor as our men in the advanced battle positions. So the birds are no better than we are, are they, Mueller?"

"Sir, I don't understand you."

Raeder shook his head. Mueller was a sound man in many ways but absolutely lacking in imagination. He had no sense of humor, and in all truth, Erik hoped that on his next assignment he would have an aide who had more spirit about him than this one. "Never mind, Mueller. I was just thinking aloud," he said as the sound of approaching footsteps and voices came from the outer office.

"I expect that would be General Rahn," Erik said.

The door opened and a tall, burly man marched inside. His dark blue eyes fell on Erik, and he threw up his arm in the ritualistic Nazi salute. "Heil Hitler!"

"Heil Hitler," Erik responded. "It's good to see you again, General."

Rahn had a face like a bird of prey, his eyes sharp and glittering. His gray hair was cut short, and on his right cheek a scar traced itself from the corner of his eye down to his lower jaw. It was, as Erik knew, a dueling scar, almost a requirement for men who had served in the war.

"Your father sends his good wishes to you, Erik."

"You saw him before you left Germany?"

"Yes, I had dinner at your parents' home."

Rahn had served with Erik's father in the Great War, and

they had forged a bond that had lasted through the years. Erik knew Rahn was the man his father admired most—next to the führer, of course. He himself, as a small boy, had been terrified of the general, and even now he was somewhat intimidated by the man. "I hope your quarters were satisfactory, sir."

"Adequate." Rahn removed his crushed hat, and a short, thin aide stepped forward to take it. He had a pasty face and never removed his eyes from General Rahn. He stood back holding the hat, waiting for his orders, and Rahn said, "You can go now, Deacons."

"Yes, sir. I'll wait outside in case you have further orders."

"Very well."

"This is Oberleutnant Mueller, my aide," Erik introduced.

Rahn merely inclined his head a fraction of an inch and said, "Leave us."

Mueller wore a startled look as he wheeled and fled out the door.

"I trust you've recovered from your wound, Erik."

"Completely, sir. I'm ready for service. Do you know anything about my orders?"

"Yes. You will remain here for the time being."

"But, sir—"

Rahn laughed harshly. "I know. You're anxious to get to the front. Well, you'll get there, my boy, but I will need your assistance for a while. This is an important job. I know you young fellows think that killing the British is the only thing that counts, but the führer's plan is complex. He has assigned you and me to the job of seeing that Holland is completely subservient to the will of the Reich. These Dutch are a stubborn bunch of fellows, but it is our job to see that all goes smoothly in the master plan."

"But now that you're here, sir, I don't think it will take long for you to take hold and crush any rebellion."

Rahn laughed. "Your father told me you would be champing at the bit, ready to go and fight. But as I told him and your mother, I will need your assistance here for a time, so let's hear no more about it."

"Yes, sir." Erik was dissatisfied. He hated his service and longed to go to the front. If it had not been for Gabby's presence, he would have been completely miserable. "Things seem to be going fairly smoothly, General Rahn," he said.

The general gave him an austere glance, almost bleak. "You think so, do you, Colonel? Well, I do not."

"You're unhappy with the situation? In what way, may I ask, sir?"

"This resistance movement. It must be crushed at once." Rahn laid his riding crop on Erik's desk. "I know it's hard to identify these traitors, but I've been studying your reports, Colonel, and I am not satisfied with them." He punctuated his statement with a slap on the desk. It made a resounding noise, almost startling Erik. "They must be rooted out, every one of them!"

"It's a little difficult, sir. They're very clever."

"I understand you're holding four of them now."

"We have four prisoners, yes, but they're merely suspects. So far they haven't confessed."

"Confessed! The fools will never confess. Shoot them immediately!"

Erik blinked with surprise, and shock ran through him. "But, General, we're not certain they're guilty!"

"You were certain enough to arrest them. That's enough for me. I want them shot at once. Tomorrow morning at the latest."

Erik licked his lips nervously. He knew General Rahn was a cold, efficient machine, but this order startled him, and he rebelled against it inwardly. "Sir, give me a few days. If they're guilty, they shall certainly be executed, but—"

"Colonel, you've been running a lax operation here. That's why the resistance has not been crushed. I want these people to understand that we are the masters, and anyone who questions us will die. Of course, a few innocent ones may get killed, but that's the nature of war. If you were at the battlefront and ordered to take a village, there would be civilian casualties. It's unavoidable. We're in a war here, Colonel Raeder, and these people would kill us all if they had the power. But they will not have it, for we will exterminate this underground—every man, woman, and child involved in it. Do you understand me?"

"Yes, sir!"

"Good. Have them shot. Now, let's get down to business." Rahn sat down at the desk and laid his hands flat. "You're a good soldier, Erik, but I want all security doubled. And I want all Jews and all gypsies rooted out." He looked up and said, "I'm expecting good things from you now. I know that some of my orders will seem harsh, but you have not yet experienced war in all of its horrors. You will be moving out to a fighting unit soon, and I want to be able to write to your father and tell him that you are totally dedicated to the cause of the Fatherland."

"Understood, sir."

"Now, I want a meeting of all officers in exactly one hour."

"I will go alert them."

As Erik left the office, he felt a great weight settling on him. He had interviewed the four prisoners—three men and one woman. The woman was a housewife who had been caught on the streets after the resistance had pulled off a spectacular feat. She denied her guilt and wept when he spoke with her. As Erik moved stiffly along the corridor, he envisioned the woman tied to a post with a cloth over her eyes. He could almost hear the commands of the officer in charge of the execution. *Ready—aim—fire!* He shuddered as he imagined the bullets tearing into her soft flesh, crushing the life within her.

Mueller was coming down the hallway toward him, and it required all of his strength to say, "Lieutenant, the four prisoners will be executed at dawn tomorrow."

Mueller's eyes gleamed. "Excellent, sir. I will see to it myself. Will you attend the execution?"

"If the commandant orders it, I will. The general has

called for a meeting of all officers in my office in one hour. See to it."

"Yes, sir. Heil Hitler!"

Suddenly, the Nazi salute seemed to be out of place, but Erik forced himself to lift his hand in a halfhearted fashion. "Heil Hitler," he muttered and watched with disgust as Mueller hurried along, pleased with the execution to come. *How can any man be pleased that people who may or may not be innocent will be shot?* he wondered. *And a woman, no less. I hope and pray to God that I will never reach that point of enjoying seeing people die!*

⋆ ⋆ ⋆

The cell had gathered in Betje's apartment. It was somewhat hazardous, but since the group had never met there, it seemed to be only a small risk. She stood facing the small group and said, "You've all heard, I suppose, that the Germans are going to kill our friends tomorrow morning at dawn." Her face was pale, and her lips were drawn into a set line. Her eyes reflected a rage that she was barely able to suppress.

"How did you find this out, Betje?" Karel Citroen asked.

"It wasn't hard. The Germans want us all to know about it. It's been announced publicly."

"Perhaps I should talk to Colonel Raeder. Or perhaps you should go," he suggested to Gabby.

"It won't do any good for anyone to try to get him to do something. Raeder is no longer the commandant. Bruno Rahn, the one they called the butcher in the Great War, is now commandant. You know his reputation."

"And Groot—he will be shot with the others?" Jan ten Boom asked.

"Yes, all four of them," Betje said.

Groot Dekker had been taken in the operation, but everyone had been hoping that he would be released, since there was no real evidence.

"We've got to do something!" Jan exclaimed. "We can't let them execute Groot and the others."

"One of them is a woman," Gottfried Vogel said, "and innocent at that. I know her. She's had nothing to do with this operation."

"The Germans don't care about that. They're out to teach us a lesson," Betje said bitterly. "We've got to break those people out of there."

"Yes!" Jan said, his eyes brightening. "We can get enough men to fight our way in."

"No we can't," Pastor Citroen said. "And even if we did, can you imagine the retribution that would come? Why, they would kill half the village if we did that."

"But we can't do nothing, Pastor!" Jan exclaimed. "We've got to help them."

Citroen's eyes dropped. He had no better answer for them. "It's impossible."

"What do you say, Dai?" Betje said.

"I agree with the pastor. I think it's impossible."

"I thought nothing was impossible for this God you serve!" Betje cried. "Isn't there a verse in the Bible that says something like that?"

Citroen was stung by her words and retorted, "Of course nothing is impossible with God, but—"

"But what? You think He wants that woman to die? And Groot and the others? Is it His will that these German swine kill our countrymen?"

"Betje, calm down," Dai said. "In a war people are lost. I may be the next one to go, and if I were there in that cell, I would tell you not to try to rescue me."

"I can't think like that!" she said.

"Of course you don't want to. We're concerned about Groot and the others, but we have to look at the big picture."

"You think of the big picture!" Betje flared. "I say if we can't save one of our own, what use is there in fighting!"

Gabby had said nothing up until this time, and now she said, "Please, Betje, I hate to hear you speak like that. We all knew when we joined this cell that we might die, and it's likely that we will. Some of us at least." She continued in a quieter tone. "I'll go to Erik. Perhaps there's something that can be done."

"You're wasting your time," Betje said. "Rahn is now the new commandant and has given the orders, and your friend will obey them." She felt defeated. She could not bear the thought of losing one of the cell. "Go talk to him," she said bitterly, resignation on her face. "Little good it'll do us!"

* * *

"I wish I could do something, Gabby, but it's impossible."

"But, Erik, can't you at least have it postponed? The woman is totally innocent. She's a poor peasant who was just in the wrong place at the wrong time."

He chewed his lower lip with a worried expression. "I've already tried to reason with General Rahn, but he won't listen. He intends to set an example."

"What good will it do to execute innocent people?" Gabby stood before Erik as he sat at his desk, her face twisted with the horror she felt. This was not someone being killed on a battlefield far away. This was her friend, Groot Dekker, an amiable, good-natured farmer. She had known Groot for years and had bought vegetables from him and laughed at his stories. The thought of him being executed was painful beyond anything she had known.

Erik shook his head slowly. "There's nothing I can do. I'm sorry, Gabby. It's not of my making."

A hot reply rose to her lips. She wanted to scream at him, *You could do something if you wanted to!* She knew, however, that he was not a cruel man; he was just caught in the complexity of the German war machine. Thousands were being slaughtered right now, and the machine would not stop for four innocent people. "All right, Erik," she managed to say. "I had to try."

"Gabby, I am sorry," he said as he came around the desk. "If it were in my power—"

"I know. But could the pastor and I at least visit the prisoners?"

"Yes, of course. I'll give the orders."

"Thank you."

Gabby walked slowly out of the office, feeling numb, and when she reached the outer office and found Karel there, she shook her head.

"At least you tried," he said gently.

"The colonel says we can see the prisoners."

"Good. I was hoping he would."

A lieutenant came into the outer office. "I will take you to the prisoners," he said. "Come with me."

They followed the officer outside the main building, and he led them to a low rectangular building set off of the square. Two armed guards stood outside holding their rifles as the lieutenant approached. They both saluted, and one opened the door. The lieutenant led them in. "You'll have thirty minutes. That's all."

Two more guards stood at attention while they passed into a room where the four prisoners were already waiting. Groot came forward at once and greeted them. "Pastor—and you, Gabby. Thank you for coming."

Karel waited until the door shut and they were alone. "I wish we could do something for you." He looked at the others, who had some hope in their eyes, especially the woman, and he knew there was no point concealing the truth. "Dr. Winslow has begged the colonel, but there is nothing he can do. The general has commanded—"

Even as he spoke, the woman began to weep. Gabby went to her at once and put her arm around her. Tears were coursing down the woman's face. "What will happen to my children? My husband is dead. They will have no one."

"I will see that your children are taken into a good home," Gabby said. "I promise you they will be cared for."

The woman looked up in disbelief. "You promise?"

"Yes, I promise. What are their names? Let me write them down."

Karel watched as Gabby took the woman over to a table and began to write the information down. He tried to think of some words of assurance he could give to Groot but for the life of him could not think of anything to say. He had spoken with dying people before, but they had always been on a sickbed surrounded by doctors with at least the possibility of life. But this big man who stood before him and the other three were as good as dead.

"You're sad, Pastor," Groot said.

"I am, brother. I would do anything to save your life, but there's nothing to be done." He lowered his voice. "Some in the cell wanted to storm the prison, but you know how futile that would be."

"Ja, they can't do that. We would lose more people."

The two men stood talking quietly, and finally Gabby came over and put her hand on Groot's arm, tears in her eyes.

"It is good that you will take care of Magda's children," Groot told her.

"It's the very least I can do. Oh, Groot, I can't help weeping for you!"

"Many have died for our cause, my doctor friend. I am an old man, and I am ready to be with my Lord."

Gabby could not keep the tears back. She removed a handkerchief from her pocket and wiped her eyes.

"One good thing has happened in here. My friend Phillip here has accepted Jesus as his Savior."

"That's wonderful!" Karel exclaimed. "I welcome you, brother, into the church of the living God."

"I should never have waited so long. I have heard many sermons," Phillip said. His face was pale, but his voice was firm. "And now I have wasted my life and can do nothing for Jesus."

"You are dying as a believer. Tomorrow you will be in His presence," Karel said with energy.

For the next few minutes they shared their faith in Christ

with one another. Finally, the guard came and told them their time was up.

As they left, Gabby embraced Groot and wept. "I've heard it said that Christians never say good-bye," he told her. "I'll be waiting for you on the other side."

Gabby managed to smile at Magda. "Never fear. I'll see that your children are safe and taken into a loving family."

"God bless you," the woman cried faintly.

"Remember, I'll be waiting," Groot said with a smile.

The door closed, and numbly Gabby followed the lieutenant out. As soon as they were outside the building, she said, "I can't stand this, Karel!"

"Yes, you can. All over the world, people are having to stand persecution of all kinds. We must trust only in God in times like this."

★ ★ ★

Erik stood in the courtyard and watched grimly as the four prisoners were led to the wall. The woman stumbled, and the largest man put his arm around her to support her. A bitter taste came to his mouth as Erik heard the man say something comforting. He glanced over at General Rahn, whose face seemed frozen. He showed no emotion whatsoever, and Erik flashed back to his argument with the man no more than an hour ago. Erik had dared to speak rashly to the general, saying, "It's wrong to shoot these people! They may be innocent!" But Rahn had silenced him with a shout. "The Fatherland must protect itself! I will hear no more of this! Your father would be ashamed."

Now the light had begun to break in the east, and the soft cooing of doves on the wall provided a contrast to the harsh scene. Erik turned his head away but heard the sound of the boots of the firing squad. When they stopped, he looked up and saw that eight men were lined up with rifles, and the prisoners were backed up against the wall. A sergeant was going along putting blindfolds over the eyes of the condemned, but when he came to the big man, the man shook his head and smiled at the sergeant.

How can he smile when he's about to die? Erik wondered. The thought tormented him, and suddenly he said, "Sir, it's not too late. Give me a few days."

"Be quiet, Colonel! You're turning into a woman!"

Erik gritted his teeth and braced himself for the scene before him. The prisoners, only three wearing blindfolds, were motionless, and the lieutenant in charge of the squad looked at the general. Rahn nodded his head, and the officer cried, "Ready!" The rifles snapped up to firing position, and after what seemed a long time, the officer gave the second command, "Aim!"

The huge old man lifted his voice and said, "Forgive these men, Lord. Show them your glory!"

The officer in charge of the squad seemed shaken, and it was General Rahn who cried out, "Fire! Fire!"

The rifles exploded, and the four prisoners were driven back against the wall. They fell to the ground, and one of the men kicked violently for a moment before gradually stopping.

Erik immediately turned and walked away. The lieutenant followed him and said, "You see what a fool religion can make of a man?"

Erik stopped. "You don't believe in God, Mueller?"

"No!"

"Then you're a fool!" Erik growled, his voice grating. He whirled and strode away, unable to face his office but eager to be alone. He felt empty, almost shredded inside, and he could not help but wonder what the future held for a man such as himself.

CHAPTER FOURTEEN

"I'M NO ANGEL"

★ ★ ★

The early morning light was a tawny glow in the east that filtered slowly through Dai's window and struck the pages of the small notebook he was writing in. He stopped writing to enjoy the peace of what he called the cobwebby time of the day. He had slept soundly, and before leaving his room, he had decided to scribble a few notes in a journal. He knew better than to leave anything in writing that could possibly be used against him, but he had found that keeping a journal was a great stress reliever. If he wrote anything of any importance, he would burn it immediately. If the enemy ever did find the entries he saved, they could make little sense of them. They were merely random, rambling thoughts of an ordinary man—nothing about wars and battles and covert cells and secret operations.

He looked at the date he had written—August 10, 1940. *What if I keep this and my grandchildren read it fifty years from now? What will they make of it? How will they feel about all this horror that's going on? Will they forget?* He shook his head and wrote carefully:

The execution affected all of us. An execution is a big ugly monster. It's very different from a battlefield, where men line up and try to kill one another.

It was terrible in a way that his mind could not accept. That human beings would line other human beings up against a wall and blow the life out of them was unthinkable. He continued writing with his stubby pencil.

The new commandant is a monster! Not all Germans are like him, but somehow many of his kind have found their way to the top of the pyramid, so that they are in command. I'm afraid they'll succeed in making monsters of those who are under them.

What troubles me greatly, aside from the injustice of the execution itself, is the way it has affected Gabby. For a few days I thought it would almost destroy her. She could not come to work for two days, and although everyone knew she was distraught by the senseless deaths, no one mentioned it. She spent this time with the dead woman's children, seeing that they found a good home. She has a gentleness that shines from her eyes and shows in her gestures. I have never seen a woman so filled with the capacity for love.

Erik has been to the hospital to see her twice, and I don't think he's had medical concerns. Gabby told me once that she had made two mistakes about men, and I have a feeling that Erik Raeder might be one of them. There's an unmistakable look in his eyes that a man cannot hide when he loves a woman. What a tragedy for both of them.

He took his pocketknife out of his pocket and carved the tip of his pencil into a sharp point. As he worked methodically, the difficulty of his mission weighed heavily on his mind. He knew he would get only one chance, and he didn't want to fail. He tested the needle-sharp tip of lead on his index finger and nodded with satisfaction.

I don't know if there's any way to successfully complete this mission, but time is running out. It always does. The longer we wait, the harder it will be to reach our man and try to convince him to come over to our side.

I have encouraged Gabby to tell me everything she can about her uncle and aunt. There must be a key to getting them out, and it lies in her. I find myself more fascinated by her as time goes by. She's built a wall around herself where men are concerned and has put up a sign that says, "No Admittance. Keep out!" That challenge makes me want to tear down her walls and get to the woman who's concealed behind all of that.

Maybe a man always wants what he can't have—what's difficult for him. I suppose I'm no different from the rest, but I cannot get out of my mind the time that I held her in my arms. At the time I told myself it was merely kindness, that I was only offering her comfort, but I know it was more than that.

"I can't believe I'm writing this drivel!" He ripped the sheet out, took a match from his pocket, and quickly burned it. As the paper curled up, he thought of what he had written—that men want what they can't have—and suddenly he remembered something that had happened years ago in Wales. He had been passing a candy shop when he noticed a boy of five or six with his nose pressed against the window and his hands on the glass. The longing in his posture was irresistible. Dai had gone inside and purchased a bagful of various kinds of candy. He went outside and offered it to the boy, who could not believe what he was seeing. He remembered laughing and saying, "Go ahead, son. It may be the last time anybody gives you what you really want."

Dai smiled as he remembered how the boy had plunged his hand into the sack and stuffed his mouth full as fast as he could.

Getting up abruptly, he laughed shortly at his own foolishness. "Enough of that! Time to face the real world, old man!"

⋆ ⋆ ⋆

Gabby carefully removed the neat stitches from what had been a gaping wound. "Now, you see, Berg, you're going to be fine," she said brightly.

The patient, a young man who had ripped his arm open

by falling into some farm machinery, grinned up at Gabby. "Good for you, Doctor. My own mother couldn't have made those stitches any neater."

"You just be careful. Next time you might get your head caught in that machine."

Berg's blue eyes danced. "I don't think I'll be doing that," he said as he put his shirt on. "I'll be going off to fight."

"How are you going to do that, Berg?"

"I'm gonna join the army in England or maybe in France."

Gabby glanced around and lowered her voice. "You need to be careful about who you say that to," she said urgently. "Do you have a way?"

"Yes."

Gabby put her hand on his and squeezed it. "God go with you, Berg."

"Thank you, Doc. I'll remember you."

Gabby walked down the corridor thinking how this war had disrupted every level of life. Even the children thought now in terms of soldiers and danger, tanks and planes overhead. This young man would be going out to lay down his life, but he was as cheerful as if he were going to a dance.

As she passed a window, Gabby glanced out and saw Dai edging the grass and remembered that she needed to talk to him. She went outside and approached him, greeting him as she would any hospital employee.

"Good morning, Dr. Winslow," he said as he continued working with his hand clipper.

"I'm taking some of the children from the orphanage out on a field trip this afternoon, and I need you to drive. We're going to the Goldmans' house so the children can play in the woods and enjoy a day out in the fresh air."

"The Goldmans? Who are they?"

"They're close friends of my aunt and uncle. They're best friends, as a matter of fact."

"The name sounds Jewish."

"They are Jewish."

"I wonder why they haven't been taken."

"I don't know. I suspect Uncle Dalton had something to do with it. Perhaps he spoke of his friendship."

Dai shook his head and looked down at the ground. "I wonder how long that will last. The way Rahn is snapping up Jews, no one is safe."

"I know, but Professor Goldman is a very important scientist at the university. Maybe they're trying to get him to go to Germany too."

"Would he go, do you think?"

"No, never. He hates the Germans, and his wife hates them too." She bent over to pick a weed that had bloomed in the grass. "Anyway, we'll plan to leave this afternoon at one o'clock."

"I'll be ready."

★ ★ ★

The children piled off the truck squealing and shouting, glad to be out of the orphanage on a nice day. Dai peered at them from under the bill of his cap and grinned. "We were once like that, weren't we?"

"I suppose we were. All children love to play outside. Oh, here come the Goldmans. You'd better keep doing your act."

"Sometimes I think it's not an act," Dai said dryly. He went to the truck as the couple approached.

"Dear, we're so glad to see you!" Sarah Goldman exclaimed. The small, thin woman always looked ill, even though she was an extremely talented woman and a fine artist. She practically worshiped her husband, Jacob Goldman, a tall man with dark hair and a pronounced hooknose. He was as untidy as was Dalton Burke. *Maybe it goes with being a professor,* Gabby thought.

"How are you, my dear doctor?" he said as he kissed Gabby's cheek.

"I'm fine, Professor. How generous of you to let us use your home for a field trip for the children."

"It's a welcome relief," Sarah Goldman said. "Make yourself at home. Go ahead and let the children roam about, and when they get tired, bring them in. I've made cakes and cookies and lemonade by the gallon."

"Fine! They turn into wild urchins when they get loose like this. It will do them good to get rid of some energy. They spend too much time inside at the orphanage."

"It's all right, my dear," Sarah said. "We love children."

Gabby called the children over so she could review the rules before letting them go off into the woods. For the next two hours the children ran wild, playing hide-and-seek, climbing trees, and collecting wild flowers.

While the children played, Gabby and Dai talked comfortably and let the time slide by in the shade of a tall elm tree. He was wearing his usual dirty garb, but his eyes were bright under the peak of his cap. His black hair had grown longer and now showed beneath the edge of the cap, and he had not shaved for several days. She couldn't help wondering what he would look like if he shaved and dressed in some fashionable clothes.

"They've got more energy than a dynamo," Dai commented.

"Yes, they do." The sun was hot, and she brushed her hair back from her forehead. The sound of the children's laughter fell on both of them like a balm. "When you're in a woods that's so peaceful, it's hard to believe there's a horrible war going on."

Dai nodded. "Wordsworth once said, 'The passions of man are incorporated with the beautiful and permanent forms of nature.' Nature is definitely prettier than a smoky building or a neighborhood, and a grove of trees is better than a neighborhood."

"I agree completely," Gabby said. "Tell me about yourself, Dai—about your boyhood."

"My father was a pastor," Dai said slowly. "He died of cancer five years ago. My mother still lives in Wales. I go there as often as I can."

"I'd love to see Wales. I've never been there."

"It's very beautiful in places, but the coal mines are bad. A lot of Welshmen have died working in the mines. I worked in one when I was a young man."

They watched as a pair of children raced by.

"Can I ask you a personal question, Gabby?"

"You're a spy," she said, smiling. "I guess you know how to find out about people."

"It's about the colonel."

"Colonel Raeder?"

"Yes."

"What about him?" Gabby grew suddenly nervous. She began plucking at the material of her blouse, a pale ivory with lace around the neckline and the cuffs of the short sleeves.

"You told me once that you had made mistakes with men twice. Was he one of them?"

"You have a perceptive mind."

"I'm just nosy maybe."

Gabby was distracted by the sun that was brightening the surface of his eyes and deepening the ruddy coloring of his skin. He appeared to have a sort of lazy indifference, yet even now she could sense the quickness and vitality that she knew lay beneath this. She sensed he was studying her as well, perhaps even comparing her to other women he had known. She forced her thoughts back to his question and decided to be completely honest.

"Yes, he was."

"You two were in love?"

"I thought so."

Dai shifted his feet, locked his hands together, and tilted his head to the side. Her answer seemed to intrigue him. "You thought so? Weren't you sure?"

Gabby mulled the question over. "Whoever knows for sure? I thought I was in love with him, and he said he loved me too."

"What about now?"

She shook her head. "I don't think much about that, Dai."

He studied her eyes and thought they were the most beautiful eyes he had ever seen, large and beautifully shaped, with thick lashes shadowing them. She had a ripe and self-possessed curve in her lips, and her summer tan added to her attractiveness.

He inhaled her perfume, which always reminded him of her strong personality. Dai knew Gabby was a passionate woman, and he admired that trait, yet at the same time, he felt the awkward emotions a man feels when he looks on a woman who is interested in someone else. "He still loves you, Gabby. I can see it when he's around you."

She shook her head in denial, and the breeze caught her hair for a brief moment. "You see too much."

"How do you feel about him?" he shot back.

"I can't say."

Dai wasn't having much success at getting beneath the barricade she had built between herself and men. "Love is a funny thing."

"Funny? You mean amusing?"

"No, I mean odd—peculiar. We often fall in love with people we don't know much about."

"What do you mean?"

"I guess just that when we're in love, we see a person as being perfect, but we find out later they have flaws."

"Of course no one's perfect. Everybody knows that."

"No, I don't think so. I didn't when I was eighteen. I fell in love with a girl in our village. I didn't think she had any flaws."

His caustic tone caught Gabby's attention. "But you found out she did?"

"Yes, I did." They both watched as a noisy pair of squirrels chased each other across the grass. "I learned that people aren't always what they seem. And it can hurt a lot when we learn the truth."

Gabby was silent for a time, wondering what heartaches Dai had gone through in his life. Then she said quietly, "You've asked me a personal question. Now I'll ask you one."

"Shoot."

"What about Betje?"

He looked up, a startled expression in his eyes. "She likes men," he said slowly.

"Don't hurt her, Dai. She's been hurt enough."

"I can promise you that."

Gabby trusted that his promise was solid and that Betje was safe from his trying to lead her on, even though she had flirted with him already. "She's so unhappy. She thinks happiness lies in getting as much love from anyone as she can, and she's so wrong."

"I won't hurt her, Gabby. You can believe that."

"I do believe it." The squirrels raced noisily up a nearby tree. "I'd like you to meet my grandmother, Dai," Gabby said. "Well, she's actually my great-aunt, but I've always called her my grandmother."

"Dalton's mother?"

"Yes. I think you'd like her. After we take the children home, we can go back to the hospital and get my car. Maybe Grandmother's housekeeper will have something good on the stove. She usually does."

"All right. It sounds good."

★ ★ ★

Dorcas was having one of her good days, and Matilda had made her specialty for supper. "These are delicious!" Dai said as he sampled the spicy sausage fried in bread crumbs. He had pulled his cap off and was sitting at the table along with Gabby and Dorcas. "What are they?"

"*Croquetten,*" Dorcas said. "And the soup is *erwtensoep*. It's the best you'll ever find. It's a thick pea soup with slices of smoked sausages."

"Very good!"

Gabby felt pleased at the visit. For some reason she had felt compelled to bring Dai Bando by to meet her great-aunt. Dai had thrown off his act as a half-wit, and despite his unkempt appearance and bristly whiskers, he had proved to be a charming guest, paying careful attention to Dorcas. Gabby listened as the two spoke rapidly in Dutch.

"What kind of name is that?" Dorcas asked. "Dai Bando?"

"It's Welsh, Mrs. Burke."

"How does it happen you speak Dutch so well?"

"Well, I've traveled a great deal, and it's very much like German. I suppose I just like foreign languages."

Dorcas was looking healthier than Gabby had seen her in some time. Her cheeks had some color, and her eyes were clear. Although she was clearly enjoying having company, from time to time she would look at Gabby, who understood that she wondered why Gabby had brought this man to meet her.

Finally, they finished the meal and went into the sitting room, where Matilda served them delicious cake and hot tea. As they enjoyed their dessert, Gabby was amused at how her great-aunt interrogated her guest. She wondered how Dai would avoid telling her his real mission in the Netherlands.

"And what are you doing in this country, Mr. Bando?"

Dai gave the old woman a direct look and answered, "I'm a British agent. I've been sent on a mission to get your son and daughter-in-law out of Germany."

Gabby gasped and dropped her fork. "Dai, I can't believe you said that!"

"I feel that this matter concerns Frau Burke." He turned his attention to the older woman. "That's why I've come, and I need any suggestions you can give me to make my mission successful."

Dorcas stared at the interesting-looking man who sat across from her. After a moment of silence, she said softly, "You don't tell everybody this, I hope."

"You and Gabrielle are the only ones I've told."

Dorcas nodded. "I think you should keep it that way. I've been praying for someone to come and help my son. I've even asked God to send an angel if necessary."

"I'm no angel," Dai said with a grin. "Ask Gabrielle."

"My son needs to get out of Germany. He is a simple man—too simple, I think, in many ways. I want to pray for your mission. Come here."

Gabby watched with amazement as Dai knelt beside Dorcas without hesitation. Her grandmother put her hands on his head and prayed softly but fiercely. When she was finished, she removed her hands, and Dai got to his feet.

"Thank you, Frau Burke."

"You may call me Dorcas, my son."

Gabby was too startled to say much, and as the two left, Dai promised to come back and visit again.

"I can't believe this is happening," Gabby said as they walked to the car.

"Your grandmother is an unusual woman. You're like her in many ways."

"Oh no, not me."

"I think you are." He hesitated and then said, "I told her about my mission because I needed to get a clear vision of what I'm doing."

"I don't understand, Dai. What do you mean?"

He shifted his feet and shook his head as if in wonder at his own actions. "I get so caught up in the details of what I'm doing that I sometimes forget this assignment is about people. Have you ever read *Robinson Crusoe*?"

"Why, yes, of course. All British schoolchildren read that book."

"Do you remember the part where he decided to build a boat?"

"Vaguely. He wanted to escape from the island."

"He threw everything he had into building that boat, Gabby. He collected the wood, he looked for other materials, he shaped and formed it—he got completely caught up in building that boat. And do you remember what happened when it was finished?"

"No, I'm afraid I don't."

"It was a very large boat, and he had built it close to his home. When he was done, he discovered it was too big to move. He couldn't get it to the sea, so it just rotted there."

"I remember that. It was funny in a way."

"Yes, it was, but that's the way I feel sometimes. I get caught up in what I'm doing, and I forget that the end is more than the elements. I want to see your uncle and aunt free from Hitler's grasp. Not only because they can help the war effort but because they're human beings. And from all I've heard, they're good human beings."

"How sweet of you, Dai." Her eyes were dim with tears. His kind words had touched something deep inside of her.

He reached for her hand and lifted it to his lips. "I know you're worried about your uncle and aunt and your grandmother. We'll just have to trust God that all will be well."

Gabby blinked the tears away. "I'm glad you came, Dai," she whispered. "And all will be well. I believe that."

The two got into the car and drove away. Inside the house the old woman prayed, and in Germany, Dalton Burke had no idea that people this far away were willing to risk their lives to save him and his wife from the evil that was slowly closing in around them.

CHAPTER FIFTEEN

A TURN OF THE SCREW

★ ★ ★

A tapping on the door brought Dai Bando instantly out of a deep sleep. He came out of the bed plucking the Walther automatic from under his pillow and released the safety as he moved across the room barefooted. The moon sent a pale silver light through the small basement window. He stopped at the door and stepped to one side. "Who is it?"

"It's me—Jan ten Boom."

"What do you want, Jan?" he asked almost harshly.

"Open the door, Dai. I've got to see you. We're in trouble."

Quickly, Dai slipped the bolt and opened the door, keeping the Walther ready. "What are you doing here, Jan?" he whispered. "What kind of trouble?"

"It's Betje," Jan whispered hoarsely. "She's drunk, and she's talking like she shouldn't. I'm afraid she'll start talking about the underground if somebody doesn't get her out of that bar."

Dai put the Walther on safety and crossed the room. He concealed the weapon behind a small chest and pulled his trousers on. As he slipped into his shirt, he said, "Where is this place?"

"It's on the edge of Amsterdam. I'll show you."

"What's she doing there?"

"Oh, you know. She's on a *kroegentocht*."

"What's that?"

"I think you British call it 'pub crawling.' She egged me to go along with her, and I did. But it's dangerous, Dai. There are German spies all over the place, and when she's had too much to drink, there's no telling what she might say."

"All right. How do we get there?"

"I've got my brother's car. Come on, but we've got to be careful. If they catch us out after curfew, they'll throw us in jail and interrogate us."

"Why don't you just tell me how to get there, and I'll drop you off at your place. You don't need to be mixed up in this." By this time Dai was fully dressed, and he listened carefully as Jan gave him directions to the Brown Café, a name that referred to the color of the walls after years of exposure to cigarette smoke. The two climbed into the ancient car and soon pulled up in front of Jan's home.

"You'd better be careful," Jan said. "The Germans are thick tonight. They've doubled up on the night guard, but you've got to get Betje out of there before she gives everything away."

"I'll take care of it. Now, you go inside and stay in."

As soon as Jan was out of the car, Dai gunned the engine. He had spent a fair amount of time getting to know the lay of the land, and he found the bar without any trouble. He parked the car, noting that there were quite a few other cars still there. He glanced at his watch—ten minutes after eleven. All the bars were supposed to shut down at twelve, according to the Nazi rule.

As he went into the narrow two-story building, he was accosted by loud music and the strong smell of alcohol. He moved out of the foyer and into the main room, noting that the decor was predominantly brown, the burnished colors of an old Dutch master. The floors and tables were made of wood, and sturdy beams held up the ceiling. There was nothing somber about the place, however. The walls were brightened with tiles and paint, and the mirror behind the bar reflected the opposite wall, filled with brightly colored paintings.

He spotted Betje sitting at a table with a large man. She was laughing and drinking, obviously intoxicated.

As Dai approached their table, he heard her say, "These swinish Nazis won't be here long. We'll take care of that."

I've got to get her out of here, Dai thought grimly. He put on a carefree exterior as he greeted her.

Betje looked up, her eyes unfocused. When she finally recognized him, she laughed loosely. "Well, if it's not the retard. What are you doing out tonight? They let you off your chain?"

"Time to go home, Betje," Dai said and moved to touch her shoulder. He noticed several empty bottles on the table in front of him.

"I'm not going home. Meet my friend. This is Wit. What's your last name?"

"Dehann," the big man said as a lock of messy blond hair fell over his forehead. He must have weighed well over two hundred and fifty pounds, and he had a belligerent look in his small eyes. "We don't need your help, retard. On your way."

"I bet the preacher sent you to get me. Or was it Gabby? I'm not going, so you can go tell them . . ." She finished with a curse and took another drink from the bottle in front of her.

Dai was desperate, but he knew he had to get Betje out of there quickly. He took her by the upper arm and said, "You're coming with me, Betje. You're drunk."

Betje struck at his hand and cursed again. "Get your hands off of me! You're some kind of a freak. Tell him to be on his way, Wit."

Wit stood up and doubled up his huge right fist. "Get out of here before I bust you up!" he growled.

"She's going with me, and that's all there is to it. Let's not have any trouble." He noticed that everyone in the room was watching now.

"I'll knock your head off!" Dehann yelled as he struck out at Dai.

Dai jerked his head back, and the fist swept by him. Dai pivoted and put everything he had into a forceful blow to the man's face, forcing him to stumble backward. When the man didn't fall, Dai realized he was in trouble. Blood trickled down from Dehann's nose, and the man blinked with surprise as he touched the blood and then stared at it. His eyes seemed to turn yellowish as they narrowed, and he came forward with his fists doubled up.

Dai moved into the clearing as patrons scrambled out of the way, and one woman screamed. He heard the bartender say, "No trouble, you fellows! Take it outside!"

But Dehann had no intention of taking anything outside. With a roar, he rushed at Dai, aiming another blow at his face. Dai easily avoided it, but the body of the huge man hit him like a tank and drove him backward. He landed on a table, sending bottles and glasses crashing to the floor, but he had no time to do more than try to get away. Dehann was like a determined bear, and Dai knew he would be demolished if one of the man's fists landed squarely on his jaw.

"Wit, leave him alone!" Betje pleaded from a safe distance.

Her cry was ignored as Dehann moved forward, his hands poised to land a deadly blow. Dai quickly pivoted on his left foot and threw his right foot forward with a savage kick, catching Dehann in the chest with a dull thump and stopping him dead in his tracks. He grunted and made an ineffectual grab at Dai's leg, but it was gone. Any other man would have been rendered unconscious with that kick, but this man was tough.

"I'll get you, little man," he threatened in a hoarse whisper. The two circled around the floor, Dai backing up and Dehann moving forward, swinging his fists but never quite connecting. One of the blows finally caught Dai in the chest, driving him back against the wall with unbelievable power, sending an icy chill through him. For a moment the bar seemed to be full of flashing lights. He heard Dehann's roar over the cheers and jeers of the customers, and suddenly he felt a massive hand on his shoulder. He pulled away, and his light coat tore away under the grasp of the big man.

"Stand still, little man, and fight!"

The two men resumed their dance across the floor, knocking tables down, Dai dodging and Dehann throwing powerful blows. Dai tried to catch the man off guard, sometimes striking Dehann's face with the edge of his palm in a slicing slash and other times landing his foot in the man's stomach.

Dai saw that the big man was becoming winded. Dai was in excellent shape, but Dehann was carrying an extra thirty pounds of fat. Dai finally landed a forceful kick directly in the man's stomach that drove his breath out. Dehann stopped still, and Dai quickly said, "Let's drop it. No sense cutting each other to pieces."

But Wit Dehann evidently did not plan to stop before his opponent lay stretched unconscious at his feet. He roared and cursed and continued the assault.

Desperately, Dai measured his opponent and threw everything he had into a tremendous kick. The toe of his shoe caught Dehann under the chin and snapped his head back with a frightening force. This time the big man simply dissolved, falling in a heap to the floor.

At once Betje moved forward unsteadily. She grabbed at Dai, and the two of them left the room as quickly as they could.

As soon as they were outside, Dai felt the pounding he had taken. He had bruises all over, cuts on the inside of his mouth, and blood was dripping steadily from his cut eyebrow. "Let's get out of here."

"Do you have a car?" she asked.

"That's Jan's car over there."

"Come on. You're bleeding like a stuck pig."

He was in no mood to argue.

"Get in. I'll drive."

"You're too drunk."

"No, I'm not. You can't see with that blood in your face. Come along."

Dai stumbled into the car and heard the door slam. She got into the other side and started the engine. "Take me to the hospital," he said.

"No, my place is right around the corner. I'll help you get cleaned up."

He laid his head back, and then the pain began to come over him in waves. His ribs hurt where one of the blows had probably cracked one or two of them, and he gritted his teeth and kept his eyes closed. When he felt the car stop, he opened his eyes and saw they were in a residential area.

"Come on up."

He got out of the car without protest, and the two of them trudged up the stairs to the second floor, where Betje's room was located. Nobody was awake in the house, and as soon as they were inside, she told him to sit down and take off his shirt so she could help him get cleaned up.

Dai pulled off the rags that used to be his jacket and then took off his shirt. He caught a glimpse of himself in a mirror and muttered, "I'm a pretty sight."

"How'd you know where I was? Did Jan tell you?"

"Yes. He said you were talking too much."

Betje did not answer. She heated some water on the stove, and by the time she got back to him, Dai was hurting badly. She took one look at his bruised torso and left to get a glass and two pills. "Take these," she instructed, handing him the glass.

"What are they?" Dai groaned.

"Never mind. Just swallow them." He took the pills and then leaned back in his chair. He watched her as she dipped a cloth in water and began washing his face. "You're going to need some stitches over your eye."

"It'll be fine. Just close it up with some tape."

Betje seemed to know what she was doing as she tended to Dai's wounds. Her face was close to his as she carefully washed the blood and then put some gauze on the deepest cut over his eyebrow.

"I was a fool," she said when she was done. She sat down on the couch.

"We're all fools at one time or another."

"I don't know why I do things like this. But I get so lonely." She patted the couch beside her, and he sat beside her and put his arm around her.

"Don't we all."

Suddenly, she began to cry in great sobs. "Why can't I be good, Dai? Why can't I?"

"You can."

"No, not me. Not ever."

"Yes, you can. You're just like the rest of us. You need help, but the only source of true help is the Lord."

Betje listened as he spoke of her need for God, and then she sighed and grew limp.

"Go to bed," he said.

"You can stay here," she said, her eyes red with weeping.

"No, I have to go. I'll see you tomorrow."

Betje waited until he was gone before making her way to her bedroom. She threw herself onto her bed and wept again. "Why can't I be good?" she kept asking herself. "Why can't I find happiness anywhere but in a bar or in the arms of a man?" But her questions had no answers, and she finally allowed herself to drift off to sleep.

* * *

Dai awoke to the sound of voices in the hall outside his door. "And so he went to help get Betje out of that bar, but he looked terrible," he heard Jan say.

"Open the door, Dai."

Hearing Gabby's voice, Dai got out of bed but stopped abruptly. His head pounded, and he swayed violently. He put his hands out to catch the wall and stood still for a moment until his head cleared. "All right. I'm coming," he said. When he opened the door, Gabby entered, black bag in her hand, along with the blinding light from the hospital hallway. He turned his face away, but Gabby had already seen it.

"You're a mess! Sit down. I need to look you over." She turned to her friend. "All right, Jan. I'll take care of him."

"It's a good thing he went," Jan said as Gabby turned on a small lamp. "Betje was talking crazy." He left, and as soon as the door closed, Dai sat down shakily on the chair.

"I don't need a doctor. I'm all right," he said, squinting from the bright light.

"I'll see if you are. Where are you hurt?"

"Ribs and some bruises and cuts in my mouth. And this one over my eyebrow is pretty bad."

Gabby gently checked his ribs. She was appalled at the sight of them, for Dai was covered with bruises. "What did he hit you with, a chair?"

"Just his fists. He was a beast."

Gabby examined his face and with one swift motion tore the tape off of his forehead.

"Ow!" he yelled. "Can't you be gentler?"

"It's easier if you do it all at once. You've got to have some stitches to close that ugly cut. Do you want to lie down, or are you okay sitting up?"

"I'm fine sitting up."

"Here, take these pills. I don't want you to feel this any more than necessary."

"I don't want any more pills. Betje gave me some last night. I could hardly drive."

"You're not going anywhere today. You need all the sleep you can get."

Dai took the pills, and she began getting the instruments she needed out of her bag. They made small talk while the pills started to take effect, and he didn't experience too much pain while she stitched the cut together.

When she finished, she bandaged it and told him he would probably have a permanent scar.

The drugs were making Dai groggy. "I think I will lie down."

He got up and started toward the bed, but the room seemed to be tilting. He felt her hands on him, strong and capable, guiding him to the bed.

"Lie down," she said.

He felt her pick up his feet and put them on the bed. She came closer as he closed his eyes.

"How was Betje when you left?" she asked.

"Sad. She felt bad about what she did."

"I'm glad you went, Dai. It could have been bad if you hadn't. She could have put everyone in the cell in serious danger."

He did not answer her, and she saw that he was drifting off to sleep. She brushed his hair back from his forehead, and for a long time, she stood over him watching him. Finally, she shook her head, thinking of how dangerous this whole business was. If a German had been in the bar, he would have arrested Betje at once. But somehow God had looked out for the two of them. With a prayer of thanksgiving, she left the room, wondering what Betje would do next. *She's so lonely and pitiful,* she thought. *She's going to break unless she finds Jesus.*

* * *

General Rahn had been yelling at his officers for fifteen minutes. There were six of them in the room, and all of them were pale and shaken by the time he dismissed them. Erik started to leave also, but Rahn said, "Not you, Colonel. You remain here."

"Yes, sir." As soon as the door closed, Rahn turned and said, "You've disappointed me, Colonel. I expected more support."

"I'm sorry, sir. I'm a soldier. I'm not fitted for this kind of work. Transfer me to a combat unit."

"This work has to be done. I've tried to tell you that. I'm

going to give you one more chance to redeem yourself, Erik."

It was strange how Rahn would sometimes call Erik by his first name and other times by his title in a formal way. He seemed to switch back and forth, and Erik never knew what mood he would be in.

"We're going to review this all again, and I expect you to do better than you have in the past."

"Yes, sir."

For the next hour Rahn went over every element of the occupation, with particular emphasis on rooting out the underground. He also addressed the presence of the Jews. "This country will be rid of the undesirables," he said. "I've been going through these papers." He indicated a stack. "What does this mean?"

"What is that, sir?"

Rahn held up a paper. "The Goldmans. That professor at the university. Why hasn't he been arrested and deported?"

"The Goldmans," Erik said carefully, "are the best friends of Dalton and Liza Burke. I'm sure you're aware, sir, of the important work Dr. Burke is doing on developing the weapon of the future. The führer is very pleased with the work he is doing for the Fatherland."

"He is not pleased when we allow Jews to hold high positions."

"If we arrest the Goldmans, Burke will be very upset. They were very close, from all I can understand. He might rebel and refuse to cooperate."

"He will obey, as will everyone else in the Third Reich. Now, I want these people arrested immediately. If Burke is so much in love with Jews, he cannot be a faithful servant of the führer, and the sooner it's discovered the better."

Erik knew arguing was useless. "Yes, sir," he said dully. "I will issue the order immediately, but I ask you to record my protest."

"Your protest is recorded!" Rahn shouted. "Now, do your duty as a good soldier."

★ ★ ★

The cell group met in the hospital basement in a room used for supplies. It was after midnight, and the meeting had not gone well. For the first time, contention filled the room as they debated over how much action they could take. Some of them, such as Jan, thought they were not doing all they could, but Gottfried Vogel, the pharmacist, always urged for caution. "We must be careful," he said. "We cannot throw ourselves away."

"But we're doing nothing," Jan said.

"Yes we are," Karel Citroen said. "We're getting people out every day, but if we're not careful, that will all come to an end. Now we must—"

"Wait. I hear someone." Betje pulled the automatic pistol from her belt and went to stand beside the door. The secret knock sounded, and she said, "Who is it?"

"It's me, Etta."

Betje opened the door, and Etta Christoffels came inside. She was a thin, intense young woman who was studying science at the university. Her eyes were wide, and she could not speak steadily. "It's . . . it's Professor Goldman," she stammered.

"What's wrong with him?" Gabby demanded.

"They've taken him and his wife. They're going to ship them to the concentration camp at Sachsenhausen."

"That can't be! You know what that place is," Karel said quickly. "It's a death camp—they'll be killed . . . executed."

"We'll have to do something now," Jan cried. "We can't let the professor be taken."

"It's too late," Etta said, and tears glinted in her eyes as she thought about her favorite professor. "They've already taken them. Shipped them out on the train. I saw them put him and his wife in one of those boxcars. They were stuffed in like cattle—it was inhuman!"

A dark feeling of despair overwhelmed Gabby. She had always respected the Goldmans. They had come to visit her aunt and uncle many times. She had been in their home, and they had always been kind to her. She could not bear the thought of them packed in a boxcar headed for a concentration camp. She left the room trembling, her hand over her mouth.

"She's taking it hard," Dai said to Betje. "She's got the most tender heart I've ever seen."

"Yes, she has," Betje said, "but if this war goes on, she'll get hard like the rest of us."

★ ★ ★

For three days after the Goldmans had been sent away to the concentration camp, Gabby attended to her duties at the hospital and orphanage with a pale face, speaking only when necessary. Everyone saw the change in her, and Hilda Schmidt, her favorite nurse, mentioned the change to the director. "She's going to collapse. She can't take things like this, Dr. Carstens."

Carstens shook his head sadly. "This occupation is hard on all of us. Where are we going, Hilda? What will happen next to our poor people?"

Late that night Gabby appeared at Dai's door. He opened the door to admit her and scanned the hallway. Luckily, it was empty. "This isn't wise, Gabby. Suppose somebody saw you?"

She ignored his words. "I think my uncle will be changed by what's happened."

"You mean about the Goldmans?"

"Yes. The Goldmans were very dear to him and to my aunt."

"I doubt if he'll even hear about it. They keep him shielded pretty well."

"You're right about that. Erik had promised me that my letters would get through to my uncle, but I've learned that they are heavily censored. I've written another one, but I don't know how to get it past the authorities so he actually learns the whole truth. Is there any way you can get this letter to him?"

Dai took the unsealed envelope. "You told him all about the Goldmans?"

"Yes, and I begged him to leave Germany before it's too late."

"He'll get the letter," Dai assured her.

"But how? How will you get it to him?"

He grinned. "I've suddenly got a new profession. I'm a postman."

Gabby looked at him in disbelief. "Why—that's impossible!"

"No, it's not. It can be done."

The lamp cast an amber light on his face. Gabby could not believe what she was hearing. She had assumed Dai would smuggle it to her uncle through various connections in Germany. If she had known he would volunteer to personally deliver the letter, she would not have brought it. Suddenly, she was afraid for him. She had not realized until this moment how much Dai Bando meant to her. "You can't go. I can't let you do it."

"We don't have any choice, Gabby."

She put a hand on his shoulder and looked up into his eyes, relishing the warmth in them. He bent to catch a better view of her face, and when he saw the expression in her eyes, he knew what she was telling him. He put his arms around her waist and drew her close, and for a moment he watched her, but he saw no anger and felt no resistance. He lowered his head and kissed her, and Gabby knew in her heart that she wanted—no, needed—the love of a man this strong. She realized that in many ways she denied her own needs, yet she could no longer ignore what she felt stirring in her heart for Dai. She had been afraid of the future, afraid to risk anything, but as she looked up into his eyes, for the first time in years she felt that the world could be safe with a man like Dai. He spoke her name, and she clung to him fiercely.

"I have to go, but I want you to know you're like the

woman in that poem I told you about, someone I could spend the rest of my life with."

Gabby's heart was racing, for this man had awakened hopes and long-lost dreams she thought would never come true. And then she remembered Madame Jana's words that God would lead her and take care of her future. She smiled but could not think of anything to say. "When will you go, Dai?"

"Tonight. You'll have to make excuses for me here at the hospital. Tell them that we had an argument and I just left."

"But how will you get into Germany?"

"I'll parachute in at night. We have an agent in place there, a German pastor who despises Hitler."

She held on to him, clinging as if she could keep him here by the sheer force of her will and spirit, but she saw in his face the grim determination and knew that he had to go. She put her face against his chest and held him tightly. "Come back to me, Dai. Please come back!"

CHAPTER SIXTEEN

A MIDNIGHT CALLER

★ ★ ★

"Professor, it is Herr Goebbels—he's coming!" Conrad Fleightmann was not easily startled, but like all other citizens of Germany, just the mention of the minister of propaganda for the Third Reich was enough to set off warnings.

"What are you talking about? You must be mistaken!"

"No, sir, it is Herr Joseph Goebbels! I was watching from the window," Fleightmann's assistant told him. "He got out of a staff car, and there are three S.S. officers with him."

Fleightmann rose to his feet, the fat around his triple chin shaking. He moved across the floor with a strange grace for such a large man but had gotten only halfway to the door when it opened, and he stopped abruptly.

Fleightmann threw his arm up and cried, "Heil Hitler," as Goebbels and his aides entered the office. He wondered nervously what the visit could mean. No one was absolutely safe in Germany these days, not even those close to the top. Anyone who displeased the führer could simply disappear and never be heard from again—or could be sent to the front, or any one of half a dozen other unpleasant situations.

Goebbels returned the salute and told his aides to wait outside.

"Herr Goebbels, if I had known you were coming, I would have prepared for your visit."

"Not necessary, Dr. Fleightmann." Goebbels was a small man who looked strangely out of place in the Nazi uniform. He was not handsome; rather, his enemies said he looked like a rat dressed up like a man. His features were sharp, his eyes small, and there was a cruelty in his mouth. Despite his small stature and lack of attractiveness, he was one of the most powerful men in Germany. Hitler trusted him without measure, and he had redefined the art of propaganda into a science. It was Goebbels who made Germany appear in a favorable light at all times. He was in charge of all printed matter, newspapers, books, scientific papers, radio broadcasts—anything that had to do with creating the image that Germany was a powerful and even a righteous nation. Only a monster like Goebbels, someone said, could write about the destruction of Poland as if it were a noble deed.

"What can I do for you, Herr Goebbels?" the professor asked in an uncertain voice.

"I've come about the Dutchman Burke."

"Is there some difficulty about him?"

Goebbels's cruel mouth twisted into a sneer. "I didn't come to give you a report, Fleightmann. I want information. Tell me, has he made any progress on the project?"

Fleightmann was apprehensive. He usually had no difficulty figuring out which direction the prevailing winds of change were blowing and getting on the fair side of them. But he could make nothing from the face of Goebbels, so he didn't know whether to praise Burke or condemn him. He chose the middle ground. "I believe the professor is making fair progress."

"You scientists never speak plainly! Are we closer to the production of the secret weapon?"

"Herr Goebbels, in all truthfulness, the work that Burke is doing is so complicated—so complex—that even I cannot understand it." He stumbled on and tried to excuse himself, but in all honesty, he was incapable of following Burke's reasoning and said as much to Goebbels. "I doubt if there are more than two or three men in the entire world who are capable of following the research of the professor."

Goebbels stood silently chewing on his lower lip, then nodded. "Very well. I wish to see him."

"I will take you to his quarters." Fleightmann led the way out of his office and took the elevator up to the third floor. Nervously, he led the way down the wide corridor, passing several startled workers who stared at Goebbels in astonishment. He opened a door and said, "This is where the professor works."

Goebbels stepped inside and saw nothing more than a large room flanked by windows along one side. A telescope stood pointed at the heavens, and bookcases lined the walls, packed with books of all sizes and shapes. In the center of the room, a man sat bent over a cheap notebook at a small desk. He was staring at the figures on the page, apparently lost to his surroundings. A phonograph was playing the music of Chopin, which displeased Goebbels. He would rather have found the man listening to a good, sound German composer like Beethoven!

He directed Dr. Fleightmann to leave them alone, and the obese man whirled and left at once, closing the door softly. Goebbels was curious. Burke was a mystery to him, as he was to the entire staff who served Hitler. The word in the scientific community was that Burke was one of the five great minds in the world and was mentioned in the same breath as men like Newton and Albert Einstein, a good German who had turned traitorous and was now in the United States.

Goebbels moved closer to the desk, but Burke didn't move. He was staring at his notebook, a yellow pencil held loosely in his left hand. Equations covered most of the page, but Goebbels could make nothing of them. He was not a mathematician and frowned slightly, for this was a situation that was out of his control. He suspected, along with others, that Dalton Burke was not a strong Nazi supporter, but the führer was convinced he was of great value to the Third Reich.

"Herr Burke . . ."

Burke jumped and looked up to find the uniformed Nazi in front of him. He flushed as he quickly rose to his feet. "I'm sorry, Herr Goebbels," he said in Dutch. "I did—"

"Speak in German please, Professor."

"I'm sorry. Old habits." Dalton ducked his head. "I was working. I didn't hear you come in. My apologies."

"No apologies are necessary." Goebbels smiled fulsomely and set out to make himself amiable. "I should have come to visit you long before this. The führer has spoken highly of your work. He appreciates what you are doing for the Fatherland."

"Why, thank you, sir. That is good to know."

"He would have come himself, but an emergency has arisen. Instead, he has asked me to invite you to a supper in his private quarters next week."

"A pleasure, Herr Goebbels."

"I will have his secretary call your secretary to arrange the details." Thinking that was enough charm spent on an obscure Dutch physicist, Goebbels said, "How goes the work, Dr. Burke? Are you making progress?"

"That is difficult to say, I'm afraid."

"How so?"

"Matters like this are so different from any other work," he explained. "It's not like making an engine, for example. There all of the basics have already been discovered. It only requires the time necessary to create the parts and assemble them. It is a job that is fenced in, you understand."

"But the work you do is different, is it not?"

"Exactly!" Dalton nodded vigorously. "It's almost like creating a symphony or painting a picture. The artist does not know what he will do until he does it. And so I sit here and I think." Burke smiled and shook his head slightly. "I know it looks like I'm wasting time. Somewhere out there the secret lies, and it can only be discovered by men like me who are not very practical, I'm afraid, but who must spend their lives sitting at a desk and staring at a sheet of paper. And even when I'm home in the bath, my mind continues to work the complexities of what we are trying to create."

"But you will find it?"

"I cannot say. I can only tell you, Herr Goebbels, I hope so."

Goebbels felt the hopelessness of urging the man on. He knew something about the creative process and was convinced that the Dutchman was telling the truth. "Well, Professor, keep at it. Work hard. We must press on to victory. Germany must have her place in the sun."

"Of course, Herr Goebbels." Burke closed the notebook on the desk. "While you're here, there is a matter I would like to consult with you about."

"Why, certainly. Anything we can do. By the way, are you being treated well? Do you like the home we've provided for you? Do you lack anything?"

"No, indeed! You've been most kind. My wife and I find the house most comfortable." A house had been provided only a few blocks away from the university. It was ornately furnished, and a car and driver had also been provided for any shopping that Liza needed to do. They were permitted to go to any events they found interesting, such as the opera. Dalton Burke did not know it, but he was a prisoner in a large and well-furnished prison.

"It's about this," he said. He picked up a newspaper from the corner of the desk and handed it to Goebbels.

"Why, this isn't a German newspaper!" He had given strict orders that men such as Burke should receive only German papers.

"No, I fell on it quite by accident. Someone left it on a bench in the park. But the story bothers me."

Goebbels ran his eyes over the front-page story. It concerned the concentration camps to which Jews were being taken throughout Germany. It spoke of the deaths and the torture that those who were carried into such places encountered. "This is all propaganda. British lies," he said with a shrug. "A few Jews have been apprehended, but they were given fair trials and proven to be traitors. They were sent to prison, of course, but you cannot believe these lies."

Goebbels ended his visit abruptly. As if by accident, he tucked the newspaper under his arm before shaking Burke's hand. "Your idea of a super weapon is exciting to Hitler."

Dalton shook his head. "I'm glad the führer is interested in my work, but I'll feel better when I have something solid to show him."

"Certainly." Goebbels smiled, exposing his teeth, but his eyes did not smile. "But the very idea of being able to destroy an entire city with one bomb is something to think about. Of course," he said quickly, "we would never use such a weapon. But just the possession of it would give Germany a victory." He smoothed the fabric of his uniform. "Well, I must go, Professor. I will leave you to your work. I will see you at the party at the führer's."

"Yes, Herr Goebbels."

Goebbels left and found Fleightmann waiting for him outside. He stalked over and shook the newspaper under his face. "You idiot! You let him get an English newspaper in his hand!" He raged, shouting and screaming, until Fleightmann was a mass of quivering flesh. Goebbels warned him not to let something like this happen again, then turned and stalked down the hall with his aides struggling to keep up.

Later that day, when Goebbels reported to his chief, Hitler asked, "Will he develop the super weapon?"

"I'm no scientist," Goebbels said, "but those who know about these things tell me he's capable of it."

"Good, and when we get it, Churchill and Roosevelt and those other capitalistic gangsters will be bombed into dust!"

Goebbels's eyes shone, and he said, "Yes, sir, into dust!"

★ ★ ★

"You look tired, my dear. Here, let me take your coat." Liza Burke took Dalton's coat and hung it on the rack in the foyer and then put her arms around him and kissed him. "You look absolutely exhausted. You're working too hard."

"I suppose so. I am tired."

She took his arm and led him toward the kitchen. She fussed over him, sitting him down and putting a slice of his favorite cake—chocolate—in front of him, along with a cup brimming with black coffee. It was a ceremony they repeated each day when he came home from work.

He took a bite of the cake. "Very good, as always. No one makes cake like you, my dear."

"You do remember that we have tickets to the opera tonight?"

Dalton stuffed his mouth full of cake and talked around it. "It will have to be a German opera," he said moodily. He was getting heavier as the years went by, and strain had begun to etch lines in a face that had once been round and smooth.

"I'm afraid so, but you do need to get out. It will be good to relax. You spend too many hours concentrating on your work."

"Oh, by the way, where is the letter from Gabrielle you told me about over the phone this afternoon?"

She took the letter out of the pocket of her apron and sat down across from him, watching his face as he read.

"Her letters aren't very informative," he said when he had finished. "She speaks only of her work and a little about our old friends and neighbors."

"Why do they censor her letters?" Liza pointed to the parts of the letter that had been blotted out by heavy black ink. "Someone feels that what she says would be dangerous to the war, I suppose."

"What foolishness! What could Gabby know that would influence the war? I would love to see her, Liza. I miss her so much."

"Can't we go home for a visit, Dalton? I'm so lonesome

for the sight of our home or for a tulip or a windmill—and especially for Gabby."

"I have asked, but they say my work is too important to leave right now. And if I finish sooner, Goebbels has promised a great reward from the führer."

She watched as he finished off the cake and washed it down with a long swallow of coffee. "What exactly are you working on, dear? Of course I wouldn't understand it, but . . ."

"It is a matter of atomic physics. There's a secret to be discovered that would give the world unlimited power. Can you imagine what would happen in undeveloped countries if they had an unlimited and inexpensive source of power for houses? It would give them a whole new economy."

"I'm not at all sure that would be good. It seems every time an industrialized nation goes into an undeveloped country, that country is ruined."

"Progress, my dear. Progress. It would keep them from starving."

Liza was puzzled, for she knew Adolf Hitler was not interested in developing poor countries. He was interested in conquering the world. She didn't voice her confusion but asked, "Are you content, Dalton? With your life here, I mean?"

He swirled the coffee in his cup while he appeared to contemplate the question. "I long for the old days, Liza. Everything then was so simple."

"Let's not go out tonight. Let's stay home. We'll listen to *Carmen* on the gramophone. But first I'll cook you a good Dutch dinner. What would you like most? Anything you can name."

"Really? Let's have *erwtensoep* and *rolpens*."

★ ★ ★

The dinner was excellent, for Liza was a fine cook. After she put the dishes in the sink, they relaxed in the living room while they listened to *Carmen*. When the last strain sounded, Liza took the needle off the record and said, "Are you ready for bed?"

"One more piece of chocolate cake."

"You're going to be as fat as Saint Nicholas if you keep eating so much."

"Then you shouldn't be such a good cook."

They had their late-night snack and went to bed.

He was tired, but Dalton was too troubled to sleep for some time. He could not get the visit of Joseph Goebbels out of his mind, and the letter from Gabby had saddened him. It reminded him of his home, and more and more of late, he had been longing for the peace of Holland. He knew it would be different now that the country was occupied by an enemy power, but still he missed their old house and the walks along the canals. And he missed his mother more than he ever intimated to Liza. He wondered how she was doing and missed the godly wisdom she often shared with him.

After tossing and turning for some time, he finally drifted into a fitful sleep. It was one of those nights in which he was more wakeful than usual.

He came out of sleep when a voice sounded close by. He opened his eyes with alarm, and fright ran through him as he saw a shadowy figure standing beside his bed. "What do you want?" he cried out and felt Liza shift and murmur faintly. "Do not harm my wife!" he pleaded. "Take anything you want, but do not harm my wife!"

"I don't mean to harm either of you."

Dalton struggled to sit up in the bed and put his arm around Liza, who had done the same. "What do you want? What are you doing here?"

A flashlight suddenly threw a cone of light onto the face of a man who stood beside the bed. He was a frightening figure, but his voice was calm. "I'm sorry to frighten you, but I'm an English agent. I've come to bring you a letter from Gabrielle Winslow."

The words brought instant comfort, for at least this man

was not a burglar. Dalton cast the cover back and threw the switch on the light beside his bed. The tall man dressed in black was pulling something from his pocket. Dalton could not focus clearly for a moment, and he put on his robe and slippers while Liza did the same. "How did you get in here?" he asked.

"It's sort of a specialty of mine."

Liza fastened her robe. "What do you want?" she asked. Her face was pale, and her voice was unsteady. She clearly did not trust the stranger. He showed no sign of having a weapon, but she knew he must have one. "What did you say about Gabrielle?"

Dai Bando took no pleasure in frightening two older people, but he had not been able to come up with a better plan to talk with them. He had been dropped into Germany and made a connection with his contact. The groundwork had been done, and he had found it amazingly simple to get into the house the Germans had provided for the Burkes. There was one guard, but he went off duty at midnight. Dai kept his voice calm as he said, "I've spent the last month in Oudekerk aan de Amstel, and I've gotten to know your niece very well."

"What is your name?"

"Dailon Bando."

A wave of reassurance came over both Liza and Dalton, for Gabby had mentioned this name more than once in her letters. She had simply said that he worked at the hospital there, but at least there was some familiarity.

"And you have a letter from her?" Dalton asked.

"Yes. Here it is."

Dalton took the letter and found his glasses on his bedside table. "Let's read it together, Liza."

She moved around the bed and kept her eyes fixed on the letter as he unfolded it.

"After you read the letter I'll tell you more about myself," Bando said quietly. He watched their faces as they read silently, clearly horrified by what they read. Gabby had shown Dai the letter and insisted that he read it. It told of the fate of the Goldmans, who had been sent to a concentration camp.

Dalton's hand began to tremble, and he sat down on the bed, hands over his face, and began to weep. Liza sat down beside him and put her arm around him, but she was weeping also. Dai silently waited while the two shared their grief.

Finally, Dalton looked up with tears streaming down his face. "This can't be true! The Goldmans are like our own family." He embraced his wife tightly. "Is it true, sir? Were they sent to a concentration camp?"

"I'm afraid it is true."

"What will happen to them?" Dalton whispered. "We are told that the camps are not bad, but I have difficulty believing that."

"I'm sorry to confirm your fears, but they are slaughterhouses. Men, women, and children are being killed and buried in mass graves. We have hard evidence of this."

Dalton's body shook as he sobbed. He realized at that moment that he had deliberately refused to face the facts. He remembered how Liza had tried to speak to him of the terrible things that were happening under Nazi rule, but he would not listen.

Liza looked up. Her arm was around her husband as she studied the face of the man who waited quietly. She knew nothing about him, but there was strength in his countenance and even compassion. "We knew some of this, Mr. Bando. Not so much about the camps, but about the slaughter of civilians by the German army."

She turned to her husband and wiped tears from his cheeks with her fingers. "We should never have come to Germany, Dalton," she said quietly. "These are not our people."

"Can we continue this conversation elsewhere?" Dai asked. "You might be more comfortable if you were dressed."

"Give us a few minutes, and then I'll come down and make some coffee," Liza said. "Why don't you wait for us in the kitchen?"

Twenty minutes later the three of them were sipping coffee in the kitchen while Dai told the couple about what was happening in the Netherlands. He painted a picture in bald terms of Germany's actions. "Your people are risking their lives every hour—and Gabby is one of them. I don't think she would mind if you knew she's working for the underground."

The two gasped. "Do you mean . . ." Dalton started.

"Yes. She and a small group of friends are helping Jews get out of the country."

"If she is captured, will she be shot?" Dalton whispered.

"Yes, she will," Dai said bluntly.

Dalton stiffened. "I will not stay in this place! Liza, we must return to Holland."

"Thank God!" Liza said. Her voice shook with emotion, and tears ran down her face. "But they will never let you go."

"Take us back with you, Mr. Bando," Dalton implored.

"I'm afraid that's not possible," Dai said regretfully. "It's a minor miracle that I got in here, and it will be another one if I get back."

"But we can't stay here," Dalton insisted.

"No, my whole mission is to get you away." Bando leaned forward, his eyes bright, and he spoke quickly. "You must deceive the Germans. Go to work tomorrow. Pretend that nothing has happened."

"I don't know if I can do that," Dalton said, shaking his head.

"You must do it, sir! There is no way that I can organize a party to kidnap you. We would never get out of Germany."

"What will we do, then? We can't stay in this place until the war ends!"

"You must find a reason for going back to Holland. I'll help you with it. It will have to be a strong reason, but it's the only way." Bando encouraged the pair, who looked at him with trust. "We'll find a way. And when the opportunity comes, you must insist on going. Refuse to work until they let you go. The Germans will send you under strong guard, but once we get you into Holland, we will see that you escape their evil clutches."

As they continued to talk, Liza asked the man about Gabby's work at the hospital. She saw something change in his face when he said Gabby's name, and Liza realized that there was more between this man and her niece than he was telling.

Finally Bando rose. "I must go. Somehow, God will get you out of this place. In the meanwhile we will do what we can."

"Thank you for coming, Mr. Bando," Dalton said. "We realize it was extremely risky for you to deliver your message to us, and we appreciate it."

"I was happy to do it, Mr. and Mrs. Burke."

When the door closed behind him, Dalton said, "I'm afraid I've ruined our lives, my dear."

"No, you haven't. God will take us from here safely."

As they clung to each other, he said, "I like that man, but he seems very hard."

"He has to be, I'm sure, to be involved in the kind of work he does, but did you hear his voice change when he spoke of Gabby? I think he's in love with her."

Dalton pulled away from their embrace. "How could you possibly know that?"

She patted his cheek. "Women have ways," she said with a smile. "Men are a little dense sometimes."

CHAPTER SEVENTEEN

NO MORE WORRIES

★ ★ ★

"Congratulations on your promotion, sir."

General Flynn shrugged off Major Ian Castleton's warm words. "More weight on my shoulders, that's all."

The two men were meeting in Castleton's office, talking about the war, which was not going well for the British. The only bright spot of the year had been the evacuation of 340,000 Allied troops from Dunkirk, but German troops had overrun Paris, and German planes continued to attack the Royal Air Force over England. The Battle of Britain was taking place at this moment, with the Luftwaffe dumping tons of explosives on Britain, killing thousands. For a time the two men spoke glumly, and then Castleton said, "One bit of good news, sir."

"Oh, what's that?"

"Regarding Operation Jonah. I think we may safely say that Dalton Burke will defect—if he gets a chance."

"What does that mean?" Flynn asked.

"It means they're guarding him like we guard our crown jewels."

"No doubt. What can we do now?"

"We're looking for a plausible excuse for the Burkes to go back to Holland. Once we get them there, we'll smuggle them out of the country and into England."

"Is it possible? Does Bando want more backup?"

"No, sir. He says the fewer in on this mission, the less chance for failure."

General Flynn dropped his head and was silent for a long moment. When he looked up, his eyes were quizzical. "Are you a praying man?"

"Well, after a fashion."

"That about describes me, and we're going to need God's help to do the impossible. The Nazis don't want to lose Burke. I have a feeling that if we can pull this off, it'll do more to win the war than anything else we'll touch."

★ ★ ★

Betje had been living with Gabby for a week. A fire had broken out in her apartment building, and the smoke damage had been considerable. The arrangement was working out fine. The two had been friends long enough that they knew each other's habits, and being together made it much easier for the cell to meet.

"This looks good, Gabby. I'm starved," Betje said as they sat down to a meal of kippers and shepherd's pie. As they finished eating, a knock sounded at the door. Betje picked up her pistol and went to the door. "Who is it?" she called out cautiously.

"It's me, Dai."

Betje opened the door, and Dai grinned when he saw the pistol. "A gun in your hand? What am I to think? And a smile on your face? Which am I to believe?"

She stepped aside so he could enter and put the gun down. Before he had time to protest, she put her arms around him and kissed him. "I'm glad you're back."

Gabby came into the living room when she heard his voice. She was so glad to see Dai that she ran toward him and wrapped her arms around him. "You're back, Dai! You're all right!"

"Yes, I am." He looked a little embarrassed at all the attention.

"I was so worried about you. Grandmother and I prayed for you every day you were gone," Gabby said.

"I appreciate that. I had some close calls, but I was able to see your relatives and deliver your letter," Dai said.

"I want to hear all about it, but you must be hungry," Gabby said. "There's plenty of supper left."

"I could eat a little."

Gabby warmed the food and listened as he told her and Betje in great detail about his mission. He dug into his meal. "This is good shepherd's pie," he said after the first bite. "Did you make it?"

"Yes."

"You're a good cook."

Gabby was pleased at his compliment but wanted to hear more about her aunt and uncle. "How are you going to get them out of Germany?"

"I'm working on that. It's complicated, since they have him guarded all the time. They do not want to lose him. It'll take something really believable for the Germans to let your uncle return to Holland."

When he had finished his meal, Dai got up, saying, "I'm tired. I'll see you ladies tomorrow." He left, and Gabby noticed the far-off look in Betje's eyes.

"Do you like him, Betje?" she asked quietly.

"I'd forgotten there were still decent men around," she said slowly. "He's got a gentleness beneath that tough exterior. I could love a man like that." She started to say more but stopped herself and said good-night.

As Gabby cleaned up the kitchen, she reflected on the evening. When Dai had come in, she had detected more than a casual interest in his eyes, even after Betje had thrown herself at him. "He cares for me," she whispered. "I know he does!"

★ ★ ★

Dai fell back into his work at the hospital, and no one seemed to have noticed his absence. He thought constantly on ways to get the Burkes back to the Netherlands, but he kept coming up with a total blank. He became glum and kept to himself a great deal.

Gabby had not seen Erik for a while, but he wrote her a tender letter expressing his love for her. *I know things look dark,* he had said, *but I can't believe that we won't be together. My love for you is so strong it will not be denied.* As Gabby read the letter, she realized that the feelings she had once felt for him were gone.

Gabby was catching up on some paper work in her office on Friday when the phone rang. She picked it up. "Dr. Winslow here."

"This is Matilda."

"Matilda, is something wrong?"

"It's Dorcas. She's unconscious."

"I'll be there at once with an ambulance." Gabby slammed the phone down and began issuing orders. She rode in the ambulance as they sped through the streets to Dorcas's house. Oskar was standing outside to direct the driver as soon as they pulled up in front of the house.

"How is she?" Gabby asked as she climbed out of the ambulance.

"She's still unconscious."

Rushing inside, she found Matilda wringing her hands, but she went straight to her great-aunt's room. At first she detected no movement from the small form on the bed, but when she got closer, she saw Dorcas's chest move slightly and gave a sigh of relief. Gabby examined her thoroughly, and when she listened to the heart, she knew that the woman's old problem had caught up with her. She had had heart problems over the past few years, and Gabby's medical training told her there was little to be done.

When Gabby removed the stethoscope, Dorcas opened her eyes.

"How do you feel, Grandmother?"

Dorcas moved her lips almost imperceptibly. "I will not . . . go to the . . . hospital," she said with some effort.

"But you must!" Gabby said. "We need the equipment we have there."

"No, my dear. My time has come . . . and I want to die at home . . . with my loved ones near."

★ ★ ★

Gabby did all she could to make Dorcas comfortable. On Saturday, the old woman was even weaker. Dai came to visit her, and he sat by her bed for a while, visiting quietly. At her request he sang hymns for her with his beautiful tenor voice, and then he read to her from the Bible.

When he said good-bye, he went to the kitchen to find Gabby and asked her if there was any hope for a recovery.

"None," Gabby said. "She's slipping away, and there's nothing we can do."

"She's hungry for heaven."

It was a strange phrase, perhaps an expression they used in Wales, she decided. "What a beautiful thing to say, Dai."

"She's a beautiful human being. I've never known anyone else like her—except for you, that is. You're a lot like her."

Gabby dropped her eyes and said, "That's a beautiful compliment."

★ ★ ★

The days went by, and Dorcas failed slowly but certainly. During one visit, she expressed concern for her son and daughter-in-law.

"Dai says Dalton and Liza will leave Germany as soon as they can convince the authorities to allow him to come home for a visit. We're hoping now they will let him come soon to see you, Grandmother," Gabby assured her. "Dai's doing everything he can to save them."

"Good. Then will they go to England until the war is over?"

"Yes, Grandmother. Dai has promised to see them to safety."

"God is so good, my dear. I have prayed for them, and God sent us Dai to help them."

Later that night Dai and Gabby were in the kitchen talking. "She's longing to go home," Gabby said. "She's made all the arrangements with the pastor."

"That's wise, but it's unusual, isn't it?"

"Yes, I guess so. She's got all the hymns picked out for the service, and she's chosen the text. I think she's even written out the sermon for Karel." She smiled faintly. "It would be like her." The two went to sit in the sickroom so they would be there when Dorcas awoke. They sat quietly until she stirred, and then both of them rose and went to the bedside.

She smiled up at them and said weakly, "I'm going to be with Jesus, so there will be no grieving."

"We'll be sad to see you go," Gabby said, "but we'll try to rejoice, knowing you're in heaven."

Dorcas nodded and closed her eyes.

When she opened them after a moment, Gabby said, "I know you're worried about Dalton—"

"Not anymore." Her grandmother reached out both hands, and Gabby and Dai each took one and held it. "They can't refuse to let him come home . . . for his mother's funeral."

"But, Grandmother—"

"It's the last thing I can do for him, and now I feel myself close to the Lord God. I will be safe in the arms of Jesus by morning." She squeezed their hands and then put her own on her chest. "You are my pride, Gabby, and it is not sinful to have pride like this." She took a couple shallow breaths. "You will serve the Lord, my precious child, all of your life."

She turned to face Dai, who leaned over to catch her

words, which were becoming more difficult to hear. "And you, my son . . . will watch over her and care for her . . . and see that she comes to no harm."

"I promise, Grandmother."

Dorcas spoke a few words of thanks and appreciation for Gabby to pass on to her grandmother's friends, and then she asked to see Matilda and then Oskar. She expressed gratitude to each one for their many years of service and friendship and then closed her eyes briefly, a peaceful smile on her face. "Now I am ready . . . to go and be with my Lord."

They all watched as she seemed to fall asleep.

"Is she gone?" Matilda whispered.

"No, she's sleeping."

They waited, but no one knew at exactly which moment Dorcas Burke went to be with Christ. She simply left in her sleep, a smile on her lips. When Gabby had not seen her chest rise for several minutes, she checked her pulse and said, "How well she endured her going forth."

Dai took Gabby's hand in both of his, and when she looked at him with a sad smile, she saw tears in his eyes.

★ ★ ★

Gabby was in Erik's office, telling him what had happened. "Dalton's mother is dead. I want to call him and tell him the sad news."

"Of course. I'll put the call through for you." Erik picked up the phone, and after some difficulty and after having spoken strictly to several underlings, he held the receiver out to her. "Here is your uncle."

"Uncle Dalton?"

"Yes."

"I have sad news."

"My mother, she's gone, isn't she?"

"I'm afraid so, Uncle."

"Did she have a peaceful death?"

"Yes. She died in her sleep with a smile on her face. Just

before she died, she spoke of you and her hope in Christ."

"That sounds like her. I'll do everything I can to get to the funeral."

"Yes, you must come. It will be the day after tomorrow at three o'clock."

"I'll get working on it right away."

"Good-bye, Uncle Dalton."

"Good-bye, my dear."

She handed the phone to Erik. "Thank you, Erik. That was kind of you."

"I'll be at the funeral. I'm sorry about your loss. I know you loved your grandmother dearly."

"Yes, I did. But I will see her again, Erik," she said with a broad smile. "I will definitely see her again."

CHAPTER EIGHTEEN

JESUS IS THE FRIEND OF SINNERS

★ ★ ★

Colonel Fritz Dietrich was sweating. His hands were unsteady, and he pulled at his collar trying to get more air. He had just endured a tongue-lashing from Joseph Goebbels that had left him weak. "But, Herr Goebbels, there's nothing we can do about this! He is determined, sir."

"It is your job to do something about it!" Goebbels said coldly. His small eyes were fixed on Dietrich, and he did not trouble himself to conceal his anger. "We cannot permit Burke to leave Germany!"

Dietrich swallowed hard. Ordinarily, he would not have thought of arguing with Goebbels, but now he had little choice. "He's a very mild man, Herr Goebbels. He's never made any demands whatsoever, and he's always been nothing but cooperative. But he's very upset over his mother's death."

"He cannot leave Germany."

"He has told me that if his mother's funeral takes place

without him, he will not be able to work."

Goebbels gritted his teeth and thought for a moment. "Very well. If you think it's the only way . . ."

"I do, sir, indeed! He has been most cooperative, but he apparently loved his mother a great deal. We cannot afford to upset him by denying his attending his mother's funeral."

"All right, but you will be in charge of the operation. I want the best squad of guards available. Major Claus Poppel will be in charge. We can't afford for anything to go wrong."

"Yes. Major Poppel is a good man indeed, sir. His loyalty to the führer is unquestionable. He will bring Professor Burke back."

"We will get Burke to Holland," Goebbels said, speaking his thoughts aloud, "just in time for the funeral, and then Poppel will bring him back on the plane at once. Burke is a simpleton, but we need to keep him in the dark. He needs to speak to as few of his countrymen as possible. You will give these instructions to Major Poppel."

"Yes, sir. All will go well, I assure you."

"It had better," Goebbels said, threat evident in his manner and his voice, "or you will suffer for it."

★ ★ ★

When the phone rang, Gabby picked it up at once. "Hello, this is Dr. Winslow."

"Gabby, this is Erik."

"Oh, Erik, have you heard anything about my uncle?"

"Yes, he is being flown in for the funeral by orders of the führer himself. You see, we are not the heartless monsters you think we are."

"We're all very grateful, Erik, especially to you."

"I'm afraid the visit must be very short. He must leave immediately after the funeral."

"He can't even spend one night here?"

"I'm afraid those are the arrangements. He will be taken to the funeral, and then he must return to Berlin at once. The work, you understand. It cannot be interrupted for long."

"Oh yes, I understand—and thank you very much, Erik. It will be good to see my uncle and aunt again, even under these circumstances."

Gabby put the phone back in the cradle. "It's all settled," she told Dai, "but my uncle and aunt will not be permitted to stay. They'll be taken from the funeral directly back to the plane."

"They don't want him speaking to anyone more than necessary. They like to keep their doings secret from people like your uncle."

"Can we do it, Dai? I mean get them away?" Gabby asked.

"You can believe that they will have a guard with them at all times, but with God as our helper we'll get them away to England." He took her hands in his and then put his arm around her and drew her close. As she clung to him, he whispered, "It will be all right. You'll see!"

★ ★ ★

The church was getting full, but there was still no sign of the Burkes. "Where are they?" Gabby whispered as Betje approached. She peered out the window again. "Erik said they would be here."

"The phone call just came," Betje answered. "The plane has landed, and they're on their way. I'll see you when it's all over."

"I'll be praying for you, Betje."

Betje hesitated, a strange look on her face. "It's odd, but ever since this operation has come up, I've been thinking about God."

Hope surged in Gabby's heart. She put her hand on Betje's. "I'm so glad to hear that," she whispered. "I think God has been after you for a long time."

"Then you'd better pray. I've been the world's worst sinner."

"Jesus is the friend of sinners, Betje."

Betje slipped away, and Gabby waited in the entryway until a large black car pulled up in front of the church. Gabby saw four men get out, three of them wearing the uniform of a storm trooper. But she had little interest in them. She started down the sidewalk and began to run when she saw Liza and Dalton emerge from the car. She threw herself at them, and the three clung to one another, all of them in tears.

Major Claus Poppel stood watching the reunion carefully. The other three men with him had spread out, their eyes darting back and forth as people arrived for the funeral. They were armed with automatic weapons, and they scanned the people making their way into the church, seeking anything out of order.

Erik Raeder had come in a separate car and now approached the tall man in charge. "Major Poppel, will you need extra guards on the return trip?"

Poppel's lips curled in disdain. "I think not, Colonel. Four of us can handle one elderly couple."

Rebuffed, Erik nodded curtly. "As you please, then."

Still clutched in an embrace, Gabby whispered to her aunt and uncle, "Don't be afraid. You won't be going back to Berlin." The three pulled apart, and without a glance at the guards, they entered the church.

★ ★ ★

The church was packed, with every seat filled and people standing along the walls. Major Poppel and the other guards had placed themselves in strategic positions within the sanctuary. Erik stood at the back, standing tall and listening intently to the service.

The music was simple old gospel hymns, all speaking of the love of God for the world and the sacrifice of Jesus for sinners.

When Pastor Citroen stood, his face was pale, but a joy shone in his eyes as he began to speak. "Funerals are usually a grim affair in which we are all saddened, but I want to speak to you this morning of one who insisted that her funeral be a celebration. Our beloved sister Dorcas Burke lived her entire life in the service of the Lord Jesus. The last thing she said to me was, 'I long for my heavenly husband, to be with Him forever and behold His glory.'"

The church was absolutely quiet as Citroen continued. "This morning, let me call to your remembrance another funeral as recorded in the twenty-sixth chapter of Matthew's Gospel:

> "Now when Jesus was in Bethany, in the house of Simon the leper, there came unto him a woman having an alabaster box of very precious ointment, and poured it on his head, as he sat at meat. But when his disciples saw it, they had indignation, saying, To what purpose is this waste? For this ointment might have been sold for much, and given to the poor.
>
> "When Jesus understood it, he said unto them, Why trouble ye the woman? for she hath wrought a good work upon me. For ye have the poor always with you, but me ye have not always. For in that she hath poured this ointment on my body, she did it for my burial.

"This incident occurred almost at the end of the earthly life of our Savior. The shadow of the cross lay before Him, and at this moment, it must have weighed heavily upon His spirit. He had spoken time and time again the words, 'Mine hour is not yet come,' but now His hour was almost come. And amidst the darkness of the last hours of the life of our Savior, this one incident shines as a light in a dark place. This woman, perhaps alone among the followers of Jesus, understood what was happening. And the Scripture tells us that she brought precious ointment worth much money, and she *wasted* it by pouring it on the head of Jesus. That was the accusation that was made. Some of the disciples complained that the ointment could have been sold for much money. It could have been sold and the money given to the poor.

"But the answer of Jesus was clear. 'She did it for my

burial,' He said. The Gospel of Mark states, 'She hath done what she could.'"

Citroen looked up and smiled. "Indeed, Dorcas Burke was much like this woman, and we might say, 'She hath done what she could.' From the time of childhood, she has served her Savior with all of her strength, and now she is in the presence of God and the holy angels."

For some time the minister spoke warmly of the good deeds of Dorcas, and finally he said, "The thirteenth verse says of the woman who poured the ointment on the head of Jesus, 'Wheresoever this gospel shall be preached in the whole world, there shall also this, that this woman hath done, be told for a memorial of her.'"

He closed his Bible. "This is the memorial of Dorcas Burke. She served the Lord Jesus, and she did what she could. She poured out her life in showing others His love and mercy. She poured out not ointment but her life and loyal service to Jesus. In our last conversation, she gave me some specific instructions regarding this service. She said, 'After you preach my funeral sermon, give an invitation to sinners.' At her request, I extend Jesus' invitation to you. He said, 'Come unto me, all ye that labour and are heavy laden, and I will give you rest.' If there sits one in the sound of my voice who does not know Jesus Christ, it takes but one cry for mercy, and then in that instant you come out of the kingdom of darkness and into the kingdom of life. You become a child of God, a servant of the Lord Jesus. Just one cry is all that is required.

"Pray with me now, won't you?" He bowed his head. "Oh, God, our immortal father, we are all sinners. We know that thy Son, Jesus Christ, died on the cross to erase these very sins from thy memory and ours. Forgive us. We are truly sorry and wish to turn away from our sinful ways. We invite Jesus to be Lord and Master of our lives now and forever. In Jesus' name we pray." He lifted his arms and continued praying. "We thank thee, Lord God, for the life of thy servant Dorcas. We thank thee that she gave herself as a living sacrifice for you, and now we pray that those who have committed their lives to thee even today might be servants of thine, obedient to the call of Jesus Christ. It is in His name we pray. Amen."

Citroen gave a few closing words and then told the crowd that there would be a ceremony at the graveyard adjacent to the church for those who cared to attend. The family filed out first, and the others followed.

As everyone gathered around the casket, Gabby's hand tucked into her uncle's arm, she caught sight of Betje, who she thought had left. She was not ten feet away, standing near the front of the crowd. Her eyes were fixed on the casket, and tears were running down her face. Suddenly, she lifted her eyes and met those of Gabby. Betje smiled through her tears, and her lips were trembling. She held up her right hand in the familiar V for victory sign that Churchill had made famous in England.

Gabby instantly knew that Betje had obeyed the call of the Savior to come! She had lost her harried look and smiled with shining eyes. Gabby said a silent prayer of thanksgiving as she returned her friend's smile.

Before Citroen prayed the final prayer over the grave, Betje suddenly turned and left.

After the prayer, Major Poppel appeared in front of the trio, saying, "I am sorry, Herr Burke, but we must hurry back."

The pair quickly hugged Gabby, but there was no time to say more than a brief farewell. The storm troopers were visible nearby in their dark uniforms, and the automatic weapons they carried seemed obscene at such a time.

Gabby caught her aunt's eye and nodded slightly, and her aunt smiled as she turned along with Dalton to get into the car. The troopers got in and then Poppel did, and the car pulled away. It picked up speed and threaded its way along the road rapidly, heading toward the airport.

★ ★ ★

Major Poppel's eyes were everywhere as they drove along the narrow road. It was Thursday, and they passed several slow trucks that were carrying produce into Amsterdam. Poppel snapped at the driver, "Lean on your horn! Get those fools out of the way!"

"Yes, Major!"

Poppel glanced back at the couple seated silently with two troopers in the rear and saw that they looked nervous. Poppel was a hardworking man whose abilities were usually put to much better use. This task was far beneath his capabilities, and it annoyed him that he had been asked to oversee it. He was anxious to get back to Berlin, where he could get on with the real work with the war.

"Major Poppel, look!"

Poppel felt the car slow and saw that they had entered a woods with tall trees lining both sides. The road was very narrow, and they were approaching a sagging load of hay pulled by two draft horses.

"What's the matter with those fools?"

"I think a wheel has come off the wagon," the driver said.

Poppel cursed, and as the car stopped, he leaped out. He pulled his Luger from the shiny black holster at his side and advanced toward the two men who were standing helplessly at the side of the road staring at the wheel.

"Get this wheel back on!" he ordered.

The two men were dressed like farmers and had on floppy hats, and both looked frightened at the sight of the major carrying a gun.

One of the men began speaking in a heavy Dutch dialect, which Poppel did not understand. He turned to the storm troopers and asked through the open windows, "Do any of you speak Dutch?"

None of them did, so Poppel addressed Dalton. "Herr Burke, come and speak to these men."

Dalton got out of the car and asked the men what the problem was. After they answered, he told the major, "They cannot lift the wagon enough to get the wheel on. They need a few more men."

Poppel glared at the two farmers and cursed under his breath. Then he waved at the guards in the car. "All right, all of you come. Get under this wagon and lift it up. Tell that man to have the wheel ready."

Dalton Burke gave the instructions, and the guards came forward.

"You will lift," Poppel said, "then these bumpkins can slip the wheel on. You tell the farmers what to do, Professor."

Dalton relayed the message, and the three storm troopers positioned themselves, along with one of the farmers, a young man with a frightened look on his face.

"All right—lift!" Poppel ordered, echoed by Dalton's instruction in Dutch. The men lifted the wagon clear, and Poppel shouted, "Put the wheel on, fool!"

But the man who held the wheel dropped it and pulled a machine pistol from under his shirt and pointed it at Major Poppel. "Don't move," he commanded in German. "Hold that wagon where it is, or I'll kill you!"

Poppel aimed his gun, but before he could squeeze off a shot, a black dot appeared on his forehead. The farmer needed only one shot. Poppel stared out of blank eyes for a moment before falling backward.

Instantly, more figures poured out of the woods, all armed with automatic weapons. The storm troopers froze as their own revolvers were yanked unceremoniously from their belts.

"Get that wheel on, then blindfold them and tie their hands," Dai instructed, for it was he who had killed the major.

"We'll have to move fast," Betje said as she emerged from the woods. "They'll be on to us quickly."

Liza got out of the car and clung to her husband when she saw that the situation was under control.

"It's all right," Betje said to the Burkes, who were both trembling. "We're going to take you to a safe hiding place."

"But what about all this?" Burke said in bewilderment, waving at the dead major and the guards, who were now being tied.

"We'll have to get rid of the car and hold them until you're out of the country."

"I'll take care of that, Betje," Dai said.

"That's not what we planned," Betje said. "You'd make a rotten husband." She smiled suddenly at Dai. "You can't take orders from a woman. Do as I say. I know this country like the back of my hand, but you need to take care of these people."

Dai smiled. "You're a quarrelsome woman, but you know best. Be sure you hide this car well and get rid of any traces of this scuffle." He looked at the dead body of Poppel and shook his head. "He would have it no other way."

A small car had pulled up behind the one that had brought the Burkes from the airport. "Get in the back," Dai told the Burkes. "Come on. We've got to go."

"Where are we going?" Liza asked timidly.

"We're going to the hospital," he said as he switched places with the driver. "You'll see Gabby there."

* * *

Dai and the Burkes entered the hospital by a back entrance that Dai had learned was rarely used. "Hurry quickly," he told them.

Inside they found themselves in a large, dank storage room. Dai pulled the light on and said, "You'll be safe here for a while."

"The danger isn't over, is it?" Dalton asked.

"I'm afraid not, Dr. Burke. We still have to get you out of Holland—and you can believe they'll throw a ring of iron around this area when they find out what's happened."

"But God has brought us safe this far," Liza said. "He will not let us down."

The three settled down to wait nervously, and time crept on interminably. Late in the afternoon, they heard someone approaching on foot.

"Over there," Dai instructed Dalton and Liza as he

pulled out his pistol. "Get behind those crates."

The door opened and Gabby whispered, "Dai, are you there?"

"Yes, come in." As Gabby stepped inside, Dai could tell something serious had happened. "What's wrong?"

"It's . . . it's Betje. She's been caught. They have her at headquarters. Oh, Dai, they'll kill her!"

Dai opened his arms to her, and she stepped into them, quickly losing control of her emotions. As she wept, the Burkes came out of their hiding places.

"There's little we can do, Gabby," Dai said quietly. "I think you know that."

"I know, but she's—" She straightened up and dashed the tears from her eyes. "Dai, something happened to Betje at the funeral. When she was at the graveside, I could see that she was touched by the message deeply. There was a victory in her that I had never seen before, and she held her two fingers up like Churchill does."

"What did it mean?" he asked.

"I'm sure it means that she found Christ at the funeral."

Dai's eyes burned with tears of joy. "Thank God, for she will need Christ now more than ever."

★ ★ ★

General Rahn was furious. He blamed Erik for the events of the day, and Erik tried to defend himself by saying, "Major Poppel would have no help. I offered it, and he refused it. He is at fault."

"Easy enough to blame a dead man!" the general declared. "We'll settle that later. These people are still in the area." A grim smile touched his face. "We'll capture them, and it'll be quite a feather in my cap when the führer hears of it." He paced the length of the office. "Now, the woman that was captured. She must be made to talk."

Erik Raeder understood that the stories he had heard of torture being used on political prisoners were true. He had tried to put the thought of people suffering unspeakable horrors from the S.S. at the back of his mind, but now the reality had become unavoidable. He was a man of honor and courage and did not agree with the Nazis' brutal techniques, but as he stood in front of General Rahn, he knew there was no escape. "I would rather someone else do that job," he said. "I will conduct the search for the others."

"All right, Raeder. You find the others, and I will take care of the interrogation."

★ ★ ★

Shadows lay under Erik's eyes, Gabby saw, as she came into his office. For two days, Erik had conducted the most intensive search for the Burkes possible. "Erik, I've come to ask for your help."

"What is it, Gabby?" Erik's tone was short, and he gazed at her moodily.

"I need to see Betje van Dych."

"Why would you want to see her? She's a traitor and will pay for her crime."

"She's my friend. She has been since we were children. She had been living with me."

"That puts you under suspicion. Everyone that this woman knows is under suspicion for treason against the Fatherland."

"I can't help that. You're going to shoot her, aren't you?"

"She has been promised she can go free if she will reveal who her friends are."

"She'll never do that," Gabby said evenly.

"She's a stubborn woman. She will be put to death first thing tomorrow morning if she refuses to speak." He could not meet Gabby's eyes.

"Please, Erik, I'd like to see her."

Finally he said bitterly, "All right. You can see her."

"I want to take the pastor with me."

"Very well. I'll make out a pass." He took a form out of a drawer and signed it.

"Have you seen her, Erik?"

"No," he said sharply, "I haven't."

"We've heard that she's been tortured."

He didn't answer. He handed her the pass and said, "That will get you in for a brief visit."

He turned away from her, and Gabby, after one look at his back, said good-bye and left his office. She knew that he was a lost soul, and she grieved that a man of his potential should be destroyed for his blind allegiance to the Third Reich.

★ ★ ★

"You'll have fifteen minutes," the lieutenant told Gabby and Pastor Citroen. "She is a stubborn woman and a foolish one!" he said as he glared at Betje.

As soon as the guard was outside, Gabby moved swiftly to take Betje in her arms. The sight of her broke Gabby's heart, for the marks of the terrible torture she had endured were evident. She held her gently and found herself weeping. "Betje," she moaned, "I can't lose you now."

Betje rested for a moment in Gabby's arms, and then she drew back. Her face was marked, but there was peace in her smile. "It's all right now. If they had caught me before the funeral, it would have been awful."

"What happened at the funeral, my sister?" Citroen said. He put his hand gently on her shoulder.

"When you gave the invitation according to Grandmother's desire, a light shined in my heart," Betje said simply. "I knew that I had been all wrong. It was like I had a vision of Jesus on the cross, and He seemed to be speaking to me. When you said, 'Come unto me, all ye that labour,' it was as if I had heard the voice of Christ, and I simply cried out to Him to forgive me." She smiled at Gabby. "It was so easy. I could have done it at any time, just like you had told me so many times before. He was waiting all the time, the Savior was."

"I'm so happy to hear that," the pastor said. "You're now a child of God."

Betje nodded vigorously, and Gabby gave her another quick hug.

"What about the Burkes?" Betje asked.

"We have them hidden in a safe place."

"Will you be able to get them out of the country?"

"Yes," Gabby said. "God will help us."

"Is there anything we can do for you, my sister?" Citroen asked gently.

"Tell them that I went out of this life into a far better one with my Savior."

This was so unlike Betje that Gabby could only marvel at the miracle that had taken place. The three stood talking for a time, and when the door rattled, they bowed their heads and prayed briefly.

"Good-bye," Citroen said, his hand on the door.

"I once heard that Christians never say good-bye," Betje said with a smile. "Think of me in the presence of the Savior."

The two left the jail and went directly to the hospital and found Dai. Karel left, and Gabby spoke of her meeting with Betje.

"They're going to execute her first thing tomorrow morning unless she gives them the names of the cell members," Gabby reported sadly. "She's ready to die for the cause."

"I'm sorry, Gabby."

"Did you love her, Dai? At times I thought you did."

"She intrigued me, but I didn't love her."

"She loved you."

"In her way she did, but we could never have been together. Betje was not the woman who was meant for me, nor I for her." He put his arms around Gabby and held her close. "You're the woman for me, Gabby, and I'm the man for you. But first," he said firmly, "we must get the Burkes to England—and that's going to be a tough one!"

PART FOUR

August–October 1940

★ ★ ★

CHAPTER NINETEEN

THE FUGITIVES

★ ★ ★

General Rahn's face was livid. His eyes flashed, and he stopped stomping around the office to point a finger at Erik as if it were a loaded gun. His voice filled the room and overflowed outside, where two guards grinned at each other, happy that someone besides them was getting severely reprimanded.

"This is all your fault, Raeder!" he shouted. "You have failed completely in your duty, and I have half a mind to strip you of your rank."

Erik Raeder stood stiffly at attention. His face was as pale as the general's was flushed, and he said with lips that barely moved, "You must do as you see fit, General."

Rahn came closer and glared up into Erik's eyes. "I don't like to do this, Erik," he said in a more reasonable voice. "Your father and I go back a long way. He would be terribly disappointed with you."

"I'm sure he would, sir. But may I remind you, I have repeatedly told you that this is not my kind of duty. I want to be sent to the front."

"As soon as this mess is cleared up, I assure you that's

exactly where I intend to send you!" he snapped. He stared out the window at some small, brightly colored birds perched on the telephone wires. He watched them for a moment as he tried to collect his thoughts; then he crossed to his chair and slumped down. "I've been talking with Herr Goebbels on the phone. He says the führer himself is aware of the situation here."

"I'd think he'd have more important things to occupy his mind, General."

"This *is* important! We must *not* let this man escape! What he has in his head could be worth more than a thousand tanks—so I expect better things from you."

"Yes, sir!"

Raeder left the room, marching stiffly, reeling from the fiery reprimand. Erik knew that part of his anger was directed at himself. He went over in his mind again and again how Gabrielle had led him on and used him. That was the thing that troubled him most. She had used him! "They won't get away," he fumed. "I'll find them if it takes every man we have in Holland!"

★ ★ ★

A knock at the door brought Dai instantly to his feet. He had been dozing in a chair, and now the revolver that had been resting in his lap seemed to leap into his hand. Stepping to one side of the door, he said, "Who is it?"

"It's me . . . Jan."

Slipping the bolt from the door, Dai put the revolver back into his belt and opened the door. Jan came in bearing a large box. "What have you got there, Jan?"

"Food." He put the box down on the table and looked around. He smiled at Gabby. "I'll bet you're hungry, aren't you, Doctor?"

"Yes, I am," she said. Actually, she was too frightened to think about food, but she wanted to put on a good face. "Come, Liza, let's see what we have here."

As the two women removed the food and two Thermos jugs from the box, Jan spoke nervously. He had always been a little high-strung, but now he seemed to have an especially hard time keeping still. He waved his hands constantly as he filled them in on the news. "The Germans are tearing the town apart. I've never seen anything like it."

"What do you mean by that, Jan?" Dai asked.

"They're searching the town house by house, tearing things apart. They came into our house this morning. They looked in every room, and they made a mess of it. They went up in the attic too. I think they've got every German soldier in the Netherlands looking for you."

"How long do you think it'll be before they get here?" Dai questioned.

"They're moving pretty fast. You'd better be out of here before tomorrow, I'd think."

"That means we'll have to leave tonight. I think that would be best."

"But even after dark they've got patrols out. I don't know how you're going to get away."

With the soldiers scouring the town, Dai Bando had no idea of what could be done. They were in a steel-tight trap and made an obvious target. The instant they stepped outside the hospital and tried to make a break for it, it would be nearly impossible to escape detection. If the Germans were as thorough as they usually were, there was a good chance they'd all be caught. Dai let none of his concern show, however. "Come back just before dark, Jan, and let us know if anything has changed." He made himself smile. "It'll be all right. We'll make it."

* * *

The four fugitives knew they were facing a long and difficult night, so they all tried to get some sleep. On a previous trip, Jan had provided them with some blankets and pillows, and they made themselves as comfortable as possible. The food and hot coffee had helped a little, but as Gabby lay still, she heard Dalton whisper, "It's all my fault. I should never have gotten you into this."

"You didn't create the horrors of the Nazis," Liza whispered back.

"If we can just get out of here, I'll do all I can to stop them."

Liza was quiet for a moment and then said, "We must pray, Dalton. That's all we can do at this time. But God will help us."

Finally, Dalton and Liza stopped talking and dropped off to sleep. Gabby heard their breathing grow slow and regular. She herself was too strung out to sleep, so she sat up and saw that Dai was also sitting up, his back to the wall. She got up stiffly and stretched and then walked over to him.

"Here, sit down beside me," he said. "We can rest together." She sat down, and Dai put his arm around her. It felt good and comforting, and she leaned over, enjoying the warmth of his strong body. "It's good to have someone to lean on," she murmured.

"Lean on me," he said. "It sounds like one of those country western songs the Americans like so much."

The two sat there quietly, listening to the steady breathing of Gabby's aunt and uncle. After a time, a dog began barking shrilly outside.

Dai stiffened. "That could be one of the German guard dogs." Gabby squeezed his arm as they waited, their bodies tense. It sounded like the dog was coming closer, and then suddenly it fell silent. Gabby could feel her heart beating and wanted to shut her eyes, as if to block out the trouble that could come, but she did not.

"I guess it was just a dog barking at the moon," Dai murmured. He looked down at her and smiled. "We'll be telling about this night for a long time. It's one of those things you don't forget."

"Do you really think so?"

"Sure. It'll be exciting to tell our grandchildren how we outwitted the German army."

"I can't think about grandchildren at a time like this. I can't even think about having children."

"You want children, don't you?"

"Yes, of course." She released her grip on his arm, embarrassed that she had squeezed it so hard. "Don't you?" Dai made a strange nose, and she realized he was stifling a laugh. "What's so funny?" she demanded.

"I'd probably make the world's dumbest father—and the world's dumbest husband too."

"I don't believe that."

"Well, I suppose there are some things I'll have to learn by trial and error."

The two fell back into silence, and Gabby was pleasantly aware of the warmth of his body and the feeling of safety that he gave her. Although she sat still, her mind was racing with thoughts of all that had happened. "I can't stop thinking about Betje," she told him.

"Neither can I."

"She had so much to live for, and now she's gone."

"Not really. She's with the Lord now."

"That's right, isn't it?"

Dai detected a change in her mood. "What is it?"

A smile turned the corners of her lips upward. "I was just thinking that Betje right now is probably saying to Grandmother, 'There, you see, I made it in spite of everything!'"

"You really think heaven's like that? Where people make jokes and talk about things just like we do on earth?"

"Oh, I don't know, Dai."

"Sometimes I get confused about heaven."

"How's that?"

"Well, the book of Revelation probably has the clearest pictures of it. Or at least the most vivid. But it sounds like the richest city on earth—walls of pearl and streets of gold and everything so ornate. Actually, I've never seen a city I thought was as pretty as a field of tulips."

"Why, I've had that same thought myself!" She laughed softly. "I think we're trapped in words. That's all we can use, so God gave us some beautiful imagery, but I'm sure heaven is better than anything we can even conceive of."

"That's a comforting thought."

The two talked some more about the dear woman Betje and Gabby had always called Grandmother, but soon the conversation turned serious again. "Let's pray about getting out of here alive, Dai."

"I'm already doing that."

"I mean together. You know the Scripture says if any two of you will agree on anything, it'll be done."

"All right, but I'm not very eloquent with prayer."

"I think that's probably a good thing. Let's just let God know what we want."

He took both of Gabby's hands in his own. They prayed silently for a while, and then she began to pray out loud. Her prayer was as simple and straightforward as she was herself. "God, you know who we are and where we are, and you know the danger we're facing. I ask that you get us all out of this trouble safely. In Jesus' name."

"Lord, I agree with Gabby on this," Dai said. "We can't do this by ourselves, but nothing is too difficult for you. So we come together and agree that this is the desire of our hearts. Let us make this escape with no loss of life, and we ask it in the name of Jesus."

"Amen," they said together.

"I think I'm going to sleep awhile," Gabby said. "Good night."

She went over to her blanket and lay down, and she fell asleep almost at once. But before long she woke up with a fresh idea in her mind. At first she rejected it and pushed it aside, but it came back even stronger. As she mulled it over, she realized that this was an answer to the prayer she and Dai had prayed. She let the thought take root, and soon it grew to a full-fledged plan.

Getting to her feet, Gabby said, "Wake up, everyone!"

"What is it?" Liza said, coming to her feet with a startled expression.

Dai and Dalton were also staring at her.

"It's time to go. We have to leave this place."

"Go where?" Dai asked quickly.

"I have never been quite certain of people who said, 'God told me to do this or that,' but I believe that after we prayed, Dai, God gave me an answer for our situation—and something to do."

"Who are we to dispute what God is telling you!" he exclaimed. "What is this plan of yours, Gabby?"

She began to explain, and they listened in silence. "Dai, the first part is up to you. You need to go to the other end of the hospital and get the ambulance. If you see the night-shift driver, tell him that Dr. Winslow asked you to make a special run to pick up a patient. Drive the ambulance around to this entrance, and we'll be waiting for you here. We'll all climb in the back, and you'll drive us to my grandmother's house." She went on, telling them what they'd do once they got to the house.

"Come on, then," Liza said firmly. "Let's do it."

While Dai left to get the ambulance, the others gathered the food they had left into a single sack and piled the blankets neatly in a corner. When they heard the knock they had agreed upon, they all slipped out the door and into the ambulance.

As Dai drove swiftly through the city, Gabby suddenly felt the pressure of her decision. She wanted to be reassured, and it was her uncle who provided the support she needed. "I'm glad you're here," he said quietly as he put his arm around her, warmth in his tone. "It's good to be in a crisis with someone that God speaks to." He squeezed her closer. "God always spoke with great clarity to my mother, and now it seems He's speaking to you in the same way."

[illegible] the place [illegible]

[illegible]

[illegible] Dorothy [illegible]

[illegible] to my [illegible]

[illegible]

CHAPTER TWENTY

"I WAS BORN FOR THIS!"

★ ★ ★

The moon was full as the party disembarked from the ambulance in front of Dorcas Burke's house. As Gabby glanced up and saw the rich fullness of the silver circle, she murmured, "It's a gypsy moon."

"What did you say?" Liza asked.

"Oh, nothing. Quick, we need to get inside."

Dai drove the ambulance several blocks down the street and around the corner before parking it and then sprinted back to the house. "We were lucky to get here without being seen," he said quietly, "but we need to get out of sight."

Gabby led them all to the back of the house. As she did, a dark figure suddenly appeared, startling her.

"Who is it?" a gruff voice said.

"It's me, Oskar—Gabby Winslow."

Oskar came forward, and Gabby saw that he was carrying a shotgun in his hands. He lowered it, and as the moonlight fell on his face, she saw him smile. "Ah, it is you!" he said. "I have been worried about you."

"We're all right, Oskar. What are you doing here?"

"I am taking care of the place until we know what to do."

He leaned forward suddenly and gasped. "Professor Burke, it is you!"

"Hello, Oskar." Burke shook the man's hand. "I'm glad to see you again."

"So, it is you they are looking for."

"The Germans? They've been here?" Dai asked.

"Down the street they are looking. They could come here soon, I think. You cannot stay here."

"We know that, Oskar," Gabby said. "I have a plan to disguise ourselves before we make our escape. I think I've come up with a workable way to escape right under the noses of the Germans."

"A disguise?" Oskar's tone was unbelieving, and he shook his head. "That will never work."

"I believe God's told me to do this, Oskar. All we need you to do is to play ignorant if the Germans question you."

He shrugged his bulky shoulders. "Of course. I will help in any way I can."

"If there's any food in the house that we could take with us, would you gather it together? If there's any dried fruit or beef jerky, that would be easy to carry. We won't be able to buy anything on the way."

Oskar screwed up his face and then asked with a voice tinged with worry, "Do you really think you can do this?"

"I was born for this," Gabby told the whole group with a face that was glowing with faith. "After all, I've always enjoyed acting, and . . . well, this will be the role of a lifetime!"

★ ★ ★

The group had planned to leave that night, but the morning was almost upon them. After a quick consultation, Gabby and Dai decided they would spend the day resting up and getting prepared and would leave the following night.

"That'll work as long as the Germans don't search the house," Dai said.

"We'll just have to hope they don't. Dai, why don't you and Dalton and Oskar put your heads together and see if you can work out an alternate plan."

"Well, the only thing I can think of right now is to go out the back door and run for it," he said, scratching his chin thoughtfully. "But we'll see what we can come up with."

"There's a loft in the barn. Maybe we could hide up there if they come here."

"I'm afraid that would be the first place they'd look."

★ ★ ★

With Oskar keeping a watch for any German search party in the neighborhood, the others tried to get some much-needed rest. Gabby didn't think she'd be able to relax with all that was going through her head, but eventually the exhaustion of the last few days caught up with her, and she slept solidly for a few hours.

When the others started to stir, Gabby asked Liza to help her, and the two went to the spare room Gabby had always used when she would visit her grandmother. She threw open the door of the closet and pulled out an assortment of German uniforms. When Erik had learned that she collected costumes of all types, he had asked her if she wanted some worn-out military uniforms, and she had jumped at the opportunity.

She and Liza sorted the uniforms into sizes on the bed. Dalton would fit the largest one they had, but they would have to turn the hem of the pants under so they weren't ridiculously long.

"Here, Liza, why don't you try this one on," Gabby said as she held up one of the smaller uniforms. Liza tried on the slacks, which were actually a pretty good fit, and then put on the tunic. It hung a little loose around her midsection, but other than that it was close to her size.

"I think I've got just the thing," Gabby said as she pulled out a dresser drawer. "Grandmother always kept extra winter clothes in here. . . ." She rummaged in the drawer until she found what she was looking for. "If we tie this around your waist"—she tied a woolen scarf around her aunt—"it'll help disguise the fact that you're a woman."

Liza checked her reflection in the mirror. "Not bad. Not bad at all."

"And with your hair cut short the way you've been wearing it recently, we won't have to do a thing with it."

"But what about yours?" Liza asked. "Are you just going to tuck it into a hat?"

"That was going to be my plan until I remembered this wig I got years ago." Gabby reached high into the closet and pulled out a box. "Do you remember the time I played the role of a man in that community theater production not long after I came to live with you? This is the wig I wore." She put her hair in a high ponytail and pulled the wig on.

"Of course I remember!" Liza helped Gabby stuff a few stray hairs into the wig. "That'll work."

"If you'll go get Uncle Dalton," Gabby said, "I'll get started on his makeup. The Germans probably have a good description of him, so we're going to have to change his appearance enough that they don't recognize him."

While Liza went to get her husband, Gabby got out her theatrical makeup, as well as her putty and fake hair. When Liza returned with Dalton, Gabby sat Dalton down and pulled another chair close for herself.

"I'd like to give you a slightly bigger nose and bushier eyebrows," Gabby explained. "How does that sound?"

"It doesn't sound very attractive," he said with a grin, "but I'll do what I need to do to get past the Germans."

"Excellent. Aunt Liza, while we're doing this, do you want to take that other uniform down to Dai and see if it'll work for him?"

"Sure. And then I'm going to look through your collection of boots and make sure we've got the right sizes for everyone."

"Good," Gabby said. "I had almost forgotten about shoes. And then when I'm done with Dalton's makeup, I'll give you and me some more masculine eyebrows and maybe a little stubble of a beard."

Gabby turned her attention to her uncle. She molded a small piece of putty and gave it a trial fitting on his nose, and when she was satisfied that it wasn't too big or unusual looking, she dabbed a little spirit gum on his nose and applied the putty, working it until it was smooth and nearly seamless. Next she got to work on his eyebrows, working in some white hair along with some slightly longer brown hair. Next she took out some foundation from a small bag and carefully applied it all over Dalton's face and neck, giving special attention to his new nose.

"Done! What do you think?" she asked as she stood him in front of the mirror.

"I hardly recognize myself! I had forgotten how good you were with your stage makeup."

"Thank you. Once we get you in a German uniform, I don't think anyone will have a chance of recognizing you."

★ ★ ★

As Gabby finally got into her own uniform, she fingered the necklace she had worn for so many years, thinking about the old woman who had given it to her. It gave her a warm feeling to remember the woman's prayers. She would never forget what Madame Jana had said, *"Jesus will make a way for you through the danger."*

She checked her uniform in the mirror and pulled on her hat. With her freshly stubbled jaw and slightly bushier eyebrows, she was pleased with her masculine appearance. She dug deep into the closet and found two old military knapsacks and a couple of canteens Erik had given her to use in one of the skits at the orphanage. She took them into her grandmother's bedroom and stuffed one of the knapsacks with light blankets.

She took a deep breath and then joined the others, who were making their last-minute preparations. "How do I look?" she asked.

"You look like a German soldier," Dai said as he looked her over in amazement.

"And so do all of you," Gabby stated with satisfaction.

Gabby handed the empty knapsack to Oskar. "We can put food and water for the journey in here." They went to the kitchen, where he filled the knapsack while Gabby put water in the canteens.

"I hope this is enough food for the four of you," he said.

"I'm sure it will be," Gabby said as she put the lid on a canteen. "I forgot to ask you if you've heard from Matilda."

"Yes, she is staying with her sister. She is very sad, as we all are, that Madam died."

"We all miss her," Gabby said gently. She put her arms around the man and hugged him. "Thank you so much for helping us. You've been a faithful friend all these years. I'll come back and see you when this is all over."

"I guess we're ready," she said as the rest of the group joined them in the kitchen.

"Let's pray, and then we'll be on our way," Dalton said.

After they finished praying that God would protect and guide them, Dalton came forward and shook hands with Oskar. "I hope you don't mind staying here at Mother's house. I want to come back to it after the war is over. I don't know what I was thinking when I sold my house."

"Ja, I will stay here. And God go with you all."

They all murmured their good-byes, and then they slipped out the back door into the night. They stayed against the house until they were sure no soldiers were nearby, and then they moved down the street.

"It's such a beautiful night, Dai," Gabby said. "I wish we were on a less dangerous mission."

"We'll make it," he said. "You'll have to help me with directions. We'll want to stay on the least-traveled roads."

"I know. Go on up to where the road forks and turn right."

"I wish it were raining and miserable," he said after they had walked several blocks.

"Why? I think the light of the moon makes it much easier to see."

"It does, but if it were raining, the Germans would be less watchful."

The two were relieved when they had made it out of the city and into the countryside. "We don't have to worry much about these country roads, I suppose. We're more likely to have trouble at the checkpoints."

"Our first checkpoint should be fairly easy," Gabby said. "They've been working on one of the main roads, and I've had to pass it several times going to the hospital. There are usually only two privates there—no officers. I don't think they're expecting anything. They just waved me by after the first time I went through."

"I hope that's the case tonight."

★ ★ ★

"The checkpoint is just ahead there," Gabby said. It was just before sunrise, and they had paused once to rest and eat a bite of breakfast.

"There are just two guards, you say?" Dai asked.

"Yes, usually only two."

"I may have to kill them."

Gabby was caught by surprise. She stared at him and saw that he was deadly serious. "I hope not."

"So do I, but we've got to get through."

As they got closer, they stood up straight and walked with authority. The checkpoint was simple enough. There was no gate, but two German privates had built themselves a shelter, and now they were cooking up some breakfast over a fire. As they approached, they heard one of them say, "Look, Heinrich, someone's coming."

As they came closer, the taller of the two, the one named Heinrich, said, "You fellows wanna play some cards?"

Dai was the one to answer, as they had planned. "Sorry, guys, we haven't got time today."

"Aw, surely you can spare twenty minutes. There's not much going on around here."

"Maybe on our way back this afternoon," Dai said as they all passed the shelter.

"Okay, then. See you later."

Gabby didn't exhale until they were well past the checkpoint. "Whew," she said, "that was easy, but my heart was pounding so hard I thought they might hear it!"

"Mine too," Liza agreed. "I feel like a man in this getup, but I was worried anyway."

"Gabby did a good job of turning you into a German soldier," Dalton teased as he put his arm around her shoulder.

"I don't see anyone nearby," Gabby said, "but we should probably play it safe and assume that we're being watched."

"You're right, Gabby. I was so relieved at getting through the first checkpoint that I lost my head for a moment."

★ ★ ★

That evening, they ate dinner by a small stream sheltered by some bushes. They were exhausted, and their feet ached from walking all day, but they were relieved and felt they could let their guard down a little when darkness closed in.

After they cleaned up after dinner, Liza and Dalton got comfortable on a blanket. They had another one gathered at their feet, but for the moment they were comfortable without one over them.

Gabby and Dai pulled out the map he had brought, and they studied it by the light of a candle.

"Where are we going, Dai?"

"If I were going alone, I would cut across country, but with the four of us together, I think we should stick to the roads." He put his finger on the map. "We're going right here."

She leaned forward and squinted. "It's right on the coast."

"Yes, it's a little place called Katwijk aan Zee. I guess that means Katwijk on the sea."

"Why'd you choose that place?"

"Well, it's isolated, and the water's deep enough for a sub to come in to within a kilometer of the shore."

Gabby traced a logical route with her finger. "We'll have to stay on the road all the way."

"Right, and when General Rahn figures out that we're not in the area around Amsterdam, he'll have all the roads watched—probably already has."

The two talked about possible alternate routes for a time, but they concluded the most direct route was probably as good as any. Dai folded the map and put it in his pocket. They leaned back on their hands and looked up at the clear sky. She pointed out some of the constellations that she recognized, and they watched as a small cloud slowly passed overhead.

"Are you cold?" he asked.

"No, I'm fine."

For a time the two were quiet, and then the ghostly sound of an owl cut through the silence. Gabby shivered and said, "I don't understand how we're going to find that submarine. And you never did tell me how you managed to arrange for a submarine to pick us up, of all things!"

"I don't think you've ever understood how important your uncle is. There isn't a country in Europe that wouldn't like to get him working for their cause in the war. Some very high people in the British navy were more than willing to divert a submarine to pick us up."

"That's incredible," she said. "I never dreamed England would put such an effort into getting him out of the Netherlands."

"Anyway, the plan is to meet the submarine a kilometer straight off shore from the lighthouse at Katwijk. I've made contact with a fisherman who'll take us out to the rendezvous area, and then the sub is supposed to pick us up at midnight on September second."

"Can you send them a radio message if we're not there right on time?"

"It would be better if we didn't. The Germans could pick it up, but we may have to if we get delayed any."

Dai moved closer to her. He reached over and picked up her hand, and then to her surprise he kissed it.

"How sweet," she whispered. She leaned over and kissed his cheek. "When this is over, I want you to court me."

"Court you?"

"Yes, you know, send me flowers and candy, and I want you to write me a love poem."

He laughed softly and put his arm around her. "I'll buy a guitar and learn to play it. Then I can sing you love songs."

The two sat there beneath the gypsy moon, as they now referred to a full moon, holding each other, not certain of what the day would bring, but knowing that they were together, and that was enough for the time being.

CHAPTER TWENTY-ONE

On the Road

★ ★ ★

Dalton Burke woke up with a stiff back. He shifted himself slightly, trying to keep from awakening Liza, who lay beside him. Accustomed to comfortable beds, Dalton had not easily found a comfortable position the night before, and it had taken some time to drop off into a fitful sleep.

The gentle warbling of a bird came floating through the air, and Dalton decided it was a mourning dove. He had always liked doves, and he had missed them when he lived in the big city of Berlin. In Holland, he had made a practice of tossing grain to the flock that gathered every morning in their garden. He always loved to awaken to their soft chirping voices.

Opening his eyes slowly, Dalton saw that the pale light of the morning sun was filtering through the branches. He watched the tiny particles of dust as they danced in the beams and, as always, wondered at the miracle of God, who he was sure knew the exact location of each tiny mote. He was a deeply religious man—not one who showed his religion a great deal outwardly, but one who loved God and saw Him in the far-flung cosmos stretched out on the evening sky and in the tiniest world of atomic particles, swirling about in a mysterious divine dance.

Liza stirred beside him, and he lay still, hoping she would go back to sleep, but she put out her arm and laid it across his chest.

"You didn't sleep well, did you, dear?" she asked.

"Oh, it wasn't too bad. I had a good dream."

Liza moved closer to him. "What was it?"

"I dreamed about the time we went to Switzerland and rented that little chalet. Do you remember?"

"Yes, that was one of our best vacations. I wish we could go back and do that again, but I don't suppose we can."

"Why not? When the war is over, we'll do it. Maybe we can get the same chalet." He rolled over to face her and touched her face gently. "You're still the same sweetheart I loved back in those days."

They lay quietly holding each other, listening to the birds and the light wind stirring the branches.

The two dozed off for a few minutes, and then Dalton heard Gabby and Dai talking quietly as they scurried around. Dalton checked to see if Liza's eyes were open. "I've thought about those two a lot—Gabby and Dai, I mean. I remember what you said about them falling in love, and I think you're right."

Liza smiled in the growing light of the morning sun. "It would be a wonderful thing for Gabby. She was born to be a wife and a mother."

Dalton lay quietly savoring the moment. He did not like adventures, and the thought of the danger that lay before them was heavy on his mind. "I've made such a mess of things," he told his wife. "I wish I could do it over again. I've ruined our lives."

"You've done no such thing. We're going to get out of this, and you're going to do great things for England. You're going to help win the war."

"I wish I could think that."

"'The steps of a good man are ordered by the Lord,'" she quoted, "'and He delighteth in his way. Though he fall, he shall not be utterly cast down: for the Lord upholdeth him with His hand.'"

"That's a wonderful passage, but sometimes people make such a mess out of their lives that I wonder if even God can straighten it up."

"In Proverbs twenty-four it says, 'For a just man falleth seven times, and riseth up again.' We've got to believe God that we're going to get out of this, and that Dai and Gabby will find a wonderful life together."

"You're a comfort to me, Liza. Indeed you are."

They were interrupted by Gabby's gentle wake-up call. "Time to get up. Breakfast is almost ready."

Liza and Dalton had slept with their clothes on. Now they pulled on their boots and got up, moving rather stiffly.

"We've got dried beef and raisins and plenty of bread to fill you up," Gabby said with a smile as they settled into a small circle on the ground. The breakfast cheered them all up, and they enjoyed the warm sun and good company.

"We've got to get moving," Dai said when they had finished. "I think walking will help us all get the stiffness out of our bones."

"Yes," Liza agreed. "It'll be good for us."

"All right. If we run into any Germans, remember to let me do all the talking," Dai instructed. "I think my German accent is almost as good as Dalton's, and they probably haven't figured out yet that I'm helping him escape."

They all nodded their agreement.

"And, women, try as best as you can to keep your distance from any guards. You look like men from a distance, but up close you still look pretty feminine." He grinned at Gabby and squeezed her hand briefly.

Both Gabby and Dai hoisted a knapsack onto their backs, and they headed south.

★ ★ ★

"This road isn't used much," Gabby said to Dai as they walked along the rutted road. He was holding her hand, but she noticed that his eyes moved constantly, never ceasing, and was glad for his constant vigilance.

He lifted her hand and kissed it, which pleased Gabby. "You're a demonstrative man. I'm glad of that. Some women have men who never show their love or speak of it."

"Oh, we Welsh are very romantic fellows," he said as he swung her hand high. "I'm working on that poem you said I was going to have to write for you."

"I look forward to hearing it. Meanwhile, say something nice. Pay me a compliment."

"All right," he said with a mischievous grin. "I'm glad you're not perfect."

"You call that a compliment?"

"Yes, I do. You're the earthy type. Just what I need. As a matter of fact, you remind me of a poem a fellow wrote a long time ago to his sweetheart. A fellow called Robert Herrick, who lived way back in the sixteenth century. It goes like this:

> "A sweet disorder in the dress
> Kindles in clothes a wantonness:
> A lawn about the shoulders thrown
> Into a fine distraction:
> An erring lace, which here and there
> Enthrals the crimson stomacher:
> A cuff neglectful, and thereby
> Ribbons to flow confusedly:
> A winning wave, deserving note,
> In the tempestuous petticoat:
> A careless shoe-string, in whose tie
> I see a wild civility:
> Do more bewitch me, than when art
> Is too precise in every part."

"So you like me because I'm a mess," Gabby said as she laughed.

"More or less. I think that the poem is true. I don't want

a woman who's all perfectly dressed and afraid to muss her hair."

Gabby patted her hat, which was pulled down over her wig.

"No, I would say you're just about rough enough for me. You do have a wild civility."

"I'm not sure that's a compliment."

"Of course it is. You've just got to learn to appreciate it." He stroked her hand. "I'm sure you've heard of the American poet named Walt Whitman?"

"Yes, of course."

"Your hand reminds me of what he said about hands. 'The narrowest hinge in my hand puts to scorn all machinery.' This joint right here"—he wiggled her thumb—"is a miracle to me."

"What else did Whitman say?"

"He said, 'A mouse is miracle enough to stagger sextillions of infidels.'"

"That's true, isn't it? All the scientists and all the laboratories that ever were couldn't begin to duplicate the amazing things God has created."

He pulled her hand up so he could examine it. "I love your hands, Gabby," he said, and then he put his arm around her. "They do good things, like healing and working hard to bless others. And they'll be good for loving a husband too."

Gabby felt content. She knew that her experience with men had not been good, but she believed, as they walked along the rutted road headed for danger, that she had found the man God had made for her.

They walked in silence past a field of windmills, and then they all grew tense as they approached a small town. Dai felt the hardness of the gun in his belt and hoped fervently that he would not have to use it. *It'll be much better if we can bluff our way through this,* he thought.

There were no more than a dozen or so shops scattered on one main street in the village. Houses, some with thatched roofs, formed other streets, all of which were quite narrow.

"I'm going into that shop to get something for supper tonight," Dai told the others. "You three stay a good distance away."

"All right," Gabby said. "Don't say any more than you have to."

Liza was desperate for a break. Her boots were not a good fit, and she had blisters on both feet.

Dai went into the store and picked out some fruit and canned meat, and after paying for them with some coins, he started for the door. As he did, he heard the roar of vehicles approaching. When he stepped outside, he saw a truck filled with German soldiers, and his heart constricted as an officer got out and walked straight toward him.

* * *

Oberleutnant Fritz Glassner was angry. He had been comfortable enough in Amsterdam enjoying the taverns and the good food. Now he had to scour bumpy country roads in an endless pursuit for some people who were trying to escape. He practically left his seat as they hit another pothole. "We're wasting our time chasing after this handful of trash, Sergeant," he said to his companion, "but orders are orders! These people must be important."

"I wonder what's so important about these people we're after," Karl Bentz responded.

Glassner grunted, "It's none of your business, Sergeant. You just drive the truck."

Bentz looked out his side window to hide his smile, for he knew that the officer had no answer. The truth was that a number of troops had been mustered and were beating every pig path in the vicinity of a hundred kilometers of Amsterdam. They had descriptions of the man they were most interested in, and all they knew was that it was important to bring him in alive. The people he was with were not so important.

They were approaching a village, and Bentz said, "Lieutenant, we've been going hard. Couldn't we stop and have some beer if there's any to be had in this village?"

"I suppose so, and I need some cigarettes. You watch over the men, and don't take more than twenty minutes."

"Yes, that should be enough, sir."

The truck stopped, and Glassner watched as the men trooped into the tavern to have a few drinks, led by the sergeant. He headed for the store to buy cigarettes, but when he got closer, he saw a soldier he didn't recognize coming out of the building.

★ ★ ★

Dai tried to angle away from the officer who was coming toward him, but the man said, "You, there, come here!" He had no choice but to turn.

"Yes, sir."

"What are you doing here? I thought my unit would be the only one passing through here today."

"Yes, sir. You're correct, sir. My commander told me there would be another unit coming through here, but we should keep to ourselves. We're on a special mission, and we need to keep moving, sir."

"Who is 'we,' soldier?"

"There are three others with me," he said as he pointed. "They're taking a much-needed rest while I buy supplies."

"Very well, soldier. Carry on."

Dai turned and moved swiftly toward the others.

Glassner watched them disappear down the road. He went inside and bought his cigarettes, and when he came out, he went to the tavern to join his men. The men were all drinking beer, and Sergeant Bentz came over to say, "Have a beer, Captain?"

"No! Get the men in the truck. We have work to do."

★ ★ ★

"What did he say, Dai?" Gabby asked. "I was worried about you."

"I told him we were on a special mission. That we needed to keep moving."

"Do you think he's suspicious?" Dalton asked.

"No, I think he believed my story."

"What a relief," Liza said. "I was afraid he would come over here and interrogate us. I can't seem to sound like a man, no matter how much I practice."

"I'm actually glad about that," Dalton said. "I like your voice just the way it is."

★ ★ ★

Later that evening, they were all getting tired and irritable as they walked into the night. They had taken a number of breaks throughout the day so Liza could rest her aching feet.

"Tell me about yourself," Gabby said, hoping to get Dai's mind off the situation.

"What do you want to know?"

"I know so little about you. Tell me about your first sweetheart."

He laughed. "You would want to know that."

"Tell me."

"Well, her name was Gorawen."

"What an ugly—I mean, what an unusual name!"

"Maybe to you, but it means joy in Welsh."

"How old were you?"

"I was fifteen, and she was the same age. We had the same birthday."

"Were you sweethearts long?"

"About six months, I think. Then she dropped me for an older boy named Evan Bryce. We had a terrible fight, which

I lost." He laughed aloud. "That's when I learned that all women are fickle."

"Not all."

"John Donne thought they were."

"You mean the poet?" she said. "I've always loved his poems."

"Do you know the one that goes like this?

"Go and catch a falling star,
Get with child a mandrake root,
Tell me where all past years are,
Or who cleft the devil's foot . . .

"I don't remember the rest of it, but he winds up by saying:

"Thou, when thou return'st, wilt tell me
All strange wonders that befell thee,
And swear
No where
Lives a woman true, and fair."

"I'd forgotten that one," Gabby said. "He must have been a cynical man."

"I think he was really two men. He was quite a womanizer in his early days, but later he became a very godly man."

"I don't like it, Dai. He shouldn't talk that way about women. You don't believe it, do you?"

"No, I don't."

He put his arms around her and pulled her close, and when he kissed her, she felt something different in him. "I see that I'm going to have quite a job on my hands educating you on the fair nature of women," she said lightly.

But Dai did not smile. "Will you have me, then?"

At that moment, trundling along a rutted road in Holland with danger imminent and life uncertain, Gabrielle Winslow knew that Dai was asking her something very important. She had to be sure. "Do you mean . . . forever?"

"Yes, forever."

"I'll have you, Dai Bando." She put her arms around him, and when he kissed her soundly, she knew that she had found her place. She was overwhelmed with her love for this man who had put himself in such danger to save her and her family. As they continued walking, she couldn't help but remember the group of gypsies she had encountered so long ago. *They said a full moon is when gypsy men and women fall in love. And here we are living like gypsies. They just might be right!*

She beamed with joy as they walked arm in arm. "Mrs. Bando . . ." she said, trying it on for size. "I don't know if I'll ever get used to being Mrs. Bando."

He stroked the back of her neck gently and smiled. "Maybe I'll take your name instead. I'll be Dai Winslow."

The two clung to each other, and both knew that their deep love would endure whatever the future held for them. "Someday we'll have children, "she whispered, "and when our daughter grows up, I'll tell her about the unusual way her father proposed, and how I told him I'd be his forever!"

CHAPTER TWENTY-TWO

PLANS GO WRONG

★ ★ ★

Carefully, Erik Raeder drew the razor down his cheek and then wiped the white foam off on a towel. He finished his shave methodically, put his shaving kit away, and slipped into his tunic. He paused to study a large map of the Netherlands on the wall. Slowly, he drew several circles with his finger around Amsterdam, getting larger each time. "They're still in this country," he murmured, "I know they are!"

He felt betrayed and humiliated by Gabrielle Winslow. She had deceived him somehow, and now as he stalked out of his quarters stiff-legged, his heels striking hard on the floor, he could not put the matter out of his mind.

He walked across the street toward the staff offices and wondered at himself. *Am I so fragile that a woman can destroy me?* The thought tormented him. He had not known that any human being could hurt him so badly—particularly a woman. Perhaps it was this that troubled him more than anything. His male pride was injured, and that made him feel vulnerable in a way he had never felt before.

The streets were quieter than usual. Ordinarily, trucks

filled with soldiers crowded the roads, but now it seemed they were all dispersed in every direction, spreading outward from Amsterdam looking for Dalton Burke. The matter had severe political and career connotations, and Raeder was sensitive to how this would affect him. He had received a sizzling phone call from his father, who had been coached, no doubt, by General Rahn, and Erik had had no defense for his harsh reprimand.

When he reached the buildings that held the staff headquarters, he found Oberleutnant Glassner waiting in his office. "What have you found, Glassner?"

Glassner blinked at the vicious tone of his superior officer. He had seen Colonel Raeder's anger growing since the affair had begun and had taken care to keep his distance from him whenever possible. "I'm sorry, Colonel, but—"

"But you've done nothing!"

"Colonel, we have a tremendous territory to cover, and our manpower is not unlimited. We're doing the best we can."

"Your best isn't good enough!" Erik exploded. He shouted for a few moments, halting only when General Rahn entered.

"Well, what news do you have for me?" Rahn demanded. "Have you found them yet?"

"No, sir, I'm afraid not," Erik said between tightly clenched teeth.

Rahn shook his head furiously. "They're keeping the phones hot from Berlin. The woods are on fire, man, don't you understand that?"

"Yes, sir, I understand it, but I can't promise any better results."

Rahn's face flushed, and his eyes narrowed. "We've got to do something. We've got to find that man. Do you understand me? He was on the verge of developing the most devastating weapon known to mankind. We can't let another country get their hands on his project!"

"Yes, sir, I understand you. Do you have any suggestions?"

"I suggest that you do your job. Use every man we have. Get the cooks out, every man that can walk, and do it now."

"Yes, sir," Erik said wearily as the general turned on his heel and left. "Come with me, Glassner!" he snapped.

★ ★ ★

Gabby pressed the heels of her hands against her eyes. Her lack of sound sleep was catching up to her. They had kept to the back roads as much as possible, but now they had been forced to take one that was more traveled. They were racing against time to reach Katwijk. The previous night they had stopped a good distance off the road, but the trucks and motorcycles and vehicles of the Germans had roared back and forth all night. Dai had shaken his head, saying, "If Liza's blisters don't get better soon, I don't see how we'll make it. We've got to make better time."

"I've tried everything I can think of to ease her pain, but there's no way to get around those awful boots."

"We'll just have to do the best we can and hope the submarine is waiting for us."

"We'll make it, Dai." Gabby reached over and put her hand on his arm. He turned to her and smiled. "God will see us through. Grandmother used to say that God doesn't sponsor failures."

"I like that."

"So do I. I keep remembering all the things my grandmother told me. It's amazing how her memory is still alive within me. And I still remember my mother, even though I was only five when I lost her."

"I suppose that's a kind of immortality," Dai mused. "We live on in what we tell our children and what they pass along to theirs."

"What a nice thought."

"That's about the end of my philosophy, I guess." He suddenly straightened up and stared down the roadway. "There's the village. There's sure to be a checkpoint there.

It's going to get harder to fool our way through them."

They turned around and waited for Liza and Dalton, who were walking several meters behind them.

"What is it?" Dalton asked. "Is there trouble?"

"A checkpoint ahead," Dai said.

"Let me check your makeup," Gabby said as she examined her uncle's nose. She got her foundation out of her knapsack and dabbed a little onto a spot that had faded. When she was satisfied that her uncle looked natural, she turned to Liza and decided she looked fine as well.

"Do I look okay, Liza?" she asked. "Do I still look like I need to shave?"

"You look good, Gabby," she said. "Just pull your cap down a little farther and you'll be fine."

The checkpoint was manned by an iron-eyed soldier who held a rifle in his hands. "Halt!" he cried out as the small group approached. "Who is your commanding officer, and what is your destination?"

Dai pulled a name out of the air and told him they were going to a small town not too far away.

"Be on your way, then."

"Thank you, sir."

"That was a close one," Dai said, releasing his breath when they were out of hearing distance.

"That German was not very thorough," Gabby said.

They walked on until a smaller road, obviously not used too often, led off to the left. "We'll take this," Dai said, "and we'll stay off the main road."

★ ★ ★

"I'm going to leave you here," Dai said. "I can hear the breakers. The village, according to my map, should be no more than a couple miles away."

"We'll be all right," Gabby said. Now that they were close to the coast, she felt encouraged. "You be careful. I wish you didn't have to go."

"I need to find my contact there—the fisherman who's going to take us out to the sub. I'm glad we got here a day early so we have plenty of time to come up with another plan if something happened to him." He pulled her into his arms. "I hate to leave the three of you without me. Here, you take the pistol."

"I wouldn't know what to do with it."

"If your life is on the line, I think you'll figure it out." He tightened his grasp and looked down into her eyes. "You're some woman, Gabrielle Winslow."

"And you're some man, Dai Bando."

They kissed, and then he released her and disappeared into the darkness. As she watched him head toward the village, a sinking feeling came over Gabby, but she straightened up and prayed a little prayer before going back to wait with the others.

★ ★ ★

The time passed slowly, but finally, after what seemed like many hours, Gabby heard someone approaching. She knew they were well hidden, but she was relieved when she heard Dai say, "It's me. I'm coming in."

They all gathered around him, and he laughed. "Well, you're not always this glad to see me."

"Did you find the man to help us, Dai? The man with the boat?"

Dai sobered and shook his head. "He almost got caught. I went to the local pub and listened in on some conversations. Apparently, someone told the Germans about him, and he left. If they had caught him, they would have shot him."

"So what do we do now?" Liza asked tremulously.

"I'll have to steal a boat."

"Do you know how to operate one?" Dalton asked dubiously. "I wouldn't know the first thing about it."

"If I don't, I'll soon learn."

"When will you go?" Gabby asked.

"I'll wait until tomorrow after dark. That should give us enough time to meet the sub at midnight."

Gabby wondered the same thing that the others did. *What if the submarine's not there?* But she said only, "It'll be all right. Come, you must be starving."

CHAPTER TWENTY-THREE

OUTBOARDS AND INBOARDS

★ ★ ★

Glancing toward the west, Dai decided he had waited as long as possible. The thin edge of the sun was still visible, but the shadows had fallen, and he knew he would have to make his move if they were going to make their rendezvous with the sub. He had figured the time closely and knew it would take about an hour to get back to where he had left Gabby and the others. Returning to the harbor would take even longer. He had no way of knowing whether the sub would be there, but he had made a grim resolve to be off the lighthouse well before midnight in case the sub arrived early.

The smell of the sea was strong as he walked along the edge of the beach. A few small dories were tied to docks, but the larger boats were down closer in a curve of the harbor. The town lay behind it, and he could hear the sound of music faintly coming through the falling darkness. Overhead, the seagulls were circling, hopeful for any scrap of food, but he did not glance up, and soon they flew away. The lapping of the waves at his feet made a sibilant sound, and he wished that the moon were not so bright. Total darkness would have been better for this kind of work.

He reached a boat that caught his interest, but when he saw that there was no motor, he moved on quickly. His knowledge of motors was more toward automobiles, but he had taken vacations several times where he did run both large outboards and inboards. The boats in this harbor, he knew, would be fishing boats, for this town was not a holiday port.

The music grew louder as he approached the edge of the town, and he froze as he saw two figures in the darkness about twenty meters ahead walking along the shore. He moved quickly and silently away, taking refuge behind a shed. As they got closer, he could see that it was a man and a woman with their arms around each other, and he waited until they passed on down the beach.

Returning to the shoreline, he reached a line of boats and began checking them. The first boat would have served perfectly, but it was chained and locked to a pier. The next boat was too large for him to handle, and just as he moved to the next, he suddenly froze, hearing voices in the distance. He paused to determine where the voices were coming from and then saw that it was a group of three people making their way down the beach. Dai drew back into the darkness, taking refuge in the shadow of a beached dory. As they came closer, he could hear them speaking Dutch.

"If the fishing doesn't pick up soon, I'm going to buy a farm."

"You couldn't be a farmer. It's too much work."

"Nothing's more work than fishing. You should know that."

The three men argued the matter, and Dai watched as their flashlight bobbed away, headed toward the town. As soon as the voices were completely inaudible, he slipped down to the boat and was relieved to see that it was simply tied with a heavy line. Scrambling aboard, he went at once to the stern and found that it had a single propeller. He pulled his flashlight from his pocket and made his way to the wheelhouse. He studied the controls and decided that they seemed simple enough, and he was tempted to try to start the engine. He hesitated but then decided, *I'll have to be able to get this thing started later tonight, and I'd better know how*. He manipulated the controls, threw the switch, and the engine burst into life at once. He let it run for only seconds before shutting it down.

He turned the light off and stood there waiting, but only the silence washed back from the town. A few gulls flew over, making their raucous calls, and then there was nothing.

It'll have to do, he thought. *I hate to steal a man's living, but I'm running out of options.*

★ ★ ★

When Dai returned to the woods where he had left the others, they descended on him immediately.

"Did you find a boat?" Dalton asked.

"Did anyone see you?" Gabby asked.

"Are there any soldiers in the vicinity?" Liza asked.

"I did find a boat, and no one saw me, and I didn't see any soldiers. Now we need to hurry. We'll leave everything here except the canteens."

"Shall we take the blankets?" Liza asked.

"No, we'll leave it all here."

"What about the boat?" Dalton asked. "Do you think you can operate it?"

"Well, I started it," Dai answered.

Dalton had more concerns. "Can you find the submarine in the dark?"

"I'm hoping they'll find us. Let's get moving. We'll have to hurry."

★ ★ ★

"Are these all the reports, Glassner?" Erik demanded.

"Yes, sir. They just came in."

"Is there anything in them?" Erik was shuffling the papers in his hand nervously. His anger had been replaced by bitterness.

"Nothing much, sir." Glassner shrugged. "Just the usual traffic on the roads."

Erik suddenly paused and held up one paper. "What's this?"

Glassner came to stand beside Erik. The two men were standing inside the office, and Glassner had to squint, being slightly nearsighted. "Oh, we ran into a group of four soldiers on a special assignment. One of them was buying supplies while the others rested. I told him we hadn't anticipated seeing anyone else in the area, but the soldier I talked to said they were just passing through."

"Did you ask him what their special assignment was?"

"No," Glassner said tersely, getting irritated over the interrogation. "It seemed innocent enough."

"Tell me what this soldier looked like."

"About my height, black hair, kind of a squarish face, cleft chin—"

"I knew it! I just knew it!"

"Knew what, sir?"

"That sounds exactly like one of the people we suspect is traveling with the man we're after. He works at the same hospital Gabby does—the man's niece—and he hasn't reported to work since this whole thing started."

"I'm a little confused, sir—"

"And you say there were three others with this soldier?"

"Yes, sir, I believe so."

"And did any of them look like women?"

"I couldn't say," Glassner said. "They were too far away, but they were all wearing uniforms."

"Show me on the map where you were," Erik demanded.

"It was right here," he said as he pointed to the small town.

"And this is only a few kilometers from the coast. . . ."

Erik said, thinking aloud. "We'll leave at once. Get a squad ready. See that they're all armed."

"They're ready, sir."

"Then let's go!"

★ ★ ★

Gabby was concerned about her uncle. He was breathing hard, for he rarely got any exercise. "Is it far, Dai?"

"No, just around the bend there."

"I don't think Uncle Dalton can make it much farther," she whispered.

"He won't have to. It's not far."

The party advanced until they emerged from the pathway that led to the town. "All right now, listen closely," Dai said. "From here on out I'll go first. The rest of you follow single file. Nobody makes a sound." He addressed Dalton. "Can you make it, sir?"

"Yes, I'm all right. Just out of wind."

"You can rest on the boat. Come along now as silently as you can."

Dai moved across the open beach until he reached the shoreline, then turned to his left. He glanced back and saw that the others were following him. He dared not show a light, so he whispered, "Stay close."

He could not hear the music from the city now and knew that it was after ten o'clock. He did not know whether the Germans kept patrols out in this small village, but he could take no chances.

The wet sand under his feet made a slight screeching sound as he moved along, and from time to time, he glanced back to see that the others were following close behind. He had asked Gabby to bring up the rear, but it was too dark to see her.

Finally, he reached the first of the boats and turned to whisper, "All right. Very quietly now. Come closer."

Dai led them around the curving shore until he reached

the boat. "This is it," he whispered. "Everyone get aboard."

Dai helped Liza climb on first, and then he gave Dalton and Gabby a hand. He looked around and said, "All of you get in the cabin. I'll cast the lines off."

He waited until all were inside and then leaped to the sand. Just as he did, a voice suddenly came out of the darkness speaking in German. "Who goes?"

"Hans Kreigan," Dai said, giving the first name that popped into his head.

"What are you doing here this late?"

The soldier flashed his light on Dai. "I have to get my engine fixed to be off with the tide," he said and waited as the German came closer. The German, he saw, had a rifle and held it loosely. "This engine is a pain," he continued. "It won't work half the time."

The German came closer, peering at Dai. He suddenly stopped and said, "You don't look like a fisherman!" He started to lift the rifle, but quicker than his movement, Dai leaped forward. His fist caught the German squarely in the jaw, harder than he had ever struck a man. The soldier fell backward, but he was still moving, so Dai struck him again until he fell silent. Quickly, Dai grabbed the rifle and leaped back into the boat.

"Who was that?" Gabby whispered, sticking her head out of the cabin.

"Sentry. We've got to get out of here now!"

He started the engine and gave a grateful sigh that it started so easily. Maneuvering the controls, he found reverse and backed the boat out into the water. As soon as he was clear of the other fishing boats, he turned and headed out away from the shore.

"But they'll find him, won't they?" Liza said fearfully as she and Dalton joined them on deck.

"Yes, and they'll find this boat missing too, but by that time the sub should be there."

"I don't understand how we'll find them," Dalton said.

"You see that lighthouse?"

They all peered forward. A dim light flickered, and

Gabby said, "Is that the one we're looking for?"

"It's the only one on this part of the coast. We'll be a kilometer off shore exactly even with that lighthouse. I don't know the latitude or the longitude, but that sub will be looking for us. At midnight tonight we'll light our lantern so they can see us."

"What if they're not there?" Liza whispered fearfully.

Dai did not answer, and the others also remained silent. Gabby came to stand beside Dai and touched his arm. "It will be there," she said confidently.

He turned to smile at her. "I believe it will."

CHAPTER TWENTY-FOUR

A Question of Love

★ ★ ★

As soon as the car braked to a halt, Erik leaped out, followed quickly by Glassner. They had reached Katwijk in record time, and the eight soldiers in the truck piled out and formed a line by the sergeant.

"Who goes there?" A soldier approached with a light on the party, and when he saw the colonel, he gasped and said, "I didn't—"

"Sergeant, we have reason to believe the fugitive we've been seeking is in this area."

"But, Colonel, we've searched everywhere."

"Have you checked the boats?"

"Yes, sir, just before dark."

"We'll check them again."

"Yes, sir! Come this way, Colonel."

Erik followed the sergeant, and when they reached the harbor, they turned and made their way along the beach. The sergeant said nothing until he practically stumbled over a form on the sand. "Sir, there's somebody on the ground!"

"Who is it?"

He bent over and said, "It's Private Mueller." He pulled

the man halfway to a sitting position. "Mueller, are you awake?"

"Is he dead?" Erik said as he knelt by his head.

"No, sir, just unconscious. I think he's coming out of it."

"Bring some water in your helmet, soldier," Erik commanded. One of the privates quickly ran to the shoreline and scooped his helmet full of water. "Pour it on his face," Erik commanded.

The soldier sputtered and shook his head to avoid the briny water. He blinked into the light and tried to get up.

"Mueller," the sergeant said, "what happened?"

The man looked at the small group gathered around him. "There was a man . . . in the boat." He pointed to where the boat had been. "The boat—it's gone!"

"What did the man look like?"

The soldier reached up and touched his mouth, which was still bleeding. "He was wearing a German uniform. I couldn't figure out why a soldier would be in a fishing boat."

"It's them," Erik said. "We need to commandeer the fastest boat in the harbor."

"That would be the one right down there. It belongs to—"

"I don't care who it belongs to. Can you operate it? Get someone here who knows boats."

"One of my men is a fisherman, sir."

"He'll do."

Quickly, Erik issued orders to the lieutenant. "I'll take this boat, Glassner, along with the driver and two others. You and the rest of the men round up as many boats as you can, and we'll throw a web around the area. There's only one marker here that can be seen at night."

"Yes, sir. What's that?"

"That lighthouse there. So they'll be making for that, I'm sure. But search the whole area. You take everything in that direction," he said as he pointed, "and I'll go the other way. They're out in those waters somewhere."

Erik turned his attention to the wounded man. "Do you

have any idea of how long you were unconscious? When were you on guard, soldier?"

"I don't think I've been out more than an hour, sir."

"Excellent. We might still have a chance."

Erik and the three soldiers quickly made their way to the boat. Before long the engine was sputtering to life, and they were heading out into the choppy waters.

"Head for that lighthouse! Everybody keep your eyes open. They won't have a light, but the moon's bright tonight. If we're on the right track, we should be able to see them."

As the boat surged ahead, Erik Raeder stood in the bow. His eyes glittered in the light of the moon. "I'll get them," he promised himself. "They won't get away."

★ ★ ★

All was quiet on the sea, and the moon lit the faces of the party, who were all on deck now, watching for interference.

Gabby watched as the lighthouse flashed its light, moving slowly in a circle, over the ocean. "How do we know we're far enough out, Dai?"

"I'll just have to make a guess. The plan was to be a kilometer off shore, but if that sub comes up, they'll see us." He had found a lantern and attached it to the top of the mast. It was not a bright light, but if they were in the vicinity, a sub should be able to spot it.

"What time is it?" Liza said nervously.

"Four minutes after eleven," Dai said, glancing at his watch. "The sub should pick us up at midnight."

The boat rocked gently from side to side, and the air was cold. "I hear something," Liza said.

Dai listened intently. "So do I."

"Is it the sub?" Dalton cried anxiously.

Dai did not answer, but he had seen a dim light approaching from a distance. "No, it's not a sub," he said. "It's a boat."

"What'll we do?" Gabby whispered. "Can we outrun them?"

"No, we'll take the light down, but they've probably already seen it, since we've seen theirs."

Quickly, he mounted the mast and blew out the light. "It's coming quick," he said as he jumped onto the deck. "I can hear the engines clearly now."

They all stood frozen, and Gabby tried valiantly to fight down her fear. *We can't come this close and then be lost,* she thought. *God, save us in this terrible hour!*

The light grew larger, and Dai said grimly, "It must be a search boat out looking for us. No fisherman would be out at this time of the night." He reached over and squeezed Gabby's arm. "I'm sorry about this, Gabby."

"It's not your fault. You've done everything you could to try to save us. No matter what happens, we're grateful."

"Maybe you're wrong. Maybe it's not a German. Maybe it's a fisherman out late," Liza said hopefully.

Her hopes were soon dashed when the engines grew louder and then over the water came a loud command in German. "You on the boat, throw your weapons down! You cannot get away! Soldiers, fire if any one of them resists."

"That's it," Dai said quietly as bitterness overcame him. To come so close and then to lose! He had known hard times and bitter moments before, but none quite like this one. He watched as the boat appeared and the German soldiers with their rifles raised became visible. "I'm sorry, Dalton," he said to the man who now stood at his elbow.

"You did very well, son. You cannot fault yourself."

"All of you put your hands in the air."

Gabby took a quick breath when she recognized Erik's voice. She obeyed, as did the others, and when the larger boat came alongside, she watched as Erik crossed over to their boat, followed by two soldiers with automatic weapons.

"So, I believe this must be Professor Dalton Burke," Erik said as he stood in front of Dalton. He had drawn a Luger from his holster but kept it lowered.

"Yes, I am Dalton Burke."

Erik stared at the man who did not look at all important enough to be the object of the High Command's interest. What he saw was a short, overweight man in an ill-fitting uniform. His attire was ragged, and his eyes were downcast. "You will be treated well, Herr Burke, but you must go back to Berlin. You and your wife."

He pointed his Luger at Dai. "You have a weapon, I suppose."

"Yes, it's in my belt."

"Take it out with two fingers and give it to me." Erik waited until he had the pistol. "What is your name?"

"That doesn't matter now."

"What is your nationality? Are you an army officer? If so, you will be imprisoned. You will be treated as a prisoner of war. But if you are a spy, you will be shot."

Dai did not answer. He simply stood there. It was all up, and now he met the colonel's eyes fearlessly. "Do what you must, Colonel," he said quietly.

"I'm curious about you. You must be a top-flight agent to have gotten this far. I will question you later."

"Hello, Erik," Gabby said quietly.

Erik Raeder was still angry with Gabby, but he also felt something else as he faced one of the hardest tasks of his life. There was no question but that Gabrielle Winslow would be shot, as would the man who had helped her, who was obviously an English agent. "Come with me," he directed. "I want to speak with you privately." He moved to the bow of the boat, and Gabby followed him.

He lowered his voice. "I'm sorry it's come to this, Gabby."

"So am I."

"Why did you do it?"

"I think you know why, Erik."

"I have my orders, you know."

"Of course."

Erik could feel the silence of the others, and he moved a step closer. Her face brought back a flood of memories. He had known many other women but never one like this one. Somehow, at that moment in this darkness with the moon beaming down on the boat that bobbed in the sea, he felt a great sadness come over him. He had become more and more disenchanted with the methods of the Nazi regime. He was smart enough to realize that there could be only one outcome. He was like many other German soldiers, trapped in a world that was not of his making. He had been entranced by Hitler's oratory, but now he had seen the results of the man's madness, and as he gazed at this woman he still loved, he knew that everything about this was wrong. "Who is this man you're with?" he asked.

"He came to help my uncle and aunt, and I agreed to help him."

"Is that all?"

"Does it matter?"

"It matters to me," he said, feeling the disillusionment grow in him. "I loved you once, and I . . . I thought you loved me."

"I did love you, Erik."

"Is love that easy to lose? What happened?"

"We believed in different things. A man and a woman have to be of one mind, Erik. I'm sure you know that. I could never be what your country stands for now."

"And if I had not been a German, it might have been different?"

"Who can say? But I did love you once."

Erik knew at this moment that he could not do what he had come to do. "I love you still, Gabby," he said softly, "and I believe I will always love you." He forced his hands to stay at his sides, although he longed to touch her.

"I'm sorry, Erik, for everything," she whispered.

Erik nodded and then his jaw tightened. He turned and said, "You two get back in the boat."

"Yes, Colonel." The two men scrambled aboard as Erik went back to stand before Dai. He leaned forward and said, "Take care of her." Then he turned and crawled back across into the waiting boat. "These are not the ones we are seeking," he shouted. "We will search farther out."

Dai watched in shock as the boat pulled away. "What was that?" he asked Gabby. "Why is he letting us go?"

"I think," Gabby said slowly, "he's two men. The one whom you saw tonight—the one who set us free—is the one I knew when I was dating him. The other is a lost man indeed."

"He let us go because of you, didn't he, Gabby?"

"Yes, he did."

"Then he's a better man than I took him for."

"He couldn't stand to hurt her," Liza put in.

"I think he could have been a great man, but he's lost," Gabby said as tears formed in her eyes. Dai put his arms around her as they watched the boat disappear.

"He'll be in serious trouble if word of this gets out," Dai said.

"I don't think he really cares," Gabby said. She walked away and stood beside the rail, staring at the boat as it turned and pulled away. For a moment she felt as alone as she had ever felt in her life.

★ ★ ★

The sub found them thirty minutes later. Liza saw it first and cried out, and then all of them came to watch as the coning tower rose and then the ocean waters washed over the decks. The hatches opened, and the decks were soon filled with sailors. "Ahoy there. Give the password!"

"Operation Jonah," Dai called out.

"Confirmed. Prepare to come aboard."

The captain, a short muscular man with hair sprouting in every direction, greeted them as soon as they were on board. "We've got orders to get you back to London as soon as possible. Who's so important here, if I may ask?"

Gabby was holding on to Dai. "We're all important, Captain. That's what this war is all about—to prove that all people are important."

The captain laughed. "You've got me there, miss. Well, let's get you all down below. You have a date in London."

★ ★ ★

Gabby walked out of the hospital at eight o'clock. She was tired after a long shift, and the sight of so many wounded men had been demoralizing, as always. She had gotten a hospital job as soon as they had reached England, and Dai had been spending much time with his superior officers. They had helped Gabby find a small apartment, for which she was grateful. Everyone had been so helpful from the moment they had arrived in England. She prayed that those she had left behind would soon experience that same kindness and freedom from the tyranny that had brought a dark shadow over all of Europe. Her uncle and aunt had been greeted with gusto by the top men in government, and they were very happy to be safely out of Germany.

As she stepped outside, Gabby saw Dai waiting for her and went over at once. It was dark outside, for London was blacked out. Streetlights were out, and there was no light coming from any windows.

"We'd better hurry. Those bombers may come at any time."

"All right, Dai."

The two walked until they came to a blacked-out pub. They stepped inside and were shown to a table in the back. When they were seated, they ordered, and as soon as the waitress was gone, Dai told her, "I've applied for active duty—and they turned me down."

Gabby was surprised.

"They want me in intelligence," he continued, "so I'll be behind a desk for the most part. That's as active as I'll be. I won't ever be a hero, I'm afraid."

Gabby felt a huge rush of relief. "You'll always be a hero to me," she said as she clutched his hand. She had been afraid to think of where Dai might end up. She would not be going back to Holland until the war was over, of course, and the Germans were driven out.

Gabby told him about some of her patients while they waited for the food to come, and then the conversation turned lighter while they ate.

"What's going to happen to us, I wonder?" Dai mused.

Gabrielle smiled and turned his hand over with a glint in her eye. "Let me tell you your fortune." She traced the lines in his palm with her finger. "I see you're going on a long journey, and you're going to meet a beautiful lady with brown curly hair. You will love her with all your heart, and she will return your love. You will have a wonderful marriage and many children and grandchildren."

Dai lifted her chin until she looked into his eyes. He smiled and said, "Do you see that in my hand?"

"No, I see it in your heart—and in mine."

"That reminds me. I've got to start courting you."

"Did you write that poem I asked you about when we were still back in the Netherlands?"

"Yes, of course I did. Why, I do everything you ask me to, don't I?"

She laughed but settled down when he started speaking the words of love he had written and memorized.

Gabby leaned forward so she wouldn't miss a word. She was happy and knew that the war might go on for a long time, but she had found her life.

Historical Fiction that Reaches Beyond its Time

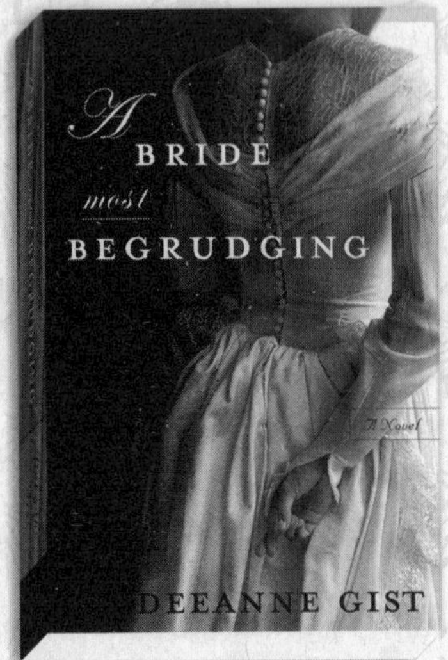

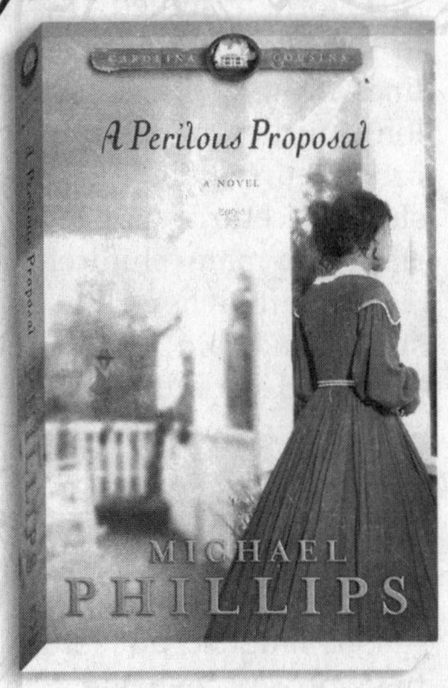

Colonial Drama and Romance

Lady Constance Morrow finds herself held against her will aboard a ship bound for the American colonies—a ship filled with "tobacco brides" and felons. Drew O'Connor, a determined Colonial farmer who is nearly as headstrong as Constance, wins her as his bride but soon realizes their marriage of convenience has become most inconvenient indeed.

A Bride Most Begrudging
by Deeanne Gist

Historical Fiction with Southern Charm

From the bestselling author of the Shenandoah Sisters series comes a new series with strong messages of equality, God's timing, and the testing of one's faith.

A Perilous Proposal follows the lives of two young women who fight to keep their home, while local whites and the newly formed KKK are furious about having blacks at their family plantation. The women wonder if life's crises are behind them as they try to maintain the freedom they have struggled to gain.

A Perilous Proposal
by Michael Phillips